The Woman's Historical Novel

Other publications by the same author

SISTERS AND RIVALS IN BRITISH WOMEN'S FICTION, 1914–39

The Woman's Historical Novel

British Women Writers, 1900–2000

Diana Wallace

823.081099287
W18w

First published 2005 by
PALGRAVE MACMILLAN
Houndmills, Basingstoke, Hampshire RG21 6XS and
175 Fifth Avenue, New York, N.Y. 10010
Companies and representatives throughout the world

PALGRAVE MACMILLAN is the global academic imprint of the Palgrave
Macmillan division of St. Martin's Press, LLC and of Palgrave Macmillan Ltd.
Macmillan® is a registered trademark in the United States, United Kingdom
and other countries. Palgrave is a registered trademark in the European
Union and other countries.

ISBN 1–4039–0322–0 hardback

This book is printed on paper suitable for recycling and made from fully
managed and sustained forest sources.

A catalogue record for this book is available from the British Library.

Library of Congress Cataloging-in-Publication Data
Wallace, Diana, 1964–
    The woman's historical novel : British women writers,
    1900–2000 / Diana Wallace.
        p.   cm.
    Includes bibliographical references and index.
    ISBN 1–4039–0322–0 (cloth)
    1. Historical fiction, English—History and criticism.   2. English
    fiction—19th century—History and criticism.   3. English
    fiction—Women authors—History and criticism.   4. Women and
    literature—Great Britain—History—19th century.   5. Literature
    and history—Great Britain—History—19th century.   I. Title.

    PR868.H5W35 2005
    823'.081099287—dc22
                                                    2004051637

10   9   8   7   6   5   4   3   2   1
14   13   12   11   10   09   08   07   06   05

Printed and bound in Great Britain by
Antony Rowe Ltd, Chippenham and Eastbourne

For my parents,
Anne and Nigel Wallace

Contents

Preface

Why a book on the *woman's* historical novel? This study starts from my belief that the historical novel has been one of the most important forms of women's reading and writing during the twentieth century. From an early age I read women's historical novels avidly, as did my mother and sister. The same was true, I later discovered, of many of my female friends and colleagues, and of many of the literary critics, writers and theorists who have been central to the development of feminist literary criticism. This book, then, asks why it is that women readers and writers have been so drawn to the historical novel in the twentieth century. This leads to a second and related question: given that a visit to any public library will offer evidence of the huge number of historical novels written and read by women, why is it that, with a few notable exceptions, there has been so little critical attention given to the genre?

The tendency has been to associate women's historical novels with romance and thus to stigmatise it as escapist. We need to reassess both the assumption that historical novels are necessarily escapist because they are set in the past, and the assumption that escapism is *per se* a 'bad thing'. When my mother went into hospital to have her first child, she took with her a book which she had been saving especially to read during labour, in the hope that it would take her mind off things. The book was the latest by Georgette Heyer (probably, given the year, *False Colours*) and it did, she remembers, get her through the early stages. The child was myself so this story, retold to me, has become part of my own personal reading history. 'Escapism' tends to be a dirty word in literary criticism but it seems to me that any book which can hold a woman's attention during labour merits at least some serious consideration.

A second personal memory which is relevant here is of being asked to write an essay on my favourite author in school when I was around 12. I wrote my essay on Jean Plaidy and explained that up until recently Georgette Heyer had been my favourite author but I had now moved on (as I saw it) to more 'serious' books. Not long after that, it became clear to me (through a teacher's comments) that even Jean Plaidy was not 'serious' reading, not suitable for an academic essay. This realisation coincided (probably not coincidentally) with my own disillusionment with history as it was taught in school because it seemed to include almost no women at all.

As numerous feminist theorists have pointed out, women have been excluded from traditional historical narratives. This offers one particularly crucial reason why women writers have turned to the historical novel as a discourse within which women can be made central. Luce Irigary has argued that western culture is posited on the 'murder of the mother' (1991, 44), that is on the erasure of the maternal genealogy. Women's historical novels, most obviously in the form of the family saga, often imaginatively reconstruct such maternal genealogies.

In *Camera Lucida*, Roland Barthes has suggested that our sense of history is intimately connected to our sense of separation from the mother's body.

> Is History not simply that time when we were not born? [. . .] History is hysterical: it is constituted only if we consider it, only if we look at it – and in order to look at it, we must be excluded from it. As a living soul, I am the very contrary of History, I am what belies it, destroys it for the sake of my own history [. . .] That is what the time when my mother was alive *before me* is – History. (Barthes, 'History as Separation', 1993, 64–5)

'History' is that time when our mother existed but we did not. 'History', however, has a radically different meaning for those who have been excluded from traditional accounts. Women writers have had to reshape the form of the historical novel to encompass this understanding. Women's historical novels, read by mothers and daughters, can offer a feminised, indeed 'hysterical', history which imaginatively returns the girl-child to her place within a maternal genealogy, and thus to a re-union with the mother. But, through the acts of cross-reading and cross-writing, they have also allowed women writers and readers access to the male domains of history – politics, warfare and adventure.

This book is an attempt to trace the development of the woman's historical novel over the twentieth century and to start to explore how and why it has been written and read by women. One of the problems with any study of the historical novel is defining exactly what constitutes 'historical' in relation to fiction. As I will argue in Chapter 1, many of the usual definitions given work to exclude women's fiction on one ground or another. Taking Barthes at his word, I have worked with a very broad assumption that a novel is 'historical' if it deals with a period set before the birth of the author, that is, a period she has not experienced herself but must reconstruct through (usually textual) evidence.

The very term 'historical fiction' is a kind of oxymoron, joining 'history' (what is 'true'/'fact') with 'fiction' (what is 'untrue'/ 'invented', but may aim at a different kind of truth). This tension is foregrounded most obviously in the convention of the 'Author's Note' (or foreword, postscript, or footnotes) in which the author explains what is 'fact' and what is 'fiction', what is historically documented and what she has invented, in her text. Many of the debates around historical fiction revolve around this tension. On a more popular level, historical fictions are often judged on their perceived 'authenticity', not only whether they get their 'facts' right but also whether they are imaginatively 'true' to their period. The postmodern recognition that both history and fiction are constructed discourses which have a complex relation to what we call 'reality' has not only shown the problems with such an approach but led to some of the most interesting historical fictions in the twentieth century.

My own interest in this book has not necessarily been in whether any given novel is an 'accurate' depiction of the period in which it is set but more usually in what it says about the period in which it was written. Although we cannot always see it at the time, our representations of 'the past' tell us a great deal about the most powerful ideologies of the present.

There are many other writers and texts I would have liked to have included here but my choices have necessarily been confined by my own reading and by the constraints of space and deadlines. I have not been able to include either historical detective fiction or children's historical fiction, although women writers have made important contributions to both genres. It is worth noting that, for instance, Rosemary Sutcliff wrote both adult and children's historical fiction, and the distinction between the two is blurred in her work. My aim has been to trace some of the most important lines of connection and development, to identify key themes and trends in each decade, and to draw attention to lesser-known writers as well as exploring important novels in some detail. My title, *The Woman's Historical Novel*, echoes not only the titles of Georg Lukács' *The Historical Novel* (1937) and Avrom Fleishman's *The English Historical Novel* (1971), but also that of Nicola Beauman's ground-breaking study, *A Very Great Profession: The Woman's Novel 1914–39* (1983), which focuses mainly on the domestic novel. My own study of historical novels by women thus both contributes to the project of recovering neglected work by women writers, and offers reassessments of what a 'historical novel' and/or a 'woman's novel' might be. This is, I hope, a beginning.

A note on nationalities

The use of the word 'British' in the subtitle of this book is a convenience rather than a definitive identity. I have used it broadly to indicate birth in Britain and a writing life spent mainly in this country. Nationality is a particularly complex issue for women, who do not usually define their identity through the easy shorthand of the football, cricket or rugby team they support. As a woman, Catholic, and northerner of Irish descent, Hilary Mantel, for instance, has written that she 'came to see that Englishness was white, male, southern, Protestant and middle class' (2002, 4). The birth of the historical novel as a genre, particularly as it has been associated with Sir Walter Scott, came out of shifts in national identity. While my primary concern has been with gender, I have tried to signal the continuing complexity of some of these issues in the twentieth century. Scottishness, for instance, was important to Naomi Mitchison and Dorothy Dunnett, while Ellen

Galford, who was born in New Jersey, USA, now defines herself as an adopted Scot. A concern with Welsh history is central to Mary Stewart's Merlin trilogy, although she herself was not Welsh. Wherever I have included brief references to Irish writers who come outside my remit, I have indicated their nationality. The American market for women's historical fiction was especially important in the 1960s and 1970s, so I have also indicated influential American texts where necessary.

Acknowledgements

I would like to thank the Arts and Humanities Research Board for a research leave grant which funded the sabbatical in which a large part of this book was written.

My colleagues at the University of Glamorgan have been generous in the practical support which made that sabbatical possible, and I am very grateful to them, particularly to Jane Aaron, Andy Smith, Meredith Miller and Henrice Altink who relieved me of teaching and administration duties.

I would like to thank Marion Shaw for her encouragement from the beginning of the project; Lynne Pearce for her support in the initial stages; and Mary Joannou for her comments as a reader on the original proposal.

I am enormously grateful to the people who read parts of the work in progress and gave me the benefit of their expert knowledge and enthusiasm. I would particularly like to thank Gill Spraggs, Jeni Williams, Maria Donovan, Meredith Miller, Gavin Edwards, Alice Entwistle, Jane Aaron, Nora Warner and John Young.

My thanks are also due to Gill Spraggs, Gavin Edwards, Alice Entwistle, Catherine Dell, Dawn Percival, Ursula Masson and Matthew Francis for kindly lending me books; to Claire Connolly for sharing her knowledge of early historical novels; and to Chris Meredith, Sheenagh Pugh, Jeff Wallace and Rosalind Marron who drew my attention to useful material. I would also like to thank Kathleen Bell and Kate Hodgkin for letting me see copies of unpublished work.

Some of the material in Chapter 3 appeared in an earlier format as an article in *Critical Survey*, and I am grateful to the publisher for permission to reuse this.

Finally, for their encouragement, support and patience, I would like to thank my parents, Anne and Nigel Wallace; my sisters Linda and Dawn; Maria and Bertie; and, as always, Jarlath Costello.

1
Introduction

History, real solemn history, I cannot be interested in. [...] I read it a little as a duty, but it tells me nothing that does not either vex or weary me. The quarrels of popes and kings, with wars or pestilences, in every page; the men all so good for nothing, and hardly any women at all. It is very tiresome: and yet I often think it odd that it should be so dull, for a great deal of it must be invention. The speeches that are put into the heroes' mouths, their thoughts and designs the chief of all this must be invention, and invention is what delights me in other books.
　　　　 – Jane Austen, *Northanger Abbey* ([1818] 1985, 123)

I had read every word of Georgette Heyer. I was a secret, illegal member of two circulating libraries to get more of her books. I had purloined exercise books to write two Regency romances and half a novel about the amours of Charles II. These were shockingly bad, and their badness led me to realise how difficult good escape literature is to write.
　　　　 – A.S. Byatt, *Passions of the Mind* (1993a, 258)

History, accurate history, is an affair of poor women, in spring, in summer, in autumn, in winter, in a country which has been invaded and conquered, talking...It's not of much account, what they say.
　　　　 – Storm Jameson, *Then We Shall Hear Singing* (1942, 83)

Women's relationship with 'real solemn history' – that catalogue of kings and popes and battles lost and won – has often been ambivalent, but they have been reading and enjoying historical novels for well over two centuries. One of the ironies of Catherine's condemnation of traditional history in *Northanger Abbey* is that her preferred reading, Ann Radcliffe's Gothic novel *The Mysteries of Udolpho* (1794), is in fact a 'historical' novel, being set (however vaguely) in the sixteenth century. Radcliffe, in contrast to the

1

writers of 'real history', uses her historical setting as a fantasy space in which she can centralise a female consciousness and explore female fears and desires. This female-centredness is partly why Catherine, bored and repelled by male-dominated 'real history', enjoys Radcliffe's books. Similarly Catherine's twentieth-century descendants have enjoyed the historical novels of Georgette Heyer, Margaret Irwin and Jean Plaidy in huge numbers. But these books have (like Radcliffe) been stigmatised as 'popular' or 'escapist' fiction. Just as Catherine felt her novel reading was something to be slightly ashamed of because 'gentlemen read better books' (Austen, 1985, 121), as a school-girl A.S. Byatt felt that her taste for Georgette Heyer had to be concealed and enjoyed secretly. Reading a popular historical novel led to an 'illegal' act, even if it was only joining a circulating library.

Yet exclusion from recorded history, whether as subject, reader or writer, is a serious business. Mussolini, Bryher records, forbade women to read history at universities (1963, 231). A knowledge of history, this suggests, has the potential to be dangerously subversive, particularly in a culture like that of pre-war Fascist Italy where women were being increasingly confined to domestic and maternal roles. It is not surprising that in women's hands the historical novel has often become a political tool. A historical setting has frequently been used by women writers (as by male writers) as a way of writing about subjects which would otherwise be taboo, or of offering a critique of the present through their treatment of the past. Perhaps even more important for women writers has been the way that the historical novel has allowed them to invent or 're-imagine' (to borrow Linda Anderson's term [1990, 129]), the unrecorded lives of marginalised and subordinated people, especially women, but also the working classes, Black people, slaves and colonised peoples, and to shape narratives which are more appropriate to their experiences than those of conventional history.

Indeed, it is the problems involved in writing traditional history which fully encompasses the experience of women – lack of records, the inappropriateness of standard periodisation and chronology, and the focus on public events – which has, Bonnie G. Smith suggests, led some women historians, including H.F.M. Prescott, to write novels instead (Smith, 1984, 720–1). Writers from Naomi Mitchison in the 1930s to the feminist writers of 'herstory' in the 1980s as well as, less obviously, popular writers like Catherine Cookson have concentrated on writing what Storm Jameson calls 'accurate history' – the lives of the conquered, the victimised and the marginalised, those left out of traditional histories written by the (male) victors.

These two uses of history – escape and political intervention – are more connected than they might at first seem. The need for escapism itself indicates a dissatisfaction with what is available: Catherine's bored inability to read 'real solemn history' is actually a form of resistance. Women's marginal and excluded position has meant that they have often understood that recorded 'history' is not straightforwardly 'what happened in the past' but has always been the result of selection, presentation, and even downright falsification based on particular ideologies and viewpoints.

Marginality or exclusion breeds a scepticism towards the grand narratives of history. Required to read history 'as men', women may well become (in Judith Fetterley's term) resisting readers of such narratives. But the understanding that much of history is 'invention' as Austen puts it, 'narrative' or 'fiction' as a postmodernist theorist such as Hayden White might argue, may also bring certain freedoms. 'History should be a hammock for swinging and a game for playing, the way cats play', writes Jeanette Winterson in *Oranges Are Not The Only Fruit*. 'Claw it, chew it, rearrange it and at bedtime it's still a ball of string full of knots' (1985, 93). For postmodern writers in the late twentieth century, history becomes a game of cat's cradle as the thread of facts is patterned and repatterned. For women readers and writers, then, 'history' has a complex and varied range of meanings, both inclusive and exclusive. 'History' has traditionally excluded women, but paradoxically the 'historical novel' has offered women readers the imaginative space to create different, more inclusive versions of 'history', which are accessible or appealing to them in various ways.

My argument in this book is that despite the extraordinary critical neglect of this area, the historical novel has been one of the most important genres for women writers and readers in the twentieth century. For very specific historical reasons, as I will show, women writers turned to the historical novel at the beginning of the century, at a moment when male writers were moving away from the genre, with the result that it has come to be seen as a 'feminine' form, a view damagingly reinforced by its association with the 'popular'. This in part explains why it has, like any form associated with women readers and writers, been neglected in critical terms. In both 'history' and 'literature', the historical novel has always been regarded as a hybrid, even a 'bastard' form, as well as being vulgar because it is a 'popular' genre – 'vulgar fiction, impure history' in Dean Rehberger's phrase (1995). In the hands of women writers it has been further hybridised, cross-fertilising with romance, fantasy, the Gothic, the adventure story and the detective novel. The overlap with romance (in its original form characterised by its setting in the past, but today meaning a love story) has been especially complicated. This is in part because the woman's historical novel has one of its roots in the Gothic historical novel or 'romance', a mode that predates the tradition of the historical novel which critics have seen as beginning with Sir Walter Scott. The dominance of the model of what Georg Lukács (1962) called the 'classical historical novel' developed by Scott has actually worked to exclude many forms of the woman's historical novel from critical attention. My own study, in contrast, is an attempt to track the development of the woman's historical novel through the twentieth century and to trace the connections between the varying different forms it has taken.

The common perception is that the historical novel is a nostalgic, reactionary genre. Umberto Eco records his irritation with people who suggest that writing about the past is 'a way of eluding the present' (1984, 73). The truth is far more complex. Although readers are often attracted to historical novels because they believe they will learn about the past time recreated in the novel, any historical novel always has as much, or perhaps more, to say about the time in which it is written. A novelist like Naomi Mitchison consciously used historical fiction to comment in a coded way on the issues of the day. So-called 'popular' fiction, however, is equally closely connected to its moment of production, not least in its relationship to whatever it is offering an 'escape' from. As Claud Cockburn writes, 'The best sellers really are a mirror of "the mind and face" of an age' (1972, 7). One of my central concerns here, therefore, is to connect these novels to the historical context within which they were written, to explore how Heyer's concern with masquerade reflects the concerns of the 1920s or what Mary Renault's decision to write about Ancient Greece tells us about the 1950s. Any historical novel is 'historical' in at least four senses: in its use of a particular period for its fictional setting; in its engagement with the historical moment (social, cultural, political and national) of its writing; in its relation to the personal life history of the writer herself; and in its relation to literary history, most obvious in the intertextual use of earlier texts.

The sheer number of historical novels published by women writers over the twentieth century is a testament to the importance of the form. The sales and public library borrowing figures indicate the wide readership for many of the popular historical novelists. Contrary to the usual dismissal of the 'popular', I believe this is a good reason for taking it seriously. The 'bestsellers' of the twentieth century included Baroness Orczy, Daphne du Maurier, Georgette Heyer, Mary Renault (Mary Challans), Victoria Holt/ Jean Plaidy (Eleanor Burford Hibbert), Norah Lofts, Barbara Cartland and Catherine Cookson (Bloom, 2002) all of whom wrote historical novels. With the exception of Renault (and possibly Orczy), these are writers who, as even the most cursory glance at the covers of their novels indicates, are marketed to a female audience. Many public libraries have a 'Historical Novels' section, just as they have a section for detective fiction. Catherine Cookson, many of whose novels have historical settings, dominated the 'most borrowed' lists compiled by the Public Lending Right Scheme for over two decades, showing signs of being toppled only in 2003 (*The Guardian*, 11 April 2003). In 1988 her novels accounted for *a third* of all books borrowed from public libraries (Bloom, 2002, 196). Despite this evidence of the appeal of these books, they have on the whole been ignored by critics until recently. (The detective novel, in contrast, has been taken much more seriously.) On the other hand, several of the most influential 'serious' women's novels of the late twentieth century which have attained cross-over 'bestseller' status, often through being Booker prize winners, have been historical, most notably A.S. Byatt's *Possession* (1990) and Pat Barker's *Regeneration* trilogy (1991–1995).

The 'woman's historical novel', then, encompasses both the 'popular' and the 'serious' or 'literary' ends of the spectrum, but one of my arguments here is that the two are intimately linked. The term as I use it here covers the whole range of women's writing within this mode from the historical romances of Heyer, the Gothic historical novels of Daphne du Maurier or the family sagas of Catherine Cookson to Naomi Mitchison's recreation of Caesar's Gallic War or Sylvia Townsend Warner's socialist realist-influenced texts. We need to read both 'serious' and 'popular' historical novels together and against each other if we want fully to understand the range of meanings that history and the historical novel have held for women readers in the twentieth century. Jean Plaidy's novels trace their literary lineage back to Ann Radcliffe and beyond, for instance, while Byatt's *Possession* is a tribute to Georgette Heyer's historical romances. What links together these often very disparate novels is their use of a historical setting in order to explore issues of gender, and a desire to rewrite history from a point of view that centralises women's concerns.

Equally important in terms of literary history and canon formation is the fact that the general critical disdain for women's popular historical novels appears to have led to the neglect of a body of historical novels by writers such as Naomi Mitchison, Sylvia Townsend Warner, Bryher, H.F.M. Prescott and Mary Renault. This in turn has contributed to the perception of the mid-century (1945–1960) as an 'empty' period for women's writing. Tracing the development of the woman's historical novel across the century shows that women were producing important fiction during these ostensibly fallow years. These connections across the decades are important to the history of women's writing in a wider sense as well as demonstrating the enduring importance of the genre.

A surprising number of women writers and critics have attested to the importance of women's popular historical novels in their emotional, intellectual and literary development, as well as to their sense that this was a slightly disreputable literary taste. This is perhaps especially true of the generation of women writers who grew up in the 1950s, and who became the influential writers and critics of the feminist era. It is perhaps not too far-fetched to argue that the roots of second-wave feminism itself can be found, ironically, in the popular historical fiction read by these women. A.S. Byatt's account of being relieved of her position on the Library Committee at her boarding school when she vetoed the purchase of Heyer's novels in an attempt to keep her own reading habits secret is especially evocative (1993a, 258). But she is not the only writer or critic to pay tribute (however ambivalent) to Heyer. Carmen Callil, the founder of Virago, suggests that her own avid reading of Heyer as a young woman actually had a 'subversive' effect on her (1996, 8). Heyer gave out mixed messages, Callil points out, suggesting that marriage was the great goal but also stressing that 'a *real* heroine should only marry on her own terms' (1996, 7). Heyer is important not only because her career as a bestseller spans such a large part of the twentieth century, but because of her influence on other writers.

In contrast, Alison Light, who has produced some of the most perceptive pieces on women's historical novels, argues that her adolescent reading of historical novels by Margaret Irwin, Jean Plaidy and Anya Seton ultimately 'fed a conservative vision' (1989, 58). Nevertheless, Light shows that novels like Irwin's 'Young Bess' trilogy offered an important fantasy of female power for women readers like herself. Anya Seton's popular historical novels concentrate on the romantic and sexual life of lesser-known women in history but even they assert the historical importance of such women in a way which echoes Austen's critique of traditional phallocentric history. Seton's 'Author's Note' to *Katherine* (1954), the story of Katherine Swynford – mistress to John O'Gaunt and thus founding ancestress of what became the Tudor dynasty – argues:

> Of [Katherine] little was known, except when her life touched the Duke's and there are few details of that [...] in the great historians Katherine apparently excited scant interest, perhaps because they gave little space to the women of the period anyway.
> And yet Katherine was important to English history. (1961, 9)

In 2003, interestingly, *Katherine* was included in the BBC's 'Big Read' 'Top 100' list of books. The popular novel, then, can offer influential models of female agency within history despite its domination by the romance plot.

As a genre, the historical novel has allowed women writers a license which they have not been allowed in other forms. This is most obviously true of sexuality where it has allowed coverage of normally taboo subjects, not just active female sexuality but also contraception, abortion, childbirth and homosexuality. As Naomi Mitchison, smarting from censorship imposed by her publishers when she wrote about sexuality in a contemporary setting, commented bitterly, 'apparently it's alright when people wear wolfskins and togas' (1979, 179). During and after the war, particularly in the rather repressive 1950s, historical novels provided an especially important space for erotic or sexualised fantasy. For Lorna Sage, as for many other women, it was the American author Kathleen Winsor's bestselling restoration romance *Forever Amber* (1944), one of her uncle's 'dirty books', which opened up 'another future [...] out of the past' (2001, 203). An active and unrepentant sexuality is the defining characteristic of the courtesan heroine, Amber, again an unexpected model of female agency. As Sage puts it, 'Her first sexual experience does it all, turns [Amber] into her own woman in one swooning paragraph' (2001, 203). Alison Light, who also read *Forever Amber* 'for its erotic content, guiltily sneaking it from my mother's shelf', argues that the popular historical novels of this period provide 'a far more plural and perverse model of desire' than one would associate with these years (1989, 64). This license has been even more important to writers such as Mary Renault and Sylvia Townsend Warner who used the genre to explore non-heterosexual desire, chiefly through the depiction of male homosexual characters.

As attitudes to sexuality shift across the period, with the sexual liberation of the 1960s marking an important turning point, so the concerns and themes of the historical novel change. Barbara Cartland famously turned to historical settings because 'it's very difficult to have virgins and all the excitement in the present day' (Philips, 1986, 28). In the 1980s the lesbian historical novel became a sub-genre in itself, while other women writers used the historical novel to write the heterosexual happy ending which became taboo in the 'serious' literary novel.

Less immediately obvious is the fact that the historical novel has also given women the freedom to adopt male narrators and protagonists, and to write about the 'male' world of public and political affairs. A number of women writers from the earlier generation, such as Naomi Mitchison, Bryher and Rosemary Sutcliff, trace their interest in the genre to the impact of the *male* writers of historical fiction they read as children, including Rudyard Kipling, G.A. Henty and J.G. Whyte-Melville, as well as Macaulay's *Lays of Ancient Rome*. For these writers, the historical novel becomes a liberating space not for erotic fantasy but for the 'boy's-own' style adventures on land and sea which they felt denied because of their gender. 'I was convinced', Bryher wrote, 'that if I wanted to be happy when I grew up I had to become a cabin boy and run away from the inexplicable taboos of Victorian life' (1963, 21). That fantasy of being a cabin boy (or a highwayman, a pirate, a Jacobite rebel or an actor on the Elizabethan stage) is one which women writers and readers have acted out in the historical novel in ways which suggest it is particularly powerful.

The pleasures offered by women's historical novels can be considerable, and in unexpected ways. The poet Patricia Beer, for instance, has written about the rapturous ecstasy she experienced as a 13-year-old reading D.K. Broster's *The Flight of the Heron* (1925) about the 1745 Jacobite rising. Beer's 'love' for the male protagonist, Ewen Cameron, was intensified by her recognition that his most important relationships were his homo-erotic friendships with men. 'Looking back', Beer writes, 'I feel sad. The feelings it roused in me were not about anything real, yet I have experienced nothing stronger since' (Beer, 1968, 118). The emotional importance of women's reactions to historical novels should not be under-estimated.

Neither should the political importance of the form. The furore in America over the publication of William Styron's *The Confessions of Nat Turner* in 1967, the fictional depiction (by a white writer) of a historically documented Black slave revolutionary, is a testament to the power of historical fiction to stir controversy (see, for instance, Woodward, 1969). The debate over whether

Styron's novel misrepresented Turner, and by implication his race, or whether a novelist is entitled to what Styron calls 'freedom of movement and choice' in writing historical fiction (Woodward, 1969, 65), raises a complex series of questions about the autonomy of art and its relationship to 'truth' and politics. Above all, it demonstrates the potential emotional and political power of the historical novel.

When I began this study I thought that I would be concerned mainly with gender in relation to femininity in women's historical novels. In fact, it quickly became obvious that the historical novel has been one of the sites where women writers have had most freedom to examine *masculinity* as a social and cultural construction. The act of reading and writing *across* gender has been central to the woman's historical novel right through the twentieth century, from Marjorie Bowen's *The Viper of Milan* in 1906 to Pat Barker's *Regeneration* trilogy in 1991–1995. One of the central reasons women writers have turned to the historical novel, I would suggest, is that a temporal viewpoint allows us to see that gender itself is historically contingent rather than essential. If gender roles are subject to change over time then they are clearly socially and culturally constructed and open to the possibility of further change.

The historical novel: history and criticism

Despite the feminist-inspired interest in women's history and what amounts to an explosion of historical novels by women in the latter decades of the twentieth century, there has been oddly little sustained critical attention paid to the woman's historical novel as a genre in its own right (especially in comparison to the body of work on romance or the detective novel). This initially surprising fact has much to do with the critical history of the genre itself and the way in which it has been treated as a male tradition.

Critical surveys of the historical novel traditionally start with Sir Walter Scott's *Waverley* (1814). As one anonymous critic put it in 1845, 'Sir Walter Scott, as all the world knows, was the inventor of the historical romance' (Clery and Miles, 2000, 274). They then trace the form through its heyday in the nineteenth century and suggest that it dies a death in its traditional form at the beginning of the twentieth century, although some critics suggest a revival of the form in the 1920s or 1930s. This is the story told, with some variations, in the major studies of the form from the seminal study by Georg Lukács, *The Historical Novel* (written 1936/1937 and published in English translation in 1962), up until the 1990s.[1]

Lukács mentions no women writers at all, other than to note dismissively that in previous criticism of Scott, 'it was the fashion to quote a long list of second and third-rate writers (Radcliffe, etc.) who were supposed to be important literary forerunners of his' (1983, 30). Some historical novels by women are mentioned in subsequent accounts, including Charlotte Brontë's *Shirley*

(1849), George Eliot's *Romola* (1863) and *Felix Holt* (1866), Elizabeth Gaskell's *Sylvia's Lovers* (1863), and Virginia Woolf's *Orlando* (1928) and *Between the Acts* (1941), clearly indicating that the major women writers were active in this genre. However, what is especially interesting here is the variation in which novels by women are included in each account.[2] *Romola* is the only text which rates consistent inclusion. This suggests a revealing uncertainty about women's historical novels and whether they are properly 'historical'.

It also indicates the extent to which Scott, regarded as the inventor of the genre, was seen as having established a model for his (male) successors to follow. Part of the problem here is to do with how the historical novel is defined, especially if Scott is used as a yardstick. Introducing Maria Edgeworth's *Castle Rackrent* (1800), seen as the first 'regional novel', George Watson comments, 'if we hesitate to call it an "historical novel" it is only because, unlike *Waverley*, it celebrates no great public event like the Forty Five. It is about a way of life, not an event' (Edgeworth, 1980, xvii). Women, of course, have been excluded from participation in the 'great public events' (think of Scott's Rose Bradwardine waiting at home while Waverley adventures in the highlands), but they may have detailed knowledge of a particular 'way of life'.

However, more recent work in the 1990s has recovered a body of work, much of it by women writers, preceding and influencing Scott (see, for instance, Ferris, 1989; Garside, 1991; Trumpener, 1993). Scott, this work shows, explicitly distanced himself from these female forerunners, most obviously in the preface to *Waverley*, and masked or played down the extent to which he was indebted to them, a move which positioned him as the father of the historical novel and ultimately of the nineteenth-century realist novel. It was therefore Scott himself who set the line followed by subsequent critics, who either saw him as being without a maternal genealogy or lauded him for rejecting it. Leslie Fiedler's argument in *Love and Death in the American Novel* (1960) that the historical novel is 'a development – more masculine, more "scientific", and more genteel' of the Radcliffean novel (1984, 162), for instance, repeats this gendering of the genre's origins in very value-laden terms. For Fiedler, Scott's achievement in introducing 'real history' (164) to the novel redeems the genre from the dirty depths to which it had sunk in female hands:

> The historical romance is the 'cleanest' of all the subgenres of the novel thus far, the creation of a self-conscious attempt to redeem fiction at once for respectability and masculinity. (170)

Obviously, only 'real history', associated with 'scientific' research, is 'masculine' enough to save literature from the clutches of female scribblers.

Scott himself, of course, has suffered from critical neglect as a result of his exclusion from what F.R. Leavis defined as the 'great tradition' of English literature. This has contributed to the wider neglect of historical fiction and especially women's historical fiction. In *The Great Tradition* (1948) Leavis condemned Scott for his lack of interest in form:

> Scott was primarily a kind of inspired folk-lorist [...] not having the creative writer's interest in literature, he made no serious attempt to work out his own form and break away from the bad tradition of the eighteenth-century romance. [...] Out of Scott a bad tradition came. (Leavis, 1962, 14, n. 1)

This amounts to a dismissal of the historical novel itself as a 'bad tradition', reinforced by his judgement of *Romola* as an artistic failure: 'Few will want to read *Romola* a second time and few can ever have got through it once without some groans' (1962, 63). For Leavis, the artist's responsibility lay in their attention to the moral possibilities of 'Life', but most importantly to the 'Life' of the contemporary moment. His deployment of the word 'serious' here is important because it implicitly aligns the historical novel with the opposite of 'serious' art – for which we can read 'popular' fiction. This Leavisite division is perpetuated by, for instance, Avrom Fleishman whose study by implication ignores 'popular' historical novels as mere escapism.[3] Associated with the 'popular', women writers have thus been doubly excluded from the established canon.

In contrast to Leavis, the most influential study of the genre, Lukács' classic work of Marxist criticism, *The Historical Novel*, uses dialectical materialism to make a strong argument for the centrality of the historical novel in the development of the realist novel. Indeed, he maintains that it is not a separate genre or sub-genre (1983, 127). What is lacking in the 'so-called historical novel' before Scott, Lukács argues, is 'precisely the specifically historical, that is, derivation of the individuality of characters from the historical peculiarity of their age' (19). The historical novel emerged as a new form, he goes on to argue, out of the new consciousness of history which was the result of the French Revolution, the revolutionary wars, and the rise and fall of Napoleon. The widespread nature of these events on a European scale, including the creation of mass armies, 'for the first time made history a *mass experience*' (23, original emphasis) for the huge numbers of people touched by these changes:

> Hence the concrete possibilities for men to comprehend their own existence as something historically conditioned, for them to see in history something which deeply affects their daily lives and immediately concerns them. (24)

History is experienced as an awakening of national sensibility, even outside France where it is evoked by resistance to Napoleon's conquests (25), as in

Britain's fear of invasion, for example. The new concept of history which developed from this understanding and found expression in the work of Hegel conceptualised human life as a historical process wherein progress is the product of dialectical conflict between social forces. 'History itself', Lukács argued, 'is the bearer and realiser of human progress' (27).

For Lukács, Scott's greatness lies in his invention of the 'classical historical novel' as a new literary form which expressed this emergent historical consciousness, and in his 'capacity to give living human embodiment to historical-social types' (35). For Scott, he argues, historical progress is a dialectical process and his novels depict the great crises or transitional moments of history as conflicts wherein two opposing forces collide and are resolved into 'a glorious "middle way"' (32). Thus in great historical art, as produced by Scott, the past is brought to life as 'the prehistory of the present', portraying those 'historical, social, and human forces' which transform popular and everyday life and produce our present (53). The clearest evidence of Scott's understanding of historical progress as a tendency towards the middle way, however, is in the construction of his novels around a hero who is not what Hegel called a 'world-historical individual' (such as Napoleon) but what Lukács terms the 'middle-of-the-road hero' (37): 'a more or less mediocre, average English gentleman' (33), typified by Waverley himself. (Here Lukács misses the complexity of Scott's negotiations with Scottish, English and British national identity.) In his 'wavering' towards each of the extremes this hero allows Scott to depict both sides of the conflict and finally represents the middle course.

The period of the 'classical historical novel' initiated by Scott lasted until the revolutions of 1848, after which Lukács argues that writers 'no longer have any immediate social sense of continuity with the prehistory of their own society' (244). For post-1848 writers, the historical novel (exemplified by Flaubert's *Salammbô*) degenerates as history becomes merely decorative background for private and subjective fantasies. However, in the 1930s, Lukács hails the arrival of the anti-Fascist historical novel of democratic humanism. This he sees as opening up new possibilities for the form, driven by the political urgencies of the period, although he deplores the tendency of these novels to 'turn the past into a *parable of the present*' (338). That is, he sees them as polemical allegories rather than engagements with the past as the 'prehistory' of the present.

Lukács' recognition that formal and compositional problems involve ideological and political choices is extremely useful but his study is restricted not only by its obvious gender-blindness but by its narrow understanding and valuation of literature itself. His valorisation of realism as a form which reflects the life of the people leads first to his rejection of the potential of any other modes of writing (whether Gothic historical novel, Modernist experimentalism or fantasy) to express a relationship to history. But, secondly, as numerous poststructuralist critiques have pointed out, realism itself despite its ostensible 'transparency' is an ideologically loaded form. Moreover, because he sees fiction only as a response to and reflection of historical and social conditions, he fails to consider its intertextual relationship with other texts. In her critique of his work, Janet Montefiore has usefully suggested that, 'A satisfying interpretation of realist historical novels needs to work with both the feminist critique of narrative as ideology, and to acknowledge with Lukács the dialectic between the present and the past which is implied in historical fictions' (1996, 153).

The concept of history (as dialectically evolving progress) and the ideal of the 'classical historical novel' which Lukács develops from Scott's work have both worked to exclude women's texts from the accepted canon. This is the case even in studies, like that of Avrom Fleishman, which actively modify or critique Lukács, to include, for instance, modernist texts. Fleishman acerbically comments that, 'Everyone knows what a historical novel is; perhaps that is why few have volunteered to define it in print' (1971, 3). In fact, the spirit of taxonomy seems to have been particularly strong in this area, as writers and critics struggle to define not only what constitutes a historical novel but also the kinds or forms within that category (see, for instance, Shaw, 1983, or Turner, 1979).

Like Lukács, Fleishman bases his understanding of the form on the relation-ship between the text and its concept of history: 'What makes a historical novel historical is the active presence of a concept of history as a shaping force' (1971, 15). This concept of history is, as with Lukács, expressed through the figure of the representative, rather than world-historical, individual. The problem here is that Fleishman, again like Lukács, consistently conceives of this representative individual as male:

> The typical man of an age is one whose life is shaped by world historical figures and other influences in a way that epitomises the processes of change going forward in society as a whole [...] the relationship of the representative hero to the society is not one of statistically determinable typicality but that of symbolic universality. (1971, 11)

As feminist critics have repeatedly pointed out, the appeal to universality has consistently been used to erase or marginalise women's experience. The 'typical' woman is one who (like Scott's Rose Bradwardine) rarely, if ever, comes into contact with world-historical figures.

Fleishman works with three other key elements in his definition which on the surface seem less gendered: that the novel is set in the past 'beyond an arbitrary number of years, say 40–60 (two generations)'; that the plot includes 'a number of "historical" events, particularly those in the public sphere (war, politics, economic change, etc.), mingled with and affecting the personal fortunes of the characters'; and that it includes at least one '"real" personage' (3). While this seems straightforward, it actually excludes novels

(such as Conrad's *Nostromo*) which Fleishman considers 'more solidly historical' (226) than other novels which do fit his definitions.

Even more so do these definitions work to exclude novels by women. The
first point, for instance, excludes the family saga which has been a very
important historical form for women writers. (Thus, Fleishman excludes
Woolf's *The Years* because it 'did little to move beyond the form of the family
chronicle novel' [245].) Given women's marginality to the 'historical' events
of the public sphere ('war, politics...etc.'), the second point is even more
problematic. Indeed, the whole question of periodisation itself is fraught
with complications for women in a way which makes Lukács' assumption that
the novel should deal with great historical crises extremely problematic.
Gerda Lerner has pointed out that

> Traditional history is periodised according to wars, conquests, revolutions,
> and/or vast cultural and religious shifts. All of these categories are appro-
> priate to the major activities of men [...] What historians of women's
> history have learned is that such periodisation distorts our understanding
> of the history of women. (Lerner, 1979, 175)

While Eliot's *Romola* with its account of the Italian Renaissance at the time of
Savonarola is clearly a 'historical novel' under any of these definitions,
Edgeworth's *Castle Rackrent*, as we have seen, does not qualify. Neither does
Fleishman give more than a tiny mention to Gaskell's *Sylvia's Lovers*, a novel
which is actually about the way in which the lives of those on the margins,
especially women and the working class, can be tragically affected by the
large historical events over which they have no control. Indeed, in dealing
with the forcible impressment of men during the Napoleonic wars Gaskell
would appear to be exploring precisely the ways in which the advent of
mass armies made ordinary people (specifically women) aware of 'history as
something which deeply affects their daily lives and immediately concerns
them' (Lukács, 1983, 24).

Finally, given the fact that historical records document far fewer female
than male '"real" personages', this is a further limiting definition for women
writers since it tends to confine them either to writing about men, or to
always seeing women in relation to men, as the mother/wife/lover/daughter
of a '"real" personage'. Admittedly, Fleishman does go beyond Lukács in
extending the tradition to include Woolf's *Orlando* and *Between the Acts*. But
he argues that Woolf reduces history to the personal and the individual, and
he sees these texts as bringing 'the tradition of the English historical novel
to a self-conscious close' (233).

Pre-1990 critical studies of the historical novel, then, have tended to
work with a conception of 'history' which excludes women's novels, thus
constructing this as a masculine tradition. In some ways more useful to a
study of women's historical novels is Eco's much broader definition which

argues that there are three ways of 'narrating the past'; the romance where the past is 'scenery, pretext, fairy-tale construction, to allow the imagination to rove freely' (1984, 74); the swashbuckling novel which 'chooses a "real" and recognisable past' and peoples it with both 'characters already found in the encyclopaedia' and invented characters (74); and, finally, the historical novel which uses made-up events and characters, yet tells us things about a period which history books do not (75). This lends itself to a gendered interpretation since the romance is associated with female readers and writers, while the swashbuckler is a 'male' form.

Post-1990 discussions of historical novels written in the twentieth century, not surprisingly, include more women writers, but these have tended to be concerned with specific areas rather than with an overview of the form. Margaret Scanlan's *Traces of Another Time: History and Politics in Postwar British Fiction* (1990) includes texts by Elizabeth Bowen, Iris Murdoch, Isabel Colegate and Doris Lessing. Scanlan's interest is in that '"other historical novel": sceptical, ironic and "discontinuous", seeking to exploit rather than cover up the boundaries between history and fiction' (1990, 3). The novels she discusses, however, are concerned with the history of the twentieth century itself (which would not qualify, for instance, under Fleishman's definition of a historical novel), and especially with the issues of de-colonisation raised by the early part of the century. Very much a writer's meditation on the genre, A.S. Byatt's *On Histories and Stories: Selected Essays* (2000) focuses on writers from the latter half of the century and is perceptive on Hilary Mantel, Penelope Fitzgerald, Pat Barker and, not surprisingly, Byatt's own work. Helen Hughes' *The Historical Romance* (1993) usefully analyses the shift from the male-centred historical romance (usually a swashbuckler) of writers such as Sir Arthur Conan-Doyle, Rafael Sabatini, Stanley Weyman and Jeffery Farnol, to the female-centred popular historical romance of Heyer and Cartland which dominates after the 1930s. With this shift the term 'historical romance' moves from being synonymous with an adventure story to meaning a love story. Julie Abraham's *Are Girls Necessary? Lesbian Writing and Modern Histories* (1996) discusses the ways in which lesbian writers have turned to history to provide narrative alternatives to heterosexual plots. Ruth Hoberman's important study *Gendering Classicism: The Ancient World in Twentieth-Century Women's Historical Fiction* (1997) is the most sustained and illuminating discussion of women's historical fiction and has been especially helpful to my own thinking, but it is concerned only with novels set in ancient Greece or Rome.

What has been missing is a survey of twentieth-century women's historical novels which would trace continuities in terms of development over the century and look at the connections between the different types of novel, including the sceptical historical novel, the popular romance and the novel of the classical world. Rather than an attempt to define the 'historical novel' by excluding the allegedly unhistorical, my own approach here has been inclusive, tracing connections between the different uses to which women have put history.

While radically modifying Lukács' account, it is important that we retain his recognition that formal and compositional choices involve ideological and political implications. The choices women writers make – in terms of narrative and plot structure (romance, quest, family saga, etc.), the historical period in which they set their novel, the deployment of point of view, the side they take in the conflicts they explore (Elizabeth I or Mary Queen of Scots? Cavaliers or Roundheads? Romans or Britons?), the decision as to whether to use period or twentieth-century language and so on – all have ideological and political implications. But they need to be seen in relation to *women*'s engagement with history and not dismissed as 'unhistorical', 'factually inaccurate' or merely 'irrelevant' according to a male-defined model.

A maternal genealogy: Sophia Lee's *The Recess* (1783)

It is also necessary, if we are not to be accomplices in the murder of the mother, for us to assert that there is a genealogy of women. [. . .] Let us try to situate ourselves within this female genealogy so as to conquer and keep our identity. Nor let us forget that we already have a history, that certain women have, even if it was culturally difficult, left their mark on history and that all too often we do not know them. (Irigaray, 1991, 44)

Given the way that adherence to Scott's novels as a model for the 'classical historical novel' works to exclude women's novels from accounts of the genre, it is more useful to trace what Luce Irigaray would call a 'female genealogy' of the twentieth-century woman's historical novel, by going back beyond Scott to the women writers whose influence Lukács so summarily dismissed. The work of Peter Garside, Ina Ferris and Katie Trumpener has, as I mentioned, uncovered a body of work, much of it by Irish and women writers, which preceded and influenced Scott. Trumpener shows how the historical novel emerged out of the national tale developed by these writers. Both the national tale and the historical novel can be seen as concerned with cultural or social difference and development but the national tale maps this in terms of geography (contrasting different areas and 'national' characters) while the historical novel traces temporal movement. The term 'historical novel' itself may, Trumpener notes, have first appeared in the subtitle of Jane West's *The Loyalists: An Historical Novel* (1812), which features a 'Sir William Waverley' who trims between opposing sides in the English Civil War (Trumpener, 1993, 694, 719). Moreover, Trumpener argues, Scott's adaptations reverse the politics of some of these novels, offering a Tory rather than Jacobin, and conservative rather than dissenting view of progress (695).

An even earlier novel, Sophia Lee's *The Recess, or A Tale of Other Times* (1783), according to its editor April Alliston, has strong claims to be considered 'the first important and fully developed text for both the "female" Gothic and the historical Gothic strains in English fiction' (Lee, 2000, xiv). A novel which influenced both Scott (most obviously *Kenilworth* [1821]) and Ann Radcliffe, it nevertheless establishes an alternative model for the woman's historical novel from that offered by Scott, one which theorises *women's* relationship to history in a very different way. As a Gothic historical novel, it highlights the continuities between the Gothic and the historical novels, rather than the discontinuities emphasised by accounts which stress Scott as the single-handed progenitor of a new form. Both models, I would suggest, have been important for women, but the domination of the *Waverley* model in standard criticism has obscured the other possibilities, and partly explains the exclusion of so many women's novels from the accepted canon. *The Recess* both exemplifies and sets precedents for the ways in which women have handled several key issues in the writing of historical novels: the choice of historical period, deployment of point of view, 'taking sides' on a historical conflict, and the question of language.

Set during the reign of Elizabeth I, *The Recess* is the story of the supposed twin daughters of Mary Queen of Scots and the Duke of Norfolk. For fear of reprisals from Elizabeth who has executed their father and imprisoned their mother, Matilda and Ellinor are brought up hidden in the eponymous 'recess', an underground structure with rooms and passages. Lee inserts these two invented characters into 'history' through their secret romantic involvements with two of Elizabeth's favourites, both of which lead to extraordinary hardships for the two endlessly victimised heroines. Matilda marries the Earl of Leicester, bears his daughter and among other vicissitudes is shipwrecked and spends several years imprisoned in a Spanish colony. Ellinor falls in love with the Earl of Essex and, disguised in masculine clothing, follows him to Ireland. There his mishandling of the campaign against the Irish is attributed to his desperation when Ellinor is captured by Tyrone, who attempts to make her his mistress.

By using invented characters in a factual historical setting,[4] Lee draws attention to the way in which she is enacting an imaginary recovery or recreation of women's lost and unrecorded history. The story is allegedly 'extracted' from a manuscript and updated into contemporary language (Lee, 2000, 5). The recess itself (once part of a convent) is an almost over-determined symbol for the way in which women have been, in Sheila Rowbotham's term, 'hidden from history' (1973). Both prison and refuge, womb and tomb, it figures the way in which the heroines are confined by their biological gender as well as their repetition of their matrilineal heritage, as they, like their mother, are imprisoned and 'murdered'. The novel dramatises what becomes one of the central concerns of the female Gothic, the erasure of women's 'maternal genealogy' within patriarchal culture and history.

Lee's novel, like many women's historical novels, was criticised for its lack of historical 'truth', that is, for its failure to adhere to the 'facts' of history, as well as its reduction of all motive (as in Essex's debacle in Ireland, or Elizabeth's jealousy of the heroines) to personal emotion. David Richter repeats such criticisms of the novel's 'anachronisms', sentimentality and 'distortions of history' though he acknowledges its parodic elements (1992, 86–7). He makes, however, the important point that while Hegel (and thus Lukács) emphasises the role of the world-historical individual who reshapes the world, for Lee it is (sexual) *desire* that shapes the world (88).

The very excesses for which the text is criticised – the lack of probability, the disregard for agreed chronology, the excessive sentiment of the heroines – all work to disturb accepted accounts of 'history' and suggest that what it offers as 'truth' is in fact equally fictional, and damaging to women. While the view of history which Lukács finds at the heart of Scott's work is one of linear progress enacted through dialectical conflict, the image of the 'recess' suggests the exclusion of women from that historical narrative and their confinement to a cyclical repetition of victimisation. Lee's fiction is closer to the model of women's history outlined by Gerda Lerner. Lerner sees women's history as 'spasmodic, uneven and often repetitive' in contrast to the 'systematic story of progress, the methodical building of thesis, antithesis and synthesis' of male history (1994, 220). Whereas Waverley, as the moderate man, 'wavers' between opposing sides, finally representing progressive compromise or 'synthesis', Lee's sisters represent a possibility denied. Matilda's daughter dies (a repetition of her mother and grandmother's fates) and it is the brother of Matilda and Ellinor, James I, who ascends the throne after Elizabeth, restoring male rule. This focus on repeated defeat and lost possibilities is particularly important in the women's historical novel, especially in the 1930s.

As Jane Spencer argues, *The Recess* transforms history into romance in order to reinstate women and the arena of private emotion. But by its excessive emphasis on suffering and victimisation it simultaneously calls into question the power of romance ideology and the 'fantasy of female power' it holds out to women. Romantic love, *The Recess* suggests, 'is an illusion standing in the way of women's access to the romance of mother–daughter reconciliation and female power' (Spencer, 1986, 200). Thus Ellinor denounces love as 'exquisite delusion! Captivating error!' (Lee, 2000, 158). It divides the sisters from their mother, from their cousin Elizabeth, and Matilda from her daughter. It also divides them from each other and, given their twinship, this suggests a damaging division at the heart of female identity itself, reinforced by Ellinor's final madness.

The first-person narrative structure of the text, memoir-letters written by the sisters, dramatises both this division and the subjective nature of historical narrative itself. The first half of the novel is narrated by Matilda. The opening of Ellinor's 'life', addressed to her 'much-loved, little-trusted' sister (Lee, 2000, 154), then throws into doubt the 'truth' of this first narrative by questioning Matilda's romantically blinded view of Leicester, whom Ellinor sees as cold-hearted and callous. This deployment of multiple viewpoints further enhances the destabilising effect Lee has produced by centring the narrative in a female consciousness which is marginalised from the main trajectory of history. This handling of narrative point of view and the use of a view from below or to the side of conventional histories is one of Lee's most important bequests to her successors, and can be seen not only in the 'Gothic' romances of Victoria Holt but also in Naomi Mitchison's histories of the conquered. Such an interest in multiple or unreliable narrative viewpoints is often used by women writers to disrupt any view of history itself as unitary and closed.

Another important precedent in terms of historical period is indicated by Lee's choice of the reign of Elizabeth I for her setting. 'The reign of Elizabeth was that of romance' she tells the reader in her 'Advertisement' (2000, 5), a comment which initially appears to echo the frequent construction of the Elizabethan period as a 'Golden Age' for Britain. Given Lee's undercutting of the ideology of 'romance', however, this is a double-edged comment, not least because Elizabeth is actually the villain of this novel, responsible for executing Mary Queen of Scots and persecuting and imprisoning her daughters. In choosing this period, Spencer points out, Lee was setting the romance as a fantasy of female power in 'a historical period when one women did wield great power' (1986, 195). It is also, however, a period when through intense public focus on Elizabeth's marriage prospects the usually private subject of courtship, the stuff of romance, becomes of national and, indeed, international importance, central to the business of the court and government. The political and strategic importance of Elizabeth's marriage made her ostensibly private emotions of historic significance.

The lives of the queens and princesses, as Bonnie G. Smith (1984) has noted, have held a particular attraction for women historians, notably Agnes Strickland who produced the successful *The Lives of the Queens of England* (1840–1848). More recently, the work of Antonia Fraser and Alison Weir suggests their continuing fascination. Given the frequent lack of recorded information about women's lives, it is not surprising that royal women, whose lives are a matter of record (however partial), have been the focus of such interest. This fascination is further based on the confluence of public and private history in their lives, and on the possibility of female power. It is this which has drawn female novelists, from Lee down to her twentieth-century successors, including Margaret Irwin, Norah Lofts, Anya Seton and Jean Plaidy (who has fictionalised the lives of most of the notable queens in Europe).

The particular attraction of the Tudor period with the first Queens Regnant of England in Mary Tudor and Elizabeth I, and their Bluebeard-like father Henry VIII with his six wives, as well as their cousin Mary Queen of Scots, is obvious. Moreover, through the names of her two heroines Lee directs our attention to earlier historically important royal women: Matilda, the daughter of Henry I, who should have been the first Queen Regnant of England but was deposed by the barons who did not want a female monarch, and Eleanor of Aquitaine, wife of Matilda's son Henry II and mother of Richard I and King John, and an intelligent and powerful personality in her own right.

It is Mary Stuart, rather than Elizabeth I, who is central to the early development of the historical novel as a genre. April Alliston has drawn attention to the way in which Lee makes intertextual use of an even earlier French text, Marie de La Fayette's *La Princesse de Cleves* (1678). This is often cited as the first psychological novel, but it is also, given its setting in the sixteenth-century French court where Mary Stuart is an important character, a very early historical novel. Lee is thus situating *The Recess* in an established female tradition of writing historiography as fiction (Lee, 2000, xv). La Fayette's focus on adulterous desire and romantic intrigue connects the psychological novel back to the ideal of courtly love which is so important to the romance in its older sense. It is also a tradition which centralises Mary Stuart as a feminine ideal of refined elegance, 'perfectly delightful' in both mind and body (de La Fayette, 1961, 16). As Jayne Elizabeth Lewis notes, Mary's tragic life has been 'inexhaustibly narrated from the sixteenth century forward' (1995, 166).[5] 'Turned by her many personal tragedies into a ruler of the private realm', Mary, Lewis suggests, represents 'the point where modern historiography meets sentimental discourse' (1995, 166, 167). Or to put it another way, it represents the possibility of a feminised historiography.

This period, then, gives us two rival queens who have constantly been assessed in relation to each other, and who are usually constructed as exemplary of contrasting forms of womanhood. If Mary is the feminine ideal, a woman victimised by her gender, Elizabeth is constructed by Lee as a 'masculine' woman because (like a man) she puts the public world of politics above the private world of emotions: her 'love was ever so subordinate a consideration' (Lee, 2000, 84). Yet Lee undercuts this by showing how Mary's daughters are victimised precisely because they subordinate all else to love. Although Lee can offer a critique of women's victimisation by romantic love, she cannot imagine an alternative female autonomy.

In taking sides with either Elizabeth or Mary, women historians and novelists signal their allegiance to both a version of female identity and a view of women's place within history. But it is the historical shifts in this allegiance which are most striking. By the mid-twentieth century, it is Elizabeth who is most often valorised as a model for female autonomy, whereas Mary is more often seen as a woman who became a victim because of her poor judgement of character, not least in her marriage choices. Writing in 1988, Susan Bassnett records having always taken Elizabeth's side even as a school-girl because 'she seemed to be a winner [. . .] she was, in short, a model of an independent woman for a girl growing up in the 1950s' (1997, 3).

The Recess, then, establishes one model (very different from that of Scott) for the woman's historical novel. It exemplifies two important potentialities in the woman's historical novel. First, the transformation of history into romance allows the reinsertion of women's concerns. At its most extreme this can become the use of a historical setting as a 'pretext' to allow the imagination to rove, but while this kind of writing is often stigmatised as 'escapism', it has, as Carmen Callil suggested, subversive possibilities. Secondly, David Punter has argued that

> the reason why it is so difficult to draw a line between Gothic fiction and historical fiction is that Gothic itself seems to have *been* a mode of history, a way of perceiving an obscure past and interpreting it. (Punter, 1996, 52)

Women writers have used the Gothic precisely as 'a mode of history' because it expresses their complex and ambivalent relationship to history as both events and narrative. Lee uses the Gothic mode to stage a coded but sustained (and angry) political protest against the ways in which women have been excluded from history.

The influence of Lee's novel in the twentieth century can often be traced through the intertextual use of the work of women writers such as Jane Austen, the Brontës and Elizabeth Gaskell, themselves influenced by Lee or her successors. Austen, of course, did not write historical novels but in one sense we now read her novels as 'historical'. (When I told one student that I was working on a study of women's historical novels she exclaimed, 'Oh, I love Jane Austen'. Her mistake is indicative not of ignorance but of the way that Austen is now seen, through the perspective offered by popular 'Regency Romances' and television costume drama, as 'historical'.) The twentieth-century woman's historical novel looks back to novels by women in earlier centuries for its inspiration, rather than traditional historiography, because novels have been a better source of information on women's past lives than 'real solemn history'. Thus a direct line of descent runs down from Sophia Lee and Ann Radcliffe via Jane Austen to Georgette Heyer and down to A.S. Byatt, just as another runs through the Brontës and Elizabeth Gaskell to Catherine Cookson.

The masqueraders: cross-writing, gender, costume

Shakespearian drama was, April Alliston points out, another important influence on Lee, especially *Cymbeline* with its ostensibly orphaned noble siblings and its cross-dressing heroine (Lee, 2000, xv). For Bryher, the girl-page in Elizabethan literature, especially Bellario in Beaumont and Fletcher's *Philaster*, was an important symbol of freedom from gender constraints: male disguise 'gave liberty in an age when freedom was unknown to women' (Bryher, 1920, 442). Whatever the historical reality, within literature such girl-pages represented, for Bryher, 'the very spirit of adventure' (452). In the woman's historical novel the cross-dressed heroine is as important a figure as the tragic queen. She can be seen as a figure for the woman novelist herself, 'cross-writing'[6] as a man in order to enter into the 'masculine' sphere of history as the Elizabethan girl-page cross-dressed to take an active part in the events of the play.

The term 'costume novel' is generally used in a derogatory fashion to distinguish the popular novel which 'tends to employ the period setting only as a decorative background to the leading characters' (Baldick, 1991, 100) from the 'serious' historical novel. But the term indicates a key element in the attraction of historical novels for women, which is quite simply the clothes: Elizabethan ruffs and farthingales, Regency pelissees and muffs, even Victorian crinolines and bonnets. Many of these were probably uncomfortable and constraining to wear (and, possibly, of doubtful cleanliness) but can be glamorous and sensual in the imagination. At one level this is a strong part of the appeal of popular historical novels like Margaret Mitchell's *Gone with the Wind* (1936), *Forever Amber*, or those of Georgette Heyer and her imitators.

Comparisons with the 'serious' or 'literary' historical novel assume that the 'costume' novel with its 'decorative' period-setting implies that people in the past were no different to us, that human psychology, our essential self, is unchanging. In fact, I want to suggest here that, in the woman's historical novel at least, the opposite can be true. The word 'costume' implies the pleasures of dressing-up, the thrills of the masquerade, of 'acting' a part. The motif of masquerade, especially of a girl dressing in boy's clothing, is a recurring one in women's historical novels and it connects in an especially suggestive way to feminist theories of gendered subjectivity as socially, culturally and, above all, historically constructed. More than just glamour and sensuality, 'costume' suggests the transgressive possibility of flexible gender identity acted out through clothes, of what Joan Riviere called 'Womanliness as masquerade', or what Judith Butler in *Gender Trouble* (1990) theorises as gender as performativity. The masquerade in women's historical novels suggests a performance which is as aware of its own theatricality as was that of Shakespeare's boy-actor playing Imogen, Viola or Rosamond playing a boy. It also suggests an understanding that masculinity itself is a masquerade.

Writing in 1979, Carolyn Heilbrun bemoaned the failure of women writers to imagine autonomous women characters and argued that they tended to project autonomy onto a male character. The exemplary figure she discusses is Mary Renault, one of the most important and under-discussed women writers of the 1950s, but whom Heilbrun regards as 'an apologist for female subservience' (1979, 77). The search for autonomous female characters as positive role models for women has meant that feminist criticism has been relatively slow to start looking at the ways in which women writers have used male protagonists and characters to explore masculinity, as well as femininity, as a social construction rather than a 'norm'.

'Women have always written about men', Jane Miller points out, 'but they have needed to be extremely circumspect about doing so' (1986, 13). Given this need for circumspection, the historical novel offered women writers a way of writing about masculinity, as well as exploring the complexities and attractions of power, both political and sexual. As novels like Marjorie Bowen's *The Viper of Milan* (1906) show, the historical novel has been *par excellence* the form which has enabled women to write about men and the male world of politics and warfare. Bowen's bestselling novel, written when she was just 17 and set in fourteenth-century Italy, opens with the despotic villain, Visconti, disposing of his parents and continues on a wild romp as he ruthlessly crushes all resistance to his reign, ending with all the main characters dead. As with several anatomies of evil (most famously *Paradise Lost*), the text is morally disconcerting because it does not offer an attractive-enough alternative to the excesses of Visconti. Indeed, the ambiguous erotic attractions of Visconti are hinted at when he dresses as a poor student in order to seduce the daughter of a painter. Historical fiction, Anthea Trodd points out, 'enabled Bowen to escape the confines of the domestic' and she used male pseudonyms ('George Preedy' and 'Joseph Shearing' – her real name was Margaret Campbell) to continue this for 40 years (1998, 111). It also offered Bowen, and other women writers, a way to escape the confines of the romance plot which, as Rachel Blau DuPlessis (1985) has shown, exercised a stranglehold over the plots of women's novels which had to be broken at the beginning of the twentieth century.

The Viper of Milan is a very different kind of woman's historical novel from *The Recess*. But both suggest that women's exclusion from traditional history has led them to think of history in a different way from the model epitomised by Scott. Equally interesting is the fact that the 'popular' historical novel has given women more freedoms than the realist version. Another hugely popular historical novel, Baroness Orczy's *The Scarlet Pimpernel* (1905) is equally interesting. As Helen Hughes (1993) shows, this combines two of the types identified by Umberto Eco, the male adventure story or swashbuckler, and the female-centred romance. While this ostensibly extended its interest to both male and female readers, I would also suggest that it gave *female* readers the double pleasure of identifying with both the heroine and, through cross-reading, the hero. This potentiality is enhanced by the novel's concern with masks and masquerade, enacted through the hero's endless disguises. In Sir Percy Blakeney, Orczy created a double-faceted aristocratic hero, whose almost feminine pose of foppish indolence and dandified love of fine clothes masks a 'masculine' brain and limitless physical courage. It also masks the psychological damage caused by the madness of his mother, and his intense passion for his beautiful wife. Sir Percy Blakeney was to prove an extremely seductive model for the historical heroes produced by women writers, not least Georgette Heyer and Dorothy Dunnett.

In cross-writing about/as men, women writers can be seen as engaged in the act of ventriloquism, adopting a male voice through the use of a male protagonist or first-person narrator. In her study of the ways in which male writers have ventriloquised female voices in texts, Elizabeth Harvey notes that: 'Historical reconstructions are always a kind of ventriloquisation [. . .] a matter of making the past seem to speak in the voice that the present gives it' (1992, 6). Given the need to be 'circumspect' when writing about men, the historical novel offers women the opportunity of carrying out a double ventriloquism – a male voice from the past – with impunity. But this also links very closely to the concern with masquerade.

While male writers, as Harvey shows, have used cross-gender ventriloquising as a way of appropriating and silencing the feminine voice, women writing as men are working from a very different position. As Ben Knights puts it:

> The woman writing her way into a man may be engaged in an activity which has much in common with post-colonial rewriting of traditional power relationships [. . .] these are male narrators reread through the lens of marginality. (1999, 139)

Most crucially, a woman cross-writing as a man exposes the constructed or performative nature of masculinity itself. Judith Butler argues that, 'In imitating gender, drag implicitly reveals the imitative nature of gender itself – as well as its contingency' (1990, 137). Similarly, a woman cross-writing makes visible the fact that masculinity is not a given, a norm against which femininity is judged lacking, but itself a learned performance. Thus, as I have suggested, the girl masquerading as a boy is a figure for the historical novelist herself, aware that 'history' is a 'fiction' but also aware that this gives her the freedom to write herself out of the 'recess' and into the mainstream.

This study of the woman's historical novel in the twentieth century is organised according to decades in order to trace the chronological development of the form. This is at best an artificial, even arbitrary, arrangement, especially where a series of books by one author overlaps decades, but it does foreground the relationship between the text and its time. In contrast to the tendency to see historical fiction as 'retreating into the past' and thus escaping the concerns of the contemporary, I want to explore the close and complex relationship between any historical novel and the moment of its production. The concern with masquerade and cross-dressing is not, for instance, a static one, but changes across the century. In the historical novel of the 1920s and 1940s, it is closely related to an understanding that femininity is a 'masquerade' and a desire to escape from its constraints. In the 1950s and the 1990s, it is the notion of masculinity as a performance that seems to fire women's imaginations. Tracing such shifts seems to me a more productive approach than any attempt to judge a novel on whether it is factually 'accurate' or 'authentic' in its representation of the period in which it is set.

2
Entering into History:
The Woman Citizen and the
Historical Novel, 1900–1929

A few women were writing historical novels in the early years of the twentieth century, including Baroness Orczy's Scarlet Pimpernel adventures, the extravagant romances of Marjorie Bowen, and the rural novels of Sheila Kaye-Smith. However, it was after the First World War that British women, entering into history as enfranchised citizens for the first time, turned to the historical novel in substantial numbers and reshaped it into forms which expressed and answered their needs and desires.

The 'Great War' made history visible in ways that were remarkably similar to the effect of the Napoleonic wars as described by Georg Lukács. As A.J.P. Taylor noted, the war transformed the 'mass of people' in Britain into citizens:

> Until August 1914 a sensible, law-abiding Englishman could pass through life and hardly notice the existence of the state, beyond the post office and the policeman. [...] All this was changed by the impact of the Great War. The mass of the people became, for the first time, active citizens. (Taylor, 1970, 25, 26)

With the imposition of British Summer Time in 1916, time itself was altered. History was visibly, as in the Napoleonic wars, 'a mass experience' on a European scale.

The key difference from the process that Lukács describes in the early nineteenth century is that this consciousness of existence within history includes *women* for the first time. Their experience of the war and of enfranchisement under the 1918 Representation of the People Act offered, to rephrase Lukács, 'the concrete possibilities for [*women*] to comprehend their own existence as something historically conditioned, for them to see history as something which deeply affects their daily lives and immediately concerns them' (1983, 24).

The war had liberated many women as they moved into the public world of work to take 'men's jobs'. They worked in munitions factories, in the

Services and the Land Army. Working as nurses and ambulance drivers on the front line, they witnessed the effects of battle. Many wore uniforms for the first time, and some even wore breeches. Such jobs gave many women a feeling of freedom and a new confidence in their own ability, as well as an earned income. The vote, the symbol of citizenship for which the suffragists had been struggling since the mid-nineteenth century, was 'given' to women after the war as a reward for these services, even as they were being pushed, in Deirdre Beddoe's phrase, 'back to home and duty' (1989).

The concept of women's citizenship was central to the campaign to get the vote extended to women on equal grounds with men during the 1920s. After 1918, the National Union of Women's Suffrage Societies changed its name to the National Union of Societies for Equal Citizenship. There was also an effort to educate women for their new role as citizens (Caine, 1997, Chapter 5). This notion of citizenship was problematic, however, in the face of the anti-feminist backlash of the inter-war period, and there was a growing sense of disillusionment. The 1919 Sex Disqualifaction (Removal) Act made it possible for women to stand for parliament and to enter the professions. But in practice, women were kept out of the centres of power. As Rose Macaulay wrote, 'the electorate, being mostly of the male sex, showed that the only women they desired to have in Parliament were the wives of former members who had ceased to function as such, through death, peerage, or personal habits' (1965, 310). 'The Act means nothing, we have been hoaxed' said *Time and Tide* in 1922 (Beddoe, 2000, 83). Women's consciousness of their participation in the State as citizens was fractured not only by their guilt that they had benefited from the sacrifices made by men in the war, but also by this suspicion that they had been 'hoaxed'.

The 'classical historical novel', Lukács argues, was born out of the new conception of history engendered by the Napoleonic wars. Similarly, the 'Great War' transformed literature. Edith Wharton, like many others, believed that the war had made a consciousness of history immediate in ways that had irrevocably changed the nature of fiction:

> Before the war you could write fiction without indicating the period, the present being assumed. The war has put an end to that for a long time, and everything will soon have to be timed with reference to it. In other words *the historical novel with all its vices will be the only possible form for fiction*. (Lewis, 1993, 423–4, my emphasis)

The majority of war memoirs and novels directly concerned with the war did not appear until 1928, but notions of 'before' and 'afterwards' inflect writing well before then. The fragmentation of form and experimentation with language in Modernism was one attempt to convey this new post-war 'wasteland' of civilisation. For Joyce's Stephen Dedalus, famously, history was 'a nightmare from which I am trying to awaken' (1971, 40).

While critics such as Avrom Fleishman and Harold Orel have seen the 1920s as the point where the traditional historical novel, associated with the nineteenth-century realism, peters out, it is actually the point where it changes direction and gains renewed vigour in women's hands. This appropriation of the form can be seen as the result of several factors: women's sense of their entry into history as citizens, the rise of the woman historian, and the emergence of university-educated women writers, usually with a degree in History or English (both then considered suitable subjects for women students). Among the university-educated novelists of these years who wrote historical fiction were Rose Macaulay, Margaret Kennedy, Lettice Cooper, Hilda Reid, Margaret Irwin, H.F.M. Prescott, D.K. Broster, Mary Renault (all Oxford University), Phyllis Bentley (London University), and Helen Waddell (Queen's University, Belfast and then lectured at Oxford). Naomi Mitchison and Mary Butts studied for but did not complete degrees. Georgette Heyer attended history lectures at Westminster College, and Sylvia Townsend Warner was a respected musicologist. The rise of the woman's historical novel is thus intimately connected to women's new access to university education.

The value of this education gained a further urgency as, after the war, women turned to the study of history, hoping that an understanding of the past could help them to prevent future conflict. Returning to Somerville College, after her time as a VAD, Vera Brittain made a conscious decision to change subject from English to History:

> It's my job, now, to find out all about it, and to try to prevent it, in so far as one person can, from happening to other people in the days to come. Perhaps the careful study of man's past will explain to me much that seems inexplicable in his disconcerting present. Perhaps the means of salvation are already there, implicit in history, unadvertised, carefully concealed by the war-mongers [. . .]. (Brittain, 1935, 471)

In her distrust of the 'war-mongers', Brittain was echoing the sentiments of her generation, many of whom felt that they had been led, or pushed, into war by the jingoistic lies of an older generation who had watched the slaughter of their sons and daughters from the safety of their armchairs. Increasingly, the post-war 'lost generation' questioned the nationalism and imperialism which they felt underpinned the war. It was associated with a Victorianism debunked by Lytton Strachey's *Eminent Victorians* (1918). Strachey's iconoclastic treatment of nineteenth-century heroes pointed to a new less-hagiographic way of writing both biography and history, a post-Freudian lifting of the veils over what the nineteenth century kept concealed.

Feminism itself had 'created a demand for information about the lives of women in history, and a need to understand how they lived' (Trodd, 1998, 110), but to supply this information the woman historian needed to develop new concepts of what constituted 'history', often using her imagination since evidence was so scant. Woolf's 'The Journal of Mistress Joan Martyn' (1906), for instance, set out 'an agenda for rewriting history by including the details of daily life, in particular those of domestic life, which means writing the excluded history of women' (Scott, 1990, 647). As a means of exploring history, Woolf's woman historian, Miss Rosamond Merridew, chooses the diary of a young woman over either household account books or a stud book. While the account books symbolise economic history, the stud books suggest the upper-class obsession with 'breeding' which ensures primogeniture. 'The history of England has been the history of the male line, not of the female,' as Woolf put it elsewhere (1979, 44). In *A Room of One's Own* (1929) Woolf noted how little information about women's lives could be gleaned from standard texts like G.M. Trevelyan's *History of England*, and urged 'Ferndean' students to search out the obscure documents and papers needed to gather the facts to 'rewrite' history (1977, 45).

Such rewriting had already begun in the work of women scholars like Eileen Power on medieval nunneries, Jane Harrison on the classical world, Helen Waddell on Medieval Latin lyrics, Enid Welsford on the court masque, Jessie Western on anthropology, and Margaret Murray on witches. The interest in women's history was intensified in 1928, the year that women finally got the vote on equal terms with men. Ray Strachey's seminal *The Cause* (1928) was published that year, together with numerous articles in periodicals such as *Time and Tide*. The interest in historical women's lives was spotted by the publisher Gerald Howe who commissioned a monograph series on *Representative Women* which was to include Naomi Mitchison's *Anna Comnena* (1928), as well as studies of Aphra Behn, Jane Welsh Carlyle and Elizabeth Barratt Browning.

Women historians were engaged in what Woolf called 'turn[ing] history wrong side out' (1979, 44) to expose its underside. The impact of their work can be traced in the portrayal of, for instance, witches and nunneries in women's historical novels. Women's attitude to history was ambivalent, characterised by that double consciousness Woolf described so well, that 'sudden splitting off of consciousness, say in walking down Whitehall, when from being the natural inheritor of that civilisation, [a woman] becomes on the contrary, outside of it, alien and critical' (1977, 93). Both inheritor and outsider, the woman historian looked for new ways of writing history which would allow her to include what had been excluded from traditional accounts with their emphasis on 'big' public events and 'great men'. As Bonnie G. Smith (1984) argues, the invisibility of women in traditional histories, the inappropriateness of conventional chronology with its emphasis on 'progress', and problems with form and narrative, encouraged women historians to focus on social history. Women turned to the historical novel because it could show 'a double world [...] in which the public moment both influenced and formed the background for domestic experience'

(Smith, 1984, 721). To extend Woolf's metaphor, such novels could expose both the 'right' and the 'wrong' side of the tapestry of history.

A university education gave women writers the skills and confidence needed for the research and this is reflected in their historical novels. Hilda Reid 'by far the best historical student' at Somerville according to Vera Brittain (1985, 324), took 7 years to research and write *Phillida* (1928), a novel about the beginnings of British imperialism in Africa set in the Commonwealth period. D.K. Broster apparently consulted eighty works before she started writing *The Flight of the Heron* (1925), the first of her Jacobite trilogy (Broster, 1929, biographical note). Broster's own career – she was for several years secretary to the Regius Professsor of History at Oxford – suggests that, despite their academic qualifications, many women found the doors of academe barred to further progress, and thus turned to fiction.

In turning to historical fiction, they were turning to a form which had lost status through its association with the kind of swashbuckling romances produced by Rafael Sabatini, Jeffery Farnol and Stanley Weyman. These used history, as Helen Hughes shows, as 'an exotic setting to add to the "escape value" of their stories' (1993, 5). In the decade of the General Strike of 1926 such 'escape value' made historical fiction extremely popular and women writers exploited this. But they also started to reshape the form in several important directions. The rural historical novel and the historical fantasy were both important forms in the 1920s but it was the historical romance of Georgette Heyer and the histories of the 'conquered' written by Naomi Mitchison which were to be the most influential developments.

The attraction of the historical romance and the rural novel during and after the war was partly connected to their presentation of English nationality. Lukács argues that the sense of history awakened by the Napoleonic wars engendered a sense of nationhood: 'the appeal to national independence and national character is necessarily connected with a re-awakening of national history, with memories of the past and of past greatness' (1983, 25). The nationhood reawakened during and after the 'Great War' was based on a concept of 'English History' which stressed the continuity of a common English past, primarily drawn from English Literature (especially Shakespeare) and associated with a rural England which was by this stage largely imaginary. The 'decay of rural England' in the face of urban encroachment, and especially the motor car, had been bemoaned well before the war by C.F.G. Masterman in *The Condition of England* (1909).

The appeal of Orczy's Scarlet Pimpernel novels, as Helen Hughes (1993) has shown, was partly their presentation of national identity through a typically 'English' hero associated with a pre-industrial, rural 'deep England'. This English gentleman is the product of a history which is represented as having evolved gradually, rather than having been shaped by bloody class revolutions. English history is thus associated with continuity, moderation and a 'democracy' in which the hierarchy of upper and lower classes co-exist happily. The animal-like revolutionary French mob in *The Scarlet Pimpernel* is contrasted with 'John Bull' in the form of the honest innkeeper Jellyband and his pretty daughter Sally.

The *Scarlet Pimpernel* had shown how the male adventure story or swash-buckler could be combined with the female-centred romance. Although Orczy went on turning out sequels after the war, it was Heyer who was to develop this form, retaining the centrality of Englishness while losing the violence of the Revolutionary setting. In her *The Black Moth* (1921), the hero, a literary descendent of Sir Percy, roams the flowery lanes of his 'beloved South Country' (1965, 90) as a gentleman-highwayman and is described by a woman he has rescued as 'so safe, and so English!' (209).

A similar notion of 'English History' was evoked in the work of the 'rural novelists', Sheila Kaye-Smith, Constance Holme and Mary Webb. These articulated a nostalgia for a lost rural England, invoking what Mary Webb called 'the wistfulness which is the past' (1928b, 9), which was intensified during the war. John Buchan wrote of Webb's *Gone to Earth* (1917), 'I read it at a time when everything that concerned the soil of England seemed precious, and one longed for the old things as a relief from a world too full of urgent novelties' (Webb, 1928a, 7). Buchan appears to be reading it as a historical novel, he thinks, set 'perhaps fifty years ago' (7). In fact, he is deceived – a reference to fruit bottled in 1909 (1928a, 117) reveals the setting to be much later but crucially pre-war. Many of the rural novels *appear* to be historical because they are set in a countryside untouched by the industrial revolution, let alone post-war modernity. Webb argued that, 'When antique things are also country things, they are easier to write about, for there is a permanence, a continuity in country life which makes the lapse of centuries seem of little moment' (1928b, 9). Although they seem to affirm rural continuity, as Trodd points out, the rural novels actually insist on discontinuity, on the gulf between the countryside and urban modernity (1998, 108). Webb's 'wistfulness' is the emotion of the present projected back onto the past.

Mary Webb's early novels, as Glen Caveliero rightly argues, had been 'weakened by the awareness that we were also in a contemporary world – or, more strictly, by a failure to imply that we were not' (1977, 142). In contrast, by setting *Precious Bane* (1924) at the time of the Napoleonic wars, Webb 'succeeds in distancing it sufficiently for it to exist in a world that is at once physically real and yet psychologically abstracted' (1977, 142). Interestingly, Stanley Baldwin emphasised Mary Webb's descent from Scott's clan in the introduction to *Precious Bane* (1928b, 5), thus suggesting her credentials as a historical novelist.

As a historical novel, *Precious Bane* is typical of the 1920s in its re-imagining of the daily experience of what its heroine, Prue Sarn, calls 'us women, leading such lost-and-forgotten lives' (1928b, 102). The novel explicitly sets itself against the exploitative values of 'great man' history: 'When folk tell me of this great man and that great man', Prue remarks, 'I think to myself, Who was stinted of joy for his glory? How many old folk and children did his coach wheels go over' (1928b, 91). Through the use of a first-person narrator, Webb gives a flexible and poetic voice to a strong heroine who appears to transmit an oral tradition through the written word.

Precious Bane celebrates the rural community which it presents through an evocation of lost customs and lore (love-spinning, harvest home and so on), which gave an important place to women and their work. Prue's physical capability and strength imply that, despite her brother Gideon's exploitation of her labour, pre-industrial women had more freedom and autonomy than their Victorian descendants. This reflects, perhaps, the experience of women who became land girls during the war. The pre-industrial age becomes a lost idyll in terms of gender as well as nationality.

But *Precious Bane* also shows how women have historically been victimised in such communities, through its reworking of two important images of women. The first is the witch, a powerful image of women's potential powers and their victimisation as spinsters, which, possibly as a result of Margaret Murray's work, appears frequently in other 1920s texts, most famously Sylvia Townsend Warner's *Lolly Willowes* (1926). Stigmatised as a witch because she has a 'hare-shotten lip' and lives alone, Prue faces being drowned at the end of the novel.

The second image is that of Venus, symbolising female beauty and the power of sexual love, invoked when Prue poses as Venus raised by the wizard Beguildy. In taking a disfigured 'witch-like' heroine and insisting on her bodily beauty and her right to sexual fulfilment by having her masquerade as Venus, Webb was being far more radical than admirers such as Buchan or Stanley Baldwin (whose championing of Webb made her reputation) recognised. Interestingly, Prue's status as a writer (if only of her own story) prefigures by some years Woolf's depiction in *A Room of One's Own* of the ducked witch as 'a lost novelist, a suppressed poet' (1977, 48).

The distancing of a historical context lends *Precious Bane* the enchantment of romance in a wider sense, but it is also more narrowly a romance in the sense that it is a woman's love story, ending with Prue literally carried off on her lover's horse. It is at this point in the inter-war years that the historical romance 'becomes predominantly a woman's genre, which it certainly had never been before' (Hughes, 1993, 3).

Women's use of a historical setting is directly connected to what were perceived as the difficulties of writing romance in a 'modern' world. In a world where women were 'citizens' equal with men, the form of romance which depended on a masterful Byronic hero and coy, virginal heroine looked a little dated. Moreover, the work of Freud, the sexologists and Marie Stopes had demystified sex and hence love. In Georgette Heyer's *Pastel* (1929) the contemporary heroine tells her mother:

You can't be romantic in these times [...] Psychologists have written so much about love and passion and marriage that it's all cut and dried, and you can look it up in the index. When you were young, Mummy, brides went away in blushing ignorance; now they pack Marie Stopes' book in their suitcase. (1977, 137)

Hence Heyer's own use of a historical setting for romance.

Moreover, in the 1920s, women were facing a population imbalance, exacerbated by the war, which had led to what the papers were presenting as a 'man shortage' and a 'million' so-called 'superfluous women' who would never be able to marry (Wallace, 2000, 16). Many women were haunted by the belief that their ideal young man had been killed off, like so many of his generation, in the war, and that any suitor who did appear would be in Rosamond Lehmann's words 'a secondary substitute, a kind of simulacrum' (quoted in Tindall, 1985, 32). The impossibility of romance in an age of sex manuals and a man shortage explains the attraction and, indeed, the perceived necessity of a retreat into the past for women during these years.

The modern woman's desire for an unattainable male ideal – as banished by modernity as the countryside invoked by the rural novels, and as illusory – is explored in Margaret Irwin's time-slip novel, *Still She Wished for Company* (1924). The ideal man desired by the contemporary heroine, Jan, is composed of fragments of her reading:

La Rochefoucauld's Maxims, Lord Chesterfield's Letters, Congreve's Valentine, Lovelace without his insatiable vanity: a man of easy ironic wit, assured composure, impossible to ruffle, and yet of fancies as fantastic as her own. (1968, 17)

But he 'can't exist in an age that hurries and scrambles and pushes' (23), so Jan falls in love with a 'Gentleman Unknown' from an eighteenth-century portrait. Paralleled with this is the story of Juliana Clare, sister of the 'Gentleman Unknown'. Juliana's own description of 'this dull year of grace 1779 [where] nothing pretty and romantic ever happened' (25) suggests that condemnation of one's own age as 'unromantic' is perennial. In a further twist, Juliana's brother, Lucien, desires a girl he glimpses only in dreams, and who is clearly Jan. His vampire-like use of Juliana as a medium to try to reach Jan nearly kills her and brings about his own death.

The moral of the novel, as both Jan and Juliana marry the unromantic but safe men who love them, is that the desire for a past which has never existed is a dangerous illusion. However, the novel acknowledges and explores its seductions. Even Donald, Jan's stolid fiancé, admits the power of such desires. Importantly, he links them to both art and love: 'Any servant girl who longs to be a duchess, anyone who has dreams of successful ambition, finds their chief happiness in something that doesn't exist. All artists do. Perhaps most lovers do also' (179).

Rather than the realism Lukács associates with the historical novel, these texts turn to fantasy. The 'abandonment of realism for fantasy and other non-realistic forms', John Lucas has suggested, is a crucial feature of the fiction of the 1920s (1999, 71). Fantasy was used especially to explore issues of gender. Indeed, Jane Marcus has argued that

> the feminist fantasy novel of the twenties [...] is the direct result of political disappointment in the power of the struggle for the vote to change anything [...] a response to realism's failure to make permanent space in the citadels of male power. (1984, 140, 141)

Marcus is mainly concerned with Sylvia Townsend Warner's *Lolly Willowes* and Rebecca West's *Harriet Hume* (1929), but she also discusses *Orlando* (1928). Women's fantasy fiction looks away from the city towards the countryside, even to the wilderness, but it also looks back into history. History functions as a fantasy space, as in Harriet Hume's fantastical description of the three trees in her garden as three ladies from a painting by Sir Joshua Reynolds (West, 1980, 38–49).

The tendency towards history in the fantasy novel is paralleled by a tendency towards fantasy in the historical novel. The use of fantasy or romance elements allowed women writers to destablise the conventions of the 'realist' historical novel associated with Scott. D.K. Broster's *The Flight of the Heron*, for instance, an ostensibly 'realistic' portrayal of the 1745 Jacobite rebellion reminiscent of Scott, is structured around five meetings between the two male protagonists, which have been foretold by a Scottish soothsayer with the 'two sights' (1927, 57). Fantasy, romance and myth are used to turn history 'wrong side out' and to allow the intrusion of elements which have been traditionally excluded and repressed: desire, the irrational, the feminine, and the homoerotic.

This period saw two high-profile court cases which made the subject of homo-eroticism a dangerous one to depict openly. Maud Allen's failed libel suit against Noel Pemberton-Billing in 1918 showed that the possession of sexual knowledge could be used to brand a woman a lesbian (see Wachman, 2001, Chapter 1). The scandalous trial, 10 years later, of Radcliffe Hall's *The Well of Loneliness* (1928) reinforced this fact, as well as showing that books which represented lesbian sexuality risked prosecution and public condemnation. 'No wonder', as Gay Wachman says, 'most representations of sexuality in women's narratives of the 1920s are oblique' (2001, 18).

Fantasy, fable, myth and the historical novel are some of the forms women turn to in order to code homo-erotic desire in oblique ways. In *The True Heart* (1929), for instance, Sylvia Townsend Warner combines history and myth to portray forbidden love in a retelling of the story of Psyche and Eros set in Victorian England. Female writers more often evoked male homo-eroticism than lesbianism, probably because it could be coded within discourses of the male comradeship during wartime, which were already central to the historical novel. Such friendships could be portrayed as reaching across barriers such as nationality, as they had in Scott's *Waverley*. In Broster's *The Flight of the Heron*, for instance, the English Keith Windham ponders the strange bond between himself and the Jacobite (and married) Ewen Cameron. He pictures their intimacy 'like the roots of two trees growing secretly towards each other in darkness' (1927, 319), a telling simile of forbidden, even repressed, attraction.

The supreme example of the historical fantasy novel in the 1920s is, of course, Woolf's *Orlando: A Biography* (1928), which is both the story of an individual, as the subtitle indicates, and a 'myth of English history' (Marcus, 1984, 142). Woolf's use of both forms is informed by that dual consciousness, that sense of being both inheritor and outsider, brilliantly illustrated through Orlando's change of sex.

A concern with history is a constant in Woolf's writing – 'we cannot understand the present if we isolate it from the past', she writes in *The Pargiters* (1978b, 8) – and her work consistently revises traditional narratives. She asserts the superiority of fiction over traditional 'history' as a means of getting at the 'truth':

> though it would be easier to write history – 'In the year 1842 Lord John Russell brought in the Second Reform Bill' and so on – that method of telling the truth seems to me to be so elementary, and so clumsy, that I prefer, where truth is important, to write fiction. (Woolf, 1978b, 9)

Despite its flagrantly fantastical form, *Orlando* is perhaps her most sustained attempt to tell the 'truth' of history through fiction.

Although he acknowledges Woolf's (modernist-influenced) transformation of the historical novel as a genre, Fleishman, curiously, reads *Orlando* as a conservative text concerned with 'the continuity of cultural tradition, expressed in personal identity, throughout the variations of history and despite the destructiveness of time' (1971, 234). Woolf, he argues, 'portrays history as a series of projections of personal style' (233). This misses the fact that Orlando's experiences of history are radically different according to her sex. Like Tiresias, she experiences both sexes but it is only as a woman that she is defined by her sex. Up to the moment of change, 'she had scarcely given her sex a thought' (Woolf, 1977, 96). The sex change, although it does not alter her 'identity' (the mind is androgynous, Woolf suggested in *A Room of One's Own*), does alter her 'future' (87), which, as a woman, is far more circumscribed. She is reduced to pouring tea for Mr Pope in the eighteenth century, and 'dragged down by the weight of her crinoline' (153) in the chilly, marriage-obsessed nineteenth century, although she is given the consolation of romantic love in the form of Marmaduke Bonthrop Shelmerdine.

The change of sex shifts Orlando from the position of 'inheritor' of history to that of 'outsider', symbolised by the fact that her female gender debars her from inheritance of her house and lands – as Vita Sackville-West, the model for Orlando, could not inherit Knole. Even when the lawsuit is settled, the property is entailed upon 'the male heirs of [her] body' (158). English history, like Orlando's house and lands, is the property of the patri-archy, entailed to the 'male line'.

In contrast to Fleishman's emphasis on the continuity of personality through history, Maggie Humm reads *Orlando* as a 'postmodern' text con-cerned with the fragmentation of experience, the multiplicities of identity and instability of gender (1998, 111–25). Woolf's play with gender in the novel suggests not only a coded representation of same-sex desire, but also the idea familiar to us now from the work of Judith Butler that gender is itself performance. On its first publication, Rebecca West noted that *Orlando* refuses the notion of a 'staircase of progress' (Scott, 1990, 593). Humm suggests that Woolf presents history as circular not linear, as a series of scenes obliquely positioned in relation to the traditional grand narratives of political, imperial and literary history and biography. However, it is only in the modern day that Orlando is able to achieve her ambition to be a writer, publishing her poem, 'The Oak Tree'. The novel finishes in the 'present moment' (186) of its publication – 'the twelfth stroke of midnight, Thursday, the eleventh of October, Nineteen Hundred and Twenty Eight' (205) – the year the Equal Franchise Act finally enfranchised women on equal terms with men. *Orlando*, then, enacts women's entry into history as fully-fledged citizens and writers.

Fleishman argues that Woolf's *Orlando* and *Between the Acts* (1941) 'bring the tradition of the English historical novel to a self-conscious close' (1971, 232). On the contrary, they herald the opening of a new act. The 1920s formed the matrix of the woman's historical novel, from which emerged two different but influential writers who were to shape the forms of women's historical fiction over the next century. Georgette Heyer and Naomi Mitchison represent the two major directions woman's historical fiction would take: the historical romance, now indubitably a woman's genre, and the historical novel, used by women to enter the 'male' world of history.

Gender as masquerade: Georgette Heyer's mask of romance

The early historical novels Georgette Heyer wrote in the 1920s are romantic adventures, in the swashbuckling tradition of Farnol and Orczy. These are the exuberant books of a young girl; her first book, *The Black Moth* (1921), was published when she was just 19. But they reveal a fascination with masks and masquerade, which, like fantasy, is used to explore gendered identity as socially constructed and therefore potentially fluid. They look forward to what we would now, following Judith Butler, understand as a notion of gender identity as 'performative' and provisional, produced through 'a stylized repetition of acts' (Butler, 1990, 140).

A consistent bestseller from 1926 until her death in 1974, Heyer has exercised an important but relatively unacknowledged influence on women's writing in the twentieth century.[1] As the founder of the sub-genre of the Regency romance, she inspired not only a host of imitators, but also, more surprisingly, the critically acclaimed A.S. Byatt (see Chapter 10). Heyer uses the romance plot, as Jane Austen did, as a formal structure within which to explore the nature of gender roles and the possibility of an ideal marriage of minds and bodies. While the period setting and the language of her romances have ensured that her historical novels have not dated, they have also meant that critics and reviewers tended to ignore them as just 'another Georgette Heyer'.

Heyer was clearly sensitive to anxieties around gender roles after the war. The four early contemporary novels she wrote are concerned with the position of an intelligent woman within a society where marriage is still her best option. *Pastel* (1929), for instance, begins as a 'spinster novel' typical of the 1920s and becomes an exploration of companionate marriage more typical of the 1930s. Heyer's decision to concentrate on historical novels reflects not only her sense that 'you can't be romantic in these times' (1977, 137) but, given her position as her family's breadwinner for much of her life, the fact that historical romances sold so well. This in itself suggests that they answered particular needs, including escapism, in her audience. *These Old Shades* (1926) made Heyer a bestseller in the year of the General Strike, when not only gender roles but the class order itself seemed to many to be threatened. In the face of this potential disruption, the historical novel, as shaped by Farnol and Orczy, offered the reassuring certainties of a previous order, when men were not merely men but aristocrats who rescued their fellows from foreign revolutionary mobs.

The historical setting in Heyer's novels is not merely escapist. It also offers a fantasy space within which to explore issues around gender which could not be addressed more explicitly. The text which offers the most fruitful way into Heyer's work here is Joan Riviere's essay 'Womanliness as Masquerade' (1929). Riviere discusses the case of a professionally successful and happily married woman, who, when lecturing to a group of male peers, would adopt an incongruously feminine manner, compulsively coquetting with father-figure types. Her anxiety, Riviere suggested, came from her identification with her father, with whom she associated such intellectual work, and her fear that her display of such 'masculine' proficiency (an 'exhibition of herself in possession of the father's penis' in psycho-analytical terms [1986, 38]) would bring retribution from the father. 'Womanliness', Riviere concluded, 'could be assumed and worn as a mask, both to hide the possession of masculinity and to avert the reprisals expected if she was found to possess it' (1986, 38). Moreover, this masculinity could be put 'at the service of the mother' (41) by aiding or assisting weaker or more helpless women.

Oddly enough, the woman Riviere describes sounds not only like Riviere herself (as Stephen Heath notes [1986, 45–61]), but also rather like the Heyer who is depicted in Jane Aiken Hodge's literary biography of her. Tall, strikingly attractive, witty and intelligent, Heyer had a strong attachment to her father which enabled her writing career. *The Black Moth* was written to amuse her younger brother and published on her father's encouragement. She developed into an immensely successful author with a formidable, almost 'masculine' personality. Yet she preferred to appear publicly sheltered behind her identity as 'Mrs Ronald Rougier', wife of a successful barrister. Paradoxically, Heyer was a woman who 'wrote mainly for women, but lived all her life among men whom she preferred' (Hodge, 1985, 210), and became increasingly dismissive of her romances.

Within Heyer's own life, there are layers of 'masks' which offer an illuminating illustration of the predicament of the woman writer at this point. If writing (especially for money) was 'masculine', then the persona of 'Mrs Ronald Rougier' provided an appropriate mask of 'womanliness' which could hide that masculine activity. But historical romance, a 'suitable' genre for a woman writer, also provided a mask behind which 'masculine' desires could be explored. Moreover, by writing 'for women', Heyer can be seen (as with Riviere's patient) as putting her 'masculinity' in the service of weaker women.

Heyer's early novels take the motif of masquerade used by Orczy and Farnol and use it to explore 'womanliness' as something which has to be learned – a 'mask' which women have to assume. The women's reward for entering this masquerade is the love of the man they desire. This is clearest in *These Old Shades*, a reworking of the Elizabethan girl-page motif. The heroine, Leonie, has been forced to dress and live as a boy in the Paris slums by her supposed brother and his brutal wife. From the age of 12 to the age of 19, that is for the 7 years immediately following puberty when most girls undergo gender-specific socialisation, she has been a 'boy'. Bought from her 'brother' by the rakish Justin Alastair, Duke of Avon, she acts as his page until he reveals that he had guessed her sex almost immediately. Her almost hysterical distress at this revelation is because she must now learn to become a girl again. 'I must wear petticoats, and not say bad words, and always be with women', she mourns, 'It is very hard, Monsiegneur. I do not like women. I wish to be with you' (1997, 96).

Taught by Avon and his ultra-feminine sister Fanny, Leonie has to learn to wear petticoats, to dance, to curtsey, and to behave and speak with decorum (even the word 'breeches' is considered improper). Her interim reward for this is that Avon also teaches her to fence: 'If I may learn to fight with a sword I will try very hard to learn the other silly things', she tells him (120). She learns her lessons well enough to captivate society when she is launched into it. Leonie's charm for the other characters as well as the reader comes from her boyishness and her disdain for the limitations of her feminine role. Her 'natural' behaviour is 'boyish', even 'masculine', but she has to learn to assume a 'mask' of femininity. Her final reward for this (once her aristocratic birth is established) is the hand of Avon himself in marriage.

Twenty years older than Leonie and not merely her guardian but also, as he repeatedly reminds her, her 'owner', Avon is clearly a father figure. His endearments for Leonie – 'Infant', 'Child' – emphasise this and his sister tells her own husband: '[Avon] will be the strictest husband in town, and the most delightful! She will always be his infant, I dare swear, and he "Monsiegneur"' (211). Despite this, the marriage is presented as one of equals not merely because Leonie's experiences have made her older than her age but because she redeems Avon. Her worship of Avon is his 'salvation' (228). Avon's friend Hugh Davenant tells him: 'You have learned to love another better than yourself, and I believe you will make your Duchess a good husband' (311). This is one of the most explicit statements in Heyer's work on the nature of love and it is the lesson almost all her male characters have to learn before they become fit husbands.

In psychoanalytic terms, the novel offers a fantasy of the seduction of the father by the daughter. Avon represents the Law of the Father but, in return for Leonie's 'good' ('feminine') behaviour as 'daughter', he offers protective yet erotic love. The attraction of remaining childlike (Leonie as Avon's 'Infant') seems to be in the license it provides for the girl to remain part *boy* – a license not allowed to adult women. There is an added complication here since the father is split between the 'good' father, Avon, and the 'bad' father, Leonie's real father the Comte de Saint-Vire, who, desperate for a male heir, exchanged her at birth for the son of one of his labourers. As punishment for his adherence to the tradition of patrilineal inheritance which disinherits all daughters, Saint-Vire is induced to kill himself by Avon.

These Old Shades is a good example of how historical fiction can provide a distanced fantasy space within which such a family romance, which could seem either transgressive or silly in contemporary dress, can work in narrative terms. As Anthea Trodd has noted (1998, 127), Heyer borrowed the basic plot as well as her cross-dressing heroine and saturnine hero (whether consciously or not) from Ethel M. Dell's *Charles Rex* (1922). A comparison between the two novels shows how brilliantly Heyer can use a historical setting and 'period' vocabulary to render 'realistic' or believable an otherwise absurd plot.

In its contemporary setting, the psychological thinness of Dell's character-isation and the preposterous nature of her plot is woefully obvious, and her contemporary slang has been dated badly. The cross-dressing Antoinette/Toby's adoration of Charles Burchester, Duke of Saltash, is merely pathetic while the aristocratic Saltash is an anachronistic cardboard cut-out, who is rather too often described as 'monkey-like'. Saltash's salvation is (as with Avon) that he has learnt to put another before himself. But the sentimental religiosity of Dell's text – 'you told me that I made you believe in God', Saltash tells Toby, 'Egad, it made me a believer too' (1922, 288) – becomes absurd. Yet for all the sheer silliness, there is an energy and an eroticism to Dell's novel, which Heyer clearly recognised and learned how to redeploy through a historical setting.

In Heyer's novel, the past is used as a distanced but eroticised setting within which romance can be made believable. *These Old Shades* is set in the mid-eighteenth century, mainly in Paris, a further distanced but glamorous setting. Leonie is presented to Louis XV and briefly sees Madame de Pompadour, and the youthful Avon's support for the failed Stuart uprising in 1745 is mentioned in passing but this is the sum total of 'real' history. The historical background is sketched in through clothes and language, both period slang and French phrases. In contrast to Dell's novel, it is this 'realistic' period background that makes the fantasy element of the text work, paradoxically by both distancing it and making it 'real'. Helen Hughes suggests that the detailed 'realism' of the historical background in Heyer's texts helps the reader to 'swallow' ideologically charged material values unaware (1993, 27). It helps us 'swallow' not merely the romance ending as the only possible ending for a woman but also Heyer's conservative insistence on aristocratic birth as connoting inherent value.

However, the historical background also allows a transformative disruption of these ideological values, most obviously through the cross-dressing but also through Heyer's use of comedy and her mockery of the romance conventions she is deploying. This is where she differs most radically from Dell, who takes her passion seriously. Heyer is closer to Shakespeare's *As You Like It* or *Twelfth Night* where cross-dressing allows the girl-page heroine the carnivalesque freedom to enter 'male' spaces and encounter the hero without a chaperone. The danger of being 'unmasked' provides an erotic frisson which is both enhanced and defused by the comedy it provides. Much of the humour in Heyer's text is derived from Leonie's trouble with her petticoats. Like an Elizabethan boy-actor, or a pantomime dame, Leonie draws attention to both the 'silliness' of femininity and its constructed nature.

The 'boyish' heroines of Heyer and Dell reflect the new fashions of the 1920s. The flapper with her short shirts, bobbed hair (echoed in the shorn curls of Leonie and Toby) and flat chest was 'boyish' rather than 'womanly'. For many women, the war had provided the first opportunity to throw off the long skirts and hair of young ladyhood and even wear trousers to do 'men's work'. Leonie's pleasure in the freedom of her breeches and her frustration over the 'cage' (108) of her petticoats probably struck a chord with many readers. Her alienation from her own image in the mirror when she first puts on a dress – 'I am not at all myself. I think that I look very strange' (114) – echoes the alienation of young girls (like Naomi Mitchison) who had been required to don long skirts and put up their hair as a signal that they were now young ladies. By directing their attention back to the even more stringent limitations to which mid-eighteenth century women were subject, Heyer is implicitly drawing attention not only to their own freedoms but also to the limitations that are still in place. Leonie's rebellion against femininity is as attractive to the reader as her eventual marriage.

If Heyer learnt about female desire from Dell, she learnt from Jeffery Farnol how to manipulate language and narrative voice to produce a 'historical' setting which flirted with parody. The sentimental education of a young man is a central theme in his work and he sends his heroes out into the world, often in disguise, to be toughened up and made into 'men'. Heyer's third novel, initially called *The Transformation of Philip Jettan* (1923) but republished as *Powder and Patch*, is in this tradition and reworks elements, including the heroine's name, from Farnol's *The Amateur Gentleman* (1913). The arch chapter headings used in *Powder and Patch* and *The Black Moth* are a clear indication of how indebted Heyer's early work was to Farnol's style. She seems to have learned from him, and adapted for her own uses, the use of 'period' slang and of a tongue-in-cheek narrative voice to produce a double-voiced discourse which both enjoys and sends up the conventions of the form. In later novels she deployed an Austenesque irony to the same ends.

Powder and Patch shows that Heyer's heroes also learn to assume a mask. The education Philip Jettan undergoes consists of learning ostensibly 'feminine' things. Rejected by Cleonie because he treats her as a possession instead of courting her, the handsome but 'boorish' Philip goes to Paris to learn 'how to dress, how to walk across a room, how to play with words, how to make love to a woman, how to bow' (1959, 45). At first he regards this as degrading but within six months he has surpassed himself, learning not merely how to dress like an exquisite but how to fence like a master. In this book, as in others, Heyer presents opposing kinds of masculinity. While Philip is 'a country bumpkin' (36), Bancroft, the man who initially ousts him in Cleonie's affections, is a 'conceited, painted puppet' (36) who represents an over-feminised masculinity. The ideal Philip is to aim for is 'something betwixt the two' (36). When Philip returns, Cleonie, mistaking him for a 'pranked-out doll', realises that she prefers a man to 'be a man' (113). Love again is an educative and redemptive force for both parties. Crucially, Philip loves Cleonie enough to change himself in order to win her.

An interesting analysis of gender differences is offered by Cleonie's aunt, Sally Malmerstoke, who suggests that women differ from men because they lack logic and the ability to reason, and that though they want gentleness they also 'like a man to be brutal [...] They want mastering, most of them' (137). Philip reverts to his 'masterful' behaviour to win Cleonie but that masterfulness is put at her service. Heyer implies that not all women want mastering: Aunt Sally will not allow herself to be mastered by the man she is about to marry.

Heyer's texts suggest that there are two different types of femininity, and that the type which uses 'femininity' only as a mask for 'masculine' qualities is the more desirable of the two. The ultra-feminine woman as represented by Fanny in *These Old Shades*, Lavinia in *The Black Moth*, Letitia in *The Masqueraders* (1928) and Cleonie in *Powder and Patch* is coquettish, illogical, often rather silly, sometimes merely because she is young. But she is usually a secondary character (Cleonie is secondary in the sense that the novel is focalised through the hero). In contrast, the centralised heroine is usually more 'masculine'. This is represented either through cross-dressing with Leonie or Prudence in *The Masqueraders*, or because she rebels against the conventions of 'femininity', like Diana in *The Black Moth* who is 'unmaidenly' (1965, 57) when she asks the hero to marry her, or as in many of the later novels because she embodies 'masculine' virtues – clear-thinking, resourcefulness and good sense. What Heyer seems to be suggesting is that 'natural' human behaviour is 'masculine' in both sexes, but that *both* have to learn a kind of masquerade which consists of 'feminine' behaviour.

The notion of the hero who wears a 'mask' is common in this period. The motif of the manly hero disguised as a fop has its roots in Orczy's dandified Sir Percy Blakeney whose 'mask of somnolent indifference' (1980, 145) conceals the daring of his alter-ego, the Scarlet Pimpernel. It also conceals a childhood embittered by the madness of his mother, as well as his passion for the wife. Heyer reworks this idea in several ways and her early heroes, like Jack Carstares in *The Black Moth*, often wear a mask of cynicism to hide past hurts. The rightful Earl of Wyncham, Jack has been disinherited and roams the English countryside disguised alternately as the foppish, dandified Sir Anthony Ferndale, or as a highwayman (wearing a literal mask). The effect of his hand-to-mouth existence has been, as with Sir Percy, to teach him to 'hide all feeling behind a perpetual mask of nonchalance and wit' (Heyer, 1965, 154). However, Jack's dual disguises also represent two parts of his personality – the 'masculine' and the 'feminine'. Both are integral to it, as they are with Philip in *Powder and Patch*.

The villain of *The Black Moth*, Tracy Belmanoir, the Duke of Andover (or 'Devil Andover'), an early proto-type for Avon in *These Old Shades*, is also presented in feminine terms – exquisitely dressed and with an androgynous given name. Lack of mother-love is the psychological explanation offered for Andover's cynical amorality (1965, 84) and Avon's brother also explains that 'We' d a spitfire for mother' (1997, 140). With Avon the studied pose is even more pronounced: even his brother refers to his 'damned mask of a face' (1997, 141). Both hero and villain are feminised through their dandyism, the satin coats, lace ruffles, high-heeled shoes, powdered wigs and paint so lovingly described by Heyer.

This gender ambiguity in the heroes serves several complex functions. First, it makes the hero more like a woman and more able to understand a woman's interests (one thinks of Henry Tilney's interest in muslin in

Northanger Abbey). Avon, for instance, frequently determines what Leonie should wear. Secondly, it suggests a 'feminine' self under the 'masculine' mask, and thus an ideal man who is able to nurture and care for (even 'parent') the heroine as well as use his masculine strength to protect her. Thirdly, this male display suggests (as Stephen Heath argues in his reading of Riviere's essay) that 'no one has the phallus', not even men, because *masculinity* is 'equally unreal, another act, another charade of power' (1986, 56).

In textual terms, this ambiguity allows the female reader to identify with the hero (who, like her, does not have the 'phallus') even in the books where the male point of view might be thought to exclude her or to position her, in Fetterley's phrase, as a 'resisting reader'. It enables a cross-gender identification which allows the female reader a *double* pleasure. First, she has the pleasure of identifying with the male hero and thus vicariously experiencing his adventures. But, secondly, the hero is constructed as an erotic object of desire for her 'gaze', an object that (through identification with the heroine) she finally attains through the romance ending.

This double pleasure is perhaps most developed in Heyer's *The Masqueraders*, published in 1928, the same year as Woolf's *Orlando*. The comparison is a useful one because both writers, in different ways, use history as a fantasy space to suggest that gender is socially constructed. Heyer provides a double cross-dressing plot where tall Prudence dresses as a young man and her shorter brother Robin as a woman in order to conceal their identity as escaped Jacobites. The interesting thing here is that Robin makes a more convincing 'woman' than his sister does. His masquerade is accomplished through adopting 'feminine' mannerisms: a tripping step, languorous attitudes, a melting voice. Watching his sister execute a curtsey, he notes, 'Not so prettily done as I can do it, my dear' (2000, 287). In contrast, Prudence with her height and cool-headed resourcefulness is one of Heyer's 'masculine' women and her reward is the admiration of the 'sleepy-eyed' Sir Anthony, who doffs his mask of lazy indifference to rescue her: 'She had spirit, this girl, in the man's clothes, and with the man's brain', he recognises (2000, 224).

What Heyer suggests here is that only a man can really be convincingly 'feminine' because 'femininity' itself is a male fantasy projected onto women, which women must then learn to assume in order to satisfy their own desires through men. Luce Irigaray's comment that 'the masquerade [...] is what women do [...] in order to participate in man's desire, but at the price of renouncing their own' (1985, 133) is pertinent here. However, Heyer suggests that if both masculinity and femininity are constructions then we, as readers of historical romance, can enjoy the pleasures of both.

The year 1928 also, of course, saw the trial of *The Well of Loneliness*, and this directs our attention to what is not said in Heyer's texts – the spectre of homosexuality raised by cross-dressing. What *These Old Shades* cannot admit is the other possible reasons for Avon to buy a young boy in the backstreets of Paris. Similarly, the friendships between Sir Anthony and 'Peter Merriot' and between Letitia Grayson and 'Kate Merriot' in *The Masqueraders* could be attributed to same-sex desires. Sir Anthony sees through Prudence's masquerade because of 'the affection for her I discovered in myself' (2000, 164), which might have been expected to indicate homosexual desires, rather than leading him to the conclusion that the young man is actually a woman. Heyer defuses such possibilities by revealing the cross-dressing to the *reader* very early on.

Heyer's early novels, like Shakespeare's comedies, provide a transgressive space within the text where rebellion can be acted out, although the 'proper' order of things is restored through the conservative happy ending. If gender is a masquerade, her work implies, then it is not merely, as Riviere and Irigaray perceive it, an enforced act but also has the potential to be a carnival space. The mask can, paradoxically, provide a disguise from behind which transgressive desires can be voiced. Thus the masquerade acts as an apt image for the way the historical romance novel itself functions as a mask for transgressive desires.

Remembering the conquered: Naomi Mitchison's anti-imperialist fictions

'The conquered is always forgotten', says the defeated Gallic chief, Vercingetorix, in Naomi Mitchison's story 'Vercingetorix and Others' (1924, 1927, 85). It has become a cliche that history is written by the victors and therefore promulgates their point of view. In contrast, Naomi Mitchison's historical fiction is a sustained attempt to remember the conquered. By focalising her narratives through the eyes of outsiders, slaves, children, women and colonised people, she offered a view from beneath which undermined and rewrote the histories of imperialist Rome and Greece which, through the 'classical education' offered by the public-school-system, underpinned Britain's own ideologies of Empire.

A member of the 'lost generation' which emerged from the First World War with a profound distrust of the ideologies of the older generation, Mitchison used fiction about the past as a political tool to intervene in the present. Her texts, although they are historically accurate, also function as allegories to draw attention to the injustices of the present. Her 1920s texts offer coded critiques of Britain's own imperialist project, especially in Ireland, but also in the wider context of the Empire. She explored the consequences of ideological conflicts in ways which offered a striking parallel to the developing confrontations between socialism and Fascism, but she always connected these issues to the issues of gender.

Mitchison's first novel, *The Conquered* (1923), established her as, according a *New Statesman* reviewer, 'the best, if not the only, English historical novelist now writing' (Mitchison, 1927, publisher's blurb). In shifting from the point of view of the victors to that of the conquered, it marked a seismic shift in the genre of the historical novel, 'the beginning of the new era' as it seemed to Peter Green (1962, 45). Thus it opened up the genre in ways that were especially important for women writers. Indeed, the epigraph of the book – 'Victrix causa diis placuit sed victa puellis' (The victorious cause is pleasing to the gods, but the conquered cause to girls [Hoberman, 1997, 121–2].) – foregrounds the special relevance of its theme to women. Mitchison was also, as she noted, 'the first to see that one could write historical novels in a modern idiom' (1979, 163). Her use of a colloquial, often deliberately 'un-grammatical' style made her fictions accessible (not least to women without the classical education their brothers took for granted), and brought the past freshly and immediately into the present.

The protagonist of *The Conquered* is Meromic, a Gaul enslaved by the Romans who defeat his tribe, execute his father and cause the suicide of his sister during the Caesar's conquest of Gaul in the first century BC. Thereafter Meromic is torn between his loyalty to his conquered people and their leader Vercingetorix, and his loyalty and affection for his Roman master, Titus Barrus, who becomes 'all I've got [...] wife and child and home and everything' (Mitchison, 1932, 182). After fighting as a Roman at Titus' side and witnessing the defeat of Vercingetorix, Meromic returns to the Gauls but is caught in the siege of Uxeldun and, along with the other survivors, has his right hand cut off as a warning to other Gauls against future rebellions. Rescued again by Titus he goes to Rome, but after hearing of Vercingetorix's execution, he metamorphoses into a wolf (his tribe's totem) and heads north. This shift into fantasy, which moves the novel out of the 'realist' realm of history into the realm of myth, is typical of the 1920s.

Caesar's *The Gallic War*, one of Mitchison's key sources, is a dry military history, ostensibly 'objective' in its treatment of facts, but actually naturalising the imperialist ideology which supported the Romans' 'right' to expand into Gaul. He depicts the Gauls as half-civilised barbarians, volatile, irrational and undisciplined, and their struggle for their freedom is portrayed as 'rebellion' against their natural masters. By using Meromic's point of view, Mitchison questions that ideology, but shows how the Gauls themselves come to inter-nalise it and think of themselves 'not as a national army driving out the invader, but as rebels up against a fixed and solid government' (1932, 239). She also details the terrible human cost of the conquest, elided by Caesar's account. The severity of Caesar's treatment of the Gauls – flogging their leaders to death, enslaving women and children, cutting off the hands of the siege survivors – is presented as military necessity in *The Gallic War*. In *The Conquered* it sickens Titus who has imbibed the Roman ethic from his cradle.

Mitchison is particularly concerned to show the plight of the non-combatants trapped between the two sides. This is symbolised most cruelly by the women and children who are evicted from the besieged Alesia by the Gauls in the hope that the Romans would enslave them and thus prevent them starving to death. Refused succour by Caesar, they were left to die between the two camps. The commentary of T. Rice Holmes, another source used by Mitchison, is illustrative of the way in which many pre-war British scholars accepted as 'common sense' the Roman ideology of conquest: 'To grant their prayer [for help] was impossible' comments Holmes (1931, 175). Mitchison's depiction of a desperate woman throwing her baby over the ramparts to Titus in the hope that he will save it disputes the inhumanity of Holmes' 'objective' judgement.

Holmes' work also illustrates the way in which Roman history was used to validate British imperialism. He notes that, for instance, 'as we conquered India with the aid of Indians, Caesar conquered Gaul with the aid of Gauls' (1931, 197). *The Conquered*, Green suggests, came 'like a slap in the face to complacent Caesar-nurtured imperialists' because it 'forced readers to perform a radical revaluation of the ethics drummed into them during their school days' (1962, 45).

Mitchison's own education should have made her one of those complacent imperialists. Her father was an Oxford Professor, her mother was a staunch advocate of the Empire, and Mitchison herself was, until she was 12, educated at the Dragon School for Boys in Oxford. Her 'Note on Books and one's Funny Idea of Ancient History' at the end of *When the Bough Breaks* (1924) surveys the books which formed her view of history and, through her irreverent approach and schoolchild vocabulary, undermines their authority. They are the standard male-authored texts imbibed by the British public schoolboys who built and maintained the British Empire: Macaulay's *Lays of Ancient Rome*, Kipling's *Puck of Pook's Hill*, Caesar's *Gallic Wars*, Gibbon, Kingsley's *Hypatia*, Whyte-Melville's *The Gladiators*, and so on. Mitchison's comments show how 'one's Funny Idea' of history is fragmentary because it is shaped in early childhood by written texts, including historical fiction and poetry. Moreover, her assertion that, 'Not unnaturally one always used to take sides with the barbarians against Rome' (1927, 316) suggests that from an early age she was a resistant reader and, through the use of the inclusive pronoun 'one', offers us that potential too. 'It's the Northerner, one's possible ancestor, who is really thrilling', she goes on, 'And that makes one interested in the Roman idea of slavery' (316).

As Ruth Hoberman (1997, Chapter 8) has shown, the effect of these canonical texts was usually to make the British reader take the side of the Romans (as Holmes so clearly does). The Romans were presented not merely as a model for the ideal of the nineteenth-century British imperial project but also, often through the depiction of inter-racial marriages, as the actual ancestors of the British. Roman history was used to nurture 'Caesar-nurtured imperialists', and to present the British as the natural inheritors of the Roman sword and mantle, and thus naturalise the ideology of Empire.

It is true that J.G. Whyte-Melville's *The Gladiators* (1863) and G. Henty's *Beric the Briton* (1892), the two texts Hoberman discusses as influences on Mitchison, take British slaves as their heroes. But they use an oedipal plot which depicts the protagonists maturing into manhood through a rejection of their British (and 'feminine' origins) and an assimilation into Roman mores via an identification with a Roman father figure. Mitchison, as Hoberman (1997, Chapter 9) suggests, invokes but then disrupts that plot through a rejection of the heterosexual marriage plot and through intimations of alternative forms of desire: Meromic's incestuous love for his sister, and his homo-erotic rather than filial love for Titus.

Mitchison's personal history suggests one reason why she might have been both particularly attracted to *and* resistant to such 'boy's own' plots of Empire. At the Dragon School, where she was 'to all practical purposes a boy' (1975, 11), and with her elder brother Jack, she seems to have developed to a fine art the practice of reading 'as a boy'. Discussing her early fascination with the idea of being one of Plato's 'Guardians', she notes that she was not put off by the fact that none of them were women: 'in my inside stories I don't suppose I was ever a Greek woman' (1975, 40). Instead, she 'always imagined myself a man, a friend no doubt of Pertinex and Parnesius in Kipling's version of the Wall' (1975, 98). As a pre-adolescent girl, like Una in Kipling's *Puck of Pook's Hill* (1906), she has access to a male world of adventure and history.

In such pre-war historical fictions, male homosocial bonds are the glue that holds the Empire together.[2] In *Puck of Pook's Hill*, Pertinex and Parnesius become Captains of the Roman Wall together, while the Norman Sir Richard befriends the Saxon Hugh and then marries his sister. The marriage not only renders their relationship safe (i.e. not 'homosexual') but symbolises the merging of Norman and Saxon, eliding the distinction between conqueror and conquered, to create the 'English'. In *The Conquered*, Mitchison makes the erotic nature of the friendship between Meromic and Titus more explicit (Titus is 'wife and child and home and everything' to Meromic). By doing this she renders it 'unsafe', destabilising the narratives and ideologies which support the Empire.

Mitchison herself was precipitously ejected from the world of male friendships when at 12 she started to menstruate, and was swiftly removed from the Dragon school. From that point until her marriage, she led the constricted life of a pre-war upper-class young lady, heavily chaperoned, sleeping in her mother's bedroom, wearing long confining skirts, and never even brushing her own hair. This contrast between her pre- and post-menstruation existences explains, first, why Mitchison writes so successfully 'as a man' through her male characters. The characters of Meromic and his sister Fiommar are based closely on Mitchison and her brother Jack, but they also represent aspects of Mitchison herself. It is as if Mitchison has to 'kill off' the adult feminine part of herself by having Fiommar commit suicide at the beginning of *The Conquered* in order to return to a pre-adolescent identification with Meromic and enter the world of 'History' which has been gendered male by those earlier fictions.

This explains, secondly, why she so often writes about the state of being female in terms of confinement and enslavement. In 'The Triumph of Faith' a young Greek girl laments to a slave, 'It's so hard being a girl! Here I am, just the same as a man really and no worse than my brother [...] But just because of two or three silly little differences I have to be treated as if I was an animal, ordered about, not allowed to decide anything for myself!' (1927, 133). The parallel between womanhood and slavery is made explicit when she realises that 'perhaps he felt a little like that too' (1927, 133). In the title story, 'When the Bough Breaks', Gersemi has the freedom to adventure and fight while she is dressed as a man and possesses her magic bear pelt, but once she becomes pregnant she reverts to her woman's dress and becomes as vulnerable as the other women and more so than the male slaves. For Mitchison, fiction functioned like that magic bear pelt, allowing her to don masculine clothes and go adventuring.

This empathy with the enslaved and the conquered through the experience of being female is the hallmark of Mitchison's work. It is what enables her to draw the comparisons and parallels which give her work depth and contemporaneous relevance. Elizabeth Maslen has drawn attention to Mitchison's use of 'Aesopian language' (1999, 139) during the 1930s, where the allegorical significance of her texts is signalled by epigraphs. Mitchison developed this technique in the 1920s with *The Conquered* where the epigraphs draw the reader's attention to the parallels with the contemporaneous situation in Ireland. Mitchison wrote that she chose her historical setting:

Because my mind was all stirred up with the troubles in Ireland in my own year of grace – 1921 – and the injustices committed by the Black and Tan troops during the British military occupation. Yet I didn't want to write directly about Ireland. [...] So it was that Gaul presented itself to me, plastic material for my parallel with Ireland. (1935, 645)

The parallel did not go unnoticed: in his Preface to the novel, Ernest Barker drew approving attention to it, while Mitchison's mother was 'shocked' by the epigraphs from 'The Irish Volunteer' and 'The Croppy Boy' (Mitchison, 1979, 162).

The use of epigraphs is a skilful way of avoiding making the text merely, in Lukács' words, 'a parable of the present' (1983, 338). Mitchison believed that in the historical novel:

the plot itself has to be a plot of its own time, and the characters must think and act within the framework of their own time [...] They must have some relationship with the present day, but it must not be overt from their side. (1935, 645)

Using epigraphs ensures that the integrity of the main body of the novel as an imaginative recreation of a historical period is not destroyed by authorial interventions or anachronistic premonitions.

The epigraphs from W.B. Yeats and from the Irish Volunteer's song point to parallels with the lengthy history of British colonisation and oppression within Ireland, which erupted into violence again with the Easter Rising of 1916.[3] The epigraph from Yeats' 'The Rose Tree', for instance, citing Patrick Pearse's assertion of the need for a 'blood sacrifice' for Ireland – 'There's nothing but our own red blood/Can make a right Rose Tree' (142) – is echoed in Mitchison's depiction of Vercingetorix 'dedicating himself and everything he had as sacrifice for his people' (1932, 217). Other epigraphs – 'The Memory of the Dead' and 'The Croppy Boy' – refer to the Irish rebellion of 1798 during which the British military (like Caesar) executed rebels like the anonymous 'croppy boy' and used brutal floggings as a deterrent (Kee, 1995, 61). Other parallels, with India and Afghanistan, were not lost on her readers: 'While reading your book,' E.M. Forster wrote to Mitchison, 'I often thought of India and the Meromics I have seen there' (Mitchison, 1979, 101).

In her second novel, *Cloud Cuckoo Land* (1925), Mitchison developed this technique further in order to critique fifth-century Athens, still usually presented as the ideal which inspired Western democracy. She signalled the allegorical nature of her text by alluding through her title to Aristophanes' *The Birds*.[4] *The Birds* can be read as an allegory of events in the Peloponnesian War, especially the Athenians' attempt to conquer Sicily (then neutral). Mitchison's novel is set at the end of the same war, and depicts a society which (like Britain in the 1920s) was struggling with the devastating impact of a long war. The epigraph to the novel, taken from Alcaeus – 'I cannot tell the direction of the wind; one wave rolls from this side, one from that and we are tossed about in the middle along with our black ship'[5] – again nudges the reader towards allegorical reading, suggesting parallels at the level of both State and individual, battered between opposing forces in fifth-century Greece or 1920s Europe.

Mitchison's protagonist, Alxenor, is a wealthy young Ionian man living on Poieessa, an imaginary Greek island (the name means 'grassy, rich in grass' but also appropriately suggests 'Poiesis', 'an act of making, a poem, a fiction'[6]), which is subject to Athens but about to be taken over by Sparta. Mitchison's exploration of the two very different political and cultural ideologies represented by Athens and Sparta provided an apposite but not an exact parallel to a Europe increasingly polarised between the ideologies of socialism and Fascism.

Athens was a democracy with a constitution, where power was held by the 'people', that is by citizens with voting rights. It had a strong navy and a highly developed culture which excelled in philosophy, art, literature and, especially important, history.[7] Athens offered a seductive model with which the British could identify themselves. Sparta, on the other hand, was an oligarchy, where power lay in the hands of elite, supported by the labour of the enslaved helots: 'We Spartans are masters in our own land', says Mitchison's Archytas, 'there are just a few of us over all the others; because of our birth and because of the way we live, they are under us for ever. It may come to be so with all Hellas' (1928, 49). This was a highly militarised state, where individualism was subordinated to the good of the state.

Both Athens and Sparta were imperialist powers who exercised hegemony over 'allies' like Poieessa. The precariousness of Poieessa's initial position is signalled by a brief reference to Melos (1928, 9), an island destroyed by Athens not long before the novel opens, when the Melians were massacred and enslaved en masse. Mitchison uses this situation to explore the dilemma of the powerless, caught between two powerful forces, and forced in the words of another of her epigraphs to choose whether to 'Eat or be eaten, / Be killed or kill' (1928, 51). Alxenor wants to walk a middle way, to 'see both sides of things' (318). But he is torn between his brother, a pro-Spartan oligarch, and his friend Chromon, a democrat, who is also the brother of Moiro, the girl Alxenor loves. When the Spartans take over Poieessa, Alxenor flees, with Moiro, to Athens, leaving there in turn when the Spartans defeat Athens. He goes next to Ephesus (representing the third power, Persia, waiting in the wings), and then on to Sparta. After the death of Moiro, he takes his young son back to Poieessa where he finds his brother and Chromon allied (democrats and oligarchs temporarily united) to remove the Spartan governor before they take up the old battle again. Finally, he joins the army of the Persian Cyrus to march east.

In this conflict of ideologies, the temptation is to make simplistic equations, to see the militarised, elitist Spartans, for instance, as Fascists, and the Athenians as the democratic ideal. However, Mitchison refuses to allow such black-and-white judgements. Through Alxenor's experiences, the reader is shown the weaknesses of both political systems, as well as the brutality of both as imperial powers. Most importantly, Mitchison makes it clear that the celebrated Athenian democracy did not extend to resident foreigners (like Alxenor), slaves, or women. 'One lives in twilight', thinks Phrasikleia (1928, 155), trying to glean information about the political events which will lead to her husband's death.

It is in her treatment of women's position that Mitchison is most radical in this novel. It is also here that she undercuts the belief dating from Thucydides that history should be concerned only with politics and the state, a belief which helped ensure the invisibility of women within standard histories. By erasing women's experiences, such histories have, Mitchison demonstrates in *Cloud Cuckoo Land*, given partial and over-idealised pictures of Athenian democracy and, by extension, other societies.

The fate of Moiro is a painful demonstration of what a Greek woman might endure. Abducted by Alxenor, who loves her because she is 'the spirit of Chromon, his dearest friend, in a maiden's shape' (125), she is dragged around Greece at his whim. After a painful childbirth, she is emotionally blackmailed into sex by Alxenor, and when she gives birth to a daughter she is ordered by him to expose the child to die. After a brief affair with the Spartan, Leon, she dies of a botched abortion. Other women in the novel do not fare much better. Theramenes' daughter, Nikodike, is beaten by her husband when she attempts to join her brother with the democratic rebels. 'It's my Athens too!' she asserts (227) but without a vote and subject to her husband's rule, this is clearly not true. An epigraph from H.G. Wells' pseudo-feminist novel *Ann Veronica* – 'For man has reason, woman rhyme, / A man scores always, all the time' (Mitchison, 1928, 114) – points the reader towards the position of British women in 1925, still not fully enfranchised and without wide access to birth control or to legal abortion.

At first glance, the women of Sparta appear to have more freedom. They are encouraged to develop their physical prowess, and seem to have more equality with their husbands. But this is based on their being subsumed (as the men are) into the state's control of the individual from birth onwards. Sparta is a totalitarian state whose religious beliefs idealise pain in the service of the State. Mitchison points to the institutionalisation of certain kinds of evil: 'Krypteia' (255), for instance, allowed for the ritual killing of rebellious helots. The rejection of individualism entailed the rejection of art, philosophy and music. Indeed, Mitchison was struck by the parallels between Sparta and the socialism of the Soviet Union. 'A lot of Sparta about all this,' was Mitchison's comment when she visited the Soviet Union in 1932 (1979, 188), and she developed this comparison in an article entitled 'New Cloud-Cuckoo Borough' (1934).

Ruth Hoberman neatly sums up the position of women within the two states when she argues that 'women are so silenced by the extremes of their inclusion (in Sparta) and exclusion (in Athens) that Alxenor's uncertainty must serve as a textual refuge for the feminine' (1997, 32). While it is true that Alxenor is feminised by his ability to see both sides and his vulnerability, Mitchison also pulls off a clever sleight of hand through her manipulation of narrative point of view. The use of Alxenor as the central consciousness of the novel initially encourages the reader to sympathise and, indeed, to identify with him, and thus to read 'as a man'. But Mitchison then uses other points of view to shake the reader out of that complacent identification into a realisation that Alxenor, while he thinks of himself as a victim, is an oppressor of women.

The same is true of the other male characters – Theramenes, Leon and Hagnon – who are all presented as sympathetic, often admirable, characters but also exposed as complicit in the oppression of women. Their unquestioning assumption that their masculinity makes them superior deforms and corrupts these men. It is shocking that, for instance, Nikodike's brother, Hagnon, laughs when he is told that his brother-in-law has beaten Nikodike: 'Women must keep to their own place', he says, 'Where would the State be otherwise?' (1928, 237). Mitchison does not, in this novel, have an answer to that question but she is asserting very strongly that no state that excludes and abuses women has any right to be considered an ideal one. This is Cloud Cuckoo Land, after all, where the oppressed become the oppressors in their turn.

Moiro's painful death from an attempted abortion is an indictment of both Alxenor and her Spartan lover, Leon. There is a strong contrast between the abortion, which is regarded as illegal, and the exposure of Moiro's daughter on Alxenor's orders, which is regarded as perfectly normal. In depicting abortion, Mitchison is breaking new ground with a vengeance,[8] but this is an excellent example of the way that historical fiction acted as a kind of screen or mask which allowed the writer to tackle taboo subjects. Like D.H. Lawrence, Mitchison shows sexuality as a potentially pleasurable and positive force but unlike him she always connects it to its possible reproductive outcome. The issues of birth control and abortion were important both personally and politically to Mitchison, as she shows in her memoirs.[9] When she tackled these subjects in a novel with a contemporary setting, *We Have Been Warned* (1935), however, she was asked to make substantial cuts and had difficulty finding a publisher. It was the hostile response to the published novel which sent her back to historical fiction again. As she put it, 'apparently it is all right when people wear wolfskins and togas' (1979, 179).

By the end of the novel, the women have been silenced and erased as the novel focuses on the homosocial bonding between Alxenor and Hagnon, who join the Persian army of Cyrus. The army represents a space within which Athenian and Spartan and even the freed Melian slave, Isadas, can accept each other – 'all Hellenes together' (1928, 330) bonded against a common enemy. But it is a delusionary unity and freedom, based on the militarism and imperialism Mitchison has already dissected. Most crucially, it is based on the exclusion of women. Even Hagnon represses his memories of his childhood closeness with Nikodike: 'after one is grown-up, one does not talk to women, not even one's own sister – what good would it be?' (1928, 345). The ending is one place where Mitchison's avoidance of ana-chronistic authorial comment can leave the reader baffled. The epigraph from A.E. Housman – 'And watch them depart on the way that they will not return' (330) – hints at what will happen to them. Cyrus' expedition was not to put down a rebellion, as he told his Greek allies, but to rise against his brother, the Great King Artaxerxes, and culminated in disaster.

This lack of closure, together with the erasure of the women, suggests unresolved issues. The future seems to lie with Alxenor's son Timas, who has been left with his two uncles 'to see two sides of life: and try to be fair' (329), but this runs the risk of him being torn between the two, as Alxenor was, or (perhaps worse) siding with one. In the face of a revival of military values brought about by the Second World War, Mitchison reflected that women are 'more likely to be sane than men, [...] more able to see two sides to any question' (1985, 65). Although she qualifies this to suggest that if they had power women might also become destructive, the ending of *Cloud Cuckoo Land* suggests that the ideal state (whether in fifth-century Greece or twentieth-century Britain) will remain an impossible utopia until women are given their proper place.

In her later writing, Mitchison centralised women protagonists, such as Erif Der in *The Corn King and the Spring Queen* (1931). In her writing of the 1920s, however, she had already broken new ground. In taking up the cause of the conquered, in her use of a modern idiom, her depiction of sexuality and desire, her handling of a male protagonist as the central consciousness of the narrative, and, above all, in showing that historical fiction could be deployed as a political weapon without losing its integrity as a depiction of an earlier time, she opened up the form of the historical novel in ways which would be especially important to other women writers.

3
Histories of the Defeated: Writers Taking Sides in the 1930s

Looking back at the inter-war period, Storm Jameson saw it divided into two parts with the energetic twenties, 'lively with ideas, dreams, hopes, experiments' (Jameson, 1984, 292), superseded by the grim political urgencies of a struggle between opposing forces in the thirties:

> I saw that two sides were struggling for mastery of the future. On one side was the idea of the Absolute State, with its insistence on total loyalty to the words and gestures of authority, its belief in the moral beauty of war, its appeal to the *canaille*: Germany awake, kill, hate, Sieg Heil, and the rest of it. On the other all that was still hidden in the hard green seed of a democracy which allowed me freedom to write and other women freedom to live starved lives on the dole. (293)

The spectre which haunted Europe in the 1930s was not Communism but Fascism. The central concerns of the 1930s – the rise of Fascism in Europe, the desire for peace, and the poverty and depression caused by widespread unemployment at home – made it impossible for writers to inhabit an ivory tower producing art for art's sake. The need to take sides, which John Lucas dates back to the 1926 General Strike (1999, Chapter 7), was intensified in the 1930s. 'I am an artist not a propagandist partisan', wrote Phyllis Bentley in 1938, 'But now I find I must take sides' (1962, 209). The questionnaire organised by Nancy Cunard, 'Authors Take Sides On the Spanish War', epitomised this, and writers like Sylvia Townsend Warner not only used their pens in defence of freedom but went to Spain to take an active part in the struggle.

The contemporary situation lent an urgency to the writing of the 1930s, a need to address the pressing concerns of the day, which might be thought to have been inimical to the writing of historical fiction. In fact, at least for women, the opposite is true and this is the moment when the historical novel blossoms in their hands. Although Lukács welcomes the renaissance of the historical novel in what he calls the anti-Fascist 'historical novel of democratic humanism' (1983, Chapter 4), the gender-blind nature of his analysis leads him to ignore the important developments in the woman's historical novel during these years.

At the very moment that they came of age as citizens, women were acutely aware of historical forces which threatened that achievement. The growth of Fascism, with its insistence that, in the words of the deputy director of the British Union of Fascists in 1934, 'We definitely prefer "women who are women and men who are men"' (Woolf, 1986, xii), threatened to deprive them of their hard-won rights and push them back into the domestic sphere. Many women during this period were concerned to show that, as Woolf put it in *Three Guineas* (1938), 'the public and private worlds are inseparably connected; that the tyrannies and servilities of the one are the tyrannies and servilities of the other' (Woolf, 1986, 162). As Jameson recognised, it was democracy which allowed the newborn woman citizen the freedom to write, although the 'seed' had done little as yet to relieve the poverty of unemployed women.

Women turned to the historical novel in the 1930s as a way of making sense of history and their position within it. In this decade, their novels obsessively examine moments of conflict between two extremes, and show how women tend to get caught between the two. Moreover, many of these novels are preoccupied with the notion of defeat, suggesting women's past defeats but also warning of future possible defeats. In Phyllis Bentley's *Freedom, Farewell!*, Brutus, confronting the disinherited and impoverished daughter of the dead Cato, rediscovers his 'strong natural dislike to be on the winning side' (Bentley, 1936, 417). This dislike of being on the winning side seems to be a characteristic of the women writers of the 1930s, reiterating Mitchison's sense that 'The victorious cause is pleasing to the gods but the conquered cause to girls.' With the exception of the historical romance, the over-riding characteristic of women's historical novels of the 1930s is their concern to write histories of the defeated.

Given what women had achieved, this seems paradoxical. Their struggle for citizenship, as Winifred Holtby indicated in a section entitled 'The Vindication of Citizenship' in *Women* (1934), her history of women's emancipation, could be traced directly back to Mary Wollstonecraft and her engagement with the French Revolution. Rose Macaulay projects the concept of citizenship even further back in *They Were Defeated* (1932), as her seventeenth-century heroine argues for her right to an education: 'I live in the State and should know of what passes in't. My father says that if I do not I should be shamed and count myself most ignorant, and not fit for a citizen' (1982, 345). For women, their duties and responsibilities as citizens included a knowledge of their history and a commitment to the political struggle to preserve democracy.

Following the Equal Franchise Act there was a flurry of histories, memoirs and biographies of the women's movement.[1] In one sense these texts view history in Lukácsian terms as 'the bearer and realiser of human progress', culminating in women's emancipation. However, any sense of 'victory' or progress was compromised by women's recognition that 'the pendulum was already swinging backwards not only against feminism, but against democracy, liberty and reason' (Holtby, 1934, 151). Women were entering a history that seemed dangerously on the edge of repeating earlier catastrophes.

This model of history as a cyclical, rather than linear, progression frequently informs the family saga which was extremely popular during these years. This reflected the sense that family structures had undergone a huge shift since Victorian times, mainly because of women's changing role. As a form of the historical novel particularly appealing to women because of its focus on the domestic, these texts explore what Lukács calls 'the present as history' (1983, 83) or 'self-experienced history' (84). Many of the family sagas written by women during the 1930s map the period from around the late 1870s to the 1930s as, in Holtby's phrase, an 'age of transition' (1934, 96). They use the story of three or four generations of women to conduct a kind of historical stocktaking, a measurement of the progress made and that still to be attained. While they present past and present as one ongoing process, they are haunted by the idea that history is repetitive rather than progressive. Rose Macaulay's earlier *Told by an Idiot* (1923), for instance, takes as its epigraph Paul Morand's 'L'histoire, comme une idiote, mécaniquement se répète'. Each generation in Macaulay's book believes it lives in 'troublous times' and civilisations are 'wrecked and wrecked all down history' (1982, 315).

Vera Brittain's *Honourable Estate: A Novel of Transition* (1936) and Virginia Woolf's *The Years* (1937) both use the family saga to trace the private, domestic history of the family, exposing Victorian family life as an 'abominable system' (Woolf, 1968, 180), which stifled the ambitions of men as well as women. While *Honourable Estate* traces the evolution of marriage from the oppressive Victorian model towards a companionate ideal, it is also aware of the looming danger of what Britain elsewhere called 'history's most grievous repetitions' (1933, 12).

Another example is Daphne du Maurier's *The Loving Spirit* (1931), set in Cornwall, where Janet Coombes is shown struggling against the constraints of nineteenth-century gender roles, while her great-granddaughter, Jennifer, has far greater liberty after the war. Yet the book ends with Jennifer fulfilled through her marriage and motherhood. As Avril Horner and Sue Zlosnik show, the opening out of opportunity suggesting progress is contradicted by an ideologically conservative closure which suggests cyclical repetition (1998, 37–44). This confirms Christine Bridgwood's argument that history is always 'a double-edged discourse' in the family saga:

at once the sharp nudge of awareness of historical process [. . .] and the soothing balm of an ideology of stoical acceptance which naturalises the social and sexual status quo, and is ultimately dependent upon essentialist categories of femininity. (Bridgwood, 1986, 178)

In its use of the marriage ending, despite its message of 'progress', the popular family saga tends towards the conservative escapism of the popular historical romance.

The predominant mood of the woman's historical novel in the 1930s is, as I have suggested, concerned with defeat. In 'Spain 1937', Auden famously suggested that 'History to the defeated / May say Alas but cannot help or pardon' (Auden, 1977, 210). Despite Auden's later suppression of this sentiment as a 'wicked doctrine' which 'equates goodness with success' (1966, 15), it should perhaps rather be seen as a recognition that 'History' has been written by the victors while the histories of the defeated (as Mitchison eloquently suggested) are lost, forgotten, or suppressed. Walter Benjamin articulated this in 'Theses on the Philosophy of History' (1940) when he wrote:

if one asks with whom the adherents of historicism actually empathise. The answer is inevitable: with the victor. And all rulers are heirs of those who conquered before them. Hence the empathy with the victor invariably benefits the ruler. [. . .] Whoever has emerged victorious participates to this day in the triumphal procession in which the present rulers step over those who are lying prostrate. [. . .] There is no document of civilisation which is not at the same time a document of barbarism. (Benjamin, 1973, 258)

In her suggestive reading of the 'Theses', Jean Radford argues that they are 'an impassioned call for the rewriting of history from the perspective of the defeated, the victims, not the victors of history' (1999b, 35). In other words, a 'history of the defeated' (37). Such a reading of the 'unrealised possibilities of the past' (36), suggests Radford, enables the novelist to grasp history not as a linear sequence of events but as what Benjamin calls a 'constellation' (1973, 265) of past and present. It thus offers the possibility of intervention in the future. Although she does not discuss historical novels as such, Radford reads several other women's texts from the 1930s as meditations on history in the light of these insights.

It is in the historical novel of the 1930s that we can most clearly see women writers embarking on the project of writing 'histories of the defeated'. Fleishman identifies a tradition of portraying 'lovely womanhood cruelly broken by the force of historical movements and men' in the work of writers like Maurice Hewlett, George Moore and Ford Madox Ford, who used victimised historical women, particularly the Tudor and Stuart queens, to symbolise human values crushed by a mechanical, masculinised history (1971, 208–11). 'The use of feminine sentiments to deny meaning or value to historical forces could not be clearer,' Fleishman argues (210). In using the passive suffering feminine as a metaphor for the human predicament during the period in which women were beginning to organise themselves politically, however, these texts not only retreat from their own historical moment but also deny female agency.

Writing at their point of entry into history as citizens, women writers of the 1930s have a somewhat different agenda. They were intensely aware of how partial and fragile their attainment was, but many were also disillusioned with how little change had actually been effected as a result: 'in the end', wrote Storm Jameson in the 1930s, 'the world is not yet a rap better because women have been let loose in it' (Holtby, 1934, 133). Rather than denying history, however, their texts open up the discontinuities and lost possibilities of history and introduce gender into Benjamin's equation of 'victor' and 'defeated'. Their texts are Janus-faced, looking back to the past like Benjamin's 'Angel of History', yet also forward to the as-yet-unrealised possibilities of the future and offering a warning to the present.

Scott, Lukács argued, always centres his novels on a middle-of-the-road protagonist, an 'average English gentleman' (1983, 33), typified by Waverley, who has sympathies with both of the conflicting forces but represents the progressive middle way of the future. Women's historical novels in the 1930s often show a young woman similarly caught between opposing historical forces but rather than demonstrating the inevitability of progress, they frequently depict her being destroyed by the conflict. Women are revealed as the victims, the defeated, in any kind of historical conflict. In addition, while Georgette Heyer's romances present love as the consolation for women's lack of citizenship, these texts present it as part of the problem.

At first glance these writers may seem, in Auden's phrase, to be simply saying 'alas' to a record of woman as victim. Margaret Irwin's *Royal Flush* (1931) is one such 'history of the defeated' which takes up the earlier theme of the victimised royal woman. Minette, sister of Charles II and married to the brother of the French King, attempts to broker a secret treaty between the two Kings to cement the alliance between their countries. Poisoned, probably, Irwin suggests, by her husband's male lover, she is the victim of male political intrigues she does not fully understand. This is a clear statement of discontent with women's marginalised position and lack of agency within history. Irwin's other novels of the 1930s, *The Proud Servant* (1934) and *The Stranger Prince* (1937), while they focus on men, are also concerned with the defeated through their depiction of the royalist cause in the Civil War.

Set in 1640, the eve of the Civil War, Rose Macaulay's *They Were Defeated* (1932) offers a particularly complex meditation on the theme of gender and the 'defeated' through a depiction of the conflict between Anglicans, Catholics and Puritans. Her androgynously named Julian Conybeare is a seventeenth-century version of Virginia Woolf's Judith Shakespeare, a woman whose desire to be a poet only makes her more vulnerable. She longs for inclusion in the culture of Cambridge, a symbol of learning and literary excellence, but is excluded because of her gender. Macaulay represents Anglicanism as the middle way between the extremes of Catholicism and Puritanism. Robert Herrick, who is Julian's tutor, espouses 'that moderate and urbane spirit and sound, unfanatical judgement that distinguished Protestants as opposed to Puritans and papists' (1982, 176). But all three religious groups are united by their active enjoyment of witch-hunting: 'Witches be fair game everywhere' comments the squire (149). The hunting of Mrs Prowse, the harmless old woman accused of witchcraft, foreshadows Julian's own later death and the victimisation of women within history.

Seduced by the Cavalier poet, John Cleveland, who refuses to read her poetry and values her only as a sexual toy, Julian is accidentally killed in a quarrel between Cleveland and her Puritan brother. Her friend Meg Yarde also dies: disguised as a man so she can fight for the King, she is killed in a skirmish. Women, denied the status as 'citizens' that Julian lays claim to, are not only caught in the conflict but also victimised by both sides despite their status as non-combatants; their deaths are merely a footnote to the main action. As the title suggests, there are several defeats in the book: of Julian; of Robert Herrick, who loses his parish to the Puritans; of the King and his Cavaliers, including Cleveland; and of the cultural heritage of Cambridge destroyed in the war. However, the most resounding defeat is that of Julian – even her final poem is appropriated and published by Cleveland as his own.

When the medieval scholar Helen Waddell read *They Were Defeated*, she was moved by its similarities to the historical novel, *Peter Abelard* (1933), on which she herself was working at that point, and wrote to Macaulay who responded encouragingly (Blackett, 1973, 95–6). The tragic story of Abelard and Heloise's illicit love and marriage, followed by the castration of Abelard and their retreat into cloisters, is another history of the 'defeated' but one where both genders are victims. Waddell's *The Wandering Scholars* (1927), a study of the medieval vagrant scholars, is the work of one who recognised a kindred spirit in Abelard, whom she described as 'a scholar for scholarship's sake' (1934, 116). Yet, writing of the genesis of the novel, she described a dream in which she herself was Heloise, 'abbess of the Paraclete, with Abelard twenty years dead' (Blackett, 1973, 220). Her recreation of history, then, is through ('feminine') emotional identification as well as ('masculine') scholarship, which enables the vividly detailed reconstruction of a lost world in dream and imagination.

The conflict in *Peter Abelard* is between sexual desire and spirituality in a medieval Christian world which insisted on the separation of the two. But scholarship, poetry and sexuality in the novel are intimately connected, and equally valued by both partners. Knowing that marriage would entail Abelard breaking his faith, Heloise declares that she wants 'no bond but your love only. I am not ashamed to be called your harlot. I would be ashamed to be called your wife' (1950, 143). Their story is thus represented as the repression of a sexual passion which 1930s readers could understand.

In contrast, in Sheila Kaye-Smith's *Superstition Corner* (1934), the boyish heroine, 'Galloping Kate', another wearer of boy's clothes, is caught between her religious faith as a Catholic during the Elizabethan persecution of Catholics, and her desire for marriage and children. She dies at the end of the novel because, stripped of family, home and friends, there is no place for her within the world she inhabits. Her defeat as a Catholic is compounded by her gender, in contrast to her brother who has a place, however dangerous, as a Catholic priest in hiding.

Margiad Evans' *Country Dance* (1932), set in 1850, explores conflicts of nationality rather than religion, possibly reflecting one of the inqualities against which feminists campaigned in the early 1930s: the nationality laws whereby a married woman could not retain her nationality of birth. Born of an English father and a Welsh mother, Ann Goodman lives literally and metaphorically in the borderland between England and Wales, crossing between the two countries and languages. The text is presented as Ann's diary, discovered by Evans. Its unconscious theme, Evans tells us, is 'the struggle for supremacy in her mixed blood' (1978, vii). Ann's daily life on the farm is detailed in her diary as if in answer to Woolf's call for information about the unrecorded lives of women.

The text revisits the nineteenth-century two-suitor plot, as used in *Wuthering Heights*. Initially engaged to Gabriel Ford, an English shepherd who works in Wales, Ann ends her diary about to marry Evan ap Evans, a Welsh farmer whose property is on the English side of the border. The choice of husband is also a choice of nationality. In choosing Evan ap Evans, Ann is identifying not only with her matrilineal heritage – her mother's country and language – but also with the 'defeated' (the colonised country). The wedding does not take place because Ann is murdered. Yet, the fact that it is never certain to outsiders whether it was Gabriel or Evan who murdered her implies their dual guilt. Like Macaulay's Julian, Ann is destroyed by the two men who fight for possession of her and who represent 'the two nations at war within [her mind]' (1978, 95).

Yet this defeat is re-imagined as victory in Evans' final commentary: 'the victory goes to Wales; like Evan ap Evans, the awakened Celt cries "Cymru am byth" [Wales for ever!] with every word she writes' (1978, 95). Ann's awakening into sexuality and subjectivity is also a coming into consciousness of nationality and therefore an awakening into history: 'that history which belongs to all border lands and tells of incessant warfare' (95). The border crossings of the novel, imaged in the title as the movements of a country dance, destabilise the binary oppositions of Welsh and English, victory and defeat and even, as Ann does a man's work on the farm, male and female.

The emphasis on defeat is also clear in the anti-Fascist historical novels, which are cogently examined as 'Parables of the Past' in Janet Montefiore's *Men and Women Writers of the 1930s* (1996). Drawing on feminist critiques of narrative as ideology in order to counter Lukács' over-privileging of traditional narrative forms, Montefiore explores the ways in which women's anti-Fascist historical novels – Naomi Mitchison's *The Corn King and the Spring Queen* (1931), and Sylvia Townsend Warner's *Summer Will Show* (1936) and *After the Death of Don Juan* (1938) – address the clash between Marxism and feminism.

Moving on from the male protagonists of her 1920s novels, Mitchison's *The Corn King and the Spring Queen* offers us another way of reading 'histories of the defeated' through its use of two heroines, one of whom is killed while the other survives. Mitchison's novel deals with the defeat of Kleomenes' attempt to effect a proto-socialist revolution in Sparta. The revolution fails partly because women are not being offered citizenship: 'the good for them was much less obvious' (Mitchison, 1983, 194). One of the two heroines, Phillyla, who represents a traditional notion of femininity as passivity, is killed in the ensuing conflict. Neither declining Sparta, nor civilised Athens, nor corrupt Egypt offer women a position much higher than that of slaves. Instead, it is the so-called 'barbarian' country, the (imaginary) Marob with its emphasis on the natural cycles of life and its respect for witches, which offers them some kind of hope for the future. Thus Mitchison disrupts the concept of a linear progress of 'civilisation'.

The primary heroine, the Spring Queen Erif Der, has to leave Marob when she kills her father in unconscious revenge for his killing of her child. The novel not only rewrites history through the use of invented characters but also offers a cross-gendered 'feminist-socialist rewriting of the Aeschylean myth [of the *Oresteia*]' (Montefiore, 1996, 165). Erif Der's quest to 'become conscious of herself in history' is also a 'search for self in community' (Benton, 1992, 65, 66). By rewriting history through myth, influenced by her reading of Frazer's *The Golden Bough* (1890–1915), Mitchison offers us not a cyclical view of history – self-defeating 'world cycles' (1983, 283) – but a new mythic structure, or 'constellation' in Benjamin's terms, which carries the possibility of future intervention. Looking backwards, Kleomenes (who is, like Christ, a 'King Who Must Die for the People') and Phillyla may be defeated. But Erif Der carries forward to Marob the possibility of a subject-hood based on responsibility to community.

Another writer who used her reading of *The Golden Bough* to re-interpret history was Mary Butts, whose *Scenes from the Life of Cleopatra* (1935) was an attempt to restore Cleopatra's reputation from the ravages of male historians. These included not only Octavian and his party who, as victors over Cleopatra and Mark Antony, promulgated 'the legend of her as a crowned courtesan' to justify 'the annexation of Egypt, her death and Antony's' (Butts, 1974, 280), but also Chaucer, Shakespeare and Bernard Shaw. In contrast, Butts presents Cleopatra as a 'girl in a desperate situation', using any weapons available to her: 'What else could she do? Walk beside her sister in Caesar's triumph or watch it as reigning sovereign' (279). Ruth Hoberman argues that Butts suggests that the power to rule is located not in gender but in the concept of 'mana' – 'a diffuse yet all-pervasive energy' (1997, 47) – derived from the work of Frazer and Jane Harrison. Butts uses this, Hoberman suggests, to make room for the concept of a 'female ruler of history' (148).

Butts was also attracted by the idea, put forward by Harrison in *Themis*, that an early female-controlled religion based on magic was superseded by a later male-controlled religion based in anthropomorphic gods and myths (Hoberman, 1997, 48). Cleopatra and her companions, who represent the ancient Egyptian and Greek cultures overtaken by the brash new Romans, are taken by Caesar to see the 'King of the Woods' at Nemi, the figure which inspired Frazer's *The Golden Bough*. The 'King' was always a runaway slave who became 'King' when he killed the slave who occupied the position before him. He then dared not sleep for fear of being similarly deposed. Butts' Cleopatra and her companions are horrified because they see this as an obscene Roman corruption of the earlier worship of Diana/Artemis. Caesar defends the ritual, arguing that, 'It all lies, if anything lies, in the continuity' (1974, 118) and it clearly offers a figure for his own rise to power and deposition. The leather phallus worn by the 'King' suggests that this cycle of victory and defeat is driven by the male will to power.

By fragmenting her text into 'scenes' rather than linear narrative and emphasising the great 'historic "Ifs"' (142), Butts disrupts the inevitability of this continuity and opens spaces for alternative possibilities – the 'unrealised possibilities of the past' in Radford's phrase – represented by a female ruler. The text ends not with the death of Cleopatra but with that of her deposed sister, Arsinoë, slaughtered at Antony's behest. One of those 'unrealised possibilities' of history is the possibility of bonds between women, who might rule together rather than always having to rule in partnership with a man.

By writing histories of those defeated in the past, these texts offer a warning to the present about the possibilities of future defeats. At the same time they suggest that the present is haunted by the lost possibilities of the past through ghostly traces in language. In *Country Dance*, for instance, commenting on Ann's use of the present tense for her diary, Evans remarks that in Ann's part of the world 'the custom of referring to past events as though they were at the moment occurring still survives' (1978, viii). Despite her death, Ann vividly inhabits the present moment through the immediacy of her written words. The experience of reading the diary offers, Evans suggests, the 'uncomfortable feeling of listening at a keyhole' (1978, ix). The text appears to open a chink in the wall between past and present. In *They Were Defeated*, Macaulay suggests that Julian's spectral presence haunts our present moment by presenting the poem 'An Epitaph on the Earl of Strafford', usually tentatively attributed to Cleveland, as Julian's only surviving poem. A meditation on the violent tragedy of extremes in conflict, it presents Strafford as

'A *Papist*, yet a *Calvinist*;/His Prince's neerest Joy & Greefe,/[...] Ye People's violent Love & Hate,/One in extremes lov'd and abhor'd' (Macaulay, 1982, 428). Thus it offers a ghostly trace of the 'defeated' within the documents of the 'victorious'.

The strength and originality of the female voices created by these writers offer a portrayal of such vibrant subjectivities that it is impossible to see these women merely as victims. In writing 'histories of the defeated' these texts offer a kind of 'pardon' or rather a belated justice to the female 'defeated' of the past. They contest any notion of 'progress' or continuity that ignores women's needs and desires, and they insist on the necessity of breaking the subservience of gender as well as that of class, nationality, religion or sexuality. Finally, they offer the hope that some of the unrealised possibilities of the past may be resurrected and realised in the future.

Driven by the urgencies of the present, the women writers of the 1930s turned to the past in ways which radically remade the historical novel. This political commitment is particularly clear in the writing of Phyllis Bentley, a bestseller of the early 1930s, and Sylvia Townsend Warner, perhaps the most important, if unaccountably neglected, writer of historical fiction to emerge in this decade.

Rooted in geography: Phyllis Bentley's regional historical fiction

The publication of *Inheritance* in 1932 transformed the Yorkshire novelist Phyllis Bentley, who had written six earlier novels, into a bestselling author almost overnight.[2] A family saga, influenced by Galsworthy's *The Forsyte Saga* (1922) which Bentley admired, *Inheritance* is also a regional novel, situated firmly in the landscape and history of Yorkshire. As such it illustrates particularly well Herbert Butterfield's contention that: 'History is rooted in geography, and the historical novel, which is a novel that seeks to be rooted in some ways in actuality, finds one of its roots in geography' (1924, 41).

Bentley's work was driven by two conscious aims: 'to write novels which should present life exactly as it really was, and by so doing help to better the world' (1962, 107). Her commitment to realism, therefore, was closely connected to her political commitment, and both inclined her towards a materialist view of history.

Bentley situated herself within the tradition of the English regional novel, itself a sub-division of the national novel as produced by Scott or Edgeworth. Despite England's relatively small size, Bentley pointed out in *The English Regional Novel* (1941), its literature is extremely rich in regional novels, because of its geographical diversity. This led to social, cultural and economic diversity as particular trades and industries developed in specific areas. As Bentley notes:

the woollen textile industry of the West Riding is entirely a product of the physical geography of the area. The rough hills of millstone grit, the grass growing on which would feed sheep but not cattle [. . .]; the many tumbling streams; the pockets of coal and iron; those, providing as they do wool, water and power, are the origins of the West Riding cloth industry. (Bentley, 1941, 16)

As the landscape influences the agriculture, industry or trade of a region, they in turn determine the working lives and the characters, customs and language of the people, and thus the historical development of the region.

The golden age of the regional novel, Bentley argued, stretched from 1840 to the 1940s with Charlotte Brontë's *Shirley* (1849) being 'the first great English regional novel' (1941, 14). Brontë, George Eliot, Thomas Hardy and Arnold Bennett perfected this genre where plot, character, language and themes are linked to regional causality, and whose transcendent merit is its 'detailed faithfulness to reality' (45). The 1930s saw a 'regional renaissance' which Bentley attributed to particular historical circumstances (13). Regional novels by writers such as Walter Greenwood, Storm Jameson, Winifred Holtby, J.B. Priestley and Lettice Cooper were a direct response to the ways in which the economic depression and unemployment of the 1930s impacted on specific areas, particularly the industrialised north. After 1939, however, improvements in communication and the need for unity in the face of war meant that the regional novel faded in significance until it reappeared in the work of Catherine Cookson and what publishers now call the 'clogs and shawl' popular family saga.

Many of these regional novels, like *Shirley*, are also historical novels. In the regional historical novel, history (temporal change) is also spatialised. That is, it is located in a particular landscape, and finds its causality in a particular culture, character and language, as much as in the impact of external factors. The 'national tale' and the regional novel depict regional/national culture, character and language as different from the 'universal' (often the colonising nation) in terms of continuity and stasis – what Katie Trumpener calls the 'thick accretion of cultural life forms' (1993, 708). In contrast, the historical novel stresses temporal change and the fragility and malleability of cultural forms in the face of historical change (708). The regional historical novel brings together the issues of spatial specificity and temporality to show how history in the regions differs from the history of the 'centre'. The experiences of local regions may be 'behind' or 'ahead' or even completely outside the linear chronological political history of the centre, represented by court or parliament. This difference was starkly illustrated in the 1930s when the Hunger Marchers marched from the impoverished industrialised regions to the political centre, a confrontation caught by T.C. Dugdale's painting, 'The Arrival of the Jarrow Marchers in London', which contrasts the dark mass of anonymous protesters with a languid upper-class couple regarding them from a window.

A further merit of the regional novel, according to Bentley, is that its valuation of the ordinary individual makes it 'essentially democratic' (1941, 45). Its strength lies in its depiction of character, and the two formative factors of 'hereditary and environment' (45). This gives it a close affinity with the family saga, which is often regional, and represents history through the depiction of several generations of a family, often connected to a specific trade or occupation.[3]

As its title indicates, *Inheritance*, the story of the Oldroyds, a Yorkshire mill-owning family similar to Bentley's own, is concerned with the issue of inheritance – both of family traits and characteristics, and of property. As Bentley put it in her own autobiography: 'we are always the heirs of the past and the begetters of the future' (1962, 167). History is understood here in terms of an organic connection between past and present. She saw the history of the West Riding as a 'perfect example' of the progress of the Industrial Revolution (1962, 14). Thus the novel traces the fortunes of the Oldroyds from the beginning of the Industrial Revolution with the introduction of frames in 1812 to the post-war slump in the textile trade and the devaluation of the gold standard in 1931. Against this she explores the relationship between private family structures and public history.

The novel deploys the two parallel temporal axes Christine Bridgwood (1986, 176–7) has argued are typical of the popular family saga. The shorter axis revolves around individuals and their family dramas, while the extended axis offers a long view which in the popular saga, Bridgwood argues, tends towards an 'ideology of stoical acceptance' of the status quo (1986, 178). Bentley, however, deploys this structure in a more radical fashion.

Her long axis shows the changing social and cultural contexts within history. The short axis shows the repetitions of key patterns of family psychology. Certain family characteristics (symbolised by the pulsating vein which shows on the forehead of Oldroyd family members when they are agitated, and by the repetition of key names) remain constant, inherited from generation to generation. Patterns of naming in the novel invoke this 'inheritance'. The name 'Will', given to both the first William Oldroyd and his son, has resonances on several levels. It indicates both the 'wilful' (1932, 11) nature of the Oldroyds – they are all 'Tartars' (353) though in different ways according to their gender, social position and political convictions – and the phallic nature of the masculine 'will' to power. It also invokes the legal 'will' which bequeaths property from one generation to another, and which is an attempt to control history by controlling the distribution of wealth. The 'will' ensures the continuity of both primogeniture (by excluding women) and class privilege (by excluding the workers).

By beginning the novel in 1812, with the Luddites attempting to prevent the introduction of cropping frames into the mills, Bentley recalls Brontë's

Shirley, where the mill-owner Robert Moore is shot and wounded by Luddite rioters. Similarly, William Oldroyd, economically hard-pressed by the fall in trade resulting from the Napoleonic Wars, brings in soldiers to ensure the frames are delivered secretly to his mill. Fearing unemployment as a result of this mechanisation, and already seeing their families short of food, four Luddites – George Mellor, Ben Walker, Thomas Thorpe and the mill's foreman, Joe Bamforth – shoot and kill Oldroyd, and are hung for his murder. Bentley then traces the after-effects of this tragic action down to her own day.

This moment creates 'a gulf between masters and men' (1932, 108) as their interests divide between the mechanisation seen by the owners as necessary to sustain the industry, and the maintenance of hand labour necessary to ensure jobs for the men. With industrialisation comes the process Marx describes as the 'alienation of labour', which Bentley depicts in terms of both the men and the masters wanting to make money rather than 'good cloth' (586), and the disempowerment of the working classes. Bentley, then, is actively showing this historical moment as the 'prehistory of the present' in Lukács' terms. In telling the history of a single family, she is also telling a wider history of the region, the period and even the country. As she puts it: 'I hope [...] that my fiction is symbolic and my valley typical' (1932, 5). The story of the Oldroyds becomes 'symbolic of all industry since the industrial revolution' (586).

The conflict between the masters and men is worked out through the novel until it reaches 'the ruin of today' (585) when the Oldroyds have lost their mill. The historical events which we think of as mainstream 'history' – the Reform Bill, the agitation for the ten-hours bill, the Chartists' demand for universal suffrage, the Franco-Prussian War, the McKinley tariffs imposed by the US, the 'Great War', the General Strike of 1926 – are depicted in relation to their effect on the West Riding textiles industry. In the economic slump of the 1930s, re-adjustment was necessary to save the cloth trade but, locked in conflict and their own interests, neither men nor employers had 'the habit of co-operation' (586).

Bentley uses shifting points of view to depict the motives of the owners and the desperation of the workers. She aims, like Elizabeth Gaskell in *North and South* (1854–1855), to promote reconciliation between the two through better understanding. Joe Bamforth is depicted as a man 'in fair compassion skilled' (585), the man who should have been able to mediate between the two sides, but was caught between them and, although technically innocent of the murder, hung.

Like Brontë and Gaskell, Bentley is concerned to show the effect of these 'public' events on 'private' lives and especially on women. William Oldroyd's son, Will, was to have married Joe Bamforth's sister, Mary, but after the murder he rejects her, unknowingly leaving her to unmarried motherhood. In the next generation, Will's two sons – Jonathan through Mary, and Brigg through the daughter of another mill-owner, Henry Brigg – quarrel because they come to represent the interests of the owners and the workers. The conflict between owners and workers is worked out within the family structure in a series of carefully plotted patterns based on marriages, frequently cross-class, and on the feuds (typical of the family saga form), which are here driven by political and class sympathies. For the women in the novel, class position depends on marriage rather than inheritance. Will's granddaughter, Janie, marries 'down' to a descendent of George Mellor, while their daughter, Carmine, marries 'up' to Francis Oldroyd. These class differences cause deep rifts in both marriages. The novel ends with the son of Francis and Carmine, David Oldroyd, who represents a 'new synthesis' (586) of all who have gone before him, both owners and workers. This intricate genealogical patterning recalls *Wuthering Heights*, another regional historical novel (although rarely read as such) concerned with kinship ties and property, which also ends with an image of synthesis and reconciliation.

The concern with property reworks Galsworthy's *The Forsyte Saga* which Bentley saw as a 'passionate indictment of all attempted ownership of human souls' (Bentley, 1948, 185). The Oldroyds' paternalistic, over-bearing attitude to their workers is mirrored in Will's treatment of Mary. He does not quite rape her but he 'beat[s] down her faint struggles' and 'drag[s] her to the settle' (18–19). 'Had he, Will Oldroyd, really done something so vile as to seduce Joe's sister?' (26), he later asks, before reassuring himself that he has merely anticipated the wedding day. Similarly, he refuses to recognise that his wealth is based on the exploitation of children's labour. Capitalism scars the workers' bodies – producing the 'cropper's hoof' (45) on the wrists of the men, and laming Jonathan, who went to work as a child. Thus the novel connects the capitalist ownership of property and male 'ownership' of women's and children's bodies.

The familial strands culminate in the 1930s in David Brigg Oldroyd who reflects that 'the blood of all those people who began the conflict in 1812 runs in my veins: [. . .] God! how deep I am in the West Riding; my roots go deep down into the Ire Valley soil' (587). In one sense this novel is a 'history of the defeated' typical of the 1930s, as David's father Francis, having lost the mill, is about to take his family south. But in the final chapter, entitled 'End or Beginning', David leaps from the London-bound train, affirming a commitment to the West Riding and a hope that, as a 'synthesis' of the blood of both owners and workers and with the understanding brought by his knowledge of history, he can begin again. This refusal of defeat and closure – of the 'dismal ending' (588) David rejects – suggests a continuity which recognises that 'the future is the heir of the present, as the present is of the past' (591). Past and present are not separate and distinct, but organically connected through the 'inheritance' of succeeding generations and this is most clearly evident when that heritage is closely connected to a place. In resisting a marriage ending for the text, Bentley also resists the kind of conservative closure Bridgwood identifies in the later popular family saga of the 1980s. This is, however, made easier by the fact that her final protagonist is male.

In Bentley's hands, the regional historical novel is used to show that 'history' is made not just by 'great men' but by ordinary people outside the metropolitan centre. The Luddites' meeting in the inn has, Joe thinks, 'almost a historical quality to it' (46). David, the inheritor of Joe's sense of history, learns that 'Really important things happen to real people in real places, and not to stage characters in velvet and ermine. And conversely [...] things that happen to ordinary-looking people in stuffy pubs may be very important' (573).

Bentley's commitment to realism – Brontë's 'something real, cool, and solid [...] something unromantic as Monday morning' (Bentley, 1941, 17) – as the most effective medium through which to convey 'phenomena as they really happen in ordinary everyday life on a clearly defined spot of real earth' (45) also allows her to show that immediate thickness and confusion of events which is clarified when the events are recorded as a neat linear chronology. 'It was all very well reading about rebellions in history books', Joe reflects, 'but when things happened in real life they were so different, so much more confusing' (73). Bentley's 'insistently realist aesthetic', Hoberman suggests, 'is also a way of making people see how things *really* are, of disrupting the process of historical interpretation by which the myriad details of experience are digested and condensed into a single plot' (1997, 156, 157). What is discarded in the 'single plot' of history books, Bentley shows, is the local, the regional, the familial and the individual. By using several generations and points of view, Bentley offers multiple 'plots' which resist absorption into a single story.

The use and abuse of power, whether by an individual, a factory owner or the leader of a state, is one of Bentley's central concerns. The year of *Inheritance*'s publication, 1932, was also the year in which Oswald Mosley founded the British Union of Fascists. A year later, Hitler became German Chancellor, and in October 1935, Italy attacked Abyssinia. Like many women writers in this decade, Bentley used the historical novel to express her anxiety over this rising flood of Fascism, looking back to Imperial Rome.

Freedom, Farewell! (1936), her novel of Julius Caesar's rise to power, was written 'on account of Hitler' (1962, 202). The novel develops Bentley's earlier analyses of the connections between public and private power structures in *Inheritance*. Indeed, the repetition of narrative patterns between the two novels signals the fact that Bentley is dealing with the same issues on a different scale. Both texts open with an almost cinematic 'shot' of a young man in a landscape about to meet the woman who will be the central love of his life, but whom he will treat badly. Both deal with a struggle for power between opposing forces, and both end with a young man meditating on the central issues of the novel and their relation to history. But whereas

Inheritance revalues what traditional history leaves out, *Freedom, Farewell!* through its focus on the 'great men' and the political 'centre' revalues the 'grand narrative' of history itself.

Caesar, like Will Oldroyd, begins his career with the near-rape of a woman, Servilia, whom he decides to 'take by force rather than wait upon persuasion' (1936, 94). Gender is thus made central to the range of power structures examined in the novel. For Caesar, Servilia represents Rome itself: 'Rome was great, Rome was noble, Rome did not lack the virtue needed to rule the world, he felt, while Rome could produce such matrons' (23). As Hoberman argues, Caesar's transformation of Servilia into a metaphor for Rome elides her personhood and demonstrates 'the compulsive figure-making of men at the expense of women' (1997, 158). As Caesar takes Servilia 'by force', so he takes Spain, Gaul, Egypt and Rome itself. At the moment of his death he realises that he has betrayed everything Rome stood for in his attempt to subdue it to his absolute power: 'He saw himself bribing, corrupting, manoeuvring, fighting, seizing men's freedom in order to make them free' (1936, 473).

The novel's final analysis is offered through the defeated Brutus' (silent) mediation on the question, 'How have we let freedom slip?' (1936, 507). His use of murder to end despotism, he now recognises, replicates Caesar's use of military might: 'Law brings forth law, but the sword only the sword' (508). Brutus' death suggests a warning, 'a fable' (509) in his own words, for later generations.

In their use of a young man to present the final argument, *Freedom, Farewell!* and *Inheritance* appear to replicate the silencing of women within history. The woman characters in *Freedom, Farewell!* 'speak' only through inarticulate suffering or silence. The novel proper closes with the haunting image of Porcia (Brutus' wife and Cato's daughter) on hearing of Brutus' death, snatching some burning charcoal from a brazier – 'holding it close against her mouth she stifled herself with the fumes, and died' (509). This image of death through stifling is, Hoberman argues, contrasted with the 'meaningless babble of the now impotent senate confirming the decrees of Augustus Caesar [...] Language itself becomes an act of submission, silence is the only weapon against tyranny' (1997, 161, 162).

In her autobiographical novel, *Life Story* (1948), Bentley returned to the question of 'cycles of power', telling the story of Hannah, a domestic tyrant whose life, despite her gender, replicates Caesar's on a familial scale. Hannah's life, Bentley suggests, falls into four stages which are replicated in 'every human being, every nation, every party, every cause':

The struggle against oppression, the achievement of power, its corruption in achievement causing revolt, its loss – the lifetime of every human organism, whether individual or collective, by nature pursues this course. (1948, 297)

The question of 'how to break this cycle of domination, how to wield authority without oppression' is, she argues, 'one of the great human problems' (297). Her novels suggest that only with an understanding of history can that cycle be broken.

Hoberman draws attention to the way in which Bentley herself was silenced as critics misunderstood *Freedom, Farewell!*, seeing it as an attempt to cash in on the success of Robert Graves' *I Claudius* (1934) (1997, 162). This failure to recognise the political engagement of women's historical novels in the 1930s, especially the way in which they consistently link patriarchal structures with other power structures, has led to the neglect of a body of important work, particularly that of the writer I want to discuss next, Sylvia Townsend Warner.

The writer as sniper: Sylvia Townsend Warner

Asked in the 1970s why she had written no more novels after 1954, Sylvia Townsend Warner replied,

> Nothing big enough was left to say. We had fought, we had retreated, we were betrayed, and are now misrepresented. So I melted into the background as best I could to continue sniping. You can pick odd enemies off, you know, by aiming a short story well. (Rattenbury, 1981, 47)

Warner was a writer who took sides with a vengeance, and the writer as sniper is a particularly good image for someone who wrote in so many ways from the so-called margins – as a woman, a lesbian, a Communist, living in rural Dorset rather than London – and who has been marginalised ('misrepresented') by literary history. Earlier, in 1939, she had said that she wrote out of 'the discovery that the pen could be used as a sword' (Dowson, 1996, 151); the metaphors change but the image of the writer as fighter remains. If Warner's work was driven by her political convictions (in terms of both party and sexual politics), she also prided herself on being 'a moral writer' (Rattenbury, 1996, 216). Like the worldly Jane Austen, whom she much admired, Warner understood that the two things – politics and morality – are intimately connected.

Warner is emerging from recent accounts of the 1930s as an important writer.[4] The earlier neglect of Warner's work has been attributed to her gender, her sexuality, her unrepentant membership of the Communist Party, and the fact that her work (poetry, novels, short stories) was too varied to be easily categorised. I would add another reason to these. Of her seven novels, five (all those from 1929 onwards) are historical novels, though they vary in period and setting from fourteenth-century England to eighteenth-century Spain and nineteenth-century France (which perhaps accounts for their perceived variability despite their common form). Moreover, she is European in her outlook. The critical neglect of the historical novel in the twentieth century has led directly to the marginalisation of Warner who is, without doubt, one of the most versatile, accomplished and sophisticated historical novelists of the twentieth century, male or female. Indeed, I would argue that she is a major writer, not *despite* the fact that she wrote historical novels but *because* her achievement is to new-mint the genre through a fusion of realist and Modernist forms and Marxist and feminist politics.

Her work shares with the anti-Fascist humanist historical novel which Lukács saw emerging in the 1930s the task of revealing 'those social-historical and human-moral forces whose interplay made possible the 1933 catastrophe in Germany' (Lukács, 1983, 342). It was, said Warner, the events of 1933, more than anything the Reichstag Fire Trial, which politicised her and led to her joining the Communist Party in 1935 and her subsequent activism in the Spanish Civil War (Warner and Schmidt, 1981, 35).

However, what Lukács would call the 'classical form of the historical novel' associated with socialist-realism is revitalised in Warner's work by a Modernist (even, perhaps, postmodernist) sensibility which is located in experimentation, as Gillian Beer has pointed out, at the level of *narrative* rather than word (1999, 77). Warner looks back not to Scott, but to Gustave Flaubert in whose work Lukács located the decline of the classical historical novel, and to the tradition of women writers that Lukács ignores: Austen, the Brontës, George Eliot and George Sand.

In 'Women as Writers' (1959), Warner suggests some of the ways in which women writers, because of their circumstances rather than their sex, might differ from many male writers. Because women enter the 'house' of literature by scrambling through the pantry window rather than as of right through the front door, she suggests, they are not hampered by heavy equipment of learning, self-consciousness, or an innate sense of moral superiority. 'Women as writers', she suggests, 'seem to be remarkable adept at vanishing out of their writing so that the quality of immediacy replaces them' (Warner, 1990, 542). Another 'pantry window trait' is 'the kind of workaday democracy, an ease and appreciativeness in low company' (542). Hence it is rare to find the conventional comic servant or countryman in women's writing.

These traits (which, she notes, are technical assets which affect presentation not content) are, not surprisingly, clearly visible in Warner's own work and they are precisely what make her a superb historical novelist. Warner herself vanishes and we are left with a sense of immediacy evoked by what Wendy Mulford has described as Warner's gift for rendering the dense texture of material reality through 'the tang of things tasted, smelt, handled, known in their quiddity and in their essence' (1988, 109–10). Rather than using 'period' trappings or language, she evokes the material reality of landscape, plants, animals or ordinary objects. This is the kind of concrete detail that trad-itionally characterises literary realism but in Warner's hands it becomes a touchstone linking past and present: 'An old teapot, used daily, can tell me more of my past than anything I recorded of it', she noted (Warner, 1982, 140). Similarly, her 'workaday democracy' was enacted through the displacement of the bourgeois protagonist from the centre of her novels, and the use of shifting points of view to depict a community.

A novel about the necessity for political engagement (the need to 'take sides'), *Summer Will Show* (1936) is the story of an upper-class English lady, Sophia Willoughby. She goes to Paris to reclaim her unfaithful husband after the death of her children, falls in love with his mistress, the Jewish storyteller Minna Lemuel, and becomes a revolutionary Communist. Warner's account of her choice of the 1848 Paris revolutions as the subject for this novel suggests her themes:

> I read how Marie-Amélie urged poor Louis-Philippe to go out and confront the mobs, adding, '"Je vous bénirai du haut du balcon" [I will bless you from the balcony on high].' 'I reflected that this nonsense coincided with the Communist Manifesto', and this shaped the argument of the book. (Warner, 1982, 40)

The confrontation of upper class and revolutionary mob, the complicity of women with the class oppressor, the false consolations of religion, and the emergence of Communism as a politics that can make sense of the processes of history are at the heart of this novel.

But Warner's novel rewrites Marx's famous assertion that, 'The history of all hitherto existing society is the history of class struggles' (Marx and Engels, 1985, 79) to show that it has also been a history of gender struggles. Her novel offers an important corrective to Lukács' theorisation of the historical novel in two ways. First, Warner foregrounds the issue of gender (of which he is sublimely unaware). Secondly, her work undermines his overvaluation of traditional realist narrative methods and his dismissal of Modernist techniques as merely 'subjective' by showing that such techniques can be (and, indeed, always are) equally political.

The choice of 1848, the date of the Paris revolutions and the *Communist Manifesto*, is a key moment on several levels. For Marxist historians, this is a crucial turning point in history: the moment when the bourgeoisie replace the aristocracy as the exploiters of the proletariat, and the proletariat 'enters upon the world historical stage as an armed mass, resolved upon the final struggle' (Lukács, 1983, 171). For Lukács, 1848 marks the beginning of the decline of the classical historical novel since after the revolutions, writers 'no longer have any immediate social sense of continuity with the prehistory of their own society' (1983, 244). The works of Gustave Flaubert, especially *Salammbô* (1862), exemplified this decline. Flaubert's disgust for modern life, Lukács argues, triggers a retreat into a history which is merely an accurately detailed but decorative background: 'a large imposing scene for purely private, intimate and subjective happenings' (1983, 199).

In *Summer Will Show*, Warner, as several critics have noted, was rewriting Flaubert's *Sentimental Education* (1869), which is about the 1848 revolution. Despite its near contemporary setting, Flaubert regarded *Sentimental Education* as a 'historical novel', researching the background to the revolution in detail (1964, 10). His protagonist Frédéric, however, is so absorbed in his own private affairs (the exploitative seduction of his friend's wife and mistress) that he misses the significance of the momentous events going on around him, regarding them as a spectacle which has no relevance to himself. Frédéric himself is a manifestation of the history he is attempting to ignore, and his retreat into the personal entails the rejection of political and moral imperatives. With its alienated, disengaged protagonist and its focus on the subjective and the psychological, rather than 'objective' reality, *Sentimental Education* is an important precursor of the Modernist novel.

When Warner's Sophia first arrives in Paris, she watches the barricade building of the February uprising from the balcony of Minna's apartment. It is an image which recasts not only Marie-Amélie's comment but also a scene from *Sentimental Education* where Frédéric spends the afternoon watching the mob from the window of an apartment belonging to the mistress of his friend Arnoux, who is about to become his mistress. Whereas Flaubert's Frédéric retreats from history into the personal, Sophia is politicised by her love for Minna and her recognition that they are both (wife and mistress) exploited by her husband, tellingly named Frederick. When Sophia goes to live with Minna, Frederick cuts off her income and retains her property. It is 'a lock-out' (Warner, 1987, 266), comments the revolutionary Ingelbrecht (loosely based on Engels), drawing a parallel between gender and class struggle. As a woman, Sophia's class is determined by her marital status in a way that Marx failed to acknowledge.

Adrift from Frederick, she is déclasseé – a 'fallen woman'. Through Sophia's emerging political and sexual consciousness, Warner traces an upper-class woman's metaphorical descent from the 'balcony' down into the streets (where Sophia acts as courier, transporting scrap iron from which the Communists can manufacture ammunition) and thus into history itself as an engaged participant. The novel ends with Sophia, reading and 'by degrees absorbed' by the *Communist Manifesto* (406). The first page of the *Manifesto*, with its striking opening, 'A spectre is haunting Europe – the spectre of Communism', is reproduced in the text. This enacts at the level of text a movement out of 'fiction' into 'history'.

This ending and the uncertainty over whether Minna, bayoneted by Sophia's half-black, illegitimate nephew Caspar, is dead has proven particularly problematic for critics. Wendy Mulford, for instance, regards it as an unconvincing 'botch' (1988, 122). The dense intertextuality of the novel and this off-kilter, indeterminate closure mean that the text both evokes and critiques nineteenth-century realism. In an important essay, Terry Castle (1993) has shown how *Summer Will Show* rewrites the male–female–male triangle which Eve Sedgwick has argued characterises the European canon (and is central to *Sentimental Education*). Warner replaces this plot of male homosocial bonding with a triangle of female desire where the man is 'between women' and finally erased. This 'counter-plotting', Castle argues, displaces the canonical texts of nineteenth-century realism which the novel summons up through pastiche and rewriting.[5] It replaces them with something which 'dismantles the real, as it were, in a search for the not-yet real' and, as a consequence, 'looks odd, fantastical, implausible, "not there" – utopian in aspiration if not design' (1993, 91). This makes it, she argues, an exemplary lesbian fiction. Castle's reading is important, yet by emphasising the 'superficial historicism' (1993, 89) of Warner's novel, as Montefiore points out, she actually *dehistoricises* it (1996, 177).

In a poststructural reading of Warner's 'unwriting' of Flaubert, Sandy Petrey (1991) returns to Flaubert's proto-modernist dissolution of objective reality, history and authorial authority in a way which re-historicises Warner's novel. Warner, Petrey argues, shares Flaubert's recognition of language as semiotic flux, the free play of signifiers rather than a representation of objective 'reality'. 'History' itself is a mass of conflicting narratives, as Warner had discovered during her research for the novel: 'Legitimists, Orleanists, Republicans, all told incompatible versions of the same events, and several times didn't even agree on dates. But their prejudice made them what I needed' (Warner, 1982, 40). In the face of this indeterminacy and subjective 'prejudice', Warner, unlike Flaubert's Frédéric, does not retreat from history but is keenly concerned about the *destination* of her writing: 'Like Barthes, she sees the death of the Author as the birth of the reader and shifts attention from proper interpretation of what words say to committed appreciation of what they do' (Petrey, 1991, 168).

In *Summer Will Show*, Warner gives us what Roland Barthes (1970) would call a 'writerly' (*scriptible*) text which demands that the reader participate in the production of its meaning. For at the end of the novel the reader has already started reading another text, the *Communist Manifesto*, and the implied natural action for her here is to find a copy of Marx's text and continue that reading. Warner's novel doubles back, returning the reader from 'history' (the year 1848) into 'history' (the year in which she exists). But, as Thomas Foster argues, because of its introduction of the issues of gender and (through Caspar) race, the ending of *Summer Will Show* positions the reader to *re*-read the *Manifesto* through her knowledge of these oppositional elements ignored by Marx (Foster, 1995, 554). Like Sophia, the reader is politicised and has come down off the balcony into the streets in order to take sides. That political transformation has been enabled precisely by the power of narrative. Within the text it is Minna's narrative of her childhood experience of an anti-Jewish pogrom which begins Sophia's political re-education. The novel ends with the defeat of the Paris revolutions but it looks forward to the continuation of the struggle through the impact of its own narrative on the reader.

That Warner, like Mitchison, was consciously using the historical novel as a cover for political commentary seems to have gone unnoticed. The reviews of *Summer Will Show*, she commented to Julius Lipton in 1936, were 'all very spotless so far, so that my pinafore is still quite presentable – just another bourgeois stylist' (Rattenbury, 1996, 214). Her next novel, *After the Death of Don Juan* (1938), was far more explicitly applicable to current events. It was, as she put it, 'a parable if you like the word, or an allegory...of the political chemistry of the Spanish war, with Don Juan – more of Molière than of Mozart – developing as the Fascist of the piece' (Warner, 1982, 51). This aligns it very clearly with the anti-Fascist novels of the 1930s.

The use of the term 'allegory' initially suggests that her novel is subject to the same weaknesses that Lukács saw in these texts: a lack of real understanding of the relation between past and present; a failure to create characters which are social types; a tendency to didacticism rather than allowing a representation of lived experience to speak for itself. Above all, he says, these texts are guilty of 'turning the past into a *parable of the present*' in a way which 'conflicts with the real historical concreteness of the content' (1983, 338). Warner's novel, although it depicts class war in eighteenth-century Spain, does not offer a direct allegory of the Civil War but something much more complex.

The novel begins 'after' the ending of the legend dramatised by Molière and Mozart, when Don Juan is carried off to hell by the statue of the Commander he has killed. Dona Ana, the Commander's daughter whom Don Juan tried to seduce, with her new husband and their entourage, travels to Tenorio Viejo to relay to Don Juan's father, Don Saturno, the account of Don Juan's death given by his servant, Leporello. She is actually driven by her unrequited lust for Don Juan, and the hope that he may still be alive. Don Saturno is inclined to disbelieve the story of Don Juan's death because it is, as he tells his visitors, just that – a story:

> This legend of the wicked Don Juan is one of our family traditions, only till now it has always attached itself to the seventh Don Juan not the twelfth. In fact, the story has passed into literature. Molière wrote a play on the theme, an uneven work, but not without merit. (Warner, 1989, 35)

The story is also the subject of a ballad sung by the villagers which emphasises indeterminacy of narrative: 'Is it a lady or is a nightingale that sings so sweetly [...]?; Is it a mattress or is it a pillow [...]?' (119). Don Juan's death, like Minna's, is uncertain.

Once again, Warner is pointing up the *fictionality* of her narrative in a way which would distress Lukács but which, as Montefiore points out,

invites debate and scrutiny of the issues raised [and] actually illumin-
ates the problem of ideological struggle in the class war. The unstable
meanings produced by the popular ballad clearly show both the power
of propaganda and the difficulty of disseminating and controlling it.
(1996, 162)

Reflecting on his own account of the Spanish Civil War, it was the difficulty
of establishing 'objective truth' in the face of propaganda which worried
George Orwell (1966, 235). He believed that 'what is peculiar to our own age
is the abandonment of the idea that history could be truthfully written'
(236), and he attributed this to totalitarian theory. Warner recognises this
textual instability but asserts the possibility of political and moral 'truth'.
Her novel enacts a series of formal shifts – out of 'fiction' into 'history'; from
melodrama into realism; from the bourgeois form of opera into the popular
form of the ballad; from the upper classes to the peasants; from a single to
multiple points of view; from the city to the country – which all expand the
form of the historical novel.

Don Juan's reappearance (as with Franco's revolt) signals the reassertion
of Fascist control of the means of production. He will implement the desperately needed irrigation scheme his liberal but ineffectual father has been
unable to bring to fruition because of the need to pay Don Juan's debts. But
he will do so by taking back the land from the peasants in order to increase
productivity for his own personal gain. In the fighting which follows, the
peasants are, like the Popular Front forces in 1936, poorly armed and
trained, fighting against professional soldiers and doomed to failure.

The parallels with 1930s Spain suggest not allegory but the way in which
the past, the shift from feudalism to capitalism in eighteenth-century Spain,
is the 'prehistory of the present' in that the struggle between the classes
is repeated. Both Warner's political analysis and her characterisation
arise directly, as Lukács required, out of the conditions which she is depicting. Every feature of the landscape she depicts 'carries social meaning'
(Montefiore, 1996, 159). The village is dominated by the castle, representing
class oppression, and the church with its 'cupola slipped awry' (Warner,
1989, 24), which has 'slipped' from its moral responsibilities. The ineffectual
priest has become a 'consenter to inequity' (Warner, 1989, 272), while the
sacristan, Don Gil, loves 'the sense of power' (154). Fascism itself is figured
as a 'hierarchy of bullying' (155) where God is the ultimate bully, but power
is devolved through Don Juan, through Don Gil who mercilessly exploits
his daughter-in-law, and so on, with the peasants at the bottom. The water
so desperately needed by the peasants represents not merely the control of
the means of production but the control of the potentiality of life itself. Just
as the river in *Summer Will Show* represents 'Liberty' (1987, 123) for Minna,
the irrigation scheme (a sharing of resources) would be one move towards
freedom from oppression for the peasants.

In Janet Montefiore's otherwise invaluable reading of *After the Death of Don Juan*, she suggests that the novel's '(relative) absence of feminist critique' is due to Warner's recognition that a character who questioned male authority would look anachronistic (1996, 163). However, I would argue that the novel offers a particularly sophisticated analysis of the way in which Fascism was rooted in and exploited traditional gender roles, an insight echoed by several other feminists in this period, notably Woolf in *Three Guineas* (1938) and Holtby in *Women* (1934). Spain, Holtby noted, was 'a country notorious for its social subjection of women' (1934, 175), where 'The laws of property, the customs of society, the whole burden of tradition and prejudice, and the influence of the Catholic Church combine to stereotype the old position' (176).

In her treatment of the issue of property, Warner shows how feudalism and capitalism are both founded on the concept of primogeniture – the passage of property from one man to his eldest son, a contract in which women can only function as conduits. Don Saturno despises his son and feels no grief over his son's possible death, yet he suffers intense 'sickness' over his lack of an heir: 'He remembered again, and acutely, that he was an heirless man, that there was no one to come after him except a wretched cousin in the female line' (1989, 193). In attempting to marry the miller's daughter for her money, Leporello is aping Don Saturno's earlier wedding of a lady with 'a fine estate of corn-land in La Mancha and some river-dues on the Ebro' (191–2). It is Don Juan's status as male heir which allows him to drain the estate and exploit the peasants to fund his libertine lifestyle, to drink wine while their land 'gasps for water' (108). But it is also why at the end of the novel he can depose his father, order in the soldiers and dispossess the peasants.

The pathologising of homosexuality, male and female, is necessary to ensure patrilineal inheritance. In *Summer Will Show*, same-sex female desire breaks that line and frustrates Frederick's control of wife and mistress. In *After the Death of Don Juan*, Warner shows how heterosexual desire has been channelled by custom, tradition and prejudice to serve the interests of the propertied classes. As a libertine, Don Juan exploits and abuses women just as he does the peasants, reducing them to sexual objects, in the same way that Fascism in the 1930s defined women only by their biology.

Barbara Greenfield's Jungian analysis of the significance of masculine archetypes for women offers a way of reading Dona Ana's seemingly inexplicable lust for Don Juan, who has attempted to seduce her and killed her father. The Don Juan figure, Greenfield argues, has the 'appeal of free and explicit sexuality' and represents the 'temptation of the instinctual and forbidden for people who are compelled by social taboos to resist these drives' (1985, 195). Don Juan is therefore especially alluring to women who have been 'kept unnaturally chaste, passive and immobile through the over-protection of the father' (196). Warner's image of Ana praying in the church – 'Rigid and ornate the church enclosed her like a cage. Rigid and ornate her stiff bodice, her massive skirts, contained the riches and suavity of her body' (71) – conveys exactly this immobility within the rigid structures of class, gender and religion. Ana's blasphemous prayer for the resurrection of Don Juan is urged by profane desires symbolised by a cat outside the church: 'Passionately, slavishly, the cat yowled and yowled, venting its shameless desolate sexual cry' (81).

In making Don Juan a Fascist, Warner shows how eroticisation of gendered power differentials involves a masochistic female worship of male power that might lead women into complicity with the atrocities of history. 'Every woman adores a Fascist' as Sylvia Plath infamously put it in 'Daddy' (1968, 8). This was a subject which had a particular relevance in the 1930s, and one thinks of the two Mitford sisters, Diana and Unity, who became apologists for Fascism.[6] This female masochism is perhaps another version of defeat, an internalisation of victimhood.

After the Death of Don Juan ends with the certain defeat of the peasants' uprising and the death of Ramon Perez, the man who is characterised by 'the steadfastness by which he lived according to his creed.' He believes that 'being born into the world man could better it, and amend what he could not abolish', that 'There should be justice to the poor', and that 'Neighbour should stand by neighbour' (248–9). This seems to reiterate Warner's own beliefs but Ramon's actions have led in part to the disaster of the uprising. His wife's consolation that 'The loaf comes out as the oven wills' (249) recalls Marx's famous comment:

> Men make their own history, but they do not make it as they please; they do not make it under self-selected circumstances, but under circumstances existing already, given and transmitted from the past. The tradition of all dead generations weighs like an Alp on the brains of the living. (1979, 234–5)

It is this weight of history which Warner is anatomising in *After the Death of Don Juan*, and which makes it more than a mere parable of the present. Like so many of the novels of this decade, this novel is a history of the defeated. But by leaving the novel's ending open, Warner indicates, as in *Summer Will Show*, the ongoing nature of the struggle and the possibility that the 'spectre of Communism' can be resurrected.

4
Writing the War and After: Wicked Ladies and Wayward Women in the 1940s

During the war, reading was an important form of escape from tension, fear and boredom. In 1944, a Mass Observation survey of 10,000 readers found that their strongest desire was for 'relaxation' and that most readers described their tastes as 'escapist' (McAleer, 1992, 94, 95). Readers frequently turned to historical fiction because it offered escape to another time. A 24-year-old woman war worker described her tastes as follows:

> I like Daphne du Maurier's books, especially *Frenchman's Creek* and also Baroness Orczy's. Books dealing with some costume period when smugglers had the rule of the seas. I like books to take me into another world far from the realities of this. (McAleer, 1992, 96)

Despite paper rationing, reading increased during the war years (Hartley, 1997, 6; Plain, 1996, 14), although publishers tended to play safe with their offerings (Hennessy, 1993, 319). Heyer, herself by now a safe bet as a bestseller, recognised the function of her own novels fulfilled, writing in 1943:

> I think myself I should be shot for writing such nonsense, but [*Friday's Child*] is unquestionably good escapist literature, and I think I should like it if I were sitting in an air-raid shelter, or recovering from flu. (Hodge, 1985, 11)

The key concept used here is 'escapism', a term which, Alison Light reminds us, only came into common currency after 1933, and therefore 'like the cinema and the best-seller it belongs to modernity' (1991, 256). In offering escape, rather than political intervention, the woman's historical novel in the 1940s becomes a very different kind of genre from the 'histories of the defeated' which were characteristic of the 1930s.

Assessing the cultural history of the 1940s, Malcolm Bradbury sees it in terms of vacancy, noting the 'relative artistic silence of the period from 1939 towards the end of the 1940s' (1987, 69). This ignores a substantial body of writing, including historical novels, published by women in this period. The wider under-valuation of women's writing during these years can be traced, Jenny Hartley argues, to the fact that, 'War is seen as men's stuff, in the field and on the page. Women should keep out' (1997, 8). Hence women turned to the historical novel to express their own particular concerns about war. But this genre was, partly as a result of the influence of F.R. Leavis, excluded from the realm of canonical literature. Leavis' dismissal of Scott in *The Great Tradition* (1948) by extension condemned any other author writing in the 'bad tradition' (1962, 14) which came out of Scott's work. Heyer's extraordinarily harsh dismissal of her own work – 'I think myself I should be shot for writing such nonsense' – suggests her internalisation of this kind of denigration of the historical novel, especially in its popular form as written by women writers.

Yet it is often in the 'escapist' historical fiction of this period that we can see the strongest traces of female rebellion against the limitations of gender roles. The very excess and melodrama of these texts code resistance not merely against the frequent drabness of wartime life but also the repressive nature of the roles enforced on women who had to suppress their own desires to 'keep the home fires burning'.

Reading women's historical novels produced in conformity with the authorised war economy standards today, I am struck by the contrast between their physical appearance, with the now-yellowing coarse paper and mean bindings, and the highly-coloured imaginative worlds which are contained within these drab covers. Their evocation of glamorous clothes, rich food and exotic travel must have been a particular draw in a culture of rationing, clothing coupons and restricted movement. This is particularly obvious in two widely read American imports during this period, Margaret Mitchell's *Gone with the Wind* (1936), the hugely popular film of which opened in London in 1940 (Hartley, 1994, 227–8), and Kathleen Winsor's *Forever Amber* (1944). But it is equally true of British texts. Heyer's *Arabella* (1949), for instance, includes a lovely example of 'Make-do-and-Mend' skills transposed to a Regency setting when Arabella and her mother transform her mother's old clothes into a new wardrobe for her London debut, as well as a lingering description of Arabella's awed experience of her first fashionable meal, including champagne. This focus on clothes, of course, gave the 'costume novels' of this period their name.

The continuing interest in the historical novel during the 1940s can be situated within a wider popular appetite for history, especially social history. Peter Hennessy has suggested that, 'This was the golden age of history not just in the British Universities but among a wider reading public' (1993, 323), with the publication of the *Penguin History of England*, and the huge sales of G.M. Trevelyan's *English Social History* (1942).[1] A.L. Rowse, author of several influential history books during this period, attributed the increase in historical reading during the war to the difficulties in travelling and the blackout (1963, 164).

This interest in history clearly also reflected the need to sustain a sense of cultural continuity and national unity in the face of desperate uncertainty. Trevelyan, for instance, argued for a distinctive racial and cultural unity of the 'English people' dating from Chaucer's time. His final footnote rather touchingly brings together past victories with present uncertainty:

> The battle of Waterloo was won, not on the playing fields of Eton, but on the village greens of England. [...] *If we win this war*, it will have been won in the primary and secondary schools (1941). (1946, 587, emphasis added)

Christina Hole's *English Home-Life: 1500–1800* (1947) stressed the importance of home life and family as the place where 'the real continuity of living can be seen', though 'Bonaparte's armies are massing across the Channel, even, indeed, though house and family may be obliterated by a German bomb before another day has dawned' (1947, vi, vii). In the 1940s, the 'Home Front' and especially the figure of the housewife, holding things together, symbolised a similar continuity.

Hole's other books in the Batsford historical series – *English Custom and Usage, Haunted England, English Folklore, Witchcraft in England* – indicate some of the key preoccupations of the period, which reappear in the historical novels. Magdalen King-Hall records that, for instance, the inspiration for her *Life and Death of the Wicked Lady Skelton* (1942) (filmed in 1945 as *The Wicked Lady*) came from a brief anecdote in Hole's *Haunted England* (1940) about a seventeenth-century lady highwayman who subsequently haunted the family mansion (King-Hall, 1946, ix). King-Hall's book opens with the destruction of the house haunted by Lady Skelton in a Nazi bombing raid. Given the prevalence of such death and destruction, it is not surprising that ghosts are a recurring motif in wartime novels. The lady highwayman is a very appealing figure of female autonomy and transgression but, as Gillian Spraggs points out, she is a figure of folklore, not historical fact. She is therefore, Spraggs suggests, important for what she tells us about women, violence and cross-dressing in the *fantasies* of the twentieth century (Spraggs, 2001, 264). More specifically, I would argue that the lady highwayman is one of the most significant of the wicked ladies and wayward women who appear in the historical novels of the 1940s.

Three general trends are strikingly clear in the woman's historical novel during this period: a concern with earlier wars as a coded way of addressing the anxieties of the present; the rise of the 'costume novel' as a specifically female genre; and an almost obsessive concern with transgressive and subversive femininities in the form of wicked ladies and wilful or wayward women. These texts mark a further turning point in the development of the woman's historical novel, after which it becomes increasingly associated with the popular historical romance.

As Jenny Hartley observes in her discussion of women's fiction of the Second World War: 'Historical novels may head for the escape hatch, but what is striking about many of them is their fondness for other wars' (1997, 149). What is equally interesting, in contrast to the 1930s, is how often these novels turn to conflicts which had a successful outcome from Britain's point of view, especially the high points of British victory over Napoleon and, earlier, the defeat of the Spanish Armada. Given that the war was a fait accompli by 1940, the protest was '"de-prioritised", demoted and marginalised by the demands of wartime unity' (Plain, 1996, 14). There are novels, like Mitchison's sadly under-rated *The Bull Calves* (1947), which continue the tradition of using the historical setting as a cover for dissent. Set after the 1745 Jacobite rebellion, Mitchison's novel deploys extensive footnotes to connect Scotland's past and present as a conquered and occupied country. As Gill Plain's important reading shows, *The Bull Calves* is a complex exploration of the gendering of war and creativity, rationality and irrationality (1996, Chapter 8). The novel's concern with the difficulties of marriage and its use of the witch as a figure for transgressive femininity also link it closely to the themes of the popular novel I want to discuss here.

The wider trend was for writers and readers to focus their energy on 'pulling together', with texts which offered escape but, at least on the surface, stressed continuity and unity. These themes are frequently conveyed through evocations of the British rural and pre-industrial landscape as a pastoral Eden. Many of the books include lyrical descriptions of the English country-side, and the names of wild flowers are often used as a kind of shorthand to evoke the pastoral. Margaret Irwin's *Elizabeth, Captive Princess* (1948), for instance, reworks this convention when the Doctor uses the country names of the flowers – 'Here's a wanton, Love-in-Idleness, though some call it Johnny-Jump-Up' (1999a, 21) – to code a potentially treasonable conversation. Novels celebrate the peculiarities and understated heroism of the British national character in the face of war. They also evoke colourful but troublingly liminal figures of the past, especially gypsies, aristocrats, witches, highwaymen and pirates. Although some texts centralise the domestic as an integral part of that unity and continuity, far more problematise it in ways which suggest that, in the interests of unity, women were suppressing particular anxieties about marriage and the family.

A preoccupation with invasion is endemic. 'England won't be invaded. She never has been', asserts the 12-year-old Elizabeth Tudor in Margaret Irwin's *Young Bess* (1944). Reminded about the Normans, she responds 'Five hundred years ago! And they were us, or they couldn't have done it' (1998, 1). In Irwin's novel, Elizabeth's confidence is reassuringly validated by the repulsion of the French fleet, which foreshadows the later defeat of the Spanish Armada in her own reign. A far more ambivalent version of the Norman invasion is given in *The Golden Warrior* (1948) written by the Canadian-born Hope Muntz who had, as G.M. Trevelyan noted in his foreword, 'a deep knowledge and love of the island she has twice seen threatened with invasion' (1949, v). By presenting her protagonist, Harold, as himself a Saxon conqueror of the Celts and as a man who not only breaks his oath to William but also betrays his handfast wife, Edith Swan-Neck, in order to become King, Muntz suggests that his defeat at Hastings was a kind of moral retribution. It is the women, Muntz suggests, who are left behind to cope with loss and grief as men fight to fulfil their own overarching ambitions: 'So my man left me. So my father rode when Odin called him; so my sons rode out. There is no sorrow like a woman's' says Edith's nurse (1949, 327).

That men fight and women wait is also implicit in Clemence Dane's *He Brings Great News* (1944), a novel which recalls *Persuasion*. It opens with a panoramic vision of the south of England and the channel seen from a balloon. It then traces the record-breaking journey of Lieutenant Lapenotiere through that landscape as he brings the news of the victory at Trafalgar and the death of Nelson from Falmouth to the King in London. Through the reactions of the people he meets along the road, Dane weaves together a celebration of an England united in both their joy at victory and their grief at the loss of Nelson, and symbolised in the person of the King. The centrality of the family and the domestic to that unity is conveyed through Lapenotiere's reconciliation with the woman he loved but was earlier unable to marry for financial reasons. In ending with Lapenotiere hearing the ghostly voices of his descendants discussing the heroic repetition of history on D-day, Dane was creating a comforting sense of continuity.

The victories against Napoleon's forces at Trafalgar and Waterloo explain in part the popularity of the Regency period, an era more safely in the past than the Victorian years, as a setting for many novels during this period. In view of Lukács' argument that it was the resistance to Napoleon in the early nineteenth century which initially produced the historical novel as a genre, it is interesting that in the face of a new threat of invasion the novels of the 1940s return to those years 'when Napoleon menaced the English channel' (Smith, 1943, 42), but do so in order to rewrite it as a comforting myth of English supremacy.

It is at this point that Heyer, having tried out several other eras, turned to the Regency period with which she has now become so strongly associated. One contemporaneous reviewer of Heyer's *The Spanish Bride* (1940), set against the Peninsular War, suggested that: 'Perhaps the best way to forget about a real war is to read about a past one presented as a rough, good humoured lark' (Fahnestock-Thomas, 2001, 128). Given Heyer's opening description of the bloody and violent British sack of Badajos, I think this reviewer is over-sanguine about this particular novel. It is more concerned with the difficulties of wartime marriage and with establishing that women have the courage and ability to play their part in a war effort. Equally important is that Heyer's novels, like so many others, suggest the enduring nature of British military supremacy (as symbolised by Wellington, the 'Iron Duke') and thus the strong probability of a successful ending to the current conflict. The message conveyed in *He Brings Great News* that 'England had always been saved in the nick of time' (1944, 187) is the implicit, and more often explicit, text of many of these novels.

The popularity of Jane Austen, the second favourite author during the war (Hartley, 1997, 4), also explains the turn to the Regency years as a setting for Heyer's historical romance. Elizabeth Wilson attributes the post-war cult of Jane Austen to a general retreat into the past by a middle class who longed 'to return to a world as ordered, as polite and as carefully ranked as hers' (1980, 148). Heyer's novels of the 1940s become increasingly Austenesque love stories, with the wartime background just hinted at through the appearance of glamorous scarlet-coated officers. Military service, Kathleen Bell (1995) has shown, is depicted as redemptive for several of her minor, young, male characters.

Rather different from the historical romance of Heyer is the new and exotic form of 'costume fiction' which, as Sue Harper (1983) has shown, arose during the war years as a genre specifically associated with women readers. Closely associated with melodrama, this differs from the historical romance in that it presents conventional marriage as something which confines and constricts women, and thus it eschews the marriage ending. Examples include King-Hall's *Wicked Lady Skelton*, Eleanor Smith's *The Man in Grey: A Regency Romance* (1941) and *Caravan* (1943), and Norah Lofts' *Jassy* (1944). The visual appeal of 'costume fiction' is suggested by the fact that several of these were also made into films by Gainsborough Studios in the 1940s, although the film versions often differed radically from the novels (see Harper, 1987). Other films based on popular historical novels at this time include *Frenchman's Creek*, *Forever Amber* and, of course, *Gone with the Wind*.[2]

The typical reader of costume fiction was a middle-class working woman (Harper, 1983, 21), but she was embarrassed by her taste in escapist literature: 'I am sometimes rather snobbishly ashamed of being seen with my current bromide', said one reader (20). These texts, Harper argues, use history to allow the expression of anxieties about groups on the boundary of permissiveness: gypsies, the aristocracy and the sexually aggressive female. Although these figures allow initial pleasure in the excesses described, she suggests, they are ultimately judged and excised: 'History becomes a country where refugees from common sense may temporarily reside, but it is a place of banishment none the less; and there, gypsy, gentry and female excess is safely placed' (Harper, 1983, 21).

The third striking trend in women's historical novels of this period is the depiction of transgressive and subversive femininities in the form of wicked ladies and wayward women. As Harper's analysis indicates, this is very clear in the costume novels. My own reading of these texts in relation to the wider trends in other historical novels of the period, however, is rather more positive than Harper's.

As I argued in Chapter 1, the term 'costume fiction' itself implies the pleasures of 'acting' a part, of 'performing' a gender role. Novels in the 1940s frequently depict women cross-dressing in men's, or more usually, boy's clothing: King-Hall's Lady Skelton, Pen in Heyer's *The Corinthian* (1940), George Sand in Doris Leslie's *Polonaise* (1944) and Christina in Leslie's *The Peverills* (1946). This undoubtedly reflected the increasing tendency for women to wear trousers, not only for factory or outdoor work but, as Daphne du Maurier did, for casual wear. In *The Corinthian*, Kathleen Bell argues (1995), this is a conservative move, suggesting that women can play the part of men as they are required to during the war effort, but that they will willingly return to their traditional roles once the war is over. *The Corinthian* may play down the erotic frisson of cross-dressing, but in texts such as *The Wicked Lady Skelton* it is connected to a far more radical escape from the restrictions of femininity and traditional female roles.

The fascination with excess and with transgressive and subversive femininities is partly a counter-reaction, a release of the suppression which, Jenny Hartley argues, 'becomes a characteristic mode for women in wartime' (1994, 7). This suppression is well illustrated by the film *Brief Encounter* (1945), where Laura with quiet heroism suppresses her own desires and the possibility of an adulterous affair in order to continue her duties as wife and mother. In vivid contrast, in the historical novels women indulge their desires, both sexual and adventurous. They dress as highwaymen (*The Wicked Lady Skelton*) or pirates (*Frenchman's Creek*), they fight duels (Kate O'Brien's *That Lady* [1946]) and commit murder (*The Wicked Lady Skelton, The Man in Grey*). Even less overtly transgressive heroines are shown resisting restrictive conventions. Rebellion is often coded through the heroine's love of riding or driving spirited horses: Lady Skelton's night-riding as a highwayman, Christina's wild rides in *The Peverills*, or the reckless phaeton-driving that kills Oriana in *Caravan*.

Above all, the historical novel, far more than the woman's domestic novel of this period,[3] is able to show a post-Freudian understanding that women too can be driven by sexual desire, and act on it outside wedlock. Araminta in Norah Lofts' *To See a Fine Lady* (1946), for instance, is betrayed by the strength of physical desire into sex with Jan, even though she knows that to marry him will mean 'life in a clod cottage with a tired, worn-out man, and a swarm of hungry little children to feed on nine shillings a week' (1968, 24). What is striking is that sexual desires are most often fulfilled through adulterous relationships. Indeed, the novels of this period seem obsessed with the adulterous woman. The protagonists of *The Wicked Lady, Frenchman's Creek, Caravan,* and *The Man in Grey* are all adulterous. Ana in *That Lady* is treated as adulterous by the King of Spain when she has an affair he regards as a betrayal of their friendship. In Jean Plaidy's *Murder Most Royal* (1949), Anne Boleyn and Catherine Howard are executed for adultery. Leslie's George Sand is 'a female Don Juan' in *Polonaise* (1944, 88), although she is divorced. Even Sylvia Townsend Warner's *The Corner That Held Them* (1948), perhaps the least 'popular' of these texts, opens with a married woman surprised in bed with her lover by her husband.

This obsession with the figure of the adulterous women relates to a tension between two anxieties about marriage which haunt men and women during 1940s. The first is the male anxiety about female betrayal. The second is the female anxiety about marriage as a place of stifling entrapment. Susan Gubar has shown how representations of women were polarised in propaganda into good or evil – either wives and mothers keeping the home fires burning, or potential spies, loose talkers or betrayers of both husband/lover and country. 'Allied propaganda', Gubar says, 'spoke directly about and to service-men's fear of their women's betrayal' (1987, 240). Moreover, the absence of men created female-only communities at home, with women taking over the role of head of the household. Warner's *The Corner That Held Them* explores, through its depiction of a twelfth-century convent terrorised by the outbreak of the Black Death, the wielding of power by women in an all-female and beleaguered community. One effect of this preponderance of women was that even 'good' women, Gill Plain argues, as their guardianship of the pre-war values moved them closer to being a source of law, were seen as dangerously other/alien (1996, 24).

Some of the depictions of powerful women in the historical novels of this period suggest that women internalised this ideology, even depicting other women (rather than, for instance, foreign men) as the enemy. This is particularly overt in Elizabeth Myers' *The Basilisk of St James's* (1945), set against the ending of the 10-years war against France, which appears to replicate and excuse the misogyny of its protagonist, Jonathan Swift. Much of this is directed at the women who are perceived to be inappropriately in power: 'I hate the intrusion of women into public life', moans Swift, 'When a woman is on the throne the high wind of it lifts every petticoat in the kingdom' (1945, 92). The bodies of women in power are presented here as gross and monstrous: Queen Anne, 'dressed in an Indian stuff gown all disorderly, dirty, oozy, malodorous bandages ignominiously tumbling off her gouty foot' (1945, 18); that 'Whig bitch, the Duchess of Somerset' (22); and the Queen's favourite, Mrs Masham, 'a quiet woman with a red nose' (12). Even Vanessa, one of the child-women Swift loves, is blamed for the way in which the seductiveness of her body entices him, unwillingly, into desire for her. Similarly, Leslie appears at best ambivalent about the 'masculine' nature of George Sand who mothers and dominates Chopin in *Polonaise*.

The villain in Norah Lofts' *To See a Fine Lady*, set in the economic decline which followed the ending of the Napoleonic wars, is Mrs Stancy, the working-class heroine's employer. A Fascist tyrant writ small, Mrs Stancy runs her dairy farm along totalitarian lines, and indulges a power complex through her physical mistreatment of her workers, culminating with the murder of one of them. Again, in Eleanor Smith's *The Man in Grey*, the husband of the protagonist Clarissa Rohan, despite being nicknamed 'the Ghost', is a benign figure. It is Clarissa's close friend, Hesther, who is the villain. Hesther becomes Rohan's mistress and then murders Clarissa in order to take her place as his wife. Hesther's ghost, the 'very essence of evil' (1941, 253), causes the death of the current Lady Rohan in the 1940s, a woman who has become obsessed with the past as an 'opiate' (252) to dull the pain of the present wartime and the death of her husband in France.

While Harper sees these novels as punishing the sexually aggressive woman and excising her by banishing her to the past, I read them as being far more sympathetic to her. These texts engage with the ideology which condemns female adultery, but they also express the understanding that marriage and traditional gender roles may entrap and stifle women's sense of their own identity. The distance provided by the historical setting allows the tension between conventional mores and women's desires to be played out through excess and melodrama, which themselves offer the reader the catharsis of escapism. The transgressive women are not, on the whole, condemned for their desires.

In *Caravan*, for instance, James, the male narrator, makes love to Oriana, the woman he has loved since boyhood but who for financial security has married another man:

> Then they made love with a fury, a violence, that left him exhausted. [...] He knew her then, at last, for what she was – a sensual woman, who had always wanted him. And as he embraced her, he remembered the sailor's talk of witch-women, of *sorcières* from whom no man could escape. (1943, 97)

This seems to replicate a condemnation of the sexual woman in line with the ideology promulgated by wartime propaganda. But this is James' view of Oriana *at this point* and Smith undermines it later in the novel when he finds it 'grotesque [...] that he had ever thought of her as a *sorcière*, a Voodoo woman' (203). Both Oriana and Clarissa in Smith's *The Man in Grey* die, but they are not condemned for the adultery which expresses their most 'natural' desires. It is not Clarissa but Hesther, her murderer, who walks as a ghost because she cannot rest in peace.

Similarly, the name of the house in which King-Hall's Barbara Skelton lives is 'Maryiot Cells', metaphorically connecting marrying and prison. Barbara's highwayman escapades are a kind of drug with which she tries to deaden her sexual disappointment in her marriage to a much older husband, and her boredom at finding herself in a household of women with whom she has nothing in common. It is also connected to the failure of her husband to provide the love she loses when her mother dies (she first turns highway-man to retrieve her dead mother's ruby pendent, lost at cards). The series of framing narratives all feature women who in some way transgress feminine norms (the Lady Skelton of 1911 is nicknamed 'Boadicea' [1946, 3]), suggesting that Barbara is not that unusual.

Many of these novels express an intense nostalgia, frequently for the England of the Regency period. While the seventeenth century is associated with bawdy excess (as in *Forever Amber*), the Regency period connotes a vanished elegance and graciousness in contrast to the privations of 1940s Britain. In *Caravan* and *The Man in Grey*, Smith constructs it as an era when people (by which she really means the privileged Whig aristocracy) 'did nothing by half-measures' (Smith, 1941, 26). Gentlemen were 'orators and pugilists and whips. Born politicians, they too turned to poetry and philoso-phy' (Smith, 1941, 26). In both texts it is the women who explicitly symbolise this lost era. In *Caravan*, which is set later in the nineteenth century, Oriana wears a Regency dress during the most idyllic moments of her relationship with James, making her 'a figure from the past' who has to reassure him 'I'm not a ghost' (Smith, 1943, 201). In *The Man in Grey*, Clarissa represents for her lover Rokeby (a privateer) 'all the charm of a gracious epoch' (Smith, 1941, 231). This point is reiterated by the contemporary Lady Rohan, who spells out its significance in the context of the war: '[Clarissa] has come to represent to me in this dark and dreadful world the symbol of a graciousness which is no longer anywhere to be found' (244).

Similarly, King-Hall makes the point that the evils of the earlier era pale beside those of the 1940s: 'The crimes that earned her the title of "The Wicked Lady Skelton" seem those of a dilettante beside the vast organised evil of the Nazis, the impersonal but deadly malevolence of a German bomber' (1946, xiii). The sightings of the ghost of Lady Skelton suggest the inevitable return of the repressed, here female sexual desire which has been unsuccessfully suppressed within marriage. It is, however, neither female sexuality nor agency which are evil in themselves. Rather, King-Hall suggests that if a woman is denied a legitimate outlet for her energies she may become dangerous.

For some women the war actually brought not a sense of suppression but a *release* from suppression within marriage. Freed by the war, Nella Last wrote of her husband, 'He never realises – and never could – that the years when I had to sit quiet and always do everything he liked, and never the things he did not, were slavery years of mind and body [. . .]' (Hartley, 1994, 143). The depictions of marriage within many of these novels (with the exception of the romances of Heyer which offer marriage as a solution to women's problems) suggest exactly that sense of repression and lack of fulfilment. Moreover, they also hint at fears of male violence. Hilda Vaughan's *Iron and Gold* (1948) retells an old Welsh folk tale of a fairy wife married to a farmer. She transforms the story into a kind of historical novel by placing it in what appears to be a realistically rendered nineteenth-century setting. The couple fail to combine their different natures ('iron' and 'gold'), despite the fairy-wife's efforts to conform to 'human' conventions. When he strikes her for the third time with iron (a symbolic rendering of domestic violence) she returns to her lake.

In the 1940s, then, women's historical novels suggest a subterranean current of resistance to the suppression which was entailed in women's wartime and post-war lives. While this is not precisely 'feminist', it certainly suggests coded protest.

'Trespasser in time': Daphne du Maurier's historical sense

'Miss du Maurier's historical sense is execrable', wrote a *TLS* reviewer in 1963, 'she has as little sense of the language of her chosen periods as of the probable behaviour, attitudes and outlooks of the people who lived in them' (Forster, 1994, 327).[4] This comment is interesting because of its assumption that a 'historical sense' is based on certain kinds of knowledge. Historical novels are frequently judged by the accuracy of their historical detail, with anachronisms of language or object pilloried mercilessly. Conversely, Heyer's novels, despite being 'romances', are redeemed in the eyes of many people by the accurate detail of their language, clothing and setting. Without the validation of that detail, a woman's historical romance is perceived as mere wish-fulfilment, projecting a desire for heterosexual love back into the past where it seems more 'natural'.

Although she shares with Heyer the distinction of having inspired a specific genre of romance (in du Maurier's case, both the modern 'gothic romance' and the 'Cornish historical romance'), du Maurier's books have none of the thick accretion of detail – the 'period' language, the descriptions of clothes and interiors – which Heyer uses to give a sense of historical 'realism' to her romances. Like Heyer, du Maurier was anti-romantic – 'There is no such thing as romantic love' she wrote (du Maurier, 1981, 99) – but while Heyer used humour to undercut her romance, du Maurier used the Gothic and disrupted the conventions of plot structure, denying her readers the happy ending. While du Maurier's 'historical sense' in the way meant by the TLS reviewer may be 'execrable', I would argue that her sense of the *gendered* social and cultural meanings of 'history' or, perhaps more accurately, 'the past', and her understanding of the ways in which the past is constructed as a space to which the reader can escape are extremely acute.

What du Maurier expresses extraordinarily well is precisely the sense in which 'the past' is seen as being *outside history*. She does this by locating the past in a geographically specific place, usually Cornwall, which is constructed as special precisely because it is a place where traces of the past are clearly visible in the landscape. The past can thus be 'visited' as a means of escaping the modern world.

Du Maurier's novels of the 1940s, especially *Frenchman's Creek* (1941) and *The King's General* (1946), explore the particular meanings of 'the past' for women during wartime, as both escape and confinement. Escape into the past is powerfully imaged through natural landscape and the sea or water, while confinement is expressed through gothic images of houses and rooms. The past, for du Maurier, is spatialised as a place which can be visited, but only in glimpses, intermittently, and even illegally. On her first visit to the woods around Menabilly, the house which was to become so central to her imaginative life, du Maurier pictured herself as a 'trespasser in time' (1981, 131), and imagined the people who had been there before her: 'what hoofbeats have sounded and then died away? What carriage wheels had rolled and vanished?' (132).

Du Maurier's books on Cornwall, *Vanishing Cornwall* (1967) and *Enchanted Cornwall* (1989), treat the landscape as a historical palimpsest – she quotes Sir Arthur Quiller-Couch's comment, 'All England is a palimpsest' (1989, 7) – on which can be read the traces of former times, partially erased by a less romantic present. Personal past and palimpsestic landscape merge in the opening of *The King's General* where Honor Harris reads the 'old hidden dreams' she thinks have been 'buried for all time' (1974, 9) in the sand and shells, momentarily revealed by the retreating tide.

The image of the (English) past as a landscape to be visited is not, of course, unique to du Maurier but what is interesting about her work is her gendering of the image. H.V. Morton's popular *In Search of England* (first published in 1927, and reaching its 31st edition in 1944), uses precisely this motif and attributes the 'long over-due interest in English history, antiquities, and topography' to 'the cheap motor-car' which has opened up the countryside to more people than in any previous generation (1944, vii). This history is perceived as being most visible in the rural (un-industrialised) 'peripheral' areas of Britain – the Border country (as Mary Webb suggested), the Lake District and, pre-eminently, Cornwall. A.L. Rowse's *Tudor Cornwall* (1941) also used this image of layers of time still visible in the landscape. Both Alison Light, and Horner and Zlosnik have shown how du Maurier draws on 'a cultural construct of Cornwall as historically unruly and ungovernable [...] a transgressive space' (Horner and Zlosnik, 1998, 68). As Ella Westland (1995) has shown, the 'Romantic' landscape of Cornwall, the 'passionate periphery', has lent itself to the depiction of 'romance' in more recent novels clearly influenced by du Maurier's work .

Du Maurier's most explicit gendering of this landscape of the past is in *Frenchman's Creek*. The novel opens with a male yachtsman, again in that evocative expression, a 'trespasser in time' (1945, 9) exploring the creek and catching 'echoes from a past that is gone' (11). There is a hierarchy of access to the past here. Like Morton, du Maurier associates the day tripper in his 'little puffing car' with vulgarity and he is 'deaf' (8) to these echoes, while the yachtsman himself is made uneasy by them, 'baffled and a little scared'

(10) by the creek. Although it is unspoken, the implication here is that it is the woman (more specifically, the woman writer/reader) who has the freedom to trespass in this hidden, vanishing past.

The creek itself, du Maurier's most potent and explicit 'symbol of escape' and 'refuge' (1945, 11), is also a blatant female landscape, a symbol of the 'spring' of female sexual pleasure:

> There, suddenly, before her for the first time, was the creek, still and soundless, shrouded by the trees, hidden from the eyes of men. [. . .] The tide was ebbing, the water oozing away from the mud flats, and here, where she stood, was the head of the creek itself for the stream ended in a trickle and the trickle in a spring. [. . .] this creek was a source of enchantment, a new escape, better than Navron itself, a place to drowse and sleep, a lotus-land. (38)

Even a 'reluctant Freudian critic', Alison Light acknowledges, cannot help reading this as 'an image of the female body' (1991, 179). The past here, then, is a female landscape where the male yachstman is an 'interloper' (9). To a less reluctant Freudian, this is a return through time to the mother's body, the first source of pleasure, forbidden to the adult woman. The discovery of the woman's pre-Oedipal desire for her mother, Freud argued in an appropriately palimpsestic metaphor in 1931, was 'like the discovery in another field of the Minoan-Mycenaean civilisation behind the civilisation of Greece' (Freud, 1977, 372). For women, du Maurier's image subliminally suggests, the desire to escape into the past is connected to the desire for a *female* body, more specifically perhaps it is a return to the lost mother's body.

In this past, du Maurier's heroine, Dona St Columb, finds the freedom both to *have* a man, to experience adult sexual pleasure as she falls in love with the French pirate, and to *be* a man, or rather a boy, as she masquerades as the pirate's cabin boy. So much the ideal of everywoman's lover that he is rarely referred to by name, the Frenchman's nationality makes him exotic ('other'), and associates him with the supposedly superior cultural and sexual qualities of his countrymen. It also feminises him. His cabin is surprisingly domestic – 'like a room in a house' (41), he cooks (admittedly the equivalent of barbequeing), and he is both maternal and erotic, undressing Dona to put her to bed. A 'fugitive' whose life is 'one continual escape' (32), he is a liminal figure who haunts the edges of the coastline, penetrating fleetingly into the creek in order to empower and enable Dona's adventures. During wartime, the coastline was ambiguous territory – both what would protect Britain from the enemy and what, if it were not rigorously policed, could allow the enemy in. Littered with landmines and barbed wire, large sections of the coastline were off-limits until after the war. Moreover, du Maurier disrupts the wartime propaganda, discussed by Susan Gubar

(1987), which played on allied fears that the enemy would seduce or rape their women. Dona suggests to the shocked Lord Godolphin that the country-women have not 'suffered' at the hands of these invading pirates but 'on the contrary, enjoyed themselves immensely' (67).

As important as the sexual fulfilment the Frenchman brings is the chance he offers Dona to 'play the part of a boy, which as a child she had always longed to be' (100). As Margaret Forster has shown, the sense that she should have been a boy was an important part of du Maurier's own persona, poignantly imaged as 'the-boy-in-the-box' (1994, 419) and linked to possibly lesbian (and therefore forbidden and repressed) desires. Dona is a few weeks short of her thirtieth birthday, a point important enough to be noted twice (1945, 85, 178). This is a key moment for female protagonists, usually marking a woman's 'sell-by-date' on the marriage market. Already married with two children, Dona experiences this state as a confinement like a linnet in a cage (18). Like King-Hall's wicked lady, she attempts to find freedom through masquerading as a highwayman in London but finds this tawdry and unheroic. Her escape from that cage to the Frenchman's ship, *La Mouette* (the seagull), is transitory, its limits marked by the age when she must relinquish adventure and accept that 'there is no escape for a woman, only for a night and for a day' (123).

The female pirate in F. Tennyson Jesse's *Moonraker* (1927), a fantasy historical novel of the 1920s, offers an interesting contrast to du Maurier's book. Disguised as the swashbuckling 'Captain Lovel', Sophie Lovel is a handsome and successful pirate who commands the respect of her men, including the cabin-boy protagonist who (knowing the stories of Anne Bonney and Mary Read) is one of the first to understand that she is female. But when Sophie falls in love and reveals herself dressed as a woman she is merely 'an unattractive spinster of thirty – that vast age' (1981, 134). Ironically, the company does not immediately recognise her as a woman and think that the Captain is merely 'masquerading' (131) as a woman. Sophie's question to the man who rejects her, 'What do I lack?' (132), implicitly draws attention to what she lacked as a 'man' (the phallus). This 'lack' now revealed, her men mutiny and she blows up herself and her ship. More radical than du Maurier, Jesse questions the cultural constructions of gender which ban women from adventure and force them to choose between 'career' and 'love'.

For du Maurier, the return to the past allows the release of a younger (pre-adolescent) self who is not ungendered but potentially male. One thinks here of Mitchison, treated as a boy until she menstruated, and Heyer's Leonie learning to be a girl. The paradox du Maurier is exploring here is that to be free to have adventures the girl must be a pre-adolescent 'boy', but to experience sexual fulfilment she must be an adult woman and that brings confinement. In terms of form, du Maurier solves this problem by merging a woman's romance plot with a boy's adventure story and allowing the reader the pleasure of both. It is only in the fantasy space of 'the past' provided by the historical novel that she can do this.

Horner and Zlosnik suggest that the success of *Frenchman's Creek* damaged du Maurier's reputation, 'giving rise to the belief that she is no more than a writer of escapist fiction' (1998, 188). If *Frenchman's Creek* is read as a novel *about* escapism, and about the ways in which 'the past' offers a space of freedom for women, however, it looks far more sophisticated.

If the romance of *Frenchman's Creek* suggests that the 'past' is a space to which we can escape, however fleetingly, then the Gothic of *The King's General* suggests that we cannot escape the 'past' which haunts us. With its carefully researched Civil War background, *The King's General* is a novel about the way in which women have been confined by and excluded from history, a process starkly highlighted in wartime through their non-combatant status. As Woolf noted in 1940: 'The defenders are men, the attackers are men. Arms are not given to Englishwomen either to fight the enemy or defend herself' (Hartley, 1994, 81). As the ambiguity of that last phrase suggests (to defend herself from whom?), a woman could often feel herself, as Dona's attitude to her fellow Englishmen shows, 'at war' with the men of her own side.

Honor Harris is crippled not as a result of the war but by an accident beforehand, which prevents her marrying the man she loves, Richard Grenvile, the 'King's General'. Her shattered legs symbolise her non-combatant status as a woman (her 'lack'). Honor's wheelchair symbolises her confinement to the domestic as she, with the other women, waits at Menabilly, enduring starvation under occupation and then making-do-and-mending the sacked house, while the war is fought by men. Yet, ironically, Honor's status as a cripple also liberates her from the usual female roles, allowing her to develop her intellect and wield power in the household. It gives her the license to spend time with Richard when he is available, even to sleep with him (and to enjoy at least some sexual activity), and to retain his affection which, she believes, would have waned in a traditional marriage.

The other image of confinement in the novel, and the most hauntingly Gothic, is the secret room in the buttress (another liminal space) where, two centuries later in the incident which inspired the book, the skeleton of the young Cavalier is found. In du Maurier's novel this is Richard's young son, who chooses to die in the buttress room after he has betrayed the Royalist cause. Effeminate, possibly homosexual, horrified by blood and violence, and rejected by both his ruthlessly masculine father and the mother he resembles, young Dick is, like Honor, a figure of ambiguous gender. His treatment of his son is the major stain on Richard's character, and through it du Maurier condemns his aggressive, cruel masculinity (the Roundheads' nickname for him, 'Skellum Grenvile', labels him a 'vicious beast' [1974, 78]). Honor suggests that war has a retrogressive effect on human beings, sending them back in history to a more primitive stage, 'like those half savages of the fourteen hundreds who, during the Wars of the Roses, slit each other's throats without compunction' (185). But she also notes that men 'are really bred to war and thrive on it' (185). Tragically, du Maurier suggests, the rigid enforcement of polarised gender roles in wartime allows no alternative modes of being for either sex.

As Horner and Zlosnik note, the buttress room 'makes concrete du Maurier's metaphor of "the-boy-in-a-box"' as Dick and 'the sexual ambiguity he represents are punished by containment of the most horrific kind' (1998, 96). Even more horrifyingly, the crippled ('castrated' in Freudian terms) Honor, who stands in the place of the mother, can do nothing to prevent this, revealing the powerlessness of the maternal within wartime society. It is the 'ghost of Richard's son' (1974, 15) confined in the buttress room, the ultimate victim of the 'agony of war' (10), who haunts Honor's dreams, a powerful image of the return of the repressed and our inability to escape history.

What Alison Light has called du Maurier's 'romantic Toryism [...] which invokes the past as a nobler, loftier place where it was possible to live a more expansive and exciting life' (1991, 156) is undercut in *The King's General*, where Honor lives a constrained and often tedious wartime life which must have resonated with many of du Maurier's readers. 'Romantic Toryism', as Light acknowledges, is only one element of du Maurier's complex and often conflicted engagement with the past (she was, Horner and Zlosnik (1998, 23) note, a Labour supporter). It is, however, a strong factor in her seemingly unquestioning, but not unusual, assumption that her novel should take the side of the Royalists, representing the parliamentary 'rebels' (66) unequivocally as the enemy.

The fact that the majority of historical novels take the side of the Royalists says much about our attitudes to 'English' history: Margaret Irwin's *The Stranger Prince* (1937) and *The Proud Servant* (1934) may criticise Charles I, for instance, while Rose Macaulay's *They Were Defeated* (1932) offers an even more ambivalent picture, but all three ultimately support the Royalists' cause. Exceptions to this are Rosemary Sutcliff, whose *The Rider of the White Horse* (1959) takes the Parliamentarian general Thomas Fairfax as its hero and, much later, Maria McCann's *As Meat Loves Salt* (2001), whose protagonist becomes a mercenary in Cromwell's New Model Army. For many of the Royalist-sympathisers, including du Maurier, it is perhaps not so much a case of, as *1066 And All That* (1930) wittily puts it, 'The Cavaliers (Wrong but Wromantic) and the Roundheads (Right but Repulsive)' (Sellar and Yeatman, 1989, 63), but that the Cavaliers were Right *because* they were Romantic. They represent not only the glamour of aristocratic personalities with better costumes, hair and horses than the Roundheads, but also the values of continuity and evolution (as opposed to revolution) underpinning a view of English history as a history of progress. In this version of history the Interregnum becomes just that, an interval or pause, out of character with the rightful order of things resumed with the 'Restoration'.

Given the need for consensus in the 1940s, it is not surprising that du Maurier does not question her allegiances. The Royalist ideology is so taken for granted that the reasons for the war are glossed over in a comment about the men's debates about 'despotism' and taxes (1974, 61), although this is consistent with her depiction of women's exclusion from the political realm. The Roundheads are portrayed as Nazi-like figures wanting to establish a totalitarian and bureaucratic state, which is especially inimical to the independent Cornish. The troopers are threateningly Gothic figures with 'close-fitting skull helmets' (139), who confine the women to the house. To Honor, 'one and all they looked the same, with their cropped heads and their drab brown leather jerkins, and this ruthless similarity was both startling and grim' (139), suggesting the crushing of individualism in a totalitarian state. Like du Maurier herself, they are trespassers at Menabilly but whereas she lovingly repaired the house, valuing its history, they wantonly destroy it.

In *The House on the Strand* (1969), du Maurier returned to the notion of the 'trespasser in time' (1992b, 87), but with a male trespasser and tragic results. Unhappy with his own world, Dick Young becomes addicted to a hallucinogenic drug which allows him to visit the fourteenth century where the landscape itself has a clarity and brightness lacking in the present. A warning about the debilitating effects of remaining in the past, the novel ends with Dick literally paralysed. Du Maurier's work suggests that for the male characters to 'trespass in time' is dangerous. Women, in contrast, have a mysterious affinity with the past which enables them to slip into a land-scape where they can trespass safely.

The new Elizabethans: Margaret Irwin's family romances

As its recent reprinting suggests, Margaret Irwin's *Young Bess* trilogy (*Young Bess* [1944], *Elizabeth, Captive Princess* [1948], *Elizabeth and the Prince of Spain* [1953]) is in some way the quintessential popular woman's biographical historical novel. The trilogy fictionalises the life of Queen Elizabeth I from the age of 12 to her coronation and the beginning of a reign which has come to be seen as a golden age for Britain. As Edith Sitwell put it, Elizabeth was 'the being in whose reign the greatness of Britain began' (1962, 3). Closely based on the well-documented facts of Elizabeth's life, it is Irwin's imaginative and quasi-Freudian interpretation of the psychology of Elizabeth herself and the way in which she makes the drama of female psycho-sexual development central to history which makes this novel so typical of the twentieth-century woman's popular biographical historical novel. The trilogy demonstrates particularly well the tendency in women's historical fiction to write the stories of historical women as 'romance', that is, to fit the facts of their lives as far as possible into the romance plot with its happy marriage ending, and the tension between historical 'fact' and fictional plot which results.

Alison Light takes *Young Bess* as her exemplary text in her discussion of the importance of women's historical novels. Although she suggests that these novels offer fantasies of female power by giving 'femininity [...] the lead role in the national drama' (1989, 60), as well as 'keeping open the potential for wayward subjectivities outside the norms on offer' (63), she concludes that they ultimately validate a conservative vision of gender and nationality.

Given the centrality of Mary Stuart to the development of the historical novel from *The Recess* on, the decision to make Elizabeth the heroine of a historical novel is not as straight-forward as it may now appear. Margaret Irwin's own *The Gay Galliard: The Love Story of Mary Queen of Scots* (1941) follows the earlier pattern to take Mary as its heroine. Irwin constructs the novel (as the subtitle indicates) as a romance centred on Mary's marriage to the Earl of Bothwell, a figure more often regarded as morally ambiguous and at worst her evil genius. The eighteenth-century emphasis on female sensibility in *The Recess* is replaced with a twentieth-century foregrounding of sexual desire.

Mary is depicted as an attractively boyish, sensitive heroine who, like so many other 1940s heroines, finds freedom in boy's clothes. She has great charm but a fatally naive tendency to think the best of others. After being twice married to clumsy boys, she finds a brief sexual and emotional fulfilment with the experienced but arrogant Bothwell who is redeemed by his love for her, before they are tragically separated. Irwin ignores the later plan to marry the Duke of Norfolk which furnishes Lee's plot, and passes over Mary's 18-years imprisonment in a couple of pages. Instead she suggests that because in her sexually fulfilled love for Bothwell, Mary knew 'the height of life' (1941, 423), 'It did not matter that the end of life was wretched any more than its beginning' (424). Romance here is used to acknowledge female desire but at the expense of denying historical and lived experience.

Far from scheming to wrench Elizabeth's throne from her, Irwin's Mary is a figure striving for unity. Mary believes that eventual union between Scotland and England is the only way both countries can find strength to withstand outside pressures. Such a valorisation of unity would, of course, have had obvious appeal during the war. Elizabeth, on the other hand, is portrayed as Mary's nemesis, and blamed for having manipulated Mary into the disastrous marriage with Darnley.

In shifting her allegiance from Mary to Elizabeth, Irwin was closely reflecting the concerns of the 1940s. She anticipates a growing interest in, even obsession with, Elizabeth I over the next decade. This was closely connected to the way in which the future Elizabeth II came to be seen as a symbol of both a new Elizabethan age and modern womanhood. Anyone reading Irwin's novels in the 1940s (and, indeed, today) would be likely to compare Elizabeth I with her twentieth-century successor. Irwin's novels were among the first of what amounts to a flood of books on Elizabeth I in the late 1940s and early 1950s in which that potential association was at least implicit. What is also interesting is the way in which Freudian psycho-analytic theory was increasingly used in both fiction and biography to explain the alleged enigma of Elizabeth I's character – that is, her refusal to marry.

The Royal family were central to the maintenance of morale during the war. The public image was very much of the Royals as a *family* undergoing the same privations and dangers as the rest of the country. They were issued with ration books, and actively promoted the ideals of 'Make Do and Mend'. They made highly publicised visits to bombed areas in London, while bomb damage to Buckingham Palace was used to suggest their shared vulnerability as civilians in this 'People's War'. 'I'm glad we've been bombed. It made me feel I can look the East End in the face', the Queen famously remarked in 1940 (Hennessy, 1993, 52).

Princess Elizabeth did her National Service and was shown in uniform, learning to be a vehicle mechanic, an image which neatly encapsulated both modern femininity and a continuing tradition of Royal female duty to others. The media coverage of Elizabeth's marriage to Philip Mountbatten in 1947 highlighted both the momentous historic and the privately romantic nature of the event as the heiress presumptive to the British throne married the man of her choice in what was popularly perceived as a love match.[5] Much play was made of the fact that the Princess was issued with clothing coupons for her wedding dress, again foregrounding the private, domestic and patriotic side of this public event. The war, as Peter Hennessy notes, vindicated a monarchy which had been damaged by the Abdication Crisis in the 1930s (1993, 436). This in itself contributed to the construction of the consensus society which emerged in the 1950s.

After the coronation in 1953 the young Queen Elizabeth with her photogenic husband and children became 'a reassuring symbol of the family which had drawn the nation into consensus' (Wilson, 1980, 11). Exploring the 'meaning of the coronation', Shils and Young (1953) empha-sise its function as society's affirmation of a shared moral consensus. They stress the way in which this was embedded in the notion of the family, with the nation itself represented as a family and symbolised by the Royal Family: 'Devotion to the Royal Family thus does mean in a very direct way devotion to one's own family because the values embodied in each are the same' (Shils and Young, 1953, 78). They use the Freudian theory of 'displacement' to argue that a particularly strong emotional charge is generated by this:

> [When] a person venerates the Sovereign partly because he [*sic*] is associated, in the seat of the emotions, with the wondrous parents of phantasy [then] there is also a sort of re-displacement at work, whereby the real parents and wives and children are thought of more highly because they

receive some of the backwash of emotion from their Royal counterparts. (1953, 78)

At the centre of the Royal Family, Elizabeth thus symbolised the stability of the nuclear family as a power for national consensus. Within this context, Irwin's trilogy looks especially interesting. Through its depiction of the early life of the young Elizabeth, not only bastardised but facing threats to her very life, it offers an account of the anxieties of instability at the level of both country and family. But, given our knowledge that this wayward young girl will become Queen, it further suggests a reaffirmation of (inevitable) national continuity, stability and greatness. However, by centralising the adolescent girl it offers an account of the Freudian family romance which suggests that the nuclear family might in fact be threatening and even deadly to women. The texts themselves are caught between the manoeuvre of transforming history into romance in order to encompass women's desire (as Irwin did in *The Gay Galliard*), and the fact that Elizabeth I was herself a serial marriage-resister.

In Freud's essay 'Family Romances' (1959 [1909]), one of the texts on which Shils and Young were drawing, he explores the way in which children use imaginative stories and daydreams to negotiate separation from their parents. These often take the form of a fantasy of being an adopted child whose 'real' parents are much grander, either aristocratic or Royal. This offers a suggestive way of reading not only, as Shils and Young suggest, our fascination with the Royal Family, but also some of the ways in which historical fiction functions for women readers.

Drawing on this essay, Carolyn Steedman has suggested that the attraction of essentially conservative historical romance (illustrated for Steedman by the child's interest in Mary Queen of Scots rather than a poor handloom weaver) is that it allows the child to 'manipulate her own family drama, and make it work to her greater satisfaction' (1989, 31). In contrast to fairy tale and myth, she points out, the events of history really did happen. Thus, while the universal drama of family relations is worked out at the exalted level of Royalty, the final message for the child is of the real difficulty of living, the fact that neither they nor their parents are kings or queens.

Irwin's novels exemplify this process, allowing the female reader to engage in precisely the kind of fantasy of being 'Royal' that Freud suggested, and thus to work through the drama of female psycho-sexual development (including the legitimacy and bastardisation which were literal in Elizabeth's case) by proxy. Light's account of the attractions of *Young Bess* – 'These opening lines can still thrill me' (1989, 57) – suggests the pleasures of identification, despite the differences of time, place and class, with this process when it is cast, as here, as a fantasy of female power.

Young Bess opens with the threat of invasion which haunted the 1940s and which underpins the entire trilogy. But a far greater threat for Bess in this opening scene is the fear that her father, King Henry, will order the death of her most recent and much-loved stepmother, Catherine Parr. As Irwin somewhat bluntly puts it, 'Family life was a difficult affair with a father who had repudiated two of his six wives, beheaded two others, and bastardised both his daughters' (1998, 8). This opening scene explores the fraught issues of female identity within this context, and suggests that for women the dangers *within* the family are greater than the threat of the enemy without.

Irigaray argues that it is the 'murder' of the mother, silenced and erased, which underpins the patriarchal structures of Western culture (1991, 34–46). In Bess' family, the all-powerful father who represents the 'Law of the Father' is literally a King, who wields the power of life and death over his family. The exaltation of the father which Freud noted as being so common in the family romance, and which signifies the child's longing to return to the days when the father seemed the noblest and strongest of men, is both conveyed and undercut through Bess' recitation of the nursery rhyme about a fisherman. Encouraged by his wife (indicating women's complicity in male power), the fisherman asked 'first to be King, and then Pope, and then God' (1998, 7), suggesting Henry VIII's over-reaching ambition.

In contrast to the figure of the all-powerful father, the powerlessness of the 'murdered' mother, silenced within the patriarchal power structure, is literally enacted in Elizabeth's life through the beheading of her mother, Anne Boleyn. It is then repeated through the death of her stepmother, Jane Seymour, in childbirth, and even more hauntingly through the beheading of her third stepmother, Catherine Howard, again on her father's orders. Elizabeth is made motherless several times over. To save her stepmother when she unintentionally angers the King, Elizabeth pretends to see the French fleet approaching and draws her father's wrath onto herself. With the exception of this incident, the murder of the mother and destruction of the maternal genealogy makes bonding between women impossible as Elizabeth and her sister Mary Tudor are consistently positioned as rivals for the approval of their father.

The question of female identity – 'What would she be? At 12 years old anything was possible' (2) – is foregrounded in the opening of *Young Bess*. This is intensified by Elizabeth's uncertainty over her own origins because of the erasure of her matrilineage, and the imputation that she is not even Henry's daughter. 'Can you tell me who I am?' (5), she asks Tom Seymour, who reassures her that she looks exactly like Henry. This affirmation of her identity with the father (and therefore her fitness to be queen) is complicated by the fact that Irwin structures the novel as a romance based around Bess' love for Tom Seymour. Seymour, the Lord High Admiral and the man who became her stepfather when he married Catherine Parr after Henry's death, is a second father figure, but one who is available as an erotic figure for female oedipal desire.

For Irwin, Elizabeth's love for Seymour, and the psychological trauma over his beheading for the treason of attempting to marry her (Irwin omits Seymour's attempt to abduct the young King Edward), is the key to Elizabeth's psychology and her later refusal to marry. 'She'll only love men who remind her of the Admiral [Seymour]' says her governess Kat Ashley after Seymour's death (1998, 246). Bess' attraction to Dudley in *Elizabeth, Captive Princess* is explained by the fact that Dudley is like Seymour (1999a, 263) that is, also like her 'father'. Her refusal to give herself to Dudley is attributed to her understanding after Seymour's death that 'Love brings terror, agony, endless suspicion' (1999a, 274).

The distorting pull of the romance plot in Irwin's shaping of her material is even clearer in *Elizabeth and the Prince of Spain* which is structured around the relationship between Elizabeth and her brother-in-law, Philip of Spain. After Mary Tudor's death, Philip did court Elizabeth, and Irwin uses as epigraphs Philip's admission that he was 'enamoured' of Elizabeth, her statement that their mutual enmity 'commenced in love', and Mary Tudor's confession of jealousy over Philip's plans to take Elizabeth to Spain with him. But while Irwin presents the relationship as a 'duel' in the earlier book (1999a, 320), the linking of the two names in the final title suggests a romance based on this rather tenuous evidence which is unrealised. It is as if without a romance plot Irwin is at a loss as to how to structure the novel. It is tempting to speculate that the name of Elizabeth II's husband, Philip Mountbatten, prompted interest in a character who remains far more peripheral, except as the enemy responsible for the Spanish Armada, in most other accounts of Elizabeth I's life. The climax of the final novel, not surprisingly given its publication in the year of the coronation of Elizabeth II, is a set-piece description of Elizabeth I's coronation. This constructs an image of the mature Elizabeth as the unifier and representative of a stable, coherent England about to embark on its most glorious years.

While Irwin emphasises the trauma of Seymour's death, other books on Elizabeth I in this period give more weight to the loss of her mother and the deaths of her stepmothers. Edith Sitwell's *Fanfare for Elizabeth*, for instance, suggests that the fates of these three women, coming as they did at impressionable ages in Elizabeth's childhood, 'were to affect her sexually, laying the chill of death on her hot blood, in the midst of passion' (1946, 29). The most detailed and Freudian analysis of this trauma as the reason for Elizabeth's assertion from the age of eight that she would never marry is in Elizabeth Jenkins' *Elizabeth the Great* (1958):

In the fatally vulnerable years [Elizabeth] had learned to connect the idea of sexual intercourse with terror and death; in the dark and low-lying region of the mind where reason cannot penetrate, she knew that if you give yourself to men, they cut off your head with a sword, an axe. The blood-stained key that frightens the girl in 'Blue-Beard' is a symbol merely of the sexual act; in Elizabeth's case the symbol had a frightening actuality of its own. It was the executioner's steel blade, running with blood. (1958, 96)

Jenkins's unequivocally 'Great' Elizabeth is very different from Irwin's, not least because Jenkins stresses her political and economic acuity. Thomas Seymour is presented here not as Elizabeth's first and lasting love, but as a criminally selfish and irresponsible man who indulges in what we would now see as sexual abuse of a child for political ends. For Jenkins, as for other historians, it is Robert Dudley, the Earl of Leicester, who is the nearest thing Elizabeth ever had to a husband. However, in invoking the story of Blue-Beard, Jenkins is still clearly using both Freudian theory and a fictional plot structure to 'explain' Elizabeth's psychology.

That both Jenkins and Sitwell returned to Elizabeth I in later books – Jenkins' *Elizabeth and Leicester* (1961), and Sitwell's *The Queens and the Hive* (1962) – demonstrates the hold Elizabeth exercised over the imaginations of women writers during the mid-century. Male historians and writers, from Lytton Strachey's influential Freudian *Elizabeth and Essex* (1928) to A.L. Rowse, were, of course, also attracted by the Elizabethan period. The story of Elizabeth, however, has a particular draw for women writers, not only because it offers, as Alison Light argues, a fantasy of female power, but because it explores the dangers of the family romance for women through a historically 'real' figure. Jenkins points to the centrality of the figure of the Blue-Beard wife-murderer in the family romance as it has been symbolised in fairy tale. This story of wife-murder, which women writers find in Elizabeth's life, is repeated again and again in the historical novel and in the related form of the popular modern gothic (see Chapter 6) as a kind of cautionary tale. Ironically, at the very point at which the association of the two female monarchs was being used to enhance the construction of Elizabeth II and her family as an image of stabilising moral consensus for the 'new Elizabethan' nation, women writers were using Elizabeth I to draw attention to the dangers of the family as a structure for women. These texts then, less conservative than they at first appear, seem to hold the seeds of an analysis of women's predicament and a resistance to the prevailing ideology which would bear fruit in the women's movement several years later.

5
Hollow Men and Homosexual Heroes: Exploring Masculinity in the 1950s

In Sylvia Townsend Warner's *The Flint Anchor* (1954), the despotic patriarch John Barnard goes down into the wine cellar of the family home to check the port wine laid down by his father. He finds there the stacks of empty bottles which are the evidence of his wife's chronic drinking habit. Anchor House, with its forbiddingly stony flint anchor motif, is surrounded by a high spike-topped wall to keep the lower classes and potential Jacobins out and Barnard's children in. But, as the empty bottles metaphorically indicate, the foundations of that family home are undermined from within, and the legacy of the earlier generation spent. His wife's indolent alcoholism and the various unsatisfactory behaviours of his unhappy children, who run off, make unsuitable marriages or simply die to escape his control, expose Barnard's own moral rectitude as a hollow sham. The 'devoted husband and father', 'deeply conscientious in the performance of every Christian and social duty', as the inscription on Barnard's tombstone puts it, is in fact, a *'Tartuffe'* (1997, 214), a hypocrite and a domestic tyrant, but one who has became what he is because this is what the rigid ideologies of his society demand. Warner's novel is an examination of nineteenth-century family structures but, in common with many novels of the 1950s, it looks back at the past not out of nostalgia, but to understand the present.

In this chapter I want to examine the ways in which the historical novel is used by Warner and several other women writers in the 1950s in order to explore the inadequacies and dangers of traditional constructions of masculinity, put into question by two world wars.[1] As Elizabeth Maslen has commented:

> The old idea of man as warrior had proved hollow, just as the links between violence in the world outside and its relation to domestic life within the family could no longer be ignored. Men began to be seen as victims of social expectations which can be quite as damaging as those which women have experienced. (2001, 18)

The image of the ostensibly solid, conventional family home in Warner's novel, the bankruptcy of its patriarchal foundations indicated by those empty bottles, is an apt symbol for the 1950s itself, at the level of both state and individual family.

With the war won and the beginnings of the Welfare State laid down in the late 1940s, the opening years of the 1950s with the Festival of Britain in 1951 and coronation in 1953 looked bright and hopeful. But the confidence of these years was built on a false premise, the belief that Britain was still a major player on the world stage. Indeed, Peter Hennessy argues that 'complacency was the real problem' (1993, 429). The Festival of Britain in 1951, which harked back to the Great Exhibition of 1851, demonstrates how much the confidence and hope was based on looking backwards – to the perceived glories of an era Warner exposes as equally fractured. In reality, Britain was undergoing a rapid process of decolonisation. Moreover, the first waves of immigration, starting with the arrival of the Empire Windrush in 1948, heralded the beginning of an increasingly multi-racial society, the tensions of which became visible in the Notting Hill race riots of 1958. The world order had already radically shifted as the freeze of the Cold War set in. The Korean War in 1950 damaged the British economy, but it also exacerbated American paranoia about Communism and kick-started McCarthyism.

Despite the election of two Labour governments in Britain, the war had appeared to vindicate the establishment and the upper classes. In 1951 the ageing and increasingly incapable Churchill was returned to power with a Conservative government. But the defection of Guy Burgess and Donald Maclean in 1951 exposed dissent and a possible rottenness at the core of the British establishment. By the Suez crisis in 1956 it was humiliatingly obvious that Britain was a third-rate power.

The 'consensus society' of the 1950s was based on a deep conservatism, bred by the uncertainties of the war, and its central symbol of unity and stability was the idealised family. Helen Taylor recalls, 'In the aftermath of the war, what [my parents] most wanted was a strong, independent nuclear family in its self-sufficient home' (1989, 7). This family unit centred around an almost mystical conception of modern woman as a happy housewife who had *chosen* to find her fulfilment through her family. Her return to the kitchen was rewarded by the new consumer goods. Even the clothes of this period, starting with Dior's 'New Look' launched in 1947, with their wide skirts and narrow shoulders, offer an exaggerated and romantic femininity which harks back to earlier ages.

This modern but feminine woman was epitomised by the young Queen, whose coronation, watched by 27 million on television, appeared to mark the beginning of a new Elizabethan age. What is striking watching the television coverage of the coronation today is how much the Queen now seems a cipher, a blank onto which the hopes of the country were projected.

The excessive pageantry and the repeated emphasis on the continuities of history both obscure and are made possible by the fact that the monarch was a figurehead, who (unlike her eponymous predecessor) would have little real power. Equally, the display of Commonwealth representatives obscures the reality of the loss of Empire.

Any possibility that the new Queen Elizabeth might represent a powerful role model for women was neutralised by the way she was represented as a 'young' and 'beautiful' wife and mother, the centre of the national 'family', but a woman who had had position thrust upon her. Her femininity was part of the mystique of her royalty precisely because it did not threaten but confirmed a status quo which was already, in fact, part of history. For, as the 1950s wore on, the 'problem that has no name' in Betty Friedan's phrase (1963), was as much an issue for women in post-war Britain as it was in America. Warner's nineteenth-century Julie Barnard is not so different to housewives in American suburbs so disillusioned by the 'feminine mystique' that they were 'taking tranquilizers like coughdrops' (Friedan, 1982, 28).

The canonical account of the literature of the 1950s is dominated by the appearance of the 'Angry Young Men', a loose group of writers (Kingsley Amis, John Osborne, Alan Sillitoe, John Wain, John Braine and Colin Wilson) whose anti-heroes expressed a seemingly radical rage against contemporary society. While many of the protagonists of these texts – Kingsley's lower-middle-class Jim Dixon, or Alan Sillitoe's working-class Arthur Seaton – are themselves marginal, their anti-establishmentism is often expressed through misogyny. 'In *Look Back in Anger*', Elizabeth Wilson comments, 'John Osborne felt justified in letting rip at women as if this were in itself an attack on convention and bourgeois values' (1980, 153). She concludes that 'just below this obsessively heterosexual world lay an absolute loathing of women' (153).

The 'Angry Young Men' was an exclusively male literary club. Until relatively recently, this decade, seen as the 'nadir of British feminism' (Pugh, 2000, Chapter 10), was also treated as an empty or reactionary decade for women's writing. Elizabeth Wilson noted 'a general sense of retreat and nostalgia for a pre-war world that had been lost' in immediately post-war writing (1980, 147). Her concern is with writers such as Rosamond Lehmann or Antonia White writing about the recent past, rather than historical novelists proper, but she goes on to suggest that:

> It is as if in the early fifties, women novelists wrote about women in the past, lost in madness, deprived completely of autonomy, because in the modern world it was not possible to suggest that a woman's normal lot was dependence and captivity, sexual frustration, and the battle with patriarchal authority. (1980, 151)

However, Niamh Baker (1989) has suggested that it was in women's fiction that opposition to post-war orthodoxy could be found. More recent work (for instance, Maslen [2001] and Dowson [2003]) has confirmed this, drawing attention to the range of women's writing being produced and its political, social and literary significance.

My own argument in this chapter is that it is in the woman's historical novel that we can find some of the most interesting and subversive works of these years. Perhaps more than with any other decade, the literary map of the 1950s looks different if we consider women's historical novels. These have been ignored, I think, because in contrast to the documentary social realism of the 'Angry Young Men', the historical novel, tainted by its association with 'escapism' in the 1940s, appeared reactionary and nostalgic. Yet contemporary commentators acknowledged its importance. In 1958, Peter Green argued that, 'The historical novel today is undergoing an unmistakable renaissance' (1962, 35), with 'major' writers moving it towards 'a form which subsumes both scrupulous scholarship and psychological insight' (35). And Helen Cam (1961) insisted that this vogue for historical fiction expressed more than merely a desire for escapism and entertainment. Dean Rehberger has usefully suggested that it was precisely the need for consensus during the Cold War period which led to scholars excluding from the canon works which do not fit within a particular defined structure, especially texts that 'demonstrated an attachment to the struggles within culture (those texts that include "foreign" elements like history and popular culture)' (1995, 64). With this in mind, the woman's historical novel, excluded as both 'historical' and 'popular' and centrally concerned with cultural struggle, starts to look rather more subversive than the ultimately conservative misogyny of the 'Angry Young Men'.

Silenced by the consensus society which relegated them to the domestic sphere, women writers used the historical novel to enter the male world, and to tackle some of the most pressing questions of the post-war world, linking them to an exploration of masculinity itself. The concern with masquerade and cross-dressing so central to the historical novel of the 1920s and 1940s is, I have suggested, closely related to an understanding that femininity is a 'masquerade'. In the 1950s, it was the notion of masculinity as a masquerade which seemed to fire women's imaginations. Many of them use male protagonists or first-person male narrators and this ventriloquism or cross-writing reveals 'the imitative nature of gender itself – as well as its contingency' (Butler, 1990, 137) in interesting ways. This is often linked to an interest in multiple or unreliable narrative viewpoints which disrupt any view of history itself as unitary and closed, and offer alternative interpretations of the grand narratives of English history.

The self-righteous tyranny of patriarchal authority figures like Warner's John Barnard is shown to result from the restrictions of a deforming model of masculinity, as rigid as the walls which block the light from Anchor House. Barnard's life is a 'malformed tree' planted in a 'bad love' (268):

For over thirty years he had been trying to turn a silk purse into a sow's ear by extending that flimsy article, a young man's fancy, into the durable zeal of a family man – trying to be patient, when in fact he was bored; to rule when he wanted to run away [...]. (Warner, 1997, 242)

Unsuited to marriage or to his role as paterfamilias, Barnard is not even, the text suggests, enthusiastically heterosexual and his wife has to resort to 'unwomanly prompting' to rouse 'a brief lust' (242). The greatest pleasure he experiences in the book comes from skating on a frozen lake in 'luxurious isolation [...] a truant from fatherhood' (79). The father in Barbara Comyns' *The Vet's Daughter* (1959), which looks back at the Edwardian period, is a far more brutal version of this figure, a Gothic wife-murderer who puts his invalid wife 'to sleep' much as he would do an animal. Even here, however, his need to marry for money indicates his precarious position within society. As with Barnard, there are moments when he becomes almost pitiable.

The hollowness or 'lack' which underlies the masquerade of masculinity is repeatedly exposed in these texts. Daphne du Maurier brings together the Gothic and the historical in *My Cousin Rachel* (1951), set in nineteenth-century Cornwall. Through the use of a first-person and unreliable male narrator, she exposes masculinity as painstakingly constructed, painfully maintained and ultimately fragile. The novel opens with the chilling statement that, 'They used to hang men at Four Turnings in the old days. Not any more though' (1992a, 5), and the tarred figure of a man hung for wife-murder. The past here is a dark and dangerous place which haunts the present, for Philip, the narrator, will cause the death of the woman he loves, Rachel, the widow of his cousin Ambrose who brought him up. Once again du Maurier sketches in the 'historical' background very lightly (little more than long skirts and carriages instead of cars), but here this suggests the uncanny repetition of this cycle of male violence. They may not hang men at Four Turnings any more, but men still murder their wives.

Young and naïve, Philip's hold on masculinity is tenuous, signalled by the way in which he clings to his pipe, itself a gift from Ambrose. Growing up 'ignorant of women' (1992a, 53), he finds them 'foreign'; 'other'. Having fallen in love with Rachel, he cannot 'read' her: is she a monstrous murderess or the victim of Ambrose's own paranoid madness? Philip's re-enactment of Ambrose's actions – he feels himself to be Ambrose's 'ghost' (8) – suggests the uncanny nature of masculinity as a repetitive performance. Both 'madness' and 'masculinity' are hereditary. Horner and Zlosnik read this as a 'male Gothic' text, expressing patriarchy's 'night*mère*', and suggest that, 'The ultimate horror for the feminist reader lies in Philip's own subjectivity' (1998, 145). Male violence, the matricide which Luce Irigaray argues underlies Western culture, stems from fear of the female, specifically of the maternal, as 'other' – the 'night*mère*'. The related fear that haunts Philip is that he is merely a ghost, a hollow man, with nothing behind the masquerade.

This is also the fear faced by Miles Lufton, an MP in Regency England in Margaret Kennedy's *Troy Chimneys* (1953). Lufton has responded to social pressures by splitting himself into two people: 'Miles', the sincere but ineffectual private man who loves solitude, and 'Pronto', the tirelessly self-promoting public persona who has enabled his successful career. When he becomes aware that Caroline Audley has long recognised this duality, he feels 'as though we had been dancing in a masquerade which had lasted for eleven years. Now the masks were down [. . .]' (Kennedy, 1985, 195). 'Troy Chimneys' is the house to which Miles wants to retire with Caroline, shaking off 'Pronto' for good. When Caroline rejects him (his failure to recognise that she fell in love with him a decade earlier has destroyed her life), he has to face the fact that both Miles and Pronto are 'dead'. The question he then has to face is 'Who then is writing this?' (216). The fact that he dies before he can get to know this 'third person' (216) suggests a vacuum behind the masks. This is reinforced by the narrative structure of the novel which consists of a memoir written by Lufton, sandwiched between letters from other members of the Lufton family which cast doubt upon his character and reliability.

That this sense of the hollowness at the heart of the masculine is intimately related to the historical context of the 1950s is made clear in Bryher's *The Player's Boy* (1957) through an implicit parallel with an earlier age. The 'player's boy' is James Sands, a failed actor for whom the 'sands' are running out, as they are for his era. 'Thou lackest something. . .', he is told by another character (1968, 52). His 'lack' echoes and represents the lacklustre Jacobean years which followed the death of Elizabeth I: 'Nothing has been the same since Queen Elizabeth died' (49). The text is suffused by a nostalgia for the lost 'Golden Age', and the decline of England is symbolised by the execution of Ralegh, the loss of the great Elizabethan actors and play-wrights, and the rise of a money-obsessed mercantile culture – the beginnings of capitalism. Sands is a figure of ambiguous sexuality who identifies with Bellario, the girl-dressed-as-boy in Beaumont and Fletcher's *Philaster*, the only part he plays with any conviction, and who also ends unloved. Sands' 'performance' of gender, then, is only convincing when he is playing a girl playing a boy, foregrounding Bryher's own act of ventriloquism in this text. The structure of the novel reinforces this as the first-person narration is fragmented into dreamlike episodes, culminating in our realisation that we are listening to the voice of a dead man.

The most sympathetic characters in women's historical novels of this period are men who are in some way 'unmasculine', such as Blondel, feminised by his position as a musician in Norah Lofts' *The Lute Player* (1951). Often they are physically damaged in ways that suggest a Freudian 'castration', such as Blondel's damaged arm, or Prescott's one-eyed younger son, Robert Aske, in *The Man on a Donkey* discussed below. Rosemary Sutcliff's Marcus in *The Eagle of the Ninth* (1954), ostensibly a book for teenagers, is unable to continue as a Roman centurion because of his wounded knee, and has to look for an alternative career. His disability enables him to empathise with the colonised and defeated British – his slave, Esca, whom he sets free and Cottia, the girl he marries. Even Heyer's heroes become less conventionally 'masculine' fantasy figures in the 1950s. Misleading outward appearances mask their sterling qualities, as in the soft-voiced, dandified hero of *The Quiet Gentleman* (1951), the seemingly dull-witted Freddy in *Cotillion* (1953), or the Yorkshire hobbledehoy of *The Unknown Ajax* (1959).

It is in their use of homosexual male characters, however, that women writers of historical novels in this period are most different from their male peers. The misogyny displayed by the 'Angry Young Men' was accompanied by what Alan Sinfield calls 'the sneer at the queer' (1997, 79). This was hostility towards homosexuals who were seen as 'effeminate' ('pansies' or 'sissies') and linked with the elitist high culture against which the 'Angries' were rebelling. For instance, Alan Sinfield suggests that in Amis' *Lucky Jim* (1954) the effeminate homosexual writer is the 'absent other' (1997, 80) against whom Jim Dixon defines himself.

This hostility reflects the increased persecution of gay men in the 1950s. When John Barnard's son-in-law, Thomas Kettle, tells Crusoe that 'For a man to love a man is a crime in this country' (Warner, 1997, 183), he could equally well have been speaking in 1954. Prosecutions of homosexual 'offences' rose five times in the 15 years after 1939 (Sinfield, 1997, 68). Bubbling under the surface of the 'consensus society' of the 1950s was a version of what Eve Kosofsky Sedgwick (1985) calls 'homosexual panic'. Homophobia is, Sedgwick argues, 'a mechanism for regulating the behaviour of the many by the specific oppression of a few' (Sedgwick, 1985, 88). Thus in the 1950s the intensified policing of homosexuality indicates a wider anxiety about masculinity itself, reflected also in concerns about spies and traitors. The scandal over the Burgess and Maclean defections in 1951 reinforced a connection between homosexuality and communist treachery. 'Once [homosexuality] could be linked, in a paranoid way, with communism, it could be invoked to reinforce the Cold War and stigmatised as treachery against the Western Alliance' (Sinfield, 1997, 76). When the police set out to trap and prosecute Lord Montagu of Beaulieu and his friends in 1954, Sinfield suggests (1997, 78), their dishonest handling of the case led to a wave of public sympathy which contributed to the pressure for reform which resulted in the Wolfenden Report of 1957 and, finally, the 1967 Act.

In the woman's historical novel the homosexual is frequently a sympathetic figure, often even a figure for identification where the openings for female agency are limited. Even Lofts' *The Lute Player*, which examines the damaging effect on women when a closeted homosexual man cannot 'perform' as a heterosexual, is relatively understanding. The man in question is Richard I, the tall, blonde and athletic 'Coeur de Lion', model of chivalry and perhaps the most ostensibly 'manly' of all English Kings. There is historical evidence which supports Lofts' interpretation of his sexuality,[2] but her interpretation is still startling to readers brought up with the heroic figure presented in children's history books. Like the patriarch, the warrior is exposed as a hollow man, not because he is a brutal tyrant but because he cannot live up to the expectations of his society. Like John Barnard, Richard is unsuited to the part he must play. Lofts suggests that this explains his retreat into the homosocial soldiers' world of the crusades, where he can sublimate his desires and find an excuse for failing to consummate his financially expeditious marriage to Berengaria. One of Lofts' narrators explains the 'very real disgust which some women do feel for this perversion' as 'Quite understandable; it threatens something that women stand for. It cuts out, disowns, disinherits them' (1951, 393). In this uncanonical 'popular' novel, Lofts anticipates by a couple of decades Sedgwick's argument in *Between Men* that male homosocial bonds mask, repress *and* express homosexual desire, and that such bonds reinforce the exclusion of women from social contracts. Lofts also makes sophisticated use of multiple narrators to destabilise the unity of traditional history and suggest that there are other stories, including those of women and other non-combatants.

For Warner, the homosexual man disrupts the rigid structures of patriarchy, offering alternative, more fluid forms of masculinity. In the fishing community of Loseby, Crusoe tells Thomas Kettle, male same-sex love is not a crime: 'Nor in any sea-going place, that I've heard of. It's the way we live and always have been [. . .] in Loseby we go man with man and man with woman, and nobody think the worse' (Warner, 1997, 183). In the light of this, we can re-read an earlier description of John Barnard at 21, seen through the eyes of the Loseby fishermen, for whom 'it was taken as a matter of course that men should feel amorously towards a handsome young man' (4). From their point of view he is 'romantically handsome', the 'image of a *man*'s young man' (4, my emphasis). This signals the alternative possibilities and pleasures Barnard has repressed, symbolised by the frozen lake on which he skates as opposed to the fluidity of the sea which takes Thomas away from Loseby.

What is, of course, even more 'unspeakable' during these years is the possibility of lesbian sexuality – of women 'going with' other women – which is regulated not by criminal prosecution but by erasure. Thus in the 1950s, women writers, like Warner, tended to depict same-sex desire through male figures. The writer who developed this strategy most fully is, of course, Mary Renault.

Ancient history: Mary Renault's dialogic histories

Mary Renault is a good example of someone who has been widely acclaimed as writer of superb historical fiction as a minor genre, but who has not been taken seriously as an important writer of *fiction per se*, much of it with direct relevance to some of the most pressing concerns of the twentieth century.

She produced six novels with contemporary settings before she turned to historical fiction and these, especially *The Friendly Young Ladies* (1944) and *The Charioteer* (1953), merit far more critical attention than they have received. Reading them in dialogue with her historical novels helps to illuminate the sophistication of her thinking about gender and sexuality, and the way in which she connects these issues to questions of history, politics and morality.

This is not to suggest that her historical novels offer simple allegories of present concerns. As she stressed in a piece which set out her own creed as a writer, the historical novelist is always unavoidably contemporary, 'a man [*sic*] of his own world situation' (1968, 85):

> We all bring to the past our own temperament, our own preoccupations, to limit the reach of our insight [...]. It seems to me that it is in the struggle to stretch these bonds, to see the universals of human nature adapting to, or intractably resisting, the pressures of life's changing accidents, that the excitement of writing historical novels lies.
>
> You cannot step twice into the same river, said Herakleitos. People in the past were not just like us; to pretend so is an evasion and a betrayal, turning our back on them so as to be easy among familiar things. This is why the matter of dialogue is so crucial. (Renault, 1968, 85–6)

There are no easy parallels to be drawn and to pretend that there are is to falsify the past. Although she, like H.V. Morton and Daphne du Maurier, conceptualises history as a palimpsest – 'Every era of man's development, from the palaeolithic upwards, is still in living existence somewhere on earth' (1968, 86) – she stresses that we cannot go to the past as a 'public utility' (87), a phrase that describes Morton's treatment of the English past as a space for tourism with uncanny accuracy. Instead, she suggests, we go to it because

> we are its products. We go perhaps, to find ourselves; perhaps to free ourselves. It is certain we shall never know ourselves, till we have broken out from the brittle capsule of Megalopolis, and taken a long look back along the rocky road which brought us where we are. (1968, 87)

For Renault, history is central to the process of self-examination implied by the Socratic injunction to 'Know Thyself', a key concept in all her works, at the level of the individual as well as the society.

It is perhaps only with recent developments in theory, particularly Judith Butler's work on gender as performative, that we have had a critical discourse which can engage fully with Renault's work. Renault herself lived for most of her life in what was to all intents a marriage with another woman, Julie Mullard, whom she met when they were both nurses.[3] Yet her historical novels centre around male same-sex desire in the classical world. While early criticism tended to evade the issue of same-sex desire, more recent feminist criticism has focused on Renault's erasure of the feminine and her failure to depict female same-sex love.[4]

The three novels Renault wrote in the 1950s – *The Charioteer* (1953), *The Last of the Wine* (1956), and *The King Must Die* (1958) – are, despite their varied historical settings, closely linked in inspiration, theme and execution. As Renault explained, in each case a 'passage of dialogue and discussion' in one text inspired the following one (1968, 81). 'Dialogue' both within and between texts is central to Renault's work. These three novels are also intimately connected to the historical context within which they were written, especially the homosexual panic of the 1950s.

Set only 13 years before it was written, *The Charioteer* is not technically a 'historical novel' but it uses history to generate its central symbol and themes. And it is essential in understanding Renault's subsequent turn to historical settings. The protagonist, Laurie, is a soldier recovering in hospital from wounds received at Dunkirk. There he meets and falls in love with a young conscientious objector called Andrew, but cannot or, rather, will not declare his love because of Andrew's sexual and emotional naivety. At a party which introduces him to the local homosexual community, Laurie re-meets Ralph Lanyon, the head boy he had idealised and who was expelled from their public school for a relationship with a younger boy. The 'queer party [...] something between a lonely hearts club and an amateur brothel' (Renault, 1993, 311), with its drunken, camp excesses, epitomises everything Laurie dislikes about the way in which fear of prosecution and rejection impels many homosexual men to live furtive, ignoble lives, defined by their sexuality rather than by their merit as human beings.

An admirable character who knows and understands his own nature, Laurie attempts to live by his ideals in the face of this pressure. In contrast, Ralph sees himself as having failed 'to make out as a human being' (345). His major sin (understood as impelled by love) is in trying to control Laurie, rather than acknowledging his maturity. Wanting the best, Laurie at first refuses Ralph's offer of a life together and attempts to hold to a chaste love for Andrew but when Andrew flees from the knowledge of his own potential desires, Laurie, to prevent Ralph taking his own life, returns to him.

Through the central symbol invoked in its title, the Socratic image of the soul as a charioteer driving two mismatched horses, one white (rational self-control) and one black (appetite), Renault places her characters in a historical trajectory which reaches back to Ancient Greece, and to the beginnings of our philosophical and political thinking. The image comes from Plato's *Phaedrus*, a copy of which Ralph gives to Laurie, and Laurie gives to Andrew. The *Phaedrus* acts as a coded signifier of homosexual desire. In symbolic terms, Laurie is attempting to balance his spiritual attraction to Andrew with the physical fulfilment offered by Ralph. The final image of the charioteer's two horses momentarily reconciled for the night suggests a compromise which is not ignoble because it is the best possible in a homophobic world.

The historical significance of Renault's inter-textual use of the *Phaedrus* in relation to homosexuality is made explicit by Ralph in a key conversation:

> They were tolerant in Greece and it worked. But, Christ, there was something a bit different to tolerate. There was a standard; they showed the normal citizen something. [...] they took on the obligations of men in their friendships instead of looking for bluebirds in a fun-fair. (1993, 200)

As Ralph indicates, in Greece, love between men had a recognised and valued public standing in state and community. Given that Laurie is a soldier and Ralph a naval officer, this has special significance in 1940, when either could have been court-martialled for homosexual 'offences'. In direct contrast to the way in which homosexuality was linked to communist treachery in the 1950s, Laurie invokes the image of an army of male lovers dying for their state at Thermopylae, and imagines Ralph fighting beside him (170).

This conversation is one of several in which Renault explores the moral and social predicament of homosexual men in 1940. Her extensive use of dialogue echoes its centrality to the Socratic method of philosophic enquiry whereby, in William Hamilton's words, 'truth emerges from the direct action of one mind on another, when both are kindled by the inspiration of love' (Plato, 1973, 10). *The Charioteer* is a thoughtful and informed argument for legal and social reform in order that homosexual men might find it easier to live full and useful lives.

As David Sweetman records, Renault's UK publishers, Longmans, were deeply anxious about the homosexual theme of *The Charioteer*, while, in the McCarthyist climate of the US, her American publishers simply refused to publish it at all (Sweetman, 1993, 145). Just a few weeks after the UK publication on 5 October 1953, John Gielgud, whose acting Renault had much admired, was subjected to the publicity surrounding a trial for homosexual soliciting (Sweetman, 1993, 146). This atmosphere of persecution in part explains Renault's subsequent turn to the historical novel as a way of coding controversial material.

In *The Last of the Wine*, Renault describes a historical society in which love between men is not merely tolerated, but central to the social and moral structures of that society and held up as the highest ideal. A *Bildungsroman*, it follows the development of a young Athenian gentleman, Alexias, born at the beginning of the 'Great War', the Peloponnesian War between Athens and Sparta. The title signals that this is the end of the great age of Athenian democracy. An imperial power, Athens has betrayed its own ideals by its treatment of Melos, whose fighting men were slaughtered and non-combatants enslaved. It is now about to launch an unprovoked attempt to conquer

Sicily. Guilty of hubris, Athens is degenerating politically and morally, vulnerable to threats of invasion and, finally, occupation by Sparta. The issues raised here were obviously of relevance to post-war Britain, as well as South Africa, to which Renault had emigrated in 1947.

At the same time, these are the years in which Sokrates taught in Athens and developed the basis of modern philosophy.[5] Alexias is part of the group of young men and boys who gather around Sokrates, and the novel includes historical figures such as Kritias, Plato and Phaedo. As Landon C. Burns has shown, Alexias' development is a dramatisation of the Sokratic 'concepts of integrity in thought and action, of self-knowledge and of devotion to truth – the primary bases on which maturity is founded' (1964, 103–4). Many of the philosophical conversations which develop the themes of the book are directly taken from Plato. As in the *Symposium* and the *Phaedrus*, it is through love of another man, Lysis, that Alexias matures into a man. Yet, Burns argues that the fact this is a homosexual love 'seems almost negligible because it is described invariably as little more than a deep friendship' (104). Reading this novel against *The Charioteer* makes it clear that this fact is not 'negligible' but central to Renault's thinking.

The relationship between Alexias and Lysis rewrites (as the names suggest) that between Andrew and Laurie, but it exists within a socially agreed set of standards and structures that both validate and regulate it, precisely what is lacking in 1940s or 1950s Britain. In the first instance, it is a relationship chosen on Sokratic principles because it represents the best possible. Pursued by other suitors, including the lecherous and amoral Kritias, because of his outstanding physical beauty, Alexias is led to Lysis (who has loved him for some time but waited until he is mature) by Sokrates who thus gives the relationship his blessing. According to the mores of the time, this is a mentor–pupil relationship where the older Lysis encourages Alexias to strive for excellence, and in so doing pushes himself further in the same search. Lysis is what Ralph could have been in a different culture. Although it is not a relationship of equals as we would understand that, it is based on trust, admiration and mutual care, signified by the way the two men nurse each other when injured and by Alexias' metaphorical 'prostitution' of his body as a sculptor's model to buy food for Lysis during the siege of Athens.

Their love is compared with a range of other possible and actual relationships between men, from the uncle after whom Alexias is named, who kills himself when his friend Philon dies of plague, to the sordidness of the brothel where Phaedo, presented here as an enslaved Melian, has to service the lusts of those such as Kritias. The relationship is an ongoing process (there is no static 'happy ever after' here) which develops and changes through time, as well as through Lysis' marriage and Alexias' honourably repressed desire for the younger lover of Plato. The two men fight together, compete at the Isthmian Games, survive the siege of Athens, and take part in the last battle to liberate the city during which Lysis is killed. They exemplify the ideal of the army of lovers who uphold the ideals of their state, even though their state has by this stage betrayed those ideals.

Their love also illustrates the two kinds of love described in the *Phaedrus*. Initially, it is the highest spiritual kind which subdues the urgings of the charioteer's dark horse and will give the lovers wings to ascend to heaven. Later it becomes physical and thus represents what Sokrates sees as a form of love 'on a lower plane' but still with the potential to lift the lovers up to the light (Plato, 1973, 65). Alexias finds that Sokrates is particularly gentle to them after this point, 'as to friends who have suffered a loss' (Renault, 1986a, 228). His own comment is that, 'What had defeated us was something beyond; and this, which had come after, seemed to us now a consolation and a joy' (228). While Renault is true to her sources in presenting physical love as a 'defeat' of the aspiration to something higher, the reader who has read *The Charioteer* may draw a different conclusion.

What is crucially important here is that the society Renault is depicting is not an imaginary utopia but an undisputed *historical* fact. In writing about a society in which homosexual relationships were not merely accepted but an ideal, Renault is implicitly demanding that the reader engage with this difference from 1950s' Britain. Moreover, the fact that both Lysis and Alexias are bisexual (both marry and have children) suggests that sexuality is more fluid than we assume. It may even be that it is because homosexuality is more highly valued in this society that men choose to have their primary relationship in that form. Ironically, Alexias has to exercise special tact with Xenophon who is incapable of feeling homosexual love.

Renault's commitment to historical 'truth' explains in part what Carolyn Heilbrun (1979, 75) regarded as Renault's failure to imagine an autonomous femininity. However, as Kathleen Bell (2003) has shown, depicting a pair of male lovers freed Renault to explore 'masculine' and 'feminine' characteristics without having them tied irrevocably to biological gender.[6] In this Renault's conceptualisation of gender, as Hoberman (1997, Chapter 6) suggests, is already moving closer to postmodern understandings of it as performative (a 'masquerade'), constructed within specific social and culture contexts. This thinking is more fully developed in *The Mask of Apollo* (1966) where Renault explores the themes of acting and masks which recur in much of her fiction. By consistently 'masquing the phallus' (dramatising or flaunting masculinity to the extent that it is turned into an explicit masquerade), Hoberman suggests, Renault exposes gender as a kind of costume or mask, a performance rather than a biological essence. (Here Renault, surprisingly, has much in common with Georgette Heyer.)

Here I want to return to the issue of voice, and suggest that Renault's interest in dialogue offers another important way of reading her texts. Language and especially dialogue were central to Renault's thinking about form. In 'Notes on *The King Must Die*' (1968), she discusses the difficulties of finding a language for historical novels which is neither 'phony archaism' (1968, 81) nor inappropriately contemporary, and which, in her case, could be used to write about people who spoke Greek. (She admired Rose Macaulay's *They Were Defeated* for its attempt to use only words which were in use in the seventeenth century.) Renault's solution was to develop a flexible prose style which eschews polysyllables and uses as far as possible 'the older and shorter' (86) English words.

This decision contrasts with Naomi Mitchison's use of a modern idiom (and explains why her books seem so much more of the period of their writing than Renault's do), but also indicates a wider difference between their attitudes to history. *The Last of the Wine* is set in the same period as Mitchison's *Cloud Cuckoo Land* and both Alexias and Alxenor are representative figures of Greek manhood, privileged and typical in many ways of the beliefs and social structures of their society. While Mitchison uses Alxenor, an increasingly unsympathetic figure, to offer a harsh critique of what is worst about his society (its exclusion and victimisation of slaves, women and other aliens), Renault uses Alexias to present what is best about it (its striving after the good and the beautiful), and link homosexuality to this endeavour in a positive way. Mitchison projects a twentieth-century consciousness back into the past and uses it to critique what she finds there (imperialism, sexism), and then through her epigraphs signals the connection to parallel contemporaneous issues. It is the characters who think most like us with whom we sympathise, and Mitchison's modern idiom enables this. Renault refuses to do this, demanding that we accept her characters within their own time.

However, in contrast to Mitchison's work, Renault's has been seen as reactionary in the way it valorises male homosexuality while erasing the feminine. Janet Montefiore suggests that Renault 'would certainly' have read Mitchison's work, and goes so far as to suggest that *The King Must Die* is an 'anti-feminist' rewriting of *The Corn King and the Spring Queen* (1996, 164). *The King Must Die* is a bravura rewriting of the Theseus myth as 'history' which translates the mythic hero into a psychologically realistic man. It presents Theseus as an unregenerate womaniser who clears away the remnants of the old matriarchal religion in Greece in a way that could easily be seen as 'anti-feminist'.

However, the concept of dialogue is central to Renault's technique here, not just at the level of characters, but also between reader and text, and, ultimately, between past and present. As I have argued, any text in which a woman writer cross-writes a male voice draws attention to the constructed nature of that masculinity. Because *The Last of the Wine* and *The King Must Die* both use first-person male narrators, this is especially the case. They are very obviously double-voiced texts (to borrow Mikhail Bakhtin's term) where the male narrator's voice is ventriloquised by the female author, with which it is *not* identical.

All Renault's texts are concerned with the ways in which meaning is produced through dialogue, as in the Sokratic method itself. In *The Charioteer*,

Renault explores the way in which language is what Bakhtin calls 'dialogic', whereby meaning is 'the effect of interaction between speaker and addressee' (Bakhtin, 1994, 35). Words are not spoken in a vacuum but are 'orientated towards an addressee, toward who that addressee might be...' (Bakhtin, 1994, 58). Renault shows how within the gay community, conversations may have a double meaning which may or may not be obvious to both inter-locutors. Certain words (most obviously 'queer') depend for their meaning on both parties sharing a common knowledge. Andrew does not share this knowledge (he thinks 'queer' means first 'mad', then 'mysterious' [1993, 55]), and it is this which reveals his sexual naivety to Laurie. With Ralph, however, Laurie recognises, 'the special phrases casually accepted, the basic assumption on which all their words had made sense' (122).

Similarly in the two later texts, Renault uses the dialogic tension between male narrator and female author, and between past and present, to produce what Bakhtin calls 'hidden polemic' (1994, 107). Both texts are orientated towards an implied addressee who is not the modern-day reader, as the opening of *The Last of the Wine* indicates:

When I was a young boy, if I was sick or in trouble, or had been beaten at school, I used to remember that on the day I was born my father had wanted to kill me.

You will say that there is nothing out of the way in this. (11, my italics)

The implied addressee – 'You' – here is one who would find the idea of exposing an unwanted child 'nothing out of the way'. Here Renault is remaining true to the mores of Alexias' time. But she is also establishing a difference between this implied reader who shares them, and the twentieth-century reader who would find them strange, even barbaric. There is a further 'doubleness', of course, in the split between the experiencing narrator (the young Alexias) and the narrator who tells the story (the older Alexias, who often comments on changes between 'now' and 'then'), and between the female author and male narrator.

It is in the dialogic tension between past and present, between the two readers and the two narrators, and especially between female author and male narrator that the possibility for alternative meanings lies. By foregrounding the strangeness, the difference, of the past, Renault exploits the dialogic nature of language to expose meaning ('truth') as something which is constructed not only inter-personally or inter-textually but also inter-historically.

Read as a dialogic text ventriloquised by a woman, *The King Must Die* becomes an account of a man who, despite his acknowledged abilities as a leader, is flawed because he is too much a man. This is made explicit in the sequel, *The Bull from the Sea* (1962), where Theseus admits that 'There is not much woman in me' (1973, 38). It is revealing that he has no capacity for homosexual love. His repression of the old matriarchal religion can be seen as a metaphor for his repression of the female in himself. In a wider sense it symbolises the repression of the feminine in the society he creates, and which leads to that in which Alexias and Lysis live, and down to the one in which we live. This is the 'rocky road' (1968, 87) Renault wants us to look back along in order to see where we came from.

Reading Jung after finishing the first novel, Renault commented:

By the end of [*The King Must Die* Theseus] has not yet reached the point of reconciliation with his anima, and of course the tragedy before him is inevitable; you could call the rest of the tale THE MOTHER STRIKES BACK. (Sweetman, 1993, 206)

Certainly this is a good description of *The Bull from the Sea*. Each of the tragedies which beset Theseus – the loss of Hippolyta, the woman he truly loves, and of their son – is directly attributable to his former transgressions against the feminine principle. This is symbolised most directly in the opening of the novel where his inability to control his lechery leads to him profaning the shrine of the mother-goddess, and causing the death of her priestess at the very moment in which his mother is attempting to cleanse him of his earlier transgressions.

Yet it is also in this novel that Renault does portray an autonomous, and bisexual, woman in Hippolyta, the Amazon Queen, whom Theseus bests in single combat and takes back to Athens. Their love is a heterosexual version of that between Alexias and Lysis, based on mutual respect and admiration, and the shared experience of fighting: 'We learned as much of each other in battle as we did in bed', Theseus asserts (Renault, 1973, 108). With Hippolyta he feels no need to assert his masculinity by breaking her as his men expect him to: 'For her I was man enough' (108). Yet in taking her from Maiden Crag, Theseus has precipitated the battle against the Amazons in which she will die defending him, as well as the later loss of their son. Her death is a chosen one, however, which positions her, like Theseus, as a 'King' who is willing to die for her people.

Renault's interest in Theseus as what Lukács (following Hegel) would have called a 'world-historical figure' connects to her interest in what it means to be a leader. In making both him and Hippolyta versions of 'the king who dies for the people' discussed in Fraser's *The Golden Bough*, she is more similar to Mitchison (who used this figure in *The Corn King and the Spring Queen*) than at first appears. When Renault later came to write her trilogy about Alexander the Great, the question of gender was central to her conceptualisation. She envisaged him as a greater leader than Theseus because his character balanced both 'masculine' and 'feminine' characteristics, and because, as *The Persian Boy* (1972) shows, he is comfortable with racial difference. Thus Alexander has the potential, tragically unfulfilled, to unify Greece and Persia, representing Western and Eastern cultures.

In the late 1950s and early 1960s, with the memories of the Second World War still fresh, and the Cold War in full freeze, the question of what it means to be a leader and how this connects to issues of gender and the traditional construction of masculinity had a particular urgency. It was the historical novel which women writers such as Renault and H.F.M. Prescott, and later Dorothy Dunnett, used to address this question.

A lost leader: H.F.M. Prescott's *The Man on a Donkey* (1952)

The Man on a Donkey, H.F.M. Prescott's 841-page *tour de force* was, Helen Cam recorded, 'widely held to be the best historical novel of our days' (1961, 17). Glen Cavaliero argues that it is 'among the most ambitious and persuasive English historical novels to be written in the twentieth century' (Henderson, 1990, 532). Peter Green puts Prescott among the 'major' writers who were reclaiming the historical novel as a genre (1962, 35), while even Avrom Fleishman acknowledges her 'impressive characterisation' (1971, 256). Yet, until 2002 *The Man on a Donkey* was out of print and Prescott's three other historical novels remain so.

H.F.M. (Hilda) Prescott, perhaps because of those disguising initials, does not appear in, for instance, *The Oxford Guide to British Women Writers* (1994). She was, however, a trained historian who read Modern History at Oxford and gained an MA from Manchester. The daughter of a clergyman, she was also a committed member of the Church of England and this clearly informs her interest in religious history. Her biography of Mary Tudor, *Spanish Tudor: The Life of Bloody Mary* (1940), which won the James Tait Black Prize, demonstrates a scholarly and imaginative use of primary documents such as Mary's account books. But it is also interesting because of its unusually sympathetic portrait of the first female monarch to rule England alone in her own right. In place of the monstrous 'Bloody Mary' of popular history, Prescott depicts a woman characterised by simplicity, sincerity and physical courage. The suffering imposed by her father's rejection of her mother and bastardisation of herself led her to cling to a rigidly narrow conception of her Catholicism with tragic results for both herself and the country she ruled. Such independence of thought, based on a careful interpretation of the available evidence, is also the hallmark of Prescott's fiction.

The Man on a Donkey, contrary to the perhaps misleading expectations raised by its Biblical title, returns to the early years of the sixteenth century. It combines a scholarly interpretation of original documents with the novelist's imaginative power in order to re-imagine the years of the Tudor Reformation. Beginning in 1495, the novel culminates in the aftermath of the Pilgrimage of Grace of 1536, the Northern rebellion of the 'commons' against Henry VIII's dissolution of the monasteries. This key transitional moment in

Britain's history marked, more than anything else, G.M. Trevelyan wrote in 1944, 'the end of mediaeval society in England' (1946, 100).

A year after Prescott's novel, Geoffrey Elton's *The Tudor Revolution* (1953) would argue that Henry VIII and Cromwell effected a revolution in government 'which equipped England with a modern, national bureaucracy which could function, and provide political stability, irrespective of the personal qualities of the king or his deputies' (Marwick, 1970, 185–6). Fleishman's comment that Prescott's characterisation is 'not matched by a historical grasp of institutions, which would allow it to take the growth of Renaissance monarchy under Henry VIII with the seriousness with which it takes the loyal Catholic martyrs' (1971, 256) seems to be based on an Eltonian valuation of political history. It misses the fact that Prescott is doing something rather different, not least in destabilizing the distinction between 'Catholic' and 'Protestant'.

The break with Rome which installed Henry as the supreme head of the English church and led to the dissolution was initially engineered to enable the annulment of his marriage to Katherine of Aragon because he needed an heir to avert a revival of Civil War (still within living memory for some). It is the additional motivation of his desire for Anne Boleyn, connecting historical change to personal and sexual issues, which has attracted many popular women historical novelists to this period.

Jean Plaidy's *Murder Most Royal* (1949), for instance, covers much of the same period but from the viewpoint of Anne Boleyn and Catherine Howard. Plaidy's novel is guilty of the charge Lillian S. Robinson (1978) brings against the woman's popular historical novel in general: of reducing women's history to the personal. Such novels suggest that women's participation in history 'consists in being a female dressed – always – in appropriate period costume', and they affirm that 'love really is what motivates and justifies a woman's life' (Robinson, 1978, 222). This is another version of the 1950s 'feminine mystique'. In Plaidy's novel, sexual desire over-rides all other motivations and this limits her understanding of key issues. Henry's religious, political or economic motivations are presented as a merely hypocritical cover for sexual urges: '[Henry's] hot tongue licked his lips and he was smiling. He thought, I must look for a new wife . . . for the sake of England' (1966, 542).

In contrast to the way the text dwells on sexual interludes, it passes over the major crisis of the Pilgrimage of Grace in just four pages. Indeed, Plaidy displays a lack of understanding of religious belief as a motivating force, consistently presenting religion as 'superstition'. Henry 'was what men called a religious man, which in his case meant he was a superstitious man' (1966, 448). Although 'less superstitious than the king', Anne Boleyn 'is not entirely free of this weakness' (345), while Jane Seymour is 'very superstitious' (451).

In contrast, Prescott is interested in the ways in which the religious changes which Henry set in motion struck right down into the heart of sixteenth-century society, threatening the beliefs and structures which bound communities together, and bringing major social, economic and political shifts. The Pilgrimage of Grace was, she remarked in *Spanish Tudor*, 'the reaction of the common people of Yorkshire and Lincolnshire to the King's doings, only now become real to the North country by the suppression of the smaller monasteries' (Prescott, 1940, 94). They feared that if the monasteries were destroyed went their parish churches, central to community life, might be next to go (95).

'The largest popular revolt in English history' according to C.S.L. Davies (Fletcher and McCulloch, 1997, 45), the Pilgrimage was very nearly successful. Had it been so, it could have altered what we now tend to accept as an inevitable progress towards a Protestant state. Interpretations of the Pilgrimage, however, vary. For historians, the controversial questions are whether it was an authentic and spontaneous popular uprising (as Prescott avers above) or a politically motivated gentry conspiracy (as Elton argued), and whether its causes were at root religious or economic and social.[7]

As a historical novel, *The Man on a Donkey* is exceptional in its ambitious scale. Prescott uses the historical novel not to provide a fantasy space for romance, to create allegories of the present, or to code controversial material (all of which I would argue, *pace* Lukács, are perfectly valid operations) but to explore historical process through the lives of ordinary people (fictional and 'real') in a period of rapid, confusing and dangerous transition. Her use of the chronicle form, itself one of the oldest forms of historiography, is central to this endeavour. She utilises it, she explains, to 'introduce the reader into a world, rather than at first present him with a narrative' (Prescott, 2002, vi). This is a world where 'he' is a stranger who must try to construct meaning, 'as in real life' (or, indeed, historical research) from 'seemingly trifling episodes' (vi).

The techniques of the realist novel, especially the naturalistic descriptions of the small details of day-to-day life, reinforce this as Prescott builds the narrative through the accumulation of incidents and events rather than through imposing a plot. The lack of authorial explication avoids the kind of dry 'summary' of historical 'facts' which often mars historical novels (exemplified by Plaidy's cursory precis of the Pilgrimage in *Murder Most Royal*). Prescott's method here illustrates Butterfield's argument that while the historian seeks to generalise, to find a formula, the novelist 'will try to reconstruct a world, to particularise' (1924, 113). Her Christian framework serves two functions in relation to this. It is necessary on a historical level to understand the meshing of religious, political and social issues during this period, and it also gives the episodic form of the chronicle a symbolic unity.

Within this chronicle, Prescott deploys multiple points of view to track the tangled web of events and personalities involved, focusing on five central but inter-connected characters. Three of these are real people: Christabel Cowper, Prioress of Marrick, a woman whose deepest drives are towards material rather than spiritual wealth; Robert Aske, the one-eyed Squire and lawyer who became the 'Great Captain' of the Pilgrimage; and Thomas, Lord Darcy, the politically shrewd but religiously conservative nobleman who held Pontefract castle against the rebels and then joined Aske as one of its leaders. The other two are fictional: Julian Savage, who loves Aske unrequitedly, is the imagined sister of the real Margaret Cheyney, who was burnt for her part in the rebellion; and Gilbert (Gib) Dawe is a failed priest who has fathered three children, and subsequently turned to Protestantism.

Both real and fictional characters are impressively imagined and through them Prescott depicts a range of perspectives on the events. With no interest in the moral or spiritual issues at stake, the Prioress, who thinks of God in 'terms of a bargain between buyer and seller' (2002, 764), is concerned only to prevent the dissolution of Marrick by bribing first the assessors and then Cromwell himself. While this worldly Prioress represents the spiritual bankruptness of the religious world, Prescott makes it clear that this is the result of the habit of consigning unmarried girls to convents, regardless of their lack of religious vocation.[8] The Protestant Gib, on the other hand, is 'intellectually convinced but morally lost' (Cam, 1961, 17). He can only conceive of God in terms of terrible judgement on those who think differently to himself and has neither love nor charity for others, even his own son.

Julian has the capacity for love that is missing in both the Prioress and Gib. An illegitimate orphan abandoned even by her sister, she finds the only security she has known during her stay at Marrick but is ejected by the Prioress when her dowry is unpaid. For Aske, she represents those most vulnerable in his society: 'This – an unhappy, frightened little wench – was one tiny fragment of the destruction that the King and Cromwell were making' (470). Her naïve, all-consuming love for Aske means she can only understand events in terms of the way in which they threaten him. She cannot translate this love into an understanding of divine love, which is the only thing which could make bearable a universe she conceives as corrupted by pain.

At a deeper level, through the visions of a sixth character, a half-crazy serving woman called Malle, and the intertextual use of Julian of Norwich's *Revelations of Divine Love*, Prescott presents what she understands as the true meaning of Christianity (above and beyond petty squabbling about forms and rituals): the redemptive power of suffering and the transcendent nature of divine love. Prescott's earlier novels are concerned to show sexual love as having its source in divine love, of which it is only one manifestation, rather than being opposed to it. In *Son of Dust* (1932), Fulcun comes to understand his love for a married woman, a love constructed as sinful by his eleventh-century society, in these terms:

> Love, mounted in him, triumphant and wounded, touched the extreme height of anguish, and still unsatisfied, proffered itself, in urgent, sharp

desire, to be crucified for love. He knew then at last the worth and power of pain. He knew [...] how God bought the world. (1958, 274)

This theme is developed in a far more complex form in *The Man on a Donkey*. It is expressed at its simplest by Julian's unloved but loving husband, Laurence: 'Love makes everything different. I love you. If I might suffer for you I would be glad' (822). And it is illustrated at its most terrible in the haunting image of Robert Aske, hung in chains above York castle to die for his part in the rebellion.

The characters of Robert Aske and Lord Darcy, as they emerge from contemporary documents used by Prescott (such as Aske's deposition written for the king, 'The manner of the taking of Robert Aske', and Darcy's letters), have been the subject of some dispute among historians. Little is known about Aske's life before the 1536, other than that he was the younger son of a Yorkshire gentry family, who had connections to the powerful Percy family, and was a lawyer in London. As the documentary evidence shows, it was Aske who gave the Pilgrimage its name, who wrote its oath and the articles which set out its aims, who restrained the rebellion to peaceful means and prevented the rebels from taking spoil, and who finally went to London to confront the King himself. It is his motives for joining the rebels in the first place which are most unclear.

Hoyle, in the most recent book on the Pilgrimage, admits that Aske 'puzzled me for years' (2001, x). In contrast to the first major account of the Pilgrimage, by Margaret and Ruth Dodds in 1915, which depicted Aske as a mysterious but saint-like leader, Hoyle argues that Aske was simply a boastful opportunist who used the Pilgrimage to further his own political ambitions. Fletcher and MacCulloch paint a more positive picture of a deeply idealistic man: 'For Aske, the essence of the rising was that it was a spiritual protest by the laity on behalf of the church' (1997, 37). His arguments, they point out, emphasise both the religious and the social and economic roles of the monasteries as the focal point of communities, providing spiritual example and teaching, as well rudimentary education, tenancies for farmers, and a place for unmarried daughters (1997, 38).

It is in interpreting such puzzles that the historical novelist has the advantage over the historian in that she can take imaginative flight from the historical evidence. As her 'Historical Note' records, Prescott worked from contemporary documents to reconstruct the personalities of the major players, and her account follows the documentary evidence wherever available. Her Robert Aske is an unwillingly messianic figure, deeply troubled by the oath of supremacy demanded by Henry VIII on both spiritual and legal grounds, and driven by his own integrity to lead the Pilgrimage as a representative of the people. An authentically human and fallible man, his major failing (symbolised by the lack of one eye) is his blindness to others' perfidy. This contrasts with the immoral manipulation exercised by the King who displays a horrifyingly inventive and calculated cruelty in exploiting Aske's honesty to betray him to a lingering death.

In her 'Historical Note', Prescott draws attention to the only major thing in which she differs from other writers on the Pilgrimage and even here she draws her evidence from contemporary documents. In her account of Aske's death (usually simply noted as hanging), she draws on Wriothesley's distinction between the hangings of Sir Robert Constable and Aske (847). The hanging of Aske alive in chains is the haunting climax of the novel and central to her Christian theme. His lingering death, troubled by the sense that God has forsaken him, is presented as a kind of crucifixion. Aske's pain and thirst as he hangs above York castle directly recalls Julian of Norwich's visions of Christ on the cross, 'hanging in the air as men hang out a cloth to dry' (Julian of Norwich, 1961, 75–6), and her descriptions of Christ's thirst and the drying of his flesh.

This is reinforced by the visions of Malle who sees Christ made human, a man riding a donkey over Grinton bridge in the Dales the day before Palm Sunday. This vision realises the words from the Latin mass which are almost the closing words of the book: *Homo factus est* [And was made man] (841). In the dangerous confusion of this period, Prescott shows people searching for some kind of sign as to God's will (what Plaidy dismisses as 'superstition'). Each of the other central characters encounters Malle and, with the exception of Aske, ignores her message. Most of them do so because they cannot believe that God would speak through such a humble mouthpiece as this crazy serving woman. In the closing image of the novel, Malle makes boats out of pages torn from Julian of Norwich's *Divine Revelations* by the men who have destroyed the Priory. She sends them sailing down the river, symbolising both human disregard for the divine and its persistence.

As a messianic figure, Aske is another version of the 'King who dies for the people', drawn from Frazer's *The Golden Bough*, who appears in the work of Mitchison, Renault and also Rosemary Sutcliff. Aske's human care for others – Julian, his drunken serving man, his niece – and his ultimate sacrifice are contrasted with Henry VIII, who wreaks havoc on the very people he should protect. At one point, Henry is seen with his foot on a chalice taken from one of the monasteries, a sacrilegious gesture which symbolises his destruction of religious structures for profane motives. Like the Prioress and Cromwell, Henry loves gold better than god, and loves it for the power it brings: 'Gold was a rod to rule with' as the Prioress reflects (695). All three are authoritarian figures who see themselves as wielding power by virtue of their position as representatives of God on earth.

The Man on a Donkey is not an allegory of the present but it does deal with issues which were of urgent concern in the 1950s. Henry VIII's actions, as Prescott presents them, can be seen as the process of setting up a totalitarian state in which all individuals are subservient to him (rather than to the Pope) and within which all dissent is brutally eradicated. Both the 1530s and the 1950s were periods obsessed with the idea of treason. The 1534 Act of Supremacy made speaking against the royal supremacy an act of treason (Hoyle, 2001, 58). This is the central moral and religious dilemma of the novel faced by Aske: should people obey the King even when their consciences tell them that to do so is to go against God's law? As Aske's servant puts it, 'there's the King's King [...] to think on' (507). Is the Pilgrimage an act of treason or, as Aske's niece Julian avers, the 'lawful petition of grievances made by all the commonalty and gentry of the North' (699)?

Treason in the 1530s was a matter of life and death, as it was again in the 1940s and 1950s, generating a climate of fear and suspicion. The post-war obsession with treason is reflected in Rebecca West's *The Meaning of Treason* (1949), which discusses the treachery of William Joyce and John Amery and others. It was updated in 1964 to include the peace-time Communist spies and the Profumo case. West's book maps shifts in the concept and motivations of treason itself. McCarthyism in 1950s America, with its 'witch-hunting' of Communists and homosexuals, was oddly reminiscent, as the phrase indicates, of the persecutions of earlier periods, including those of both Protestants and Catholics in the sixteenth century. It reached its peak with the execution of the Ethel and Julius Rosenberg as alleged Communist spies just a year after the publication of Prescott's novel.

The Man on a Donkey is particularly interesting for the way it disrupts what Herbert Butterfield called the 'Whig interpretation of history' – that 'tendency in many historians to write on the side of Protestants and Whigs, to praise revolutions provided they have been successful, to emphasise certain principles of progress in the past' (Butterfield, 1951, v). The Reformation is one of Butterfield's central examples of the way in which 'Whig' historians have interpreted history in over-simplified terms, constructing a narrative of inevitable linear progression, with Protestants fighting for the religious toleration and freedom of thought which leads to the future and our modern world, and Catholics clinging to the past.

This is the story Prescott rejects, not least because applying the labels 'Catholic' and 'Protestant' to participants in the conflict in the 1530s is a distortion of what was a far more fluid and confused situation. While her use of a Christian framework could be seen as a reactionary move, I think it is much more sophisticated. Her novel presents the Pilgrimage of Grace in terms of the 'clash of wills' which Butterfield saw as a more accurate depiction of the processes of history-writing than a simple linear progression (1951, 46). Through her sympathetic characterisation she also depicts the human costs of the confusion which accompanies such a conflict.

The Man on a Donkey is a history of the defeated, of an unsuccessful revolution, of a vanquished leader and of a lost possibility, but it uses its Christian framework to redeem that defeat. This is not a fashionable stance today. With the advantage of hindsight, we can now see how nineteenth-century historical novels imposed a Victorian religious sensibility on their depictions of earlier times. Twentieth-century novels with their obsession with sexuality as motivation often either ignore the issue of religion, as Heyer does, or, like Plaidy, treat it as a bizarre form of superstition. Even a novel as accomplished as Sylvia Townsend Warner's *The Corner that Held Them*, in many ways similar to *The Man on a Donkey*, could be seen as flawed by a failure to engage with this issue. Prescott, like Rose Macaulay, takes it seriously. To do otherwise is to fail to understand a period when people were prepared to die for their faith. This, perhaps above all, is the strength of *The Man on a Donkey*, a powerful and important novel which deserves to be far better known.

Far from being an empty period for women's writing, as the canonical emphasis on the 'Angry Young Men' implies, the 1950s produced some powerful and important work, particularly in the historical novels of Prescott, Renault and Warner. Their analysis of masculinity has still to be properly appreciated.

6
The Return of the Repressed: Maternal Histories in the 1960s

Penguin's victory in the *Lady Chatterley* trial in 1960 seems, in retrospect, to mark the opening victory of liberated modernity over the old guard (those stuffy elders who, famously, would not want their wife or servant to read Lawrence's book). It is the moment when sex came out into the open to be freely discussed – and in literary terms stepped out of the coded pages of the historical novel and into the contemporary moment.

The popular images of the 1960s are images of youth, liberation and modernity – the Rolling Stones and the Beatles, Marianne Faithful in a mini-skirt, pop art, plastics and acrylic colours, James Bond with his gadgetry, even Albert Finney in the bawdy film of Fielding's *Tom Jones*. The Who's 'Hope I die before I get old', released in 1966, was the mantra of 1960s youth.

But there is, of course, the other side of the 1960s – a post-war Britain, temporarily affluent, but having to cope with the loss of her position as a world power and undergoing a process of decolonisation which focused attention on the historical meaning of that loss of Empire. Moreover, memories of the Second World War were still vivid, kept in the public eye by, for instance, the revelations of suffering and atrocities during the trial in Frankfurt, between 1963 and 1965, of staff who had served at Auschwitz concentration camp; a trial attended by the novelist Sybille Bedford. The memory of Hiroshima, the shadow of the Cold War and American involvement in Vietnam kept the threat of violence and even nuclear annihilation ever-present.

The historical novel of this period is often engaged with these issues though an engagement with the tragedy of history. A character in Iris Murdoch's novel about the 1916 Easter Rising in Ireland, *The Red and the Green* (1965), reflects:

> But after all what could one do? The begging mother, the starving children, the men in the trenches, the Germans down in the U-boats. It was a mad and tragic world. (Murdoch, 2002, 120)

This sense of a 'mad and tragic world' initially seems at odds with the bright new world of the sexually liberated, even hedonistic, young women we associate with the 'Swinging Sixties'. At first sight, Murdoch is evoking the image of a superseded and completed past, a past precisely consigned by the use of the past tense to 'history'.

However, as Juliet Mitchell notes, 'The late fifties and early sixties marked the rise of youth politics – the Campaign for Nuclear Disarmament, the New Left, the Committee of One Hundred, were dominated by young people' (1975, 230). This new generation was in rebellion against an older generation who seemed to have lost the right to respect. But the risk of the 1960s, as this youth politics recognised, was the risk of the repetition of violence – the fear that it had not, in fact, been consigned to the past.

The teenager as a phenomenon, Ruth Adam points out, was created by prosperity (1975, 180). This in itself enabled rebellion. The healthy young women of the 1960s – the 'tallest, strongest, healthiest generation on record' – matured early because they were the products of the post-war Welfare State, privileged ration-books, free cod-liver oil, and subsidised milk and school meals (Adam, 1975, 182). In an expanded education system they began to compete with boys for the new university places, and were trained for both marriage and career. They were the first generation to benefit from the new sexual permissiveness, not only the availability of the Pill and the Abortion Act of 1967 but also a new openness which meant that pregnancy outside marriage was less likely to be covered up, with the result that illegit- imate births soared, peaking at 70,000 in 1967 (Adam, 1975, 187). The youth of the 1960s could afford (literally) to rebel because the Welfare State, combined with the relatively affluent economic situation, provided a safety net which had not been available to their parents. It was this unique moment, before the system began to contract again, which enabled the development of youth politics and the beginnings of feminism.

The paperback revolution, headed by Penguin, disseminated not only fiction but radical new ideas – R.D. Laing on sanity, for instance, one of the key texts in the youth rebellion because of its attack on the family – on a far wider scale than ever before through cheap, easily accessible paperbacks. It also brought a change in marketing strategies as books were increasingly sold as products within categories and genre divisions. Penguin used a simple colour coding – orange for fiction, green for crime and so on.

As Clive Bloom notes, the 1960s confirmed rather than changed the genre categories in existence – crime, historical romance, science fiction and so on – but 'the paperback revolution meant that authors on the bestseller list could reach unprecedented numbers of readers' (2002, 100). This reliance on genre categorisation, together with the increased use of authors as brand names,[1] was important in shaping the development of the woman's historical novel and its increasing association with popular, even pulp, fiction during these years.

The crossover with the American market was also important for British women writers of popular historical fiction. Heyer's novels, for instance, were republished by Dutton in the US in 1960s, while Dorothy Dunnett was first published in the US when she was unable to find a British publisher. Reviewers noted that the interest in these historical novels coincided with a resurgence of interest in British history after the death of Winston Churchill in 1965 (Fahnestock-Thomas, 2001, 203), but also that they provided welcome escapism. As one reviewer commented in 1967: 'In a world that is concerned with the intense and serious problems of world peace, a war that is not a war, racial injustice and civil disobedience, an escape into the world of Georgette Heyer's Regency period has some merit in itself' (Fahnestock-Thomas, 2001, 214).

The best example of this genre categorisation, however, is the work of Eleanor Hibbert, who used different pseudonyms to market the various types of novels she produced. Hibbert had been writing popular historical novels under the name 'Jean Plaidy' since 1945, and these were republished in paperback in the 1960s by Pan. The Plaidy books were biographical historical novels, usually based on the lives of royal women, and came in sets or series – the 'Mary Queen of Scots series', 'the Tudor series', 'the Stuart saga' and so on. The reader was buying not only a 'Jean Plaidy' but also a period category within the larger 'historical novel' category.

In 1960, on the suggestion of an American agent, Hibbert published *Mistress of Mellyn*, a popular reworking of *Jane Eyre* and *Rebecca* set in a vaguely nineteenth-century setting, under the new pseudonym 'Victoria Holt'. The first of what came to be known as the 'modern gothics' (also called 'popular gothics', 'gothic romances' or 'drugstore gothics'), *Mistress of Mellyn* sold more than a million copies (Radway, 1987, 31) and sparked off a boom of such novels which lasted until the early 1970s. One of the attractions of Holt's novels in 1960s' America was precisely their *Britishness*. Nancy Regan comments that her mother and her friends liked books by Holt, Mary Stewart and Daphne du Maurier because they offered 'romance with a decidedly British accent' (Henderson, 1990, 692).

The pervasiveness of the model was such that even Georgette Heyer produced the gothic-influenced *Cousin Kate* (1968). In 1971, *Time* magazine paid tribute to the genre's continuing status as a boom area in a generally depressed publishing industry. It also noted that literary reviews of the modern gothic were rare and had little influence: 'What sells is the author's name on the jacket and that illustration showing a girl and a castle' (Duffy, 1971, 65). The lurid pinks and greens of the covers used by Fontana for Holt's books in the UK indicated their strongly generic nature and marked them out as 'pulp' fiction.

The association of the woman's historical novel with such popular, even pulp, fiction had a damaging effect on women's historical novels in critical terms. Indeed, by 1968 it seems to have led to the downgrading of the genre as a whole. In America, William Styron commented at a meeting of the Southern Historical Association in 1968 that, 'Historical fiction has been largely discredited in this country, doubtless due to the fact that its practitioners, most of them, have aimed at titillating a predominantly female audience' (Woodward, 1969, 65). In 1969, Ursula Brumm thought that, 'In our time [...] the historical novel has almost disappeared' (1969, 327).

Brumm was mistaken, partly because she was working with Lukács' theorisation of the genre, and thus with a model of historical fiction which excluded a wealth of work by women in this decade. This includes not only the popular woman's historical novel by Hibbert, Heyer, Norah Lofts and Daphne du Maurier, but also Dorothy Dunnett's Lymond series, and work by Mary Renault, Bryher, Rosemary Sutcliff, Iris Murdoch, Rebecca West and Sybille Bedford.

Many of these novels obviously refract specifically post-war anxieties. Bryher's novels of the 1960s explored her belief that history repeated itself in cycles of destruction. As she explained it in her memoir, *Days of Mars* (1972):

A civilisation rose. It would not listen to the wise, it neglected its own protection and was over run and destroyed by the barbarians. The circumstances were repeated several times and was it not just what had happened in 1940? (Bryher, 1972, 55–6)

The Second World War seemed to her to parallel the Norman Conquest. 'The Normans were the Nazis of their time' (1972, 166), she wrote, who destroyed the superior culture of Britain in order to take the land they needed to survive.

In *This January Tale* (1966), Bryher turned to the post-Conquest period to explore the aftermath of defeat, as a warning of what could have happened had Germany successfully invaded. She saw the options as exile, and loss of a loved home and identity, or an attempt to live under the invaders. The protagonist, Eldred, like most of her heroes, is an outsider, a damaged arm disabling him as a fighter, and he chooses to become an exile. After his death in Ireland his wife returns home, where she prefers to be even if she has to face the destruction of the language, culture and landscape she loves. A very bleak novel, *This January Tale* offers a radically different view of the Conquest from Kipling's myth of the synthesis through marriage and male friendship of the best of both Norman and Saxon in *Puck of Pook's Hill*.

Very obviously of the 1960s is Daphne du Maurier's time-slip novel, *The House on the Strand* (1969), with its hallucinogenic drug which allows the protagonist, Dick Young, to take a 'trip' – 'the LSD phraseology was certainly apt' he remarks (1992b, 54) – into the fourteenth century. Its most haunting images are of fourteenth-century Cornwall, devastated by the Black Death: 'a place resembling, in its barren desolation, all the most hideous features of a twentieth-century landscape after disaster, suggesting a total abandonment of hope, the aftertaste of atomic doom' (283). 'Bubonic plague', notes Dick's doctor, 'Endemic in the Far East – they've had a number of cases in Vietman' (287). The present is infected by a past which will not stay dead.

Given Brumm's contention that the historical novel had disappeared, it is interesting that several women who are not usually associated with the genre produced fine historical novels during this decade – including Murdoch's *The Red and the Green*, Rebecca West's *The Birds Fall Down* (1966), and Sybille Bedford's *A Favourite of the Gods* (1963) and *A Compass Error* (1968). These texts look to the recent past in order to trace the roots of the present, so they would fall outside Lukács and Fleishman's definitions of the genre.

In *Traces of Another Time* (1990), however, Margaret Scanlan argues that there is an alternative tradition of historical novels, the proto-type of which is Thackeray's *Vanity Fair* (1847). These novels, she suggests, are ironic, sceptical, decentred, 'seeking to exploit rather than cover up the boundaries between history and fiction' (1990, 3). Focusing on defeat rather than victories, they marginalise the great events of history in order to explore the 'question of how private lives or consciousnesses intersect with public events; how it is that we experience our history' (7). Scanlan connects this other, sceptical historical novel with 'the diminishment of British political power that followed the war [which] created the sort of sharp break with the recent past that promotes a greater consciousness of history or historical process' (5).[2] That break can be seen at its sharpest in the 1960s. Sked and Cook pinpoint 1963 (following the collapse of Britain's nuclear independence and de Gaulle's veto of Britain's application to join the European Common market) as the year after which Britain could no longer see herself as a world power (1993, 10).

These novels, Scanlan suggests, are particularly distrustful of any sense of a clear progress from past to present, including that of classical Marxism (1990, 6). D.J. Taylor who draws on her argument for his own reading of what he sees as the 'decline' of post-war fiction connects this deconstruction and decentring of long-standing myths with the loss of a sense of 'shared history' (1994, 53).

Although Scanlan's correction of Fleishman's account is extremely valuable, it underestimates the importance of gender. Given that women have never been a part of that 'shared history', their historical novels have always eschewed the grand narrative of progress in favour of an emphasis on the marginal and discontinuous, from Mitchison's histories of the conquered back to Lee's 'recess'. Two things are especially interesting about the 1960s in relation to this. First, the extent to which this interpretation moves into the mainstream. And, secondly, a widening of the concerns of the woman's historical novel as it moves outside the 'recess' to Ireland, Europe, Russia and Britain's former colonies.

Iris Murdoch's *The Red and the Green* is a typical example of Scanlan's sceptical historical novel. Published just one year short of the fiftieth anniversary of its central event, the Easter Rising of 1916, it presents the events of the week running up to the Rising through the relations between members of one family, exploring the tangled politics of the Anglo-Irish relationship through a tangled mesh of kinship shadowed by incest. Through a series of parallels, Murdoch emphasises the similarity between the two cousins who represent the young men on opposing sides of the conflict: the Anglo-Irish Andrew Chase-White, a British Cavalry officer, and Pat Dumay, an Irish rebel. Both, for instance, fear sex and associate it with death but both become entangled with the same women, the feminist Millie Kinnard, and Andrew's putative fiancée Frances.

History is exposed as subjective – 'There's no such thing as European history', remarks Frances' husband in the Epilogue, 'Each country tells a selective story creditable to itself' (2002, 315) – but also as inseparable from literature. As Scanlan points out, Murdoch's novel deconstructs both Yeats and Joyce, as well as other texts, like the popular song from which the title comes, in order to examine the ways in which literature (even 'bad' poetry) *shapes* history (Scanlan, 1990, 24–8). Art – Yeats' 'Easter 1916', Picasso's 'Guernica', the poem Frances quotes about the Irish soldiers who fought for the French at Fontenoy (2002, 315) – determines what is remembered but also determines how it is remembered. By exploring the human complexity and mess of experience that constituted the Rising, Murdoch suggests that historical events are often glamorised and simplified in art in a way which offers a dangerously heroic example to those who come after.

The Red and the Green is typical of women's historical novels in the 1960s in that its exploration of the wider political sphere always *connects* this to the issues of the private and the personal in terms of family structures. In particular, Murdoch exposes the inadequacies of Yeats' attitude to gender, the contradictions involved in his personification of Ireland as tragic queen in Cathleen ni Houlihan while he believed that women, such as Maud Gonne, should stay out of politics. Thus Frances remarks, 'I think that being a woman is like being Irish [...] Everyone says you're important and nice, but you take second place all the same' (Murdoch, 2002, 36). Cathleen ni Houlihan is countered by the unheroic figure of Kathleen, a woman with 'an intuitive gift' for 'jumbling together the personal and the impersonal' (2002, 153). Kathleen rejects both the personification of Ireland as a woman which is used to justify patriotism – 'She! She! Who is Ireland indeed?' (227) – and the male violence of the rising: 'One can't live by violence. The whole world's mad with violence [...] It's a man's world, a world of hate' (153–4). But she is powerless to prevent the deaths of both her sons.

The novel ends with an epilogue in which Frances recalls the names of those who died in the Rising, the First World War and the Irish Civil War, for her son, echoing Yeats' roll call of the dead in 'Easter 1916'. However, the question Frances cannot bear to ask is whether these 'inconceivably brave men' (318), frozen in the perfect moment of their youth, had died 'for nothing' (318): 'Because of their perfection she could not bring herself to say so. They had died for glorious things, for justice, for freedom, for Ireland' (319). Yet, even as she speaks, Frances is haunted by the fear that her own son is about to be drawn into the Spanish Civil War, and the cycle of male violence and death and women's tears which make up this 'mad and tragic world' will be repeated.

Rebecca West's *The Birds Fall Down* (1966), set in 1900–1902, similarly connects public history, here the birth of the Russian revolution, to private family structures, paralleling public political violence and treachery with private male tyranny and treachery. Like her *The Meaning of Treason* – updated in the 1960s to cover the Profumo affair of 1962, notorious for its mix of Russian spies, pretty girls and government ministers, as well as the defection of Harold Philby in 1963 – the novel examines the 'meaning of treason', and its fatally tragic effects.

Her heroine, Laura, is witness to a conversation between her grandfather, the exiled Russian Count Nikolai Niklaievitch, and his revolutionary adversary, Chubinov. Chubinov reveals that Nikolai's most trusted aide, Kamensky,[3] is a double agent, working for both the Tsarist police and the revolutionaries. This revelation kills the old Count.

West shows patriarchal family structures are replicated in political and religious structures, all of which are damagingly dominated by the Law of the Father. Nikolai Niklaievitch, who sees women as inferior and closed down the schools for women doctors when he was in Russia (West, 1966, 44), takes the family as the model for the state and vice versa. He regards the Tsar as divinely sanctioned, a representative of God, the Father. By extension, he tells Laura, within her own family her father is 'the image of the Godhead' (West, 1966, 57). But Laura's father is engaged in his own act of betrayal through an affair with his wife's best friend, and this renders him unable to protect Laura when her life is threatened by Kamensky.

West's novel engages with Hegel's theory of the 'dialectical process' of history (West, 1966, 25), but not as the positive progressive force theorised by Lukács. Each of the three central male characters finds in Hegel's work 'the messages they wanted' (300) to vindicate their beliefs. Most dangerously of all, Kamensky uses it to justify his position as a double agent, arguing that by working for both sides at once he will hasten their destruction in order to bring about a synthesis which will create a superior organisation (302–4). Kamensky sees himself as a Christ or Buddha-like figure who will 'have the satisfaction of knowing that he has controlled history' (305). But his actions will lead, West indicates, to Lenin's assumption of power.

West sees the dialectic as a theory of the *necessity* of extremes, which validates violent conflict and the debilitating separation of male and female into public and private spheres. In the metaphor of the woodcock shoot which provides the book's title, the cocks fight and the hens watch, until both are shot by the men they have been too preoccupied to notice. The only positive relationship in West's novel is the unconditional and protective love between Laura and her Russian mother, Tania.

Victoria Glendinning suggests that the novel most comparable to West's in its international scope and grasp of history is Sybille Bedford's earlier *A Legacy* (1956), which examines, through the story of two German families, the roots of the First World War. Indeed, Bedford commended *The Birds Fall Down* because 'it has everything: characters, living people, the sense of history and movement of history, time, action, Fate' (Glendinning, 1988, 230).

In the 1960s, Bedford's two linked novels, *A Favourite of the Gods* (1963) and *A Compass Error* (1968), again examine the connections between family relationships and the wider political sphere on an international level. She traces divisions, specifically those caused by nationality, within a family centred on the marriage of an American heiress to an Italian Prince, against the background of two world wars and the growth of Fascism. The question posed by their daughter, Constanza, 'shall we never escape the muddling consequences of our family history?' (2000a, 241), is in turn echoed by her daughter, Flavia: 'How is one to live – if one step leads to another?' (303).

A substantial portion of *A Compass Error* is the retelling, from Flavia's point of view, of her mother and grandmother's story, already told in the first novel. This retelling is necessary for her to understand how she has arrived at the point at which she stands. The issue of historical causation is thus explored through the tracing of a matrilineal genealogy, wherein Flavia's 'compass error' can be seen as both caused by and a repetition of a crucial act of denial (a refusal to see something) by her grandmother in the first novel. The second novel is a meditation on betrayal within the private world of the family. Flavia falls in love with a woman she may or may not realise is the wife of her mother's lover, thus destroying her mother's happiness. But Flavia, Bedford noted, 'can only be accounted guilty if she *knew*' (2000b, 4). The questions which are being raised here – the relationship between knowledge, guilt and justice – were being asked on a grander scale, not least in the trial of the Auschwitz staff which Bedford attended and which she mentions in the introduction to *A Compass Error*.

The concern with family structures and with maternal histories which are themes in these novels are central to the growth of feminist thinking during this decade. Feminism in Britain is typically dated from 1968 and often seen as inspired by the American movement. The historical fiction of the period, however, suggests that a pre-feminist consciousness was developing earlier in ways that are closely tied to attitudes towards the past, the family and the repression of the feminine. These are expressed at their most schematic in the popular gothic.

Captive women: 'Jean Plaidy' and 'Victoria Holt'

The sudden and phenomenal success of the modern gothic novel developed by Eleanor Hibbert under the pseudonym 'Victoria Holt' between 1960 and 1972 suggests that it articulated particular needs during those years. While the modern gothic has attracted considerable critical attention, much of it drawing on psychoanalytic theory, the biographical historical novels Hibbert published under the name 'Jean Plaidy' have received almost none. Hibbert herself distinguished between the two, saying that the 'Plaidy' books were written for 'a very special, very loyal public, who want to learn something' and the 'Holt' books for 'the housewife in the mid-west of America who has never heard of Louis XV and doesn't want to' (Shattock, 1994, 212).[4]

Yet there are important similarities between the two types of novel. The central motif of the modern gothic, encapsulated by the cover image of the girl and castle, is that of the captive woman. This is also a recurring image in the 'Jean Plaidy' novels, as well as in other women's historical novels of the period such as those by, for instance, Norah Lofts. It has its most sophisticated expression in Jean Rhys' *Wide Sargasso Sea* (1966), itself, like *Mistress of Mellyn*, a rewriting of *Jane Eyre*. The image of the captive woman and the language of the gothic are central to the development of pre-feminist thought and language in the early 1960s.

What psychoanalytic readings of the Holt books obscure is the fact that, like the 'Plaidy' books, they also have a 'historical' or, perhaps more accurately, 'period' setting. Critics have usually read these texts as the enactment of a female psychic drama where women's ambivalence towards her husband or lover is worked out in a version of the Freudian family romance.[5] Joanna Russ' evocatively titled essay, 'Somebody's Trying to Kill Me and I Think It's My Husband: The Modern Gothic' (1973) was the first to draw attention to the repetition of key elements: the independent but vulnerable Heroine, the possibly haunted House, the brusque but attractive Super-Male, the Other Woman, the quiet Shadow-Male, and the repressed Secret. In what Terry Carr, editor at Ace books, called '"pure" Gothics' the tension is produced by the handsome and magnetic husband or suitor who 'may or may not be a lunatic and/or murderer' (Russ, 1973, 667). He suggested that the attraction of these books was to women who 'begin to discover that their husbands are strangers' and concluded that 'they were frightened of their husbands' (667).

Why, however, should this drama be set in the *past*? While the Plaidy books range across several centuries, almost all the Holt novels, with the exception of *Bride of Pendorric* (1963), are set in the late nineteenth century.[6] One reason is that the proto-type, *Mistress of Mellyn*, is recognisably a reworking of *Jane Eyre* (via *Rebecca*) in which the governess heroine discovers the dead body of her employer's wife and subsequently marries him.

According to Fleishman's definition of the genre, Holt's modern gothics are barely 'historical novels' at all. Although they are set 60 years or more in the past, the historical background is so lightly sketched in that one has to read very carefully to pick up the signifiers (usually clothes like the cape and bonnet worn by Martha in the opening of *Mellyn*) which situate the novel in any particular time. History here is a pastiche derived from earlier literary texts, particularly *Jane Eyre*. There are no real historical personages (even in *Menfreya* [1966], where the hero is an MP, there are only vague references to 'Balfour', for instance) or 'historical' events, and no concept of 'history as a shaping force' (Fleishman, 1971, 15). Instead, the shaping forces in these texts are desire and fear: the desire for a man, and the fear that he will turn out to be a murderer.

The psychic drama which the plot enacts is exactly the same whether it takes place in the 'historical' setting of *Mistress of Mellyn* or the modern setting of *Bride of Pendorric*. (The heroine on the 1965 Fontana cover of *Pendorric* wears a long negligee which at first glance is indistinguishable from the 'period' costume of the other covers.) Moreover, the first-person narrative voice, a technique borrowed from *Jane Eyre* and *Rebecca*, which facilitates a strong identification between reader and heroine, is exactly the same whatever the historical or geographic setting. This interchangeability suggests the transhistorical continuity of the psychic drama the texts enact.

History is central, however, to two elements in the texts, whether the setting is modern or period. The first is the house itself. Always ancient and imposing, this is strongly identified with the hero, having belonged to his family for generations (thus symbolising continuity through history) and often bearing the family name reiterated in the book's title: Connan TreMellyn in *Mistress of Mellyn*, Bevil Menfrey in *Menfreya*, Roc Pendorric in *Pendorric* and so on. This sense of the continuity of patriarchal familial history is connoted in *Menfreya* by family portraits, an 'ancient clock which was never allowed to stop', and 'suits of armour worn during the Civil War by the Menfreys of the day' (1968, 92). Thus the house symbolises the class status and security the heroine can attain through marriage, and her place within the historical narrative of generations it represents. There is a conservatism in the representation of the vanishing 'good old days'. In the modern setting of *Pendorric*, Roc's ownership of the family estate is threatened by 'crippling taxation' (1965, 140). 'The end of the old way is not exactly imminent, but it's creeping towards us', he remarks, 'I'd be sorry if we fell to the National Trust in my time' (141).

The geographical setting of the house (as in *Rebecca*) reinforces these connotations of 'history' and 'mystery', especially in the books set in Cornwall. In *Mistress of Mellyn* the heroine reflects:

> In this moorland country it was possible to believe in fantastic dreams; as some told themselves that these tracts of land were inhabited by the Little People, so I told myself that it was not impossible that Connan TreMellyn would fall in love with me. (Holt, 1963, 163)

As with Heyer and du Maurier, history functions as a fantasy space for romance but it is a romance which will ensure the heroine her place in (family) 'history' – her picture in the gallery of family portraits as it were. The possibility that the house is haunted links to the second element where history is important. This is the heroine's fear that she is repeating the fate of a woman from the past, a woman who has often been imprisoned within the house and died a violent or unpleasant death. In *Mellyn*, the heroine is locked into a priest hole with the body of the first wife and seems to merge with her: 'Was I Martha? Was I Alice? Our stories were so much alike. I believed the pattern was similar' (1963, 247). In *Menfreya*, the heroine believes she and the nursery governess are fated to re-enact an earlier incident where a governess, who had become pregnant by the husband of the house, died in a secret room after giving birth. The heroine comes to believe the governess may have been murdered by the wife. In *Pendorric*, the legend is that the house is haunted by the murdered 'Brides of Pendorric' who can only rest when another bride has died to take their place, and at one point the heroine is locked into the family vault.

The motif of imprisonment is eerily repeated in the present, increasing the heroine's paranoia, even in seemingly innocent comments. Connan tells Martha in *Mellyn*, 'I want to marry you because I want to keep you prisoner in my house' (1963, 212). For Martha, the 'unthinkable thought' (Russ, 1973, 688) is that it is Connan who is trying to kill her: 'How could I say', asks Martha, 'I suspect the man I am engaged to marry of being involved in a plot to murder me' (1963, 238). This is the fear which drives these texts, but is repeatedly deflected as the murderer is discovered to be someone other than the husband in novel after novel.

Uncanny repetition is the keynote of the modern gothic, both within the text, as each heroine fears that she is repeating a pattern, and as each text itself repeats the same plot. Reading these novels as 'paranoid texts' which help women to cope with enforced confinement, Tania Modleski has argued that this sense of the uncanny is connected to the heroine's fear of both repeating her mother's fate and of *being* the mother in the sense of failing to separate from her (1984, 70–1). In order to detach from the mother she has to attach herself to the 'father', previously seen as the enemy because of the way in which he controlled the mother.

Interestingly what few critics have picked up is the fact that in most of Holt's books the villain is revealed to be a woman.[7] In *Menfreya* it is the nurse who has been the heroine's surrogate mother, and she attempts to kills the heroine out of love. In *Pendorric* it is the husband's mother, who has been masquerading as her own twin sister. Thus the oedipal drama seems to be completed when the 'mother' is recognised as the true 'enemy', and the heroine transfers her affection to the husband as father-substitute.

This compulsive re-enactment of the 'history' of the family romance is why the historical setting is so necessary to these texts. It suggests that for women 'history' is not a matter of progress but rather a series of cyclical patterns of victimisation, as daughters repeat their mothers' fates. Julia Kristeva's theorisation of 'women's time' (1981) as 'cyclical' while men's time is 'linear' has obvious relevance here, but in the modern gothic this is a terrifying prospect. Janice Radway (1981) has persuasively argued that the modern gothics offer a 'feminist' protest by giving form to disaffection and discontent but then contain this through the imposition of a conservative ending. They offer but then withdraw the suggestion that men are the real problem (1981, 159). While voicing female fears of male violence within the domestic space, the texts suggest that the only way of breaking this cycle of violence is to find the 'right man'.

The Plaidy novels of the 1960s are ostensibly very different to the Holt novels, hence Hibbert's use of different pseudonyms. Despite the fact that they are much more clearly 'historical novels' by at least two of Fleishman's definitions (they are set over 60 years ago and contain real historical personages and events), Plaidy's novels have been virtually ignored by critics, with the exception of Alison Light. This probably has much to do with the fact that Plaidy 'novelises' history (in Trevor Allen's term [1967]) by presenting it from the point of view of the women involved, who are usually royal or the mistresses of kings or princes. Moreover, she adheres very closely to known facts and standard interpretations rather than offering rewritings.

The novels are loosely constructed and episodic rather than being tightly plotted, with chapters broken up into smaller sections. The prose style is bland with short paragraphs and relatively simple sentence construction. There is virtually no figurative language, very little description (except of emotions and, to a lesser extent than one would expect, clothes) and the dialogue is resolutely ahistorical. Language, like clothing, is one of the primary signifiers of period in fiction. In contrast to Heyer, who created a 'period' language for her Regency novels, Plaidy's characters speak twentieth-century English, whatever period or country the novel is set in. (She does avoid the contemporary idioms and slang which date some of Mitchison's novels.) For 'historical novels', Plaidy's texts are remarkably lacking in real detail of the culture, beliefs, morals and manners of their chosen periods. In this they contrast with Heyer's novels which are packed with the details which give her texts the appearance of 'realism'.

While the Holt novels use first-person narration, the Plaidy novels use third-person or impersonal narration, and the point of view often shifts to other characters to convey information not available to the central figure. The reader is not invited to identify with women from the past in such an intense way as in the gothics.[8] The implication here is that the 'history' conveyed in the Plaidy novels is objective, hence the impersonal narrator. In contrast, the modern gothics are highly subjective, as the reader is trapped inside the narrator's point of view.

However, the Plaidy novels repeat many of the themes and motifs of the Holt novels: male violence, the imprisonment of women, family structures, desire and power. Ultimately, they disprove the conservative and reassuring endings of the Holt novels because they show that the heroine's paranoia *is* justified. Plaidy's *The Captive Queen of Scots* (1963), *Daughters of Spain* (1961), *The Princess of Celle* (1967), *Queen in Waiting* (1968), *Caroline, The Queen* (1968), *The Third George* (1969), as well as earlier novels like *Murder Most Royal* (1949) demonstrate that it is a matter of historical fact that women have been locked up, mistreated, violently abused, raped, and even killed, often by their husbands. 'Happy women, like happy countries, they say, have no histories', says Harriet in *Menfreya*, 'so there is little to report of the first weeks of my honeymoon' (Holt, 1968, 152). Plaidy's novels suggest that history has been full of unhappy women, who discovered once the honeymoon was over that marriage was not all that they had been promised.

Despite their conservatism, Plaidy's texts offer the historical evidence of women's oppression across history. They suggest an implicit argument for many of the reforms for which second-wave feminists were to struggle: control of their own bodies, the right to sexual fulfilment, easier divorce and the right to retain their children, access to abortion and so on. This sense of oppression is expressed most vividly in the figure of the captive woman who is a recurring motif in both the biographical historical novel and the modern gothic.

These captive women include Mary, the 'captive Queen of Scots', Sophia Dorothea in *The Princess of Celle* (wife of George I) and her grand-daughter Caroline Matilda (sister of *The Third George*). The latter two are imprisoned as punishment for sexual indiscretions after disastrous marriages, and Plaidy draws attention to the fact that Caroline Matilda's fate directly replicates that of her grandmother, since she is also imprisoned in the castle of Celle (Plaidy, 1976, 262–3).

In *Daughters of Spain*, Juana goes mad because of her husband's heartless philandering, while Catalina, as Katherine of Aragon, will be repudiated by Henry VIII. Mothers in these texts – Caroline of Ansbach, the wife of George II, Isabella of Spain, and Eleonore (mother of Sophia Dorothea) – are powerless to prevent their daughters being married off for dynastic reasons, even when they recognise that the husbands are brutes or bullies, grotesquely deformed (in the case of William of Orange who marries Caroline's daughter Anne), or mad (in the case of Christian of Denmark, husband of Caroline Matilda or, latterly, George III himself).

Other women, like Caroline of Ansbach, are metaphorically 'imprisoned' within marriages which stifle their independence. Even though it is Caroline who, in partnership with Robert Walpole, is *de facto* ruler of England in *Caroline, The Queen*, she must pretend to defer in everything to her vain and stupid husband, George II, who consistently humiliates her in public to prove that he wears the trousers.

In Plaidy's novels the shaping forces of history are reduced to interpersonal relations, particularly familial and sexual relations. Although in one sense this corrects the exclusion of these elements from 'real solemn history', it is equally reductive. 'History' is narrowed down to the family relations of Royalty. Far more space is dedicated to the admittedly complex family life of the Hanoverian kings, for instance, than to the political and religious context of the Georgian period. Family or sexual relationships shape the form of the texts, and other historical events – political, social, religious, cultural – are introduced only as and when they immediately affect family members, often in language which is reminiscent of school textbooks. While in *The Heart of Midlothian* (1818) Scott weaves an entire novel around the Porteous riot and Jeanie Deans' journey to London to obtain a pardon for her sister from Queen Caroline, Plaidy disposes of the riot in around a page and a half and the Jeanie Deans incident in a six-line paragraph (1975b, 346–7). Sometimes this produces even more banal effects, as in the following passage where Caroline regrets the return of George II from a visit to Hanover:

> Life had been so peaceful; and she and Walpole had achieved so much. Now the King was on his way home and they would have to be so careful. How easily they had dealt with the tricky Portugese affair and the even more important Treaty of Seville! (Plaidy, 1975b, 119)

Given that Janice Radway found that the readers she surveyed valued historical romances as a source of information about history – 'You don't feel like you've got a history lesson, but somewhere in there you have' as the bookshop owner, Dorothy Evans, put it (Radway, 1987, 107) – such passages suggest that the information they are getting from Plaidy's novels is sparse to the point of being unintelligible. Plaidy even underplays the political and intellectual abilities of many of her subjects. The historian J.H. Plumb, for instance, although he contended that Caroline 'bullied' her husband, admitted that she was a woman 'of singular accomplishment' (1966, 69, 72). This is not evident from Plaidy's portrayal of her.

Other novelists create less reductive portraits of several of the same figures. In *Saraband for Dead Lovers* (1935), another novel about George I's imprisonment of his wife, Helen Simpson depicts Sophia, Electress of Hanover (cousin of Charles II and mother of George I), as an intelligent but dry woman with a passion for theological debate. This is very different from the vindictive and narrowly obsessed woman who victimises Sophia Dorothea in Plaidy's *The Princess of Celle*. Likewise, Norah Lofts' version of Caroline Matilda's life in *The Lost Queen* (1969) creates a more believable version of the political context within which the Queen's lover attempts to free the serfs and create an 'English-style' democracy within Denmark. The sight of a pregnant woman harnessed to a plough symbolises the hardships of the serf system for Caroline Matilda, but it is also another vivid image of a captive woman.

Alison Light has commented that Plaidy's depiction of Mary Queen of Scots in *Royal Road to Fotheringay* (1955) as 'the passionate Queen [...]

commanding [Darnley] to be her lover' (Plaidy, 1967a, 283) offers a 'far more plural and perverse model of desire' than one would expect in novels of its period (Light, 1989, 64). There are, however, major problems with Plaidy's persistent emphasis on Mary as an impulsive, passionate woman. For Plaidy, sexual desire is the *only* motivating force for Mary's behaviour and, indeed, often for the men who fall in love with her. Plaidy asserts in her 'Author's Note':

I believe that [Mary's physical charm] was largely due to an extremely passionate nature which was but half awakened when she met Darnley and not fully so until it was recognised by that man – so experienced in amatory adventures – the virile Bothwell. (Plaidy, 1967a, 6)

As in Irwin's *Gay Galliard*, this involves Plaidy in attempting to justify Mary's connivance in Darnley's murder. It also supposes that it was Bothwell's *rape* of the Queen which was the 'emotional climax' of her life (Plaidy, 1967b, 32), and that by thus awakening her sexuality, Bothwell made her his 'passionate mistress and most willing slave' (1967a, 400). Plaidy is less successful than Irwin, partly because her depiction of Bothwell is sketchy and unappealing, but also because by continuing Mary's story into imprisonment in *The Captive Queen of Scots* she has to deal with Mary's willingness to divorce Bothwell (by then imprisoned in Denmark) in order to marry Norfolk. Despite Plaidy's best efforts, Mary comes across as a silly and inconsistent woman, a danger to herself and others.

The villain in the Mary Queen of Scots books is Elizabeth I, who is held responsible for Mary's death and is presented as coldly unfeeling, an unnatural and unfeminine figure (as in *The Recess*): 'The Queen of England was governed by ambition; the Queen of Scots by her emotions' (1967a, 396) as Plaidy puts it. This use of a female villain accords not only with the Victoria Holt books I have discussed but also with many of the other Plaidy novels, such as *The Princess of Celle*, where it is Clara von Platen and Sophia, Electress of Hanover, who actively plot the downfall of Sophia Dorothea. Although Plaidy is concerned to demonstrate women's oppression within patriarchal structures (especially marriages), she is more comfortable valorising the emotional and 'feminine' woman than the woman who likes and uses power. Her heroine is Mary the tragic victim, not Elizabeth the survivor.

The image of the captive woman and the language of the gothic novel reappear in the non-fiction texts which mark the beginnings of feminist theory in a way that suggests we should not underestimate the power of popular, or even pulp, fiction to express dissent. Writing about Judith Hubback's *Wives Who Went to College* (1957), a study of graduate wives, Elizabeth Wilson notes that, 'The themes of escape and imprisonment were in fact the dominant metaphors used by these women to describe their condition'

(1980, 57). Wilson herself deploys the language of the gothic to express the resurgence of feminism in the 1960s, calling it 'the return of the repressed' (1980, Chapter 10). She notes the necessity for each generation of women to 'turn back to history [...] a past that continues to remain hidden' (195) to rediscover women's oppression. This repetition of the turn to the past, to uncover the imprisonment of the 'mother', is precisely what is enacted in Holt's modern gothics.

The use of gothic imagery is most striking in *The Captive Wife* (1966), the title given by Hannah Gavron to her sociological study of the invisible and housebound young mothers in London. The notion of confinement was picked up by newspapers in their reviews of the study which were given titles like 'Prisoners in their own Home' or 'Walled-in Wives' (Gavron, 1983, xiii). Gavron's survey exposed the conflicted and ambivalent feelings of young women who found that the reality of marriage and motherhood, especially after the birth of their first child which tied them to the home, did not live up to the romantic image they had been sold in advertisements. Many were bored, frustrated and lonely. Two of Gavron's findings are especially interesting in relation to fiction. First, the number of women who saw their own childhoods as unhappy, often because of rows between their parents, paternal violence or maternal unhappiness (1983, Chapter 6). Secondly, that their own husbands were not seen as enemies but as allies enlisted 'against the institution of parenthood' (1983, 134). The modern gothic seems to reflect this in the way it explores the woman's fear of repeating her 'mother's' unhappiness, and suggests that marriage to the 'right man' is the only way to prevent this.

The 'captive wife' can be seen as the gothic shadow of the liberated teenager of the 1960s. She haunts the fiction of the period in a way which suggests that what the young woman of the 1960s feared most was being recaptured and imprisoned within home and family – in short, being forced to repeat her mother's life. Both Margaret Drabble and A.S. Byatt, for instance, have written of the frustrations and anger of their own mother, a highly intelligent woman confined to the role of wife and mother. 'We wanted "not to be like her"', Byatt has written (1991a, ix). Drabble's *A Summer Birdcage* (1962) and Byatt's *The Game* (1967) suggest that women in the 1960s were faced with a choice between a life of the mind *or* wife and motherhood – both in their own ways 'birdcages'. 'You can't be a sexy don', remarks Sarah in *A Summer Birdcage* (1967, 183), while Julia in *The Game* writes about 'the lives of those trapped in comfort by washing machines and small children' (1983, 47). 'The captive housewife spoke' was Drabble's sense of the way in which her novels caught the mood of the 1960s (Brannigan, 2003, 108).

In America this sense of the repetition of women's imprisonment, the fear of returning to the nineteenth century, was articulated by a woman quoted in Betty Friedan's *The Feminine Mystique* (1963):

In the past 60 years we have come full circle and the American housewife is once again trapped in a squirrel cage. If the cage is now a modern plate-glass and broadloom ranch house [. . .] the situation is not less painful than when her grandmother sat over her embroidery hoops in her gilt and plush parlour and muttered angrily about women's rights. (Friedan, 1982, 25)

The first written text of second-wave British feminism, Juliet Mitchell's 'Women: The Longest Revolution' (1966), offered a critique of the socialist movement's failure to address family structures. It also used (although less obviously) the language of imprisonment, arguing that it was women's 'confinement' (1984, 51) to the family which was the problem.

Mitchell's later *Psychoanalysis and Feminism* (1974) argued that the work of R.D. Laing, which included 11 case studies of female schizophrenics in *Sanity, Madness and the Family* (1964), was instrumental in the development of feminism because it developed a theoretical analysis of family structures and offered a 'vocabulary of protest' (Mitchell, 1975, xix). Laing's work attributed women's schizophrenia to the oppression and repression of young women within the family, and particularly to the *mother* who frustrated her daughter's attempts to attain autonomy and independence. This evidence of women's role in policing their daughters' behaviour suggests another reason for the prevalence of the female villain in the modern gothic and the biographical historical novel – the mothers (like Caroline of Ansbach) who watch their daughters married to monsters or who, like the nurse in *Menfreya*, kill them out of love. The language of feminist protest can thus be seen evolving in women's popular fiction.

Indeed, the true daughter of the 1960s modern gothic and the biographical historical novel is the feminist literary criticism of the 1970s and 1980s with its focus on female desire, doubling, images of confinement and imprisonment, and the 'madwoman in the attic'. For Gilbert and Gubar in *The Madwoman in the Attic* (1979), *the* paradigmatic female story is *Jane Eyre*, 'a story of enclosure and escape, a female *Bildungsroman*', which provides 'a pattern for countless others' (1984, 338, 339) – including, of course, Holt's novels.

The most powerful revision of *Jane Eyre*, and a far more complex and accomplished novel than anything by Hibbert, is Jean Rhys' *Wide Sargasso Sea* (1966). Rhys situates her analysis of maternal histories and the cyclical repe-tition of women's imprisonment within an understanding of the subjective nature of history and language. 'There is always the other side, always', says Antoinette to the Rochester who will rename her 'Bertha' and imprison her in Thornfield (Rhys, 1968, 106). The connections Rhys made between gender and race, and between patriarchal and colonial structures, were so far in advance of their time that it was not until the 1980s that feminist criticism recognised the way in which she had anticipated postcolonial and post-structural theory and made her novel central to a new feminist canon.

In the 1970s, the modern gothic relinquished its pre-eminent bestseller status to a new genre, the 'erotic historical' or 'bodice-ripper', pioneered in America by Kathleen Woodiwiss' *The Flame and the Flower* (1972) and Rosemary Rogers' *Sweet Savage Love* (1974). Rather than focusing on the heroine's domestic captivity, these more often depict a heroine who travels across a broad American landscape. The bodice-ripper had an important influence on British women's historical novels, not least in its reworking by Philippa Gregory (see Chapter 8). However, novels by Victoria Holt and Jean Plaidy still have a strong presence in British public libraries today.

Chess games: Dorothy Dunnett's Lymond Chronicles

Dorothy Dunnett's monumental Lymond series, with its male protagonist and broad European scale, is ostensibly very different from the popular woman's historical novel associated with Hibbert. The six novels – *The Game of Kings* (1962), *Queens' Play* (1964), *The Disorderly Knights* (1966), *Pawn in Frankincense* (1969), *The Ringed Castle* (1971) and *Checkmate* (1975) – follow the career of Francis Crawford of Lymond, between 1547 and 1558, as he ranges from his home in Scotland through England, France, Malta, Turkey and Russia, participating in some of the key events of these years.

Chess is a traditional metaphor for history,[9] as well as warfare and diplomacy. The extended chess motif of the series was inspired by Caxton's *The Game and Playe of the Chesse*, the first book to be printed in England. A guidebook for life, rather than chess, it provides the epigraphs for *The Game of Kings* (Morrison, 2001, 62). Dunnett then elaborates this controlling metaphor throughout the series: in titles, chapter headings, epigraphs and plot structures. Perhaps her most memorable use of it is in the lethal chess game using live pieces in *Pawn in Frankincense*. It is particularly appropriate because the most powerful piece on the chess board is the queen, and Dunnett, like Plaidy, is concerned with the importance of maternal history.

Dunnett's texts exploit the tension between 'fact' and 'fiction' which is inherent in the historical novel as a genre. This is encapsulated in her comment about her fictional hero, Lymond, in the Foreword to the Penguin reprints of the series: 'while he cannot change history, the wars and events which embroil him are real'. This is the central conundrum of the historical novel: because it purports to tell 'what happened', its 'real' events are always predetermined. The novelist cannot herself 'change history' without breaking her unwritten contract with the reader.

Dunnett's novels are in the tradition of the popular historical novelists she herself enjoyed: Alexander Dumas, Rafael Sabatini and Baroness Orczy. Like Orczy, Dunnett combines male and female forms (the 'male' swashbuckler and the 'female' romance) and centres the narrative around a complex male figure who plays a dual role as heroic man of action and psychologically damaged romantic hero. Her novels offer the pleasures we have come to associate with popular historical fiction – the fast-paced narrative action of the swashbuckler and the happy ending of the romance. She is, however, particularly sophisticated in her treatment of the intersection of 'history' and 'fiction'.

These are also undeniably historical novels according to Fleishman's definition: they are set over 60 years in the past, interweave fictional characters with historical personages and events, and have a strong sense of history as a shaping force on a national and, indeed, international scale. History here is not merely a decorative background for modern characters in period costume (as Orczy uses it), although part of the pleasure of the texts is in their painterly detail.[10] The intensive nature of Dunnett's research into her period – between the death of Henry VIII and the accession of Elizabeth I – is evidenced by the publication of two *Companions* compiled by Elspeth Morrison (1994, 2002), which document her sources and literary references. Dunnett makes extensive use of intertextuality, figurative language and symbolic structures in a way that we associate with 'high' art rather than popular fiction.

Dunnett is interested in the European Renaissance as the beginnings of what we regard as the modern world, especially in the building of nation-states, but also as a period which saw a flowering of art and culture, the extension of the known world through exploration and trade, and in which warfare was still tempered by the ideals of chivalry. Politics at this period were intensely familial, and the balance of power in Europe was shaped through alliances forged through marriages. While women were frequently 'pawns' in such marriages, this period also saw an unusual number of women taking power in their own right as 'queens', as well as those like Diane de Poiters who wielded power as mistresses or courtesans.

The 10-year period Dunnett maps was one of particular instability for Scotland, a small nation caught up in the power-struggles of larger countries, especially the rivalry between France and Spain, and continually threatened by its neighbour, England. Its vulnerability is epitomised by the accession, after the defeat at Solway Moss and the death of James V, of the young Mary Queen of Scots. Both 'queen' and 'pawn', she is sent to France for safety and married to the Dauphin.

As popular historical fiction, Dunnett's novels are very good indeed, not least in her self-conscious play with the conventions of the form. As Cleo McNally Kearns (1990) has pointed out, Dunnett uses several techniques which foreground the tension between 'fact' and 'fiction' in the historical novel. She 'makes drama of what could have happened' (1990, 46) – such as the frustrated assassination attempts in *Queens' Play*. She plays with the notion of predestination through her use of astrologers and prophetic visionaries: John Dee, Nostradamus and the fictional Dame de Doubtance (a figure, perhaps, for the author herself). She allows her characters to be 'self-conscious anachronisms within their own time', most obviously through Lymond's vision of 'a secular, tolerant state' that will take a 100 years more to achieve (Kearns, 1990, 46).

Finally, she blurs the line between fiction and history by the use of intertextuality. As Kearns comments:

> The sudden intrusion [of quotation] complicates the texture of the narrative by adding both another dimension of time and another level of reality, so that a 'real' character and a 'fictional' one mutually destabilise each other. [...] These interpolations increase the 'reality effect' of the novels by offering us characters who can quote texts we ourselves know or at least know to have existed, historically, but they also de-realise these texts in return by making them part of a fiction. (1990, 42, 44)

This technique is at its most complex in the central figure of Lymond, 'the kind of man who remembers everything he has ever read', who 'uses his learning as a weapon, and also as a defence' (Dunnett in Morrison, 2001, ix).

Dunnett's treatment of her protagonist is the opposite of Scott's use of Waverley as a middle-of-the-road hero. In contrast, Dunnett takes as her protagonist 'a classical hero' (Dunnett, Foreword, 1999a), a 'Renaissance man'. The chess metaphor for history centralises the importance of 'great men' or leaders as 'players' who can manipulate events. Lymond is a man of extraordinary abilities – a soldier and a scholar, a polyglot, a musician and, of course, a skilled chess player– who becomes a gifted and charismatic leader. He has the potential to be what Hegel called a 'world historical individual', a great leader who could revitalise and unify Scotland, but because he is fictional, *he cannot change history.*

In her interest in what it means to be a leader, Dunnett is typical of the 1960s.[11] The exercise of power was, Taylor comments, 'very much a 60s subject' (1994, 204). Historical fiction, such as Mary Renault's *Alexander Trilogy* and Rosemary Sutcliff's *Sword at Sunset* (1963), looked to the exceptional leaders in the past in relation to this. In Lymond, Dunnett updates the swashbuckler hero of Orczy and Sabatini to combine two figures which were central 1960s' concerns – the charismatic leader who can use his power for good or bad, and the spy, particularly the double agent, who may or may not be a traitor. The fascination with the figure of the spy can be seen in the James Bond films, John Le Carré's *The Spy Who Came in from the Cold* (1963), and the fictions of Philby discussed by Margaret Scanlan (1990, Chapter 4).

In writing historical novels, Dunnett was using a genre pioneered by a Scotsman (Sir Walter Scott) to write about Scottish history and nation formation, and she was doing so during a time when nationalism in Scotland and Wales was undergoing a revival. After the Scottish National Party won Hamilton in 1967 their membership rocketed (Sked and Cook, 1993, 241). The original of Lymond, Dunnett said, was her husband Alastair Dunnett, editor of *The Scotsman* from 1956 to 1972, who was knighted in 1995. *Checkmate* is dedicated to him: 'In the end, as in the beginning, for Alastair, who was the inspiration of the legend of Francis Crawford, and whose love for Scotland, in word and deed, has done more for her than Lymond ever could' (1999c, dedication). In its subordinating of the fictional to the 'reality' of history, this dedication seems slightly clumsy in comparison to the sophisticated interweaving Dunnett has achieved but it makes a strong political point. In looking back to the past to create an ideal leader, Dunnett is expressing the need for such a leader in the present.

The Game of Kings opens with Lymond returning to Scotland after being outlawed as a traitor for 5 years. It ends with Lymond tried for treason against Scotland and offering in his own defence a passionate plea for nationhood and for a leader who can make patriotism a force for good rather than a 'hothouse for maggots':

> Is there no one will take up this priceless thing and say, Here is a nation, with such a soul; with such talents; with these failings and this native worth? In what fashion can this one people be brought to live in full vigour and serenity, and who, in their compassion and wisdom, will take it and lead it into the path? (Dunnett, 1986, 532)

The need for a leader is explored again in Oonagh O'Dwyer's search for a 'Messiah' (1999a, 369) to lead Ireland against English colonisation in *Queens' Play*, and again in the bitter struggle for leadership between Lymond and his double and rival, Graham ('Gabriel') Reid Mallett, a false Messiah, in *The Disorderly Knights*. The final novel, *Checkmate*, ends with the union of Lymond and his English wife, Philippa, and their pledge to work together for the future. This can be read as symbolising a 'marriage' of the two countries on equal terms, as opposed to the 'rough wooing' Henry VIII had used to attempt to force the marriage of Mary Queen of Scots and his son Edward, or the prostitution of herself Oonagh contemplates with whatever man will answer her political purposes.

It is Dunnett's treatment of gender and its relation to history as a fantasy space that is most interesting in relation to the concerns of the woman's historical novel. In Lymond, she has constructed an enigmatic and mysterious but ultimately ideal hero seen from a woman's point of view. Like Orczy's Sir Percy Blakeney and Sabatini's Scaramouche, Lymond is a performer and a trickster figure. A consummate actor, he constructs a mask that conceals his own psychological vulnerability, which stems from his fear that he is the product of his mother's adultery and therefore not only a younger son but also a bastard.

As a trickster-hero, Lymond's participation in the interstices of history both mirrors women's marginality and fulfils female fantasies of power through reinstating maternal history. Barbara Greenfield's Jungian discussion of the significance of the trickster as a figure of liberation is especially relevant here. She argues that, for women, the trickster represents 'the son who over-throws the authority of the father in the name of freedom and transformation'

(1985, 192). Throughout the series, although most explicitly in *The Game of Kings* where he is an excommunicated outlaw, Lymond is an outsider who operates in the interstices of 'real' history and *outside* the law. In *Queens' Play*, for instance, he infiltrates the French court disguised as an Irish bard, Thady Boy Ballagh, in order to try to protect the young Queen from assassination. His actions, and his loyalties, are therefore open to the kind of misinterpretation that leads to the accusation that he is a traitor.

This problem of interpretation is repeated at the level of the text, as Dunnett manipulates point of view to withhold important information from the reader. The reader usually sees Lymond through the eyes of other characters, and therefore according to their (mis)judgement of him. The reader, like the other characters, has to 'read' Lymond, to penetrate his mask, and is continually in doubt about his actions and motives. In *Queens' Play*, Dunnett takes this to an extreme in the opening sections where it is not until nearly 50 pages into the book that Thady Boy is revealed as Lymond in disguise. His drunken excesses on a later occasion are explained only afterwards as the result of belladonna poisoning. Dunnett uses this control of point of view to even more dramatic effect in an extraordinary sleight of hand in the final novel where she appears to kill off Lymond (it is actually his sister) and then resurrects him to provide a happy ending.

The 'unreadable' hero is a familiar motif from romantic fiction where women are continually attempting to work out men's motives. Dunnett develops this to a more complex degree, partly through Lymond's use of quotation as a defensive mask. This also foregrounds the ways in which Lymond is himself a 'text' to be read for *women's* pleasure. In *The Game of Kings*, it is the blind girl, Christian Stewart, who 'sees' Lymond more clearly than anyone else. His titular wife Philippa feels that leaving him is 'like losing unfinished a manuscript, beautiful, absorbing and difficult, which she had long wanted to read' (Dunnett, 1973b, 565). Reading here is a sensual act and Lymond is an erotic object for the female gaze. His body is fragmented – again, a technique used in romantic fiction where it is more often the woman's body which is fragmented. It is repeatedly signified through references to his hair (usually 'gilt', 'yellow' or 'golden'), his eyes ('cornflower blue') and his hands ('fine', 'flawless', but also scarred by his time as a galley slave). Historical fiction here is a space which privileges the female gaze and women's pleasure in both text and male body.

However, despite his masculine athleticism, Lymond is also feminised in ways which construct him as an object of identification for the female reader. He is frequently referred to as catlike and has 'kitten's eyes' (Dunnett, 1986, 22). He is most effective operating outside male power structures, often in disguise or as a spy. He is repeatedly shown at the mercy of a body which renders him physically incapable, through belladonna poisoning, opium addiction and debilitating migraines which make him blind. He is often outrageously camp, especially in his use of irony and parody. And he becomes the object of male desire for Robin Stewart in *Queens' Play* and for Jerrott, who marries Lymond's half-sister as a surrogate for Lymond himself.

Ventriloquised by a female writer, male gender identity here (as in so many women's historical novels) is a matter of performance, a kind of drag act. Tellingly, the poem which Dunnett gives to Lymond to reveal his love for Philippa, '*Tant que je vivre mon cueur ne chanera*' [Long as I live my heart will never change...] (1999c, 96), was probably originally written by a woman, Marguerite of Austria, and addressed to a man (Morrison, 2001, 343). Lymond is a woman-identified man and a male-impersonator – he is, indeed, a woman author posing as a man in order to rewrite history.

The theme that unites and structures the series is Lymond's search for 'the history of his origins' (1999c, 407) or rather, since he refuses to undertake the task, Philippa's search for his origins on his behalf. This echoes Sabatini's *Scaramouche*, with its famous opening lines: 'He was born with a gift of laughter and a sense that the world was mad. And that was all his patrimony. His very paternity was obscure' (Sabatini, 2001, 1). Sabatini's André-Louis Moreau, lawyer, actor and swordsman, is an important precursor for Lymond but Dunnett reworks the issue of legitimacy in important ways.

While it is André-Louis' 'patrimony' which has to be established for him to take his rightful place in society, Dunnett foregrounds Lymond's matrilineal genealogy. This is a search into history as, in Barthes' words, 'the time when my mother was alive before me' (1993, 65). It is Lymond's mother, Sybilla, the most significant person in his life, who holds the key to his origins, and his estrangement from her is represented as psychologically devastating. His most powerful enemy is also female: Margaret Lennox, the woman who seduced him as a vulnerable 16-year-old, had him set up as a traitor and deported to the French galleys as a slave, thus separating him from his family and his country.

The books enact a common male plot line: the flight from the mother which Berthold Schoene-Harwood (2000) aptly calls 'domophobia'. But they then reverse this to bring about a reconciliation with the mother. *The Game of Kings* ends, unusually, with Lymond in his *mother's* arms. This is repeated in *Checkmate*, which ends with his union with Philippa, sanctioned by his mother through the final revelation of the secret of his birth. This complicated secret, finally revealed through the aegis of Philippa, is that Lymond is his mother's son, but that his father was not Gavin Crawford, the husband who tormented her, but the man she really loved. Lymond is thus the child of a reciprocated love rather than merely a lawfully sanctioned marriage. The twist to this is that Sybilla's lover was Gavin's father, the man Lymond had regarded as his grandfather, and the original legendary Francis Crawford. The final twist is that Sybilla had been married to him before she married Gavin, thus making Lymond not only legitimate but also the rightful heir to Cultar.

Dunnett's plot structure coincides very closely with Freud's account of childhood fantasies in 'Family Romances' (1909). He argues that a 'younger child' uses imaginative stories:

> in order to rob those born before him of their prerogatives – in a way which reminds one of historical intrigues; [...] he often has no hesitation in attributing to his mother as many fictitious love affairs as he himself has competitors. (Freud, 1959, 240)

Moreover, Freud goes on to offer an 'interesting variant' where 'the hero or author returns to legitimacy himself while his brothers and sisters are eliminated by being bastardised' (240). This exactly describes Dunnett's version of the 'family romance'. However, Dunnett genders this so that her texts result in the 'exaltation' of the mother, not, as in Freud's, the father. While the final plot revelations ostensibly replace Lymond within the line of *patrilineal* inheritance, the 'Law of the Father', his burning of the marriage lines which provide legal proof symbolises his acceptance of a place outside it. His alignment is with what might be seen as a 'Law of the Mother', which operates in the interstices of patriarchy. The figure and power of the Father is doubly erased and displaced here. The 'bad father' Gavin is not in reality Lymond's father at all, but the 'good father' is his 'grandfather', a less powerful figure despite his legendary status because of his displacement by generation and age.

The text rejects the kind of patriarchal masculinity represented by Gavin Crawford and replaces it instead with the matriarchally sanctioned masculinity represented by Lymond, a man who unites 'feminine' and 'masculine' virtues and acknowledges the power of the feminine. The important lineage here is the maternal history represented by Sybilla, who is repeatedly affirmed by the texts as the central figure in Lymond's life. History here, for both man and women, is a matter of matrilineal genealogy.

This emphasis on maternal power is echoed on the larger stage of history where Europe itself has a sudden excess of female rulers. 'In a hive of Queens, Russia holds the last masculine cell. [...] The Tsardom which does not admit the power of women', one character tells Lymond (Dunnett, 1999b, 207). Although Lymond's journey to Russia is a domophobic flight from the feminine, it is significant that his influence there is a civilising one, curbing the masculine excess and violence associated with the Tsar's rule. It is also significant that the Tsar, a rampantly male ruler, who will not 'admit the power of women', descends into a spiral of mad violence after Lymond leaves.

When Lymond's brother remarks that Lymond needs 'a master', it is Sybilla who replies, 'Or a mistress' (Dunnett, 1973a, 493). That 'mistress' is variously his mother, Philippa, and his country. Throughout the series, Sybilla is identified with Scotland, linking mother-love with love of the mother-country.

Lymond's reconciliation with Sybilla is also a return to the country he loves, and an affirmation of his commitment to serve that country, reinforced by his marriage to Philippa. It is his feminine qualities which make Lymond an ideal leader, as Alexander's bisexuality makes him exceptional in Renault's trilogy. Both men are as equally at home in the 'East' as in the West, suggesting openness also to racial difference.[12]

The woman's popular historical novel in the 1960s moves in two directions. It is used by Hibbert to expose women's victimisation in history. It is used by Dunnett to suggest that history, like gender, is a kind of text, and that as such it can be rewritten by women to encompass their own desires and pleasures. In both, history is rewritten at the level of family and nation as a matter of maternal influence and power. But because we 'cannot change history', this can only be done in the interstices of known history through the intervention of popular fiction.

7
Selling Women's History: Popular Historical Fiction in the 1970s

In the 1970s the woman's historical novel was widely visible but in a range of sub-genres regarded as *popular* fiction and therefore disregarded by literary critics: the historical romance associated with Mills and Boon and Barbara Cartland; the family saga reinvigorated by Susan Howatch; the American-influenced 'bodice-ripper' or 'erotic historical'; the social histories of Catherine Cookson; Mary Stewart's Arthurian novels. Like the modern gothic of the 1960s which they replaced, these texts are associated with the mass-market paperback. They are also associated with an author or publisher marketed as a 'brand-name' easily recognised by readers – 'Barbara Cartland', 'Catherine Cookson', 'Mills and Boon' and so on.

The high visibility of these authors and the promotion of such popular genres in 1970s Britain were the result of strategies developed by publishers in response to economic uncertainties. The demise of the commercial lending libraries in the 1960s left the public libraries with the sole responsibility for lending fiction. Given that libraries accounted for 20 per cent of all books sales, the effect of financial cut-backs during periods of recession was to force librarians to make conservative choices in their book-buying (Bloom, 2002, 74). Thus publishers increasingly marketed authors as tried and tested 'brand-names', and they looked for potential 'bestsellers' which could be promoted through television tie-ins and other marketing strategies (Bloom, 2002, 75).

The global market became increasingly important. Clive Bloom notes that Futura paid £160,000 for the rights to the Australian Colleen McCullough's *The Thornbirds*, and used £60,000 in its promotional budget (2002, 75). The 'erotic historicals' or 'bodice-rippers' of the Americans Rosemary Rogers and Kathleen Woodiwiss were 'probably the most valuable finds any paperback publisher made in the 1970s' according to John Sutherland (1981, 76).

Television also fed the appetite for popular 'historical' genres with high-profile adaptations of novels by Catherine Cookson, Susan Howatch, Mary Stewart and Colleen McCullough.[1] The television serial of Colleen McCullough's *The Thornbirds*, Cora Kaplan recorded, so 'profoundly affected' her that she rushed out to buy the paperback (1990, 120). Over two decades later, I still have a vivid memory of the rape scene in the television drama-tisation of Catherine Cookson's *The Mallens*.

One of the paradoxes of the 1970s is that the rise of feminism was accompanied by the rise of the paperback popular romance novel in both Britain and America. At first glance, this turn to romance, particularly historical romance, might seem to mark a reactionary shrinking from the politics of feminism, a nostalgic desire to return to a simpler and more conservative world of class and gender certainties. The picture is, as usual, more complex.

In *The Romance Revolution* (1987), Carol Thurston argues that the popular romance of the 1970s divided into two basic types – 'the sweet romance and the erotic romance – with the fundamental difference being the presence or absence of specific sexual behavioural norms and explicit sexual activities' (1987, 7). As Thurston sees it, the 'erotic historical' sparked the romance revolution by developing a new, independent, and adventurous heroine, who combines the chaste heroine and sexual Other Woman of previous texts (1987, 8). Although the 'erotic historical' clearly influenced the British market, it seems to have been a particularly American phenomenon.[2]

Another crucial player in the paperback market was Mills and Boon, who merged with the North American Harlequin in 1972 and changed to paperback publication, increasingly selling through newsagents and mail order service, rather than bookshops and libraries. Their business expanded rapidly, with 33 per cent increase in sales between 1972 and 1974 (Sutherland, 1981, 85). Finally, the romance revolution also heightened the demand for Barbara Cartland's novels. She produced around 136 novels during the decade (Henderson, 1990, 112–18).

Two things are especially interesting here. First is the fact that publishers were responding to the realisation that *women* made up the bulk of both buyers and borrowers of fiction, so they were producing and marketing novels which explicitly appealed to women. Clive Bloom notes that almost three-quarters of all fiction is bought or borrowed by women and that this pattern has remained consistent from 1900 to 1999, with genres 'mutating' rather than changing over time to suit new tastes. Thus 'women readers are vital to the book trade' (2002, 51). The 1970s, Sutherland points out, proved that women's fiction could provide profitable 'blockbusters' (1981, 74). The phenomenal success of Mills and Boon was a direct result of their ability to tap this female market.[3]

The second interesting factor is that a considerable proportion of this mass-market popular women's fiction is 'historical' in one way or another, even if it is not in ways which critics of the 'classical historical novel' would recognise as such. This is particularly obvious in the case of the 'erotic historical' discussed by Thurston, Barbara Cartland's novels or the historical romances published in the 'Masquerade' series Mills and Boon launched in 1977.[4]

By 1979, Mills and Boon had published 46 novels in this series. Given the sustained popularity of Georgette Heyer's work, it is not surprising that publishers turned to historical romance for sure-fire sales. Heyer herself died in 1974, leaving a gap in the market which Mills and Boon were clearly trying to exploit through their use of the name 'Masquerade', a concept she repeatedly deploys in her early work. However, the family sagas of Susan Howatch and the majority of Catherine Cookson's novels are also historical.

These historical novels are in direct contrast to the fictional form most closely associated with the feminist movement in the 1970s, which is the 'confessional realist' novel. A form of consciousness-raising, these centralised women's experience in the contemporary moment in order to expose the ways in which women suffered through oppression. As Nicci Gerrard puts it, they answered the need for novels that 'tell it as it is' (1989, 112). Within feminist thinking, romance was rejected as an ideology which sugar-coated the economic and social realities of gender inequality within sex and marriage. The exposure of male violence, both rape and domestic violence – for instance, the fact that 58 per cent of all women murdered were killed by their husbands (Rowbotham, 1997, 420) – and the campaign for the 1976 Domestic Violence and Matrimonial Proceedings Act, made that sugar-coating look especially thin.

Germaine Greer derided the popular romance in *The Female Eunuch* (1971), taking Heyer as her example, and declaring that, 'The traits invented for [the hero] have been invented by women cherishing the chains of their bondage' (1993, 202). In *The Dialectic of Sex* (1971), Shulamith Firestone similarly argued that romantic love was 'love corrupted by its power context – the sex class system – into a diseased form of love that then in turn reinforces this sex class system' (1972, 139). The rejection of the romance plot by 'serious' women writers goes back into the 1960s. In 1974, Rebecca West wrote an astute piece entitled 'And They All Lived Unhappily Ever After', where she pointed to the preoccupation with the pain and unhappiness resulting from relationships between the sexes in the novels of Margaret Drabble, Edna O'Brien and Penelope Mortimer.

Women's fiction at this point splits between the 'serious' novel, typically confessional realism concerned with women's predicament in the contemporary moment and consciously eschewing the romance plot, and the 'popular' novel, epitomised by the popular romance with its happy ending. Although a handful of serious women writers (Naomi Mitchison, Julia O'Faolain, Rosemary Sutcliff) are still writing other kinds of historical novels (which have also been critically neglected), on the whole the woman's historical novel at this point is most closely associated with the popular forms.

Despite the increased attention to sexual politics, however, 'women's desires', as Sheila Rowbotham puts it, 'remained decidedly murky' (1997, 433). It was, she suggests, often popular culture which 'grasped the ambiguities that politics bypassed' (462). jay Dixon, in her study of Mills and Boon novels, illustrates this point when she notes that her reading of popular romance novels was at its height at the point when she was most actively involved in feminism. 'It may have been', she suggests, 'that at the time I was splitting my emotions into two: using feminism to express my anger and romances to express my needs and love' (1999, 41). The number of feminists who later came out as closet romance readers suggests that Dixon was not alone, and that romance reading answered needs not satisfied or acknowledged by the feminist confessional realist texts. Lillian Robinson's discussion of her enjoyment of Heyer in 'On Reading Trash' (1978) was a particularly astute analysis of the phenomenon.

From the early 1980s, critics such as Janet Batsleer, Ann Rosalind Jones, Janice Radway and jay Dixon generated increasingly sophisticated readings of the popular romance. Most recently, Dixon has argued that Mills and Boon romances, like feminism, 'argue for a change in the way society is organised, from male-orientated to female-orientated' (1999, 9). They give women power, she suggests, by transmuting sex into love, a move by which the hero is drawn into the heroine's world. Most critics, however, with the exception of Janice Radway and Carol Thurston who discuss American historical romances, have discussed contemporary romances. Since readers themselves see significant differences between historical and contemporary romances (Dixon, 1999, 34), it is clearly not appropriate to treat them as a single genre.

As with the modern gothic, the key question here is *why* so many of these texts, particularly the romances, used historical backgrounds. As Gillian Beer noted, romance is 'a peculiarly precise register of the ideals and terrors of the age [...] it forms itself about the collective subconscious of an age' (1970, 58). Hence it has always flourished in periods of rapid change. Beer believed that by 1970, romance had been degraded into 'the insipidity of women's magazine fiction' (1970, 78). In fact, we can now see that the popular romance of the 1970s precisely registers women's 'ideals and terrors' in a period when feminism was exposing them to the cold light of day.

Since romance, as Beer notes, depends on distance between its subject matter and its audience to enable its fulfilment of desire, it has frequently deployed the past as a setting to provide that distance (1970, 5). The popular historical romance of the 1970s offers a good example of that 'necessary mingling of "distance" and "reality"' which Helen Hughes argues enables the working out of the hopes and fears of its readership (1993, 1). The 'realism' is provided by description of a 'real' period not too distanced from the reader (hence the popularity of the Regency and nineteenth century), while the historical distance simultaneously provides an exotic setting for the fantasy of romance. The historical setting both validates the romance as 'real' through its putative verisimilitude and exposes it as 'fantasy' by locating it in a lost and irretrievable 'past'. Moreover, the centralisation of women's fears and desires is dramatically enhanced in the historical romance where what we normally think of as 'history' – the 'public' and 'masculine' sphere of politics and war – is pushed into the background in favour of the 'private' sphere of love and home where women are depicted as having power. .

The erotic historical, Thurston argues, acted as a kind of 'testing ground for women readers struggling to find new ways of seeing and thinking about themselves and their place in the world' (1987, 87). This is particularly true of the *historical* romances. Even the most cursory historical background, as Lillian Robinson argues, 'forces the reader into some definition, whether considered or superficial, of history and historical process' and thus 'serves to promote a vision of historical possibilities for the woman reader herself' (1978, 206). By foregrounding historical change, woman's historical novels offer the reader a retrospective view of how things *were* (particularly in relation to the restrictions imposed upon women) and thus point the way to possible change in the future.

It is important, however, to distinguish between the different types of historical romance and the ways in which they use history. Even Mills and Boon novels, Dixon demonstrates, are not monolithic but change in response to historical shifts, and, indeed, according to individual author. The popular tendency to use Barbara Cartland, self-styled 'Queen of Romance', as a byword for what is worst about women's historical romance has damaged other writers, such as Heyer, who have been mistakenly aligned with her. This association of women's historical fiction with the popular romance (that is, with 'trash' or 'pulp' fiction) is one of the factors which has led to the neglect of women's historical fiction as a genre.

Cartland's reasons for turning to historical settings are both revealing and, at first sight, simply reactionary, particularly in contrast to the erotic historical. Publishers, Joseph McAleer notes, wanted Cartland to write about sex but she kept saying, '"No" That's why I write in the past. Everyone's a virgin in the past; it was alright' (McAleer, 1992, 121). By 'everyone' Cartland means the middle-class young girls who are her protagonists, since her worldly and rakish heroes are clearly *not* virgins. Cartland turned to historical romances, set between 1870 and 1914, in order to continue to write about virginal woman, and to validate a double sexual standard which was being eroded, but which had, she implies, given women a bargaining tool which they lost in the emancipated 1960s. This reverses the ways in which the historical novel had been used to circumvent the taboos against writing about sexuality earlier in the century. In a post-Pill and newly feminist decade, it was virginity and romance, as well as the happy ending, which had become taboo in *serious* fiction.

In Cartland's books it is the heroine's virginity which transforms male lust into 'divine' love and thereby redeems the hero. In *No Time for Love* (1976) and *Love Has His Way* (1979), Cartland not only uses a period setting (the former is set in 1904, the latter in the Regency), but invokes an even earlier 'history' in the form of classical Greece to posit this transcendent 'divine' love which (in contrast to Renault's use of the same culture) is *always* heterosexual. Larina in *No Time for Love* is typical in both her naivety and her ellipsis-ridden discourse: 'I am not... really sure... about what men and women... do when they... make love... but it must be... wonderful... because the gods used to... assume human disguise...' (1967, 169). When she and the hero kiss, 'It was as if he lifted her up to Olympus where they were both gods' (1976, 171).

The perceptive readings by both Janet Batsleer (1981) and Rosalind Brunt (1984) suggest that Cartland's texts are more in tune with the feminist movement than Cartland herself admitted. Batsleer recognises that the gendered conflicts of Cartland's fiction – conflicts *between* private and public spheres, and *within* the private sphere of the home itself – 'are the conflicts which have produced feminism itself' (1981, 55). Brunt goes further and argues that Cartland's avowed moral message as a romance writer is undercut by her storytelling which offers a materialist account of gender relations, suggesting that love is 'the economically rational career for a woman under most forms of patriarchy' (1984, 148).

Much of the scorn directed at Cartland comes from the fact that her (short) books endlessly repeat the same basic elements – the aristocratic and rakish hero, the innocent and fragile heroine with a name ending in 'a' (Larina, Romana, etc.), the upper-class 'period' setting, and so on. Brunt suggests that the pleasure of these texts is this 'bricolage' effect which eases the reader into a familiar world (1984, 146). This marks three key differences from Heyer. First, despite her use of 'Author's Notes' to signal her 'research', Cartland gives a minimum of 'historical' detail. Secondly, her language, as Brunt points out, has an 'oral' quality (1984, 146)[5] with very short paragraphs and bland prose which contrasts with Heyer's delight in linguistic richness. Thirdly, Cartland's bricolage offers none of the ironic gameplaying with generic conventions which is evident even in Heyer's earliest novels.

The historical novels in Mills and Boon's 'Masquerade' series fall somewhere between Heyer and Cartland. The series' title recalls Heyer's deployment of the motif of masquerade and draws attention to the way in which the 'historical' settings act as a 'mask' for desires which are otherwise inexpressible. Even within this series, however, there is considerable variation in the way in which history is deployed. Some texts are blatant imitations of Heyer. Imitations of Heyer's work began as early as 1950 (Hodge, 1985, 92), and they are especially interesting because they show the extraordinary influence this under-rated author has had on women's imaginations.

Jane Wilby's *Eleanor and the Marquis* (1977) recycles both plot elements (the Yorkshire daughter of a Vicar is made the 'rage' of the London 'ton' and marries the foremost 'Arbiter' of fashion) from Heyer's *Arabella* (1949) and language ('fustian', *convenable*, *tendre*, 'Tulips of Fashion') from the Heyer canon in general. Even the characters' names are lifted from Heyer: the hero's name 'Justin' is from *These Old Shades*, while Wilby's Eleanor, like Heyer's

Arabella, has a brother called 'Bertram'. Marguerite Bell's *A Rose for Danger* (1977), with its gentleman highwayman and Bow Street Runner, is another Heyer-influenced text, although with less grasp of either narrative consistency or the historical nuances of fashion than Heyer.

'History' here becomes pastiche – an imitation of an imitation. Heyer herself, of course, borrowed plot elements from other texts in her early work (notably from Ethel M. Dell and Jeffery Farnol), while her later language increasingly became a knowing pastiche of Jane Austen. The difference is that Heyer's novels were based on extensive original research and knowledge of the Regency period, while these authors' 'historical' knowledge comes second-hand from Heyer herself. The woman's historical novel is often a recreation of a historical period which has been filtered through the eyes of a woman writer who centralises women's experience and privileges women's desire. Thus Jane Austen offers a woman's eye view of the Regency years which makes them available as a background for later writers. In her later texts, Heyer's self-conscious play with romance conventions and her use of 'Austenesque' language draw attention to the artificiality of the form while acknowledging the reality of women's desires. 'History' in Heyer's novels *is* text, a linguistic construct just as much as in the work of postmodernist theorists. And the pleasure of the text is as much in the reader's recognition of Heyer's construction of this artificial world as in her acknowledgement (like Austen) of female desire.

Female desire is also central to the imported American bodice-rippers, starting with Kathleen Woodiwiss' *The Flame and the Flower* (1972) and Rosemary Rogers' *Sweet Savage Love* (1974), which move in the opposite direction to Cartland in transposing a post-1960s sexual permissive back into a pseudo-historical context. 'History' here becomes a fantasy space for a form of soft pornography which invokes shades of de Sade. As John Sutherland comments, in the bodice-rippers: 'The unliberated condition of women – incarcerated, flagellated, degraded, violated – was celebrated time and time again, with a great deal of accurate sexual and inaccurate historical detail' (1981, 85). The 'unliberated' position of women in history excuses them from responsibility for what happens to them. Both Rogers' and Woodiwiss' heroines are raped by men who later come to love them.

This replicates a general pattern in 1970s romance when sexual violence together with the aggressively dominant hero became common in Mills and Boon (Dixon, 1999, 63). Dixon connects this to Susan Brownmiller's influential argument in *Against Our Will* (1975) that all men can use the threat of rape to keep women in a state of fear (1999, 144–5). The Mills and Boon novel, Dixon argues, depicts men who use sexual coercion as a form of domination in order to argue that they must learn to recognise sex as an expression of love. This is taken to an extreme in the bodice-ripper but not all readers responded favourably: Rogers was 'universally detested' by the group of American romance readers Radway interviewed (1987, 69).

In the 1970s the British Mills and Boon historical romance encompasses both attitudes to sex. Some use the historical setting (as Wilby and Bell do) to confine the expression of sexual desire to a kiss, while others become more explicitly sexual. Elizabeth de Guise's *Puritan Wife* (1977), for instance, uses the opposition between Puritan and Cavalier to map gender differences. The sexually experienced Cavalier husband initiates his naïve Puritan wife into the pleasures of the bedroom, while she introduces him to the emotional happiness produced by the fidelity implied by her name 'Constance'. Her Puritanism is the reason for her lack of sexual knowledge.

However, de Guise also uses the marriage between Puritan and Cavalier – they are 'not so very different after all' (1977, 87) – as an image which conflates the necessary unity of the sexes with that of the nation as a whole. 'The breach between Cavalier and Roundhead will have to be healed if England is to prosper', comments the Earl (1977, 115). This desire for both national and gender unity rather simplistically replicates key concerns of the 1970s, conscious of 'civil war' between the sexes as well as divisions between the components of the 'United' Kingdom, with the 'Troubles' in Northern Ireland and the revival of Scottish and Welsh nationalism.

Far more complex and playful use is made of the conventions of the historical romance in the work of the sisters Jane Aiken Hodge and Joan Aiken. As Hodge admitted in her perceptive study of Georgette Heyer, her own early novels 'show far more of a debt to [Heyer's] than I like to recognise now' (1985, 92). Her texts are less politically conservative than Heyer's, with particularly sympathetic treatment of revolutionary movements. In *Judas Flowering* (1976), a text which uses an American Revolutionary setting which would have appealed to bodice-ripper fans, the heroine Mercy Phillips lives a double life as the 'Reb Pamphleteer', printing revolutionary pamphlets, while she is ostensibly acting the ideal hostess to British troops. This interest in masquerade is also obvious in *Red Sky at Night* (1978) where the heroine cross-dresses to pose as her feckless brother. Hodge pushes the romance plot to the edge of parody by pairing up the classically saturnine Earl of Hawth and the heroine's *mother*, while the heroine gets the brash American heir who starts off courting her mother.

This intertextual play with the romance conventions is even more sophisticated in the work of Joan Aiken, better known as a writer of historical fantasy for children. Like Heyer, Aiken is fascinated and delighted by archaic language, especially underworld slang, and the ways in which this can be used to convey the 'difference' of the past. As Roland Barthes pointed out in 1967:

> The only feature which distinguishes historical discourse from other kinds is a paradox: the 'fact' can only exist linguistically, as a term in a discourse, yet we behave as if it were a simple reproduction of something on another plane of existence altogether, some extra-structural 'reality'.

> Historical discourse is presumably the only kind which aims at a referent 'outside' itself that can in fact never be reached. (Barthes, 1970, 153–4)

As a form of historical discourse, archaic language foregrounds the difference and impenetrability of the past. An intuitive understanding of this textual construction of history where 'reality' can 'never be reached' seems to free both Heyer and Aiken to recreate the past as a space for desire. Their language play signals the status of the historical novel as a constructed artifact which does not represent the past but recreates it as 'fantasy'.

Aiken repeatedly teases the reader by invoking and then subverting the conventions of the form. In *The Smile of the Stranger* (1978) the capable heroine, Juliana, escapes from revolutionary France in a balloon, aided by the unromantically tubby Herr Welcker. Aiken parodies the attractions of the historical romance hero by having Juliana want a lover resembling Charles I, rather than Herr Welcker, whom she fends off with a bodkin when he tries to kiss her. At the end of the novel, Herr Welcker, having shed the excess poundage, is revealed as a Count and Juliana discovers that kissing him is actually rather pleasant.

Aiken's heroines are intelligent and informed 'readers' of books, situations and people (though not always of the heroes). Sometimes they are also writers. The later *Deception* (1987) takes her parody of form to the extreme, using intertextual references to Austen and the Brontës as well as Byron and Scott. The heroine is not only masquerading as someone else, but is also the author of the evocatively named *Wicked Lord Love*. The 'deception' of the title is carried out at a textual level on the reader who thinks she is reading a historical romance, only to find Alvey rejecting her suitors and turning to her writing. Alvey is ultimately concerned with a 'horrible choice', not between men, but 'between my own imagination and the real world' (1988, 412). Romance novels, Aiken is slyly hinting in a novel dedicated to 'all Female Writers, past and present', fulfil female desires more fully than any real man. This is not least because they offer women the opportunity to *be* men, as Alvey's satirical hero indulges in the excesses forbidden to a well-brought-up young lady. Aiken's work anticipates some of the genre and gender-play which we have come to associate with the feminist writing of the 1980s and 1990s.

The second important historical form used by women writers in the 1970s was the family saga reinvented by Susan Howatch in *Penmarric* (1971) and *Cashelmara* (1974), and used by Catherine Cookson in the *Mallen Trilogy* (see pp. 159–67). Both authors rework the saga form used by Galsworthy and Bentley, making it a more explicitly historical form. Whereas Galsworthy and Bentley bring their sagas up to the contemporary moment, Howatch and Cookson end theirs in a period which is still 'history' to most of their readers.[6] The result is to distance the treatment of class and gender in a way which makes it far more politically conservative.

The central unit which drives the narrative structure of the saga is not the couple (as in romance) but the family. Thus these texts do write beyond the marriage ending. Howatch's lengthy blockbusters use their eponymous houses to stand for the family as a social structure. Within this structure, inheritance determines the relationships between property and gender. Women's status *as* property is the major theme signalled in the opening sentences of both books. While Bentley used the family saga form in *Inheritance* to represent a much wider public history, Howatch's family sagas relegate 'public' history to a backdrop against which private family relationships are played out through the generations.

Howatch's texts are what Joseph Turner calls 'disguised historical novels' (1979, 337). As the epigraphs indicate, *Penmarric* takes the story of Henry II, Eleanor of Aquitane and 'Fair Rosamond' and replays it in nineteenth-century Cornwall. *Cashelmara* transplants the stories of Edward I, II and III from fourteenth-century England to nineteenth-century Ireland. The effect of this, despite the 'regional' settings, is to deny the social, cultural and economic specificity of different periods of history and, indeed, national and geographic specificity, and to suggest that nothing changes (at least up until the post-war period). Family relationships are extreme in their disfunctionality but the repetition of family patterns through the generations suggests their universality. Howatch does suggest the subjectivity of historical narrative through her use of several first-person narrators but since these are not stylistically differentiated, this again blurs specificity into similarity.

Penmarric illustrates particularly well the way in which historical distance functions in the family saga 'to clear a site for the representation of class and sexual inequalities without being obliged either to criticise or defend them directly' (Bridgwood, 1986, 179). This is why the family sagas of Howatch and those who followed her (including Cookson) do not extend into the post-war era because to do so would be to invite comparison between 'then' and 'now', and to acknowledge their interconnectedness. These texts deny precisely the comparison that Bentley demanded her readers to make in *Inheritance*, where she presented the past as the 'prehistory' of the immediate present. The same can be said of the historical romance of the 1970s in general.

The 'self-experienced' past: Catherine Cookson's social histories

The phenomenal success of Catherine Cookson's books, given that the majority deploy a historical setting, suggests a popular and influential version of the woman's historical novel which is worth investigating.[7] Cookson had an extremely strong profile during the 1970s which saw the publication of her most successful novel, *The Mallen Streak* (1973), which sold 1,27,000 copies by 1993 (Goodwin, 1994, 310). The *Mallen Trilogy* (*The Mallen Streak*, *The Mallen Girl* and *The Mallen Litter* [both 1974]) was made into a television series by Granada in 1979. Like Heyer, Cartland and Plaidy, Cookson became an authorial brand-name but she wrote a very different kind of historical fiction. In Cardiff Public Library, for instance, while Heyer, Cartland and Plaidy are shelved under 'Historical Fiction', Cookson's novels, even those with nineteenth-century settings such as *The Dwelling Place* (1971), *The Girl* (1977) or the *Mallen Trilogy*, are shelved under 'General Fiction'. This is more than an accident of shelving. It reflects the particular version of 'history' which Cookson constructs in her novels, which is concerned with working-class people rather than historical personages or even imaginary aristocrats, and is strongly regional in the specificity of its setting in the North East where she grew up. This history *appears* to spring out of her own experience rather than research in history books.

In one of the few critical studies to take Cookson seriously, Bridget Fowler has argued that she is 'the leading exponent of what can be called the "social democratic" subgenre' of popular romantic fiction (1991, 73), and that her work alternates 'strands of realism with redemptive utopia' (3). Cookson herself deeply resented having the label 'romance writer' 'tacked on' to work she saw as realistic (Cookson, 1999, 29). But, as Fowler notes, the realism of Cookson's descriptions of working-class experience and values is always in tension with her formulaic plot structures which offer the reader 'refuge in conservative myths' (Fowler, 1991, 97). Cookson's novels map an upward trajectory, the classic rags-to-riches structure of the regional saga novel, in which the protagonist overcomes poverty to rise into wealth and middle-class status. Her attainment of this is frequently indicated by marriage to a man of higher-class status which symbolises a utopian vision of class reconciliation – 'a fantasy of love binding together the servant and gentry spheres' (Fowler, 1991, 75).

Cookson's use of history is central to both her realism and her conservative utopianism. Much of the 'realism' of Cookson's novels stems from her regional settings (only one is set outside the North East). This produces a materialist sense of the ways in which economic and social factors shape historical movements and the lives of ordinary people. Over the last two centuries the landscape of the North East has undergone huge transformations. From an agricultural community it changed to a booming industrial economy in the mid-nineteenth century, when the area became 'an empire of coal mines, steel works and railway, not forgetting glassworks' and 'a few outstanding men rose from muck to millions' (Cookson, 1999, 81). The 1930s saw the depression which spawned the Jarrow Hunger Marchers. The mid- and late twentieth-century brought de-industrialisation and a Welfare State which eradicated much of the poverty. Ironically, the landscapes of industrial Tyneside and the Northumberland countryside have now become a tourist destination, a kind of historical theme park known as 'Catherine Cookson Country'.

Like Scott, Cookson is interested in how major historical transformations affect everyday life and people, and she is particularly concerned with the class struggles these engender. But Cookson's books present themselves as being about what Lukács called 'self-experienced history' (1962, 84), or as what could be called 'autobiographical history', even when they are written about a period well before she was born. Conversely, her novels present themselves as being 'historical' (about 'the past') even when she is writing about a time which she herself experienced. Thus although Cookson is writing, as Fowler notes, 'Condition of England' novels, she is writing about the past 'condition' of the North East rather than, as Elizabeth Gaskell writes, about the immediate present.

This sense of retrospection is in part explained by the fact that Cookson did not start writing until she had moved from the North East to live in Hastings where she married into the middle classes. Even when they are set within her own lifetime, therefore, her novels look back in time to a 'past' landscape which is part of her own personal 'history' and which has now changed radically. Moreover, as a kind of 'expatriate' she was looking back to a period before the post-war Welfare State, a watershed moment in eradicating much of the poverty and the physical landscape which her books detail.

Cookson herself regarded her work as an accessible version of 'social history', describing her early novels as:

the social history of the North East, readable social history interwoven with the lives of the people; and it is after all, simply the people who make history, whether they are ascending to thrones or fighting wars; it is people who create not only replicas of each other but atmosphere, environment and the meat for writers. (Cookson, 1999, 30)

While people 'make' history, Cookson is equally interested in how history, as both environment (economic, social and cultural factors) and family inheritance (genetic and property), makes people.

The other key factor here is class. While Cartland and Heyer produce historical romances set in upper-class milieus, and Plaidy chronicles the lives of royal women, Cookson centralises the kind of working-class people who are left out of 'real solemn history' or, indeed, historical romances, except in bit parts or crowd scenes. This is history seen from below and from the regional 'margins' through the eyes of some of the most oppressed and disenfranchised people in society, particularly illegitimate women and children. She has also written of those stigmatised because of race, such as the half-black Rose-Angela *Colour Blind* (1953), or of disability, such as the deaf Barbara in *The Mallen Girl* (1974).

The novel Cookson herself saw as marking a key turning point in her writing career in terms of her use of historical research rather than simply her own experience was *Katie Mulholland* (1967), which captured the American market for the first time (Cookson, 1999, 30). Set in Jarrow and South

Shields between 1860 and 1944, it tells the story of Katie, starting with her as a 15-year-old scullery maid, against the rise and fall of Sir Charles Palmer's shipyard, the industry which shaped the social and economic history of the area. It took Cookson 18 months to research the background (Goodwin, 1994, 190), and among the authors she read were the historians G.M. Trevelyan and Arthur Bryant, and the socialist M.P. Ellen Wilkinson (Cookson, 1999, 11–12, 30).

This research led to other historical novels in the 1970s, including *The Dwelling Place*, a text which illustrates many of the themes and patterns repeatedly deployed in her fiction. The eponymous 'dwelling place' is another version of the image of the 'recess' which I have suggested is a powerful image for women's position in relation to history. In Cookson's novel it symbolises class marginality. The 'dwelling place' is a cave or more accurately a hollow in the Northumberland fells which becomes the home of Cissie Brodie and her nine siblings when their parents die of fever in 1832. Determined that they shall not be sent to the workhouse, Cissie moves her siblings to the cave and, with the help of the wheelwright Matthew Thornton, they build walls to enclose the space. The 'dwelling place' thus symbolises the plight of the poor working classes (rather than semi-royal women as in Lee's 'recess'), and their exclusion from the rest of the community.

Although the centre of her novels is always in the private sphere (the 'home' even though it is only a cave) of family relationships, Cookson details the exploitation of the poor through her treatment of child labour and the brutal physical punishments invoked for small infringements of the law. Cissie's mother worked in the mines as a 12-year-old and was bought out of them for a gold sovereign by the man who became her husband. To survive, Cissie has to send her two terrified brothers, both under ten, into the mines. Following a strike at the mine, several other families are forced to set up home on the fells but, far from creating a community, this simply makes Cissie fear that the gentry will enclose the land.

The class structures in the novel are spatially mapped through the opposition of the 'dwelling place' on the fell and Houghton Hall, the home of Lord Fischel and his family. The 'dwelling place', furthermore, represents the class struggle over land rights enacted through the Enclosure Act. The Fischels have enlarged their estate by enclosing land, but have not yet enclosed the fell on which the 'dwelling place' stands. Cissie's dwelling is legally allowed only because the land has not yet been enclosed and because it has no foundations. In contrast, Houghton Hall, with its gallery showing the portraits of all the male Fischels, the first of whom was given his title by Elizabeth I, represents the Fischels' privileged class position founded in unearned wealth.

This spatial representation of historically shifting class structures is repeated in the *Mallen Trilogy* where Cookson uses the family saga form to show how class structures shift over time. The action is divided between High Banks

Hall, built in 1767 by the original Mallen, himself an *arriviste* from the Midlands, and Wolfbur Farm, home of Donald Radlet, one of the current Thomas Mallen's many illegitimate sons known as his 'streaks' because each carries a white streak in their hair. In all four novels the gentry's economic exploitation of land and tenantry is paralleled by their sexual exploitation of working-class woman. But the class structure is itself subject to historical shifts as the economy of the area changes. Bankruptcy forces the Mallens to leave High Banks Hall, and they are replaced by the Benshams who have come up through the new industry developing in the North East in the 1850s. This instability allows lower-class women to ascend the class ladder. It is Anna Brigmore, the déclassée governess, who survives the rest of her generation to inherit High Banks Hall after the First World War. She passes it on to Ben Bensham and Hannah Radlet, whose marriage represents the utopian fantasy of class reconciliation and hope for the future.

As a kind of womb symbol, the 'dwelling place' represents working-class female and specifically 'maternal' strength in adversity, one of Cookson's most consistent themes. It is women, especially surrogate mothers like Cissie or Anna Brigmore, who hold families together in times of trouble, and whose strength invigorates weakened men. Cissie is able, through sheer force of will, to transform the cave into a domestic space which, however bleak, is better than the workhouse. It is, as another character notes, cleaner than many of the homes in the village. It is characteristic of Cookson's realism that she even details the sanitary arrangements: Cissie instructs her siblings that 'even for number ones they had to go to the holes she had dug' (1973, 46). It is in the dwelling place that Cissie, after she is raped by Clive Fischel, gives birth to her illegitimate child.

The rape illustrates Cookson's ambivalent treatment of gender and masculinity. She frequently represents gentry men spreading their seed among working-class women, through irresponsibility or rape. Clive Fischel's grandfather was 'the terror of the country', who left his mark in children sporting 'the Fischel nose and the black eyes' around the villages and farms (1973, 70). Similarly, Thomas Mallen leaves his mark in the form of the 'Mallen streak' displayed by his male bastards, and even, in a drunken stupor, rapes the girl he has brought up as a daughter.

Despite this, men, even rapists, are represented as redeemable in a way that exploitative or callous women are not. Cissie finally achieves status and security through her marriage to Clive Fischel, an extraordinary domestication of her former rapist. This is a troubling ending since Cissie's earlier marriage to Matthew Turnbull, the working-class man who helped her throughout her poverty, is presented as problematic because of his possessiveness and her lack of sexual passion for him. Clive is represented as her rightful partner or 'mate': 'Cissie had been nobody's except this man's from the day [Cissie's sister Ruth] had watched him *mate* her' (1973, 350, my emphasis). Cookson's male characters are frequently 'feminised' or domesticated through injury

(Ned in *The Girl*), loss of money and status (Thomas Mallen), mental instability (Ben's shellshock in *The Mallen Litter*) or loneliness (Clive in *The Dwelling Place*), and therefore in need of the kind of mothering her working-class female protagonists can provide.

The utopianism of Cookson's class reconciliation and her depiction of female strength are based on a conservative notion of gender roles. Margaret in *The Girl* voices what seems to be Cookson's own view:

> It is strange that in the main woman are always stronger than men, yet they have to be subordinate to them. They can't claim any of men's rights, they are chattels; and yet in most cases happy to be chattels. I suppose love helps. (1977, 157)

It is this combination of strength with subordination that makes women cruel. 'Women [...] were much more cruel than men', reflects Hannah, 'men could be brutal, physically brutal but women seemed to have the knack of torturing you mentally' (1977, 240). The real villain of *The Dwelling Place* is Clive's sister, Isabelle, who provoked him into the rape in the first place. In *The Girl*, it is Hannah's stepmother, who nearly flays her to death. At the end of the novel, Hannah gives away the money she has inherited because it would unbalance her relationship with Ned, the man she loves: 'I know Ned', she says, 'he's all men rolled into one in that he must be master' (1977, 302). Despite the difference in their treatment of class, Cookson, like Heyer and Cartland, offers love as the consolation prize for women's subordinate position in society, and as the medium which will transform 'girl' into 'woman': '*The Girl* was gone, buried in the past. [...] Whatever the future might bring she could face it as a woman, Ned Ridley's woman' (1977, 307).

Cookson's historical novels represent the past as 'self-experienced' in two senses. First, her fascination with the historical construction of class structures and especially with the stigma of illegitimacy very obviously comes from her own experience. The illegitimate child of an unmarried working-class mother and a 'gentleman' who disappeared before she was born, Cookson was brought up by her grandmother and, until she was eight, believed that her mother was her sister. Her novels are recognisably 'autobiographical' in the sense that, as Piers Dudgeon's biography *The Girl from Leam Lane* (1997) shows, she repeatedly reworks elements from her own life: illegitimacy, rejection, mental breakdown, incest, cross-class marriage. 'He was a bastard and all bastards know rejection', says Matthew of his half-brother Donald, one of the Mallen 'streaks' (1979, 142). The 'autobiographical' elements of these novels are also foregrounded by her repetition of names or versions of names from her own family. This is most obvious in her repeated use of versions of her own Christian name – Catherine, Kate, Katie, Kitty – which she shared with her mother, as in *Kate Hannigan* (1950), for instance, and *Katie Mulholland*, or even 'Cissie' (aurally very close to 'Kitty') in *The Dwelling Place*.

Cookson's step-grandfather's name, and her own maiden name, McMullan is echoed in 'Mallen'.

Thus Cookson's own experiences are projected back in history. The fact that attitudes to illegitimacy (like those to virginity) had changed by the 1970s explains why she turned to historical settings in order to explore the stigma attached to illegitimacy and its importance in terms of inheritance. In *The Mallen Streak*, the stigma of illegitimacy is marked on the body in the form of the 'streak' of white hair inherited by the male 'flyblows' of Thomas Mallen. This sense that she is retelling her own 'personal history' is enhanced by the emphasis on family relationships in the family saga form of the *Mallen Trilogy*, where wider social history is subordinated to immediate 'family history', dramatised through inherited traits (like the Mallen 'streak'). Cookson further explores the theme of genetic inheritance (she herself inherited a rare blood disorder from her father) through the curse which ensures that the Mallens neither reach old age nor die in their own beds.

The impression of authentic 'self-experienced history' is also conveyed through the oral style of her novels. 'History' in Cookson's texts is not what is written down in history books (even when she has researched it herself) but what is handed down by word of mouth, particularly within families. Her husband emphasises the importance of the oral to her work in his description of her as a realist rather than romantic writer:

> One must remember her upbringing in the years prior to and during the First World War: no wireless – this came in the 1920s – no TV; only reading, if possible; but certainly there was the listening to tales told and retold by members of the family, detailing events which had occurred much earlier, perhaps even going back even to her great-grandmother's time before the 1850s. (Cookson, 1999, 11)

Cookson's history is both *oral* and *maternal* in origin. It is telling that her first novel, *Kate Hannigan*, opened with a barely fictionalised version of Cookson's own birth (Dudgeon, 1998, 1–2). Thus, even in looking back to the 1850s, Cookson is still writing about her own personal history in that she is writing about the lifetime of her grandmother or great-grandmother.

After 1963, Cookson dictated her books (1999, 25) and her prose style retains the immediacy of the spoken narrative, especially through her use of the North East idiom. Words such as 'oxters', 'hunkers', 'flyblow', 'fiddlefartin', and the ideologically loaded phrase 'taken down' to describe a raped woman, lend an aura of oral authenticity. So does her use of indirect reported speech to convey the 'people's' view of history, as in a description of the reaction to the outbreak of war in 1914: 'Everybody said they had seen it coming. Why, look at the number of German bands that had been going about this last few years. [...] They weren't German bands at all, they were spy bands' (Cookson, 1975, 199).

This is a technique she also uses when reporting reactions to events in the protagonists' lives, such as the village's reaction to the appearance of Matthew Thornton's illegitimate child on the same day as the coming of age of 'young Master' Beaumont: 'By! That was a day and a half wasn't it; something to be remembered for years ahead' (1977, 4). Both international and local history, at all class levels, are reported in the same idiom and given the same weight in this kind of oral narrative.

Furthermore, the history in Cookson's novels appears to have its source in her memory because she does not provide the kind of scholarly documentation of her 'sources' – an 'Author's Note', bibliography, footnotes, glossaries of place names – which historical novelists often give. Margaret Irwin, for instance, may mock the convention – 'A Bibliography has always filled me with awe. How do people know so exactly what they have read?' she asks in a note in *The Stranger Prince* (1966c, 9). But she and many other women novelists – Plaidy, Bryher, Mitchison, Sutcliff – have followed Scott in their use of scholarly paraphernalia which asserts the authenticity of their use of 'real' history. Perhaps the most extreme (and self-reflexive) example is Mitchison's *The Bull Calves* which includes 126 pages of endnotes, giving background information, drawing attention to parallels between past and present, and documenting what 'actually' happened. Even Heyer, who usually carries her research lightly, appends an 'Author's Note' and a Bibliography to *An Infamous Army* (1937). In omitting such evidence of research, Cookson is basing her claim to historical 'reality' on another kind of perceived authenticity, that of orally transmitted stories of the 'self-experienced past', whether her own or her foremother's. When she does use an 'Author's Note' in *The Girl*, for instance, it pays tribute to a local figure, referred to in familial terms as Mrs M.J. Westcott's 'grandfather'.

An autodidact, Cookson was widely read despite her lack of formal education but she brings a sharp class consciousness based on the authenticity of lived experience to her use of intertextuality. In *The Mallen Litter*, for instance, she notes that in the 1890s 'more women were reading, and not only those from the middle classes' (1975, 165). She adds that the working classes do not need to read John Stuart Mill's 'The Subjection of Women' 'because they knew all about it, they lived it' (165). Choice of reading matter is shown to reinforce the class-blindness of her middle-class protagonist:

> Neither the events of the world nor the struggles of the working class towards emancipation touched Brook House and its inmates during those years. Mrs Dan Bensham occupied herself mostly with reading the works of the Brontë sisters, never Dickens or Mrs Gaskell. (1975, 165–6)

Cookson reworks the governess theme of *Jane Eyre* in her treatment of Anna Brigmore. But in this passage she suggests that Brontë's gender politics ignore class issues.

Despite her concern with the poverty of the working classes of the past, Cookson explicitly defined herself as apolitical. Although her books can be seen as potentially politically radical in their centralisation of the plight of the working classes, that radicalism is defused by the fact that it is always placed in the past, precisely part of 'history'. As with the other sagas Bridgwood discusses, historical distance 'clear[s] a site for the representation of class and sexual inequalities without being obliged either to criticise or to defend them directly' (1986, 179). Poverty and deprivation are documented as 'what actually happened' in the past tense, and with no connection to what might be happening now. Furthermore, Cookson's use of the formulaic rags-to-riches fantasy structure validates individual solutions (marriage to a wealthy, upper-class man) to the problems of poverty. Her sense of both life and history as cyclical, 'a pattern that is already cut' (1979a, 246) – she uses 'Full Circle', for instance, as a title for parts of both *The Mallen Litter* and *The Dwelling Place* – reinforces a sense of the rightness of the current status quo, whatever the wrongs of the past may have been.

'Merlin was me': Mary Stewart's Arthurian trilogy

Mary Stewart began her career as a writer of gothic thrillers but in the 1970s she produced a rewriting of the Arthurian legend from the point of view of Merlin. Stewart's trilogy (*The Crystal Cave* [1970], *The Hollow Hills* [1973] and *The Last Enchantment* [1979]) and an earlier novel by Rosemary Sutcliff, *Sword at Sunset* (1963), mark the moment when women writers appropriated one of the most enduring of our national narratives.

From the Welsh tales recorded in *The Mabinogi* through Geoffrey of Monmouth's *History of the Kings of Britain*, Chrétien de Troyes' romances, Malory's *Le Morte d'Arthur*, Tennyson's *Idylls of the King*, T.H. White's *The Once and Future King* (1958) and countless others, the Arthurian story has been endlessly remade. What is most interesting about any given version is its ideological implications: who is retelling the story, and for what reason? As Stephen Knight has succinctly argued:

> The Arthurian legend, especially in its most sophisticated literary versions is about power in the real world: the texts are potent ideological documents through which both the fears and hopes of the dominant class are realised. (1983, xiv)

Given this, it is not surprising that the Arthurian legend has been a male-authored tradition, used to legitimise male power from Edward I through Henry Tudor to John F. Kennedy's 'Camelot'.

This was the case, as Marion Wynne-Davies (1996) has shown, right up until the mid-twentieth century.[8] It is also not surprising, given the highly stratified gender roles which come to dominate Arthurian legend, where men fight and women love, as well as the emphasis on women's perfidy – the treachery of Morgan le Fay and Morgause and the adultery of Guinevere – that women writers found this material somewhat recalcitrant.

So when Sutcliff and Stewart produced Arthurian literature in the form of historical novels in the 1960s and 1970s, this marked a radical appropriation and reinterpretation of a dominant male narrative.[9] It is significant that both writers were writing outside mainstream literature. Rosemary Sutcliff first approached the Arthurian material through the form of juvenile fiction in *The Lantern Bearers* (1959). Mary Stewart was already aligned with the 'popular' through her modern gothics.

The Arthurian scholar Geoffrey Ashe acknowledged Sutcliff's groundbreaking status when he remarked that her decision to make Arthur himself her narrator was 'a bold course for a woman to take' (1971, 199). These texts come out of the interrogation of women's relationship to leadership, power and authority which I have suggested is typical of the 1960s. Through their exploration of the gendering of power and authority, Sutcliff and Stewart progressively opened up the Arthurian legend to make a space for the feminine which enabled subsequent women writers to further appropriate the story.

This appropriation was possible because, as I have argued, the historical novel as a form has traditionally allowed women to write about 'male' subjects and to ventriloquise male voices. Both Sutcliff and Stewart use a first-person narrator, a technique borrowed from nineteenth-century realist novels, which foregrounds internal psychology. These novels are particularly fine examples of women cross-writing to ventriloquise male voices – Sutcliff voicing Arthur, whom she calls Artos, while Stewart voices Merlin. They rewrite the legend not as heroic romance or medieval fantasy but as realistic historical fiction, emphasising psychological realism, rationality and verisimilitude. Lukács argues that the historical novel is the closest that we now get to epic, but the epic is predominantly a 'masculine' form. It seems that it is only by translating the material of the epic or the legend into the bourgeois and 'feminine' form of the novel (making it 'real') that women writers are able to appropriate it.

The realistic treatment of the Arthurian material at this point was made possible by an explosion in scholarship focusing on both the historical and the legendary Arthur. Starting in the 1920s, this peaked in the 1960s.[10] Both Sutcliff and Stewart include 'Author's Notes' that acknowledge the influence of this scholarship, particularly Geoffrey Ashe's work, and explore its relation to their own thinking in terms of what is 'fact' and what they have imagined. Sutcliff points out that 'almost every part' of her novel, even the most unlikely, 'has some kind of basis outside the author's imagination' (1963, 8). *Sword at Sunset* is frequently cited by scholars, including Ashe himself (1971, 199), as the best fictional treatment of the historical Arthur.[11] Although Stewart's initial inspiration came from Geoffrey of Monmouth's *History of the Kings of Britain*, her trilogy is informed by this later scholarship, and she describes it as a 'work of the imagination [...] firmly based in both history and legend' (1974, 458).

It seems to be the very paucity of actual historical fact, in contrast to the elaborate accretions of the male-authored literary tradition, which provided a space for women writers which was liberating in its very emptiness. Both authors use the historical evidence provided by this new scholarship, as well as the techniques of the realist novel (the use of naturalistic detail, specific locations, psychological realism and a first-person narrator), to 'rationalise', to borrow Maureen Fries' term (1977), the Arthurian material, especially the supernatural elements which shift the legend into the realm of fantasy. Both writers also self-reflexively explore the processes by which raw human experience is transmuted through memory, narrative and art, especially oral 'gossip' and story-telling, into history and legend.

Watching the Northern Lights, Sutcliff's Ambrosius anticipates this process:

And later, all Britain will tell each other that there were strange lights in the sky on the night before Aurelius Ambrosius died; and later still, it will become Aquila's dragon, or a sword of light with the seven stars of Orion set for jewels in the hilt. (1963, 327)

Stewart's Merlin, a harpist, actively manipulates this process in Arthur's service. Retelling the story of 'Macsen's Dream' (from *The Mabinogi*), he comments that the part which asserts Ambrosius's descent from Maximus 'at least was true', but

The rest of the legend, like all such tales, was a kind of dreaming distortion of the truth, as if an artist, reassembling a broken mosaic from a few worn and random fragments, rebuilt the picture in his own shimmering new colours, with here and there the pieces of the old, true picture showing plain. (Stewart, 1974, 157)

The fragmentary nature of history enables Merlin, as it enabled Sutcliff and Stewart, to intervene, retelling the story for his own ends.

Sutcliff's *Sword at Sunset* attempted to piece together the historical fragments to re-imagine what kind of man Arthur might have been. Her Artos is not the romanticised figure of Malory or Tennyson but a 'Romano-British War leader' who fought against the 'Barbarian darkness' brought by the Saxons (Sutcliff, 1963, 7). Artos is both historically and psychologically realistic, a gifted leader who fights for a dream of a unified Britain. His life and marriage are blighted by incest with his half-sister, inadvertent on his part but planned by her in revenge for their father's desertion of her mother.

Here Sutcliff gives psychological realism to her treatment of what she saw as the 'original framework' of the story, the 'Sin that carries its own retribution' (1963, 7). Both Ygerna's motivation for the incest (Sutcliff gives the traditional name of Arthur's mother to his half-sister here, doubling the incest motif), and Artos' consequent failure to be a loving sexual partner to his wife, Guenhumara, are psychologically 'real' rather than mythic. Guenhumara's adultery (both Sutcliff and Stewart use Bedwyr rather than Lancelot, a later French addition to the legend, in this role) is explained as the result of Artos' impotence, and her later belief that Artos is responsible for the death of their daughter.

Sutcliff creates a space for the 'feminine' within the story, through her sympathetic and psychologically realistic treatment of the women characters. But she also makes Artos a man who contains both male and female, Roman and British/Welsh:

Half of me is Roman [...] My right-hand people are those who built squared forts and drove the great roads straight from city to city through whatever lay between; men who deal in law and order and can argue a question in cold blood – a daylight people. The left side is the dark side, the woman's side, the side nearest the heart. (Sutcliff, 1963, 27)

This binary is not essentialist or rigid in its gendering. Artos' mother's people are the Welsh, but his father's 'Roman' side may include the blood of the 'Dark Ones', or the 'People of the Hills', the even older Celtic inhabitants who live outside the Romano-British culture. Similarly, Bedwyr, both poet and soldier, encompasses duality, symbolised by his curiously mismatched 'ugly-beautiful' face (1963, 55). On the other hand, while Artos respects and works with the 'Dark Ones', Guenhumara is terrified of them.

As with Dunnett's Lymond and Renault's Alexander, it is Artos' ability to encompass both 'right' and 'left' sides – to see 'the oneness of all things' (1963, 210), including the competing religions of the period – which makes him an exceptional leader. Sutcliff depicts both Ambrosius and Artos as versions of the 'King Who Dies for the People', merging religions ('Christian' and 'pagan') which are usually conceptually and historically differentiated into 'oneness': 'the king-sacrifice, older than either Christos or Mithras, reaching back and forward into all time until the two met and the circle was complete' (1963, 335). It is striking here that women writers so often turn to the notion of the sacrificial (rather than all-conquering) leader as a model of the moral and humane use of power. In using this mythic structure they also conceptualise history in terms of the circular repetition of this pattern.

Women writers also frequently deploy the theme of illegitimacy to feminise both leaders and their narrators.[12] Illegitimacy is central to both Sutcliff and Stewart's conceptualisation of their narrators' place (or lack of it) in history and their sympathetic and humane use of power. Artos' illegitimacy legally debars him from succession to the High Kingship, setting him outside the Law of the Father. There is no Freudian fantasy of legitimacy restored as with Dunnett's Lymond. Instead Artos has to prove his capacity as leader at the battle of Badon, after which he is spontaneously crowned Emperor by the army.

Mary Stewart's approach to the Arthurian material is similar to Sutcliff's in its rationalisation of the legend and its use of a first-person narrator, but she differs dramatically in her retention of the supernatural or fantastic elements which are held in tension with the realism of the text.[13] Like Sutcliff, she uses the techniques of the realist novel to produce what Barthes called the 'reality effect' (1970, 154). This is most obvious in her treatment of the timeless elements of natural history and place which suggest continuity, and the way she invokes the senses. Descriptions of natural objects such as plants, trees, water, landscape and animals, especially horses, produce an effect of sensual and vivid immediacy, as in the following passage from the opening of the trilogy:

> It had been raining all day, and from the branches near the mouth of the cave water still dripped, and a steady trickle overflowed the lip of the well, soaking the ground below. Several times, restless, he had left the cave, and now he walked out below the cliff to the grove where his horse stood tethered. (1971, 27)

This is juxtaposed with the technique, borrowed from Geoffrey of Monmouth, of noting toponymic shifts that indicate historical change over time:

> Maridunum lies where the estuary opens to the sea, on the river which is marked Tobius on the military maps, but which the Welsh call Tywy. [. . .] Even when I was a child, I heard the town called Caer-Myrddin: it is not true (as they say now) that men call it after me. The fact is that I, like the town and the hill behind it with the sacred spring, was called after the god who is worshipped in high places. (1971, 27)

In its geographical exactitude this passage connotes (to borrow Barthes' phrase again) 'what really happened' (1970, 145), or rather 'what really exists' and therefore 'what really exist*ed*'. Stewart provides maps which enhance this 'reality effect'. The doubling of names, both Roman and Welsh, indicates historical shifts over time, but it also acknowledges the palimpsestic co-existence of two or more cultures and religions.

The supernatural or fantastic elements of the texts are focused in Stewart's narrator, Merlin, but rationalised by their position within this highly realised setting. It was possibly the difficulty of rationalising the magical elements which led Sutcliff to omit Merlin from her novel. Stewart only partially rationalises them. Her Merlin (or Myrddin Emrys) is the illegitimate son of a Welsh Princess and Aurelius Ambrosius[14] (rather than the prince of darkness as Geoffrey of Monmouth has it). This interpretation of Merlin's birth was inspired by Geoffrey's probable conflation of two historical figures in the phrase, 'Then saith Merlin, that is also called Ambrosius...' (Stewart, 1971, 464). Merlin's illegitimacy makes him a marginal figure, an outsider who, even when recognised by Ambrosius, is debarred from legal inheritance of the throne and thus from recognised power in the public sphere. A solitary and celibate figure, he works outside the Law in the interstices of history, watching rather than fighting, and orchestrating events rather than taking a central role in them.

Metaphorically speaking, illegitimacy is the weakness in the 'masculinity' of the Arthurian legend which allows women writers to open it up to provide a space for the feminine. As with Sutcliff's Artos, it is Merlin's illegitimacy which disempowers him as a 'man', puts him outside the 'Law of the Father', and 'feminises' him in a way which makes it possible for a woman writer to ventriloquise his voice. Stewart foregrounds the theme again in her treatment of Arthur, who is brought up thinking himself a bastard and is conceived out of wedlock. For her final, and less successful, Arthurian novel, *The Wicked Day* (1983), Stewart chose as her protagonist the illegitimate Mordred.

Homosexuality, as Renault demonstrates, also makes male figures available for appropriation by women writers. Merlin is celibate for most of his life, but his closest relations are with other men, especially his servants, and a homo-erotic interpretation of this is hinted at when Uther, for instance, accuses him of being Ambrosius' 'catamite' (1971, 193). When he does finally consummate a relationship with a woman, it is with Nimuë whom he knows first disguised as a boy called 'Ninian'. Sutcliff's Artos is heterosexual but she makes him tolerant of male homosexuality, and treats sympathetically the homo-eroticism of his love for Bedwyr. Merlin's ambiguous sexual and social standing is further complicated by Stewart's treatment of his supernatural abilities. It is the other-worldly figure of Merlin which, as Lewis Thorpe notes, more than anything marks how far Geoffrey of Monmouth's narrative is from 'anything which can ever approach *real history*' (Geoffrey, 1966, 20–1, my emphasis). It seems, then, paradoxical that Stewart chooses the most supernatural figure of the legend as the narrator of what she explicitly regarded as a 'historical novel' (Thompson, 1989) rather than a fantasy or a romance.

However, it is precisely Merlin's 'otherness' that makes him a superlatively appropriate figure for the woman historical novelist, herself reassembling the mosaic of the past. Stewart herself was well aware of this, telling Thompson that 'Merlin was me' (Thompson, 1989), a fascinating echo of Flaubert's famous 'Madame Bovary, c'est moi.'

On the one hand, Stewart demystifies events like the legend of Merlin's conception by the prince of darkness, which is revealed as a story told by his mother to conceal the fact that his real father is Ambrosius, or his rebuilding of Stonehenge, which is attributed to his superior engineering skills. On the other hand, Stewart's Merlin really does have supernatural gifts, primarily of the 'Sight', inherited from his mother, which enables him to see events at which he is not present. In technical terms this has two advantages. It is a device which allows Stewart to overcome the limitations of first-person narrative and show events at which Merlin is not present. But the gift of prophecy also 'explains' the sense of predetermination which haunts all historical novels where the outcome is known to the reader.

The description of the cave quoted earlier is thus especially complex because it is part of an account of Merlin's conception, or rather of the meeting between his mother and father which immediately preceded it (again, history as 'the time when my mother was alive before me' [Barthes, 1993, 65]). Merlin could not have witnessed this but he explains it thus:

> It is not my own memory but later you will understand how I know these things. You would call it, not memory so much as a dream of the past, something in the blood, something recalled from him, it may be, while he still bore me in his body. (1971, 12)

As Wynne-Davies notes, the story of Merlin's conception is retold five times in the text, foregrounding the tension between 'magic' and 'reality' which is at the heart of the Arthurian narrative and embodied at its most complex in Merlin himself (1996, 169).

It is through her treatment of Merlin's magic that Stewart most obviously explores the gendering of power and authority. Merlin makes a distinction between the 'Sight', which women can also have and which he retains until the end of his life, and what he calls the 'Power', which is 'doing and speaking with knowledge [. . .] bidding without thought, and knowing that one will be obeyed' (1980, 469). Although it is his mother from whom he inherited the Sight, Merlin connects his vision of the primal scene of his conception to his father – 'something recalled from him'. His mother renounces the Sight when she retires into a Christian nunnery (1971, 155). The 'Power' is linked to masculinity: 'a man takes power where it is offered', as Merlin's father tells him (155). But it is paradoxically dependent upon Merlin's virginity, that is, on him not being 'a man'. He loses it when he falls in love with Nimuë. Merlin uses his power not to intervene in history but to foresee what will happen and advise accordingly. In contrast, the power of kingship is associated with active heterosexual 'manhood': Uther shies away from anything supernatural, while Arthur's power comes from his 'full fierce manhood' (1980, 290).

In *The Last Enchantment*, where she is treating elements of the Arthurian legend associated with the later literary versions of Malory and Tennyson rather than the earlier 'historical' Merlin of Geoffrey of Monmouth, Stewart seems to find the material relating to women and power especially difficult to rework. While Merlin loses his power when he falls in love with Nimuë, she does not lose her power when she marries Pelleas. Women's 'power' is connected to their sexuality in ways which reiterate some of the more misogynistic elements of male-authored texts, although Stewart distinguishes between Nimuë's benign and Morgause's evil use of it. Yet it is in this text that Stewart makes her most obviously 'feminist' statements, as in Arthur's explanation of Guinevere's predicament:

> Does it not occur to you that [women] lead lives of dependence so complete as to breed uncertainty and fear? That their lives are like those of slaves, or of animals [. . .] Why, even royal ladies are bought and sold [. . .] as the property of men unknown to them. (1980, 312)

For the woman reader who has been able to identify with Merlin by 'cross-reading', as Stewart herself clearly did, this depiction of women as victims is remarkably unappealing.

The crystal cave in Bryn Myrddin (one of 'the hollow hills' which are the 'physical point of entry between this world and the Otherworld' [Stewart, 1973, 460]) is the generative matrix of Stewart's texts and of Merlin's narrative. In metaphorical terms it is another version of Sophia Lee's 'recess', a liminal space which is both outside and inside 'history', refuge and prison, womb and tomb, but this time for a male character. It is where Merlin is conceived, where he first sees his reflection in a mirror (1971, 55), affirming his separate identity, where he is educated in magic and learning by Galapas, where he makes his 'home' for much of his life, and where he is put living into the tomb by Nimuë. It is the place from which the narrating self speaks, from which the old Merlin looks back at his younger experiencing self in the past. It also symbolises Merlin's position as the nexus between the real world and the 'Other world'. His namesake Myrddin is the 'wayfarer between heaven and earth' (1980, 332), and as narrator Merlin connects past and present, magic and reality, history and legend, and reader and text.

In locating the matrix of the narrative in Bryn Myrddin, Stewart is also *re*-locating a legend which has been appropriated by the English to construct a notion of 'British' nationality which is essentially Anglo-Saxon, and returning it to one of its probable origins in Wales. Gwyn A. Williams has argued that, for instance, it was only once the Welsh had been conquered that the English could embrace the Arthurian legend and blur 'England' with 'Britain' (1994, 134). T.H. White inverted Malory, Williams points out, to make Arthur a Plantagenet and the *Celts* his enemies (213). Stewart, who consciously set out to differentiate her work from White's, reverses this. Like Sutcliff, she emphasises the palimpsestic historical mix of races, cultures and languages out of which the legend has evolved, including its Welsh elements. It could be argued that as a non-Welsh writer, Stewart is re-enacting another form of colonisation, retaining the association between the Celts and magic which positions the Welsh as 'Other' within the narrative.

However, she was writing at a moment when the issue of Welsh and Scottish nationalism was very clearly on the public and political agenda, most obviously in the gains made by Plaid Cymru and the SNP since the 1960s. The possibility of assemblies for Wales and Scotland, for instance, was included in the Queen's speech in 1974 (Sked and Cook, 1993, 300). With devolution being mooted as a real possibility, Sutcliff and Stewart depict Arthur as a possible model for a unifying leader and both retain the centrality of Welsh identity in the Arthurian material.

Both Sutcliff and Stewart, although ostensibly pre-feminist, are sophisticated in their presentation of gender as neither ahistorically essential nor immutably fixed to biological sex. Yet their texts have been neglected partly because of the tendency in feminist criticism, especially in the 1980s, to look for positive depictions of female characters as possible role models, or to focus on female victims as evidence of the oppression of women within patriarchy. Their work is important not only because it opened up the Arthurian legend for later women writers to reinvent further,[15] but also because it offers ways of thinking about gender, including the pleasures of cross-reading, which feminist thinking has been slow to address.

8
'Herstory' to Postmodern Histories: History as Dissent in the 1980s

The 1980s saw the beginnings of a renaissance in the 'serious' or 'literary' woman's historical novel, a stream of novels which broadened into a veritable flood in the 1990s. This was part of a general resurgence of interest in the historical novel also marked by the popularity of male writers like John Fowles, Umberto Eco and Peter Ackroyd, who were reworking the genre in ways which were formally, if not politically, radical.[1] While these male-authored historical novels frequently elided the female, either erasing women altogether or presenting them as the enigmatic 'Other', women's historical novels were politically driven, refashioning history through fiction as part of the urgent need to tell 'her story'. Women's history had to be recovered and reconstructed before it could be deconstructed.

In the wider national context, interest in the historical novel can be seen in part as a response to a widespread and ideologically reactionary (re)turn to history during the 1980s, a return strongly signalled in Britain by the Conservative victory in 1979. The Conservative election campaigns in 1979 and 1983 appropriated history to support their right to power through a narrative of Britain's degeneration, attributed to Labour and the 'liberal' legacy of the 1960s (including, of course, feminism). 'I cannot bear Britain in decline' was Margaret Thatcher's theme. The Conservative project was to restore Britain to the glories of its imperial past and to reassert the virtues of Victorian values, famously to put the 'Great' back into 'Great Britain'. As Beryl Bainbridge acerbically noted, for Margaret Thatcher and her American ally Ronald Reagan, 'Progress [...] should have led backwards not forwards' (1999, 91). The language of Conservatism foregrounded the notion of *re*turn – *re*covery, *re*storation, *re*vival, *re*solution – in the name of continuity, appropriating the past for its own reactionary ends.

For women writers, however, dissent from this project combined with the feminist recovery of women's history to produce a renewed interest in the historical novel. The early fiction of second-wave feminism had been dominated by the confessional realist novel, but in the mid-1980s women writers increasingly turned to genre fiction (reworking forms like the detective novel, for example) and to history.[2] While criticism of the fiction of this period has drawn attention to the importance of history as theme and content in these novels, it has rarely attended to them as 'historical novels' as such, or situated them within a tradition of women's historical novel writing which stretches back to the 1920s and earlier.[3] By the late 1980s the historical novel, especially in the hands of women writers who had come to political consciousness in the 1960s and 1970s, had become an important signifier of dissent from the Conservative project.

The impetus towards the historical novel can be linked closely to the project of *recovering* women's history, rather than the deconstruction of history associated with male authors such as Fowles. The recovery of 'herstory', which had begun with the second-wave of feminism in the late 1960s and 1970s, was politically motivated, partly through the desire to find suitable role models. By the 1980s, feminist activism was under threat from a conservative anti-feminist backlash. But despite, or perhaps because of this, 'women's history' had moved into the academy and there was a boom in feminist publishing led by presses like Virago and the Women's Press. As in the 1930s, a body of historical research about women's lives became available to women writers. As the title of Sheila Rowbotham's ground-breaking *Hidden from History* (1973) indicates, research also drew attention to the gaps and silences in the records, the kinds of gaps which have always inspired historical novelists. What Linda Anderson (1990) called the 're-imagining' of women's history became the province of the novelist, who had the freedom to reinvent the past on behalf of the marginalised and excluded.

This is the premise on which Ellen Galford draws in the 'Historical Note' to her lesbian historical novel, *Moll Cutpurse: Her True History* (1984): 'Some of the episodes in this story are derived from these sources', she writes, 'others may be as close – or closer – to the truth' (1985, 221). Building on the fragmentary evidence about *Moll Cutpurse* which appears in sources such as Middleton and Dekker's *The Roaring Girl*, Galford re-imagines Moll's story as a glorious herstorical romp, reworking both the popular historical romance and the swashbuckler in order to encompass lesbian desires (for both sex and adventure). Her Moll is a cross-dressing trickster heroine, a pickpocket and one-time 'highwayman', who has a life-long love affair with Bridget, an apothecary. Moll's considerable courage, strength and abilities are used to defend the rights of women, mainly against the wealthy and the Puritans. In one central episode, for instance, she rescues Bridget's aunt from an accusation of witchcraft brought by a farmer who wants her land. This is history as lesbian feminist fantasy. As such, it clearly reflects the desires of 1980s feminists rather than offering a realistic picture of women from the sixteenth and seventeenth centuries.

In contrast, a far bleaker version of 'herstory' can be found in Kathy Page's *The Unborn Dreams of Clara Riley* (1987), which explores the hidden history of infanticide and illegal abortion in Edwardian England. The novel parallels the story of two women: the working-class Clara Riley, who has abandoned one child and smothered another, and her employer, the upper-class suffragist Mrs Audley Jones. When Clara becomes pregnant again, Mrs Audley Jones procures an abortion for her but the discovery of what they have done leads Clara to prison and Mrs Audley Jones to an insane asylum. This is history as consciousness-raising, a novel which strives to make readers aware of the injustices done to women in the past.

Writing about the development of feminist fiction in the conservative 1980s, Nicci Gerrard suggests that censorship led to allegories and political concealment in fiction (1989, 155). Women's historical novels of the 1980s can clearly be seen within this context. Galford's celebration of same-sex desire and Page's assertion of women's right to abortion, for instance, both look more radical in the context of the sexual conservatism which followed the AIDs-inspired panic of the mid-1980s and the homophobic panic surrounding Clause 28 of the Local Government Act, which banned the promotion of homosexuality by local governments and became law in 1988. As in the 1920s and 1930s, women turned to the historical novel in the 1980s to provide allegorical critiques of the economic individualism of the 1980s and the increasing gulf between the 'haves' and the 'have-nots'. They also used it as a way of reviewing earlier history as the 'prehistory' which led to the present moment. This increasingly involved refashioning concepts of history itself and the form of the historical novel.

Indeed, Galford's and Page's novels are less conventional in terms of genre than they at first appear, and both self-consciously centralise figures who are marginalised in traditional historical narratives: the working-class woman and the lesbian. Page's novel re-values working-class women's history, but it also explores how gender oppression crosses class boundaries through its focus on shared biology. Although the novel initially looks conventionally realist (and thus resembles feminist confessional realist texts), it is written in the present tense in a way which transforms 'then' into 'now' and suggests a continuum of oppression of women through time.

This re-valuation of working-class women's history is central to several other novels of the period, including Pat Barker's *Liza's England* (1986).[4] While it would not qualify as a historical novel under Lukács' or Fleishman's categories, Barker's text is one of the most important novels to engage with history in the 1980s. It is, as Lyn Pykett notes, 'a "condition of England" novel which examines the social and economic crisis of the eighties through the perspectives of other twentieth century crises, most notably the 1930s' (1987, 73). Barker parallels the story of Liza Jarrett, born at the exact beginning of the twentieth century, with that of Stephen, a gay social worker in the 1980s who listens to her stories of the past. The use of parallel narratives to draw historical comparisons was a popular device during the 1980s. Barker uses a blend of 'social realism, dream and symbol' (Pykett, 1987, 74) to expose the marginalisation and silencing of working-class women, and to parallel this with the similar silencing of male homosexual experience. Working as a cleaner for an upper-class family, Liza's mother is required to remain unseen by her employers. Another maid, Ellen, describes the sense of erasure this induces when she looks into the mirror: 'there was nothing there. Nothing. Not a bloody thing. I could see the wall behind me [...] It was like I didn't exist at all' (1986, 56). She has been erased from history.

To counter this, Barker reconstructs a matrilineal history (symbolised by a painted box passed from mother to daughter) which asserts these women's strength as survivors. Women's shared bodily experience, especially child-birth, binds them together: Liza and her daughter are 'links in a chain of women stretching back through the centuries, into the wombs of women whose names they didn't know' (1986, 211). This continuum is contrasted with the fragmentation of modern life which Stephen witnesses during his work with disaffected youth in a north-east community disintegrating under the pressure of de-industrialisation. The physical destruction of the landscape, including the local pub, is the erasure of unwritten working-class history: 'It's history, this pub', comments one of the characters (1986, 248). The new world of the 1980s with its imperative to 'spend, spend, spend' (218) is a world without hope or a sense of coherence. Liza refuses to feel nostalgia for the past – in the 'good old days', she reminds us, 'women wore out at thirty' (252). Yet, her generation concurs, 'we had something then that we've lost now' (252). Part of that something, Barker suggests, was a sense of community.

Liza's England illustrates Beryl Bainbridge's non-fiction analysis of the 'condition of England' in *Forever England* (1987). 'Progress must always be achieved at the expense of something else' (1999, 90), Bainbridge points out. Communities, which 'come into existence because people are forced through circumstances to rely on each other' (90), disappear with a rise of living standards. 'It could be', Bainbridge speculates, 'that the consequences of comparative poverty are less debilitating than the effects of general afflu-ence' (90–1). By paralleling Liza's past with Stephen's present, Barker is able to critique both times without falling into nostalgia or espousing a false notion of progress.

In appropriating the popular historical romance for lesbian desire, Ellen Galford paved the way for the new genre of the lesbian romance which (like the lesbian detective novel) took off in the 1980s.[5] Her later comic novel, *The Fires of Bride* (1986), shows an awareness of the fragmentary and constructed nature of history, particularly the history of Christianity. It parallels the story of a contemporary feminist researcher, Lizzie, with that of a community of heretical nuns living on a remote Scottish island. Con-sidering the island's history, Lizzie thinks, 'Which history?' (1994, 9), acknowledging that it could be 'political', 'romantic', 'spiritual' or 'sexual' history. Increasingly seen as a genre in its own right, the lesbian historical novel gained added impetus after the publication in 1988 of the diaries of

Anne Lister, written between 1791 and 1840. Lister's frank accounts of her sexual life put paid to the idea promulgated by the Lillian Faderman's concept of 'passionate friendship' (1981) that women in the past did not have genital sex with each other. In the light of this evidence, historical accounts had to change.

As Linda Anderson points out, the quest to recover women's hidden history involved a 're-visioning' of history itself: '...women cannot simply be added on to history – expanding the boundaries of historical knowledge empirically – without putting under pressure the conceptual limits that excluded them in the first place' (1990, 130). This re-visioning of the concept of history itself was paralleled and, to a certain extent, fed by 'a kind of radical suspicion of the act of historiography' (Hutcheon, 1988, 90) in the work of poststructuralist thinkers like Hayden White, Dominic LaCapra, Michel de Certeau, Roland Barthes, Frederic Jameson and Michel Foucault. They drew attention to the 'fictionality' of history. This led not to a rejection of history but to an understanding of it as fragmentary, plural and subjective, as a form of discourse which was constructed or emplotted (in White's terminology[6]) through narrative devices and rhetorical strategies in ways similar to fiction. This in turn enabled the understanding that, in White's words, 'every representation of the past has specifiable ideological implications' (1985, 69).

From the mid- to late 1980s women writers began to write increasingly playful and sophisticated 'postmodern' historical novels or, to borrow the term used by Linda Hutcheon (1988), 'historiographic metafictions', which drew on these understandings. Hutcheon defines 'historiographic metafictions' as novels 'which are both intensely self-reflexive and yet paradoxically lay claim to historical events and personages' (1988, 1).[7] Historiographic metafiction, she argues, is 'what characterises the postmodern in fiction' (viv). In women's writing, however, the formal experimentation of historiographic metafictions is not mere intellectual gameplaying but urgently linked to the political and moral necessity of recovering women's history.

The radical potential of the reconceptualisation of history as plural and subjective becomes clearer in the context of the Conservative appropriation of history during the 1980s. This was at its starkest in Margaret Thatcher's personal involvement in the drawing up of the National Curriculum between 1988 and 1990. The 'hardest battle', Thatcher recalled, was over the history curriculum (1993, 595). Given that Thatcher's own academic expertise was in chemistry, her involvement in the minutiae of the history curriculum is remarkable. As she recalled:

> Though not a historian myself, I had a very clear – and I had naively imagined uncontroversial – idea of what history was. History is an account of what happened in the past. [...] No amount of imaginative sympathy for historical characters or situations can be a substitute for the

initially tedious but ultimately rewarding business of memorising what actually happened. (1993, 595)

Her conception of history as undisputed 'facts' was at odds with the views of the professional historians on the History Working Group. She was 'appalled' by their interim report in July 1989 because it 'put the emphasis on interpretation and inquiry as against content and knowledge' and gave 'insufficient weight' to British history (1993, 596). The final report in 1990 was, she thought, 'still too skewed to social, religious, cultural and aesthetic matter rather than political events' (596). This is more than a misunderstanding between academic disciplines. The strength of Thatcher's language – 'appalled', 'exasperated' (596) – suggests the ideological importance of a unified notion of history to her own project.

Thatcher herself turned to the nineteenth century to evoke 'Victorian values' – or 'the phrase [she] originally used – Victorian virtues' (Thatcher, 1993, 627) – to imply the continuity of the politics she was endorsing. The Victorians, she asserted, 'had a way of talking which summed up what we were now discussing – they distinguished between the "deserving" and the "undeserving" poor' (1993, 627). The economic individualism Thatcher espoused, which prioritised the market over everything else, was seen at its sharpest after the so-called 'Big Bang' of 1986 when the city was deregulated and the 'Yuppie' was born. The country increasingly seemed split between prosperous south and poverty-stricken de-industrialising north in a way which echoed the 'two nations' of Victorian England described by Disraeli in *Sybil* – as Bainbridge implied when she used a quotation from that novel as the epigraph to *Forever England*.

Two other key periods were also mobilised to harness Conservative policies, both domestic and foreign, to a notion of a restored sense of national identity. Simon Barker (1986) has shown how the history of the sixteenth and seventeenth centuries was used to manufacture consent and to neutralise resistance, particularly in relation to the Falklands. The notion of a 'smooth historical continuum' was reinforced in television, books, newspapers and even literary criticism in ways which neutralised opposition and naturalised consent to policies which included immigration control, nuclear 'defence', and the sinking of the *General Belgrano* (Barker, 1986, 175). Yet this very desire for continuity in the 1980s, as Patrick Wright has argued, suggests a sense of crisis and discontinuity (1985, 166). This negates any sense of history as process, offering instead a version of 'the past' as a timeless utopia to which we can only attempt to return.

The choice of historical events and periods invoked by the dominant ideologies is crucial here. The consensual historical continuum did not include either the General Strike of 1926 or the Jarrow Hunger Marchers of the 1930s. Either of these would have provided an important context for the year-long miners' strike in 1984–1985 which attempted to prevent colliery closures and the subsequent loss of jobs. Indeed, Thatcher's characterisation of the miners as 'the enemy within' positioned them as that which threatened British national unity. Nor, indeed, did it include the Peasants Revolt of 1381, which was to be echoed in the riots of 1990 protesting against the poll tax or 'community charge'.

Writing in 1986, Simon Barker saw both literature and literary criticism as playing a leading role in the shaping of this notion of history as a continuum which encouraged consensus. He draws particular attention to the contribution of the critic G.R. Wilson Knight to the pamphlet *Authors Take Sides on the Falklands* in June 1982. Wilson Knight, he noted, invoked Shakespeare in support of a notion of 'democracy in strict subservience to the crown as a symbol linking love to power and the social order to the divine' (Wilson Knight quoted in Barker, 1986, 185). This was used, Barker noted, to validate Wilson Knight's 'unreserved acceptance of parliament's decision' (185). In contrast, Barker called urgently for a literature and criticism which aimed to 'disrupt the continuum of history and produce a knowledge of the sixteenth and seventeenth centuries as a period of crisis and rapid change' (1986, 188). As he saw it, the historian Christopher Hill was the only writer embarked upon such a project at that point.

My own argument here is that we can see in women's historical novels of the period precisely the kind of disruption and critique Barker was calling for. Conservative attempts to control and censor history actually helped to generate a counter discourse of dissent during the 1980s. Similarly the attempt to control discourses about homosexuality through Clause 28 mobilised political opposition to the Act. And the arrival of American cruise missiles at the base at Greenham Common in 1983 ignited a highly visible women's peace movement in response. This counter discourse is, as I suggested above, articulated particularly clearly in the woman's historical novel of the 1980s, which often explicitly registers dissent from the notion of history as a continuum. Nicky Edwards' *Mud* (1986), for instance, used parallel narratives and oral history to make connections between the trenches of the First World War and the women's peace camp at Greenham Common.

Given Thatcher's lauding of Victorian values, it is not surprising that several novelists turned to the nineteenth century to show that the Victorianism Thatcher invoked was a carefully constructed fiction, which ignored the seamier side of nineteenth-century life in favour of its supposed 'values' of civic duty, charity, hard work at home and imperial expansion abroad. The nineteenth century produced both the realist novel and narrative history. Both of these, as feminists were pointing out, have either excluded women's lives and experiences or shaped them in particular ways. By using the historical novel, women writers were able to disrupt conventional historical accounts of the Victorian period and offer a critique of Thatcher's appropriation of it.

Perhaps the most outstanding of the novels which return to the Victorian period is Beryl Bainbridge's *Watson's Apology* (1985), a fictionalisation of a real murder case in 1871 when a respectable clergyman and headmaster murdered his wife after nearly 30 years of marriage. 'Mrs Thatcher', Bainbridge acidly commented in *Forever England*, 'grieves over the loss of attitudes rooted in and dependent on an oppressed and deprived society' (1999, 91). In *Watson's Apology*, Bainbridge showed how 'oppressed and deprived' even the 'respectable' middle classes of Victorian England could be. The novel is a study of historical cause and effect in both private and public life. Bainbridge knits together the documents from the case and supplies 'what has defeated historical enquiry' – 'the motives of the characters, their conversations and their feelings' (2001, 6). She re-imagines the accumulation of abrasions and unhappinesses over nearly 30 years of marriage between two people, both disappointed and frustrated by their lives and who, kept to their separate spheres by Victorian ideology, have nothing in common. Both J.S. Watson and his wife are, in their own ways, what might be called mad. Through this act of imagination, Bainbridge calls attention to the fragmentary nature of historical records and the problem of interpretation, thus implicitly undermining Thatcher's insistence on the unproblematic nature of 'facts'.

The parallels with 1980s Britain are also clear. Living through the industrial revolution and the development of competitive commercial opportunism in Victorian England, Watson is 'a victim of progress, that shifting tip beneath whose load it is always someone's turn to be buried' (Bainbridge, 1999, 57). His career as headmaster and as an author and translator of the classics has been only semi-successful. But as the old classical education is superseded by the new sciences, Watson finds himself summarily dismissed from his job and ignored by his publisher. This was a time, like the 1980s, when 'a man's labour could be dispensed with as easily as falling off a log' (1999, 57).

One of the more bizarre elements of the case was a series of letters to the newspapers from public-school-educated men who disputed the correct translation of a Latin sentence left by Watson after the murder. While this draws attention to the indeterminacy of meaning in historical research, for Bainbridge the most interesting element here is the status of Latin as a privileged discourse which functions as a signifier of identity shared by the ex-public-schoolboys who rule the country. As she notes in *Forever England*, 'men from the same educational institutions still hold political power' in 'the clearing banks, the discount houses or the merchant banks' (1999, 112). There is a historical continuum here but it is not the one invoked by Thatcher.

Another common strategy for undermining Thatcher's invocation of 'Victorian virtues' was the exposure of repressed Victorian sexuality, a theme already made popular by Fowles' *The French Lieutenant's Woman*. Margaret Power's *Goblin Fruit* (1987) made extensive intertextual use of Christina Rossetti's poetry and Pre-Raphaelite painting to explore such sexual repression, but she linked this to an exploration of the sexual and emotional exploitation of women in art. Power developed this technique in *Lily* (1994) which looked at the effects of syphilis in a marriage of convenience, using it as a symbol of the rot concealed beneath the veneers of middle-class Victorian society. Power uses the Gothic to expose the desires and fears beneath the smooth surface of the nineteenth-century realist novel.

Perhaps the most ambitious refashionings of the historical novel to recover 'herstory' in the early 1980s are Michèle Roberts' rewriting of the New Testament in *The Wild Girl* (1984) and Angela Carter's *fin de siècle* fantasy *Nights at the Circus* (1984). Both texts reinsert women into history, using techniques (such as first-person narrative) which make them the speaking subjects, not the objects, of historical narrative. Through this and their use of non-realist discourses (myth and fantasy), they stretch the form of the historical novel well beyond the realist conventions lauded by Lukács.

Presented as the lost fifth gospel written by Mary Magdalene, *The Wild Girl* is an ambitious attempt to re-vision Christianity by recovering and re-symbolising the feminine which Luce Irigaray argues has been repressed in Western thinking. In re-visioning Christianity, Roberts is, of course, tackling *the* grand narrative of Western history. In 'Theses on the Philosophy of History', Walter Benjamin imagined history as a game of chess played by a puppet representing historical materialism, whose strings are actually pulled by a hunchback seated under his chair who represents theology (1973, 255). Roberts' project is to expose how the theological thinking which still invisibly controls the 'strings' of our thinking has consistently erased the female from historical narratives.[8]

The main body of *The Wild Girl* is the familiar narrative of the gospels, but told in the first person by Mary, a former prostitute, who becomes Christ's lover and accompanies him to Jerusalem as one of his disciples. Embedded in this narrative are Mary's dreams and visions which provide a mystical and poetic recovery of the repressed maternal-feminine. In Kristevan terms, these approximate to a kind of timeless semiotic or feminine unconscious underlying the realist narrative which unfolds in linear historical time. Mary's visions recover a matrilineal genealogy which links her with the female divine in its many manifestations. The Mother, Salome, is 'she who has many names' (1985, 125): Sophia, Ishtar, Astarte, Artemis, Aphrodite, Inanna, Hecate, Demeter and Persephone.

In Roberts' re-visioning of the Christian story, Christ himself acknowledges the importance of the feminine and the body, and speaks of God as 'our Father and Mother' (1985, 37). It is through Mary's visions that he comes fully to understand that, 'We have lost the knowledge of the Mother' (1985, 110). The subsequent separation of man and woman is a sickness and exile which can only be healed through a rebirth which is 'the marriage between the inner woman and the inner man' (110). However, the disciples ignore this final message from Christ, relayed to them by Mary, and found the andro-centric version of Christianity which has dominated Western culture. Roberts' use of the historical novel to offer an analysis of Western culture as founded on the repression of the feminine – what Irigaray has called 'the murder of the mother' (1991, 44) – situates her own work in the matrilineal genealogy of the woman's historical novel which reaches back to Sophia Lee's *The Recess*.

While Roberts uses myth to disrupt the realism with which the historical novel traditionally insists on the 'truth' of its narrative, Carter's *Nights at the Circus* uses fantasy. Indeed, Carter distrusts myth which, as she put it in *The Sadeian Women*, deals in 'false universals' (1979, 5). Her fiction always locates itself within history because she sees gender as culturally and therefore historically constructed: 'relationships between the sexes are determined by history and by the historical fact of the economic dependence of women upon men' (1979, 6–7). Or, as she puts it even more bluntly, 'our flesh arrives to us out of history like everything else does' (1979, 9).

Despite its fantasy elements, *Nights at the Circus* is specifically set in 1899, at the 'fag end [. . .] of a nineteenth century which is about to be ground out in the ashtray of history' (1984, 11), a period which has clear parallels with the pre-millennial 1980s. Whereas Lukács insisted that the protagonist of a historical novel should be typical in the sense of being an average man rather than a world-historical figure, Carter's heroine is an outrageous fantasy figure, a cockney circus performer with real wings. Raised in a brothel, Fevvers is a parody of both the Victorian 'Angel in the House' and Helen of Troy, who has learned to live by manipulating and exploiting her enforced position as an object for the male gaze. Seen through the eyes of Walser, the American journalist to whom her life story is initially addressed, she is an enigma, the 'Other', a mystery to be solved. 'Is she fact or is she fiction?' (1984, 7), he asks, itself a question which subverts the premise that a historical novel is based on 'fact'. Through Fevvers' wings, the text, in Lorna Sage's words, 'escapes the gravitational pull of realism's settings' (1992, 176).

Fevvers' early career consists of posing as a static object for the male gaze – the brothel, an underground museum of monsters catering to men with macabre tastes, the circus itself. Her stage act explicitly presents her as a 'Bird in a Gilded Cage', who invites the audience to 'LOOK AT ME' (1984, 15). However, this static objectification, which positions her in a form of pornography, is dangerous. As Carter points out in *The Sadeian Women*, 'our contemporary pornography does not encompass the possibility of change, as if we were the slaves of history and not its makers' (1979, 3). Fevvers may think that she is able to control her transactions with men, trading her appearance only – she is 'not [to be] handled' (15) – for hard cash, but the tenuous nature of her control is demonstrated when she is very nearly trapped in the cage for good by the lecherous Grand Duke.

In fact, Fevvers has failed to recognise her own unique potential. As her Marxist foster mother Lizzie tells her, 'You are Year One. You haven't any history and there are no expectations of you except the ones you create' (198). Thus Fevvers has to learn to cast off the 'long shadow of the *past historic*' (240) which holds her static and fly completely free of its oppressive institutions, seeing herself as a 'maker' of history, not its slave. Carter shifts the novel into the picaresque to signal that Fevvers' quest must take her outside the confines of Western history. As Lizzie argues, 'It is not the human soul that must be forged on the anvil of history but the anvil itself must be changed in order to change humanity' (1984, 240). Thus Carter sends Fevvers and Walser to Siberia, a carnivalesque space whose inhabitants exist outside Western history because they do not distinguish between past, present and future.

In Siberia, both Walser and Fevvers are reborn. Fevvers, symbolically equipped 'only for the "woman on top" position' (292), becomes an active subject within history, and Walser, having acquired an inner life through the knowledge of love, becomes a fit mate for her. Their union coincides with the first stroke of the twentieth century and heralds the possibility of the millennium as a time when 'all women will have wings' (285). Carter thus goes back into the past to use history as a springboard into the future, a utopian future which is not outside history but holds the potential that 'the anvil of history' itself can be reforged.

Fevvers herself is a new feminist vision of Walter Benjamin's 'Angel of History' (1973, 259). While Benjamin's Angel is irresistibly propelled into the future with his face turned towards the debris of the past (in a mode oddly reminiscent of Thatcher's backward-looking 'progress'), Carter's Fevvers is actively winging her way towards the future with her face firmly looking forward, a maker not a victim of history.

Popular fictions: Philippa Gregory's Marxist–Feminist novels

The covers of Philippa Gregory's Wideacre trilogy – *Wideacre* (1987), *The Favoured Child* (1989) and *Meridon* (1990) – with their provocative female figures and raised gold and red lettering make them look like typical bodice-rippers, a British updating of the 1970s' American erotic historicals. The trilogy also deploys the typical structure of the family saga, tracing three generations of women – Beatrice Lacey, her daughter Julia and granddaughter Meridon – and their claims to the ancestral estate of the Laceys, Wideacre Hall in Sussex, between 1760 and 1805. However, their popular appearance belies the political content of these texts and the seriousness of their engagement with history.

In a review of *Wideacre* reproduced in the blurb for *The Favoured Child*, Peter Ackroyd remarks that 'This is a novel written from instinct, not out of calculation, and it shows.' This slightly ambiguous comment indicates the way in which the ostensible artlessness of Gregory's texts conceals both her commitment to historical accuracy and the ways in which her texts subvert the conventions of the popular forms they borrow, smuggling in radical politics under the guise of entertainment.

Gregory uses the forms of popular historical fiction, both erotic historical and family saga, to offer a Marxist–Feminist critique of the economic individualism of the 1980s. This critique is at odds with both the conservative sexual politics of the typical family saga and the glamorisation of female suffering in the typical erotic historical. In contrast to the usual denial of historical process in both erotic historical and family saga (which more often use the past as an exotic pretext for erotic titillation and as a conservative reassertion of the status quo respectively), Gregory presents the past as the political and economic prehistory of the present and connects a Marxist analysis of the growth of capitalism to a feminist analysis of the relationship between women, property and ownership.

Gregory's concern with historical accuracy is not surprising in an academically trained writer, who turned to historical fiction when she found other career options closed.[9] After a precociously political career at school – she 'founded a sixth-form union, organised uniform strikes and insisted the library order Mao's Little Red Book' (Gregory, 2004, 7) – she completed a PhD on eighteenth-century fiction at Edinburgh University in 1984. She then wanted to pursue an academic career but 'at that time Margaret Thatcher's government was cutting back on "non-useful" university work, so I had to think of other ways of earning a living' (Zigmond, 2003, 4).

Gregory's doctoral thesis, 'The Popular Fiction of the Eighteenth-Century Commercial Circulating Libraries', was a detailed analysis of the plots and themes of 127 of the most popular fictions between 1739 and 1801 (including The Recess, which Gregory calls 'a glorious assault on the rules of historical accuracy' [1984, 169]). Her thesis is not explicitly Marxist in either its analysis or the secondary material she deploys, but is interesting in the way it pinpoints what is left out of the fictions she discusses – what Marxist critics would see as the 'not-said' of these texts (although Gregory does not use the term).[10]

Fiction seems to have allowed Gregory to be more radical in her approach. Her Wideacre trilogy returns to the eighteenth century, the moment at which the novel emerges, in order to refashion the form from a twentieth-century perspective and to lay bare what was concealed or absent in the earlier fictions. This is not to say that Gregory privileges the modern period as the superior result of 'progress'. Instead, she indicates how the historical shifts of the eighteenth century led to those of the 1980s. She locates the origins of economic individualism in the years of crisis between 1760 and 1805, and allows us to see the connections between two major historical shifts. The first is the replacement of traditional agricultural practices by 'farming for profit' in the late eighteenth century, partly in response to the development of new markets overseas, which enabled the industrial revolution and the development of capitalism. This foreshadows the erosion of the traditional manufacturing base (steel, coal mining, shipbuilding, textiles) in the 1980s. Both shifts can be seen as being made at the expense of the most vulnerable people in society.

In her thesis, Gregory argues that the eighteenth-century fictions present an idealised picture of a timeless pastoral English countryside, which ignores the reality of an agricultural revolution which was transforming both the landscape and the relations between the classes:

> From 1650 the feudal-style village life of Britain had been changing as a result of the increasing number of enclosures which destroyed the open field system of sharing land and with it the traditional relationship of landlord and peasant or tenant farmer. In place of the old ways of farming, a new relationship was developing based on maximising crop yields by experimental farming methods, and increasing profits by using a seasonal, landless, work-force on high-rent farms. (Gregory, 1984, 6)

In *Capital*, Marx argues that it was this expropriation of the people from the land, beginning with the Norman Conquest and reaching its height with the enclosures and land clearances of the period between 1765 and 1780 when 'the law itself became now the instrument of the theft of the people's land' through the Enclosure Acts (Marx, n.d., 678), which enabled the development of capitalism by 'freeing' a pool of people to sell their labour. As he puts it: 'the expropriation of the mass of the people from the soil forms the basis of the capitalist mode of production' (Marx, n.d., 719). It is this process, with its consequent rural tensions, sporadic violence and bread-riots, which is absent from the eighteenth-century fictions Gregory examines. This absence, Gregory suggests, can be attributed to the guilt felt by the literate elite who produced and consumed these fictions (1984, 6).

In her trilogy, Gregory traces this historical shift from feudal agricultural practices – the 'old ways' as Beatrice Lacey calls them – to the development of 'capital farms' or 'merchant farms' (Marx, n.d., 678), through the story of Wideacre. Deep in the heart of Sussex, Wideacre represents the quintessentially English rural countryside. The Norman Laceys ('Le Says') took Wideacre from its Saxon inhabitants by force during the Norman Conquest. The landscape itself still bears the scars in the 'Norman Meadow', site of the old battlefield which cannot be enclosed because a plough would turn up old skulls and bones (Gregory, 1987, 441). But even after the conquest, the villagers retain their (unwritten) rights to the strips of land on which they can grow their own crops, and their rights to graze animals and collect firewood on the common land. In the 1770s this feudal system is violently destroyed by Beatrice Lacey and her brother Harry, as they enclose the common land and introduce new farming practices to grow wheat for profit, selling it to London merchants at a price out of reach of the people on the estate who had traditionally bought it.

Gregory links together the appropriation of the common land by the privileged classes with the damaging consequences of excluding women from property ownership under the system of primogeniture. This system, Gregory pointed out in her thesis, made the eldest son heir to the estate and thus of supreme importance, allowing him to control the rest of the family and giving him precedence even over his mother (Gregory, 1984, 226). In the late eighteenth century it was being reinforced by the increasing popularity of entail – 'the legal process of tying up a great estate so it is always handed on to the next male heir – be he never so distant, even if there are a hundred daughters loving the land before him' (Gregory, 1987, 27).

As a young girl, Beatrice Lacey is outraged to discover that her almost mystical love of the land counts for nothing because of her gender. Beatrice, like Julia and Meridon later, is shown actively *working* on the land, and her detailed knowledge of estate management comes from this intimate daily contact. This depiction of a woman working is in itself at odds with the norms Gregory identifies in fiction. Yet despite Beatrice's labour, the system of entail ensures that her brother Harry, despite his ignorance of farming, will inherit the estate, while she will be expected to marry. The appropriation of land by the men of the upper classes is directly paralleled with their 'ownership' of their wives. As Beatrice's daughter Julia discovers: '[My husband] owned me as surely as he owned the land I had once called mine, my land, my horse, my little box of trinkets, my gowns, even my own body' (1989, 556).

Gregory traces the practice of primogeniture to the arrival of the Normans, who were: 'fighting men [...] hungry for land. Women for them were carriers and breeders and rearers of soldier sons. [...] Of course they settled it that boys and only boys should inherit' (1987, 389). Generations of women 'inherit responsibility but no power' (389). They are 'serfs without hope of recompense' (391).

The exclusion from property-ownership corrupts Beatrice's love of the land into a mania for possession, and transforms her from a victim into a villain. She turns to murder and to incestuous sex with her brother to retain her position as *de facto* 'Squire' of Wideacre. When she becomes pregnant by her brother, she marries and then encourages her husband's alcoholism. Finally, she nearly destroys Wideacre in an attempt to wring out of it the money she needs to break the entail. Ironically, she does this so that the estate can be inherited not by her daughter Julia, who has been brought up as the daughter of Harry and his wife Celia, but by her *son*, Richard, jointly with Julia.

When Harry starts to farm Wideacre 'for profit' according to the new theories, enclosing the common land and using gang labourers, he does so because he sees himself as 'part of a process of historical change' for which he can be neither blamed nor held responsible (1987, 455). Understanding the estate better than he does, Beatrice knows the human price which will be paid in terms of starvation and death among the villagers whose livelihood is destroyed.

Beatrice's connection to the land is explored through her identification with the pagan corn goddess, predating Norman feudalism. Here Gregory, like Mitchison in *The Corn King and the Spring Queen*, turns to myth to express a sense of female power and agency which has been erased from conventional history. Corrupted by her desire for possession of the land, Beatrice becomes a life-destroying figure, the 'Wideacre witch' rather than a fertility-affirming 'goddess' (1987, 621). Likewise, her lover Ralph, who has lost his legs in the mantrap set for him by Beatrice and has become the leader of bread-rioters known as 'the Culler', becomes a mythic figure: 'another of the old gods, half-horse, half-man' (621). He finally kills Beatrice while the villagers burn Wideacre. This mythic/folkloric level, like Julia's second sight in *The Favoured Child*, suggests kinds of knowledge which cannot be assimilated to the conventional narratives of history, or indeed the realist novel, but which offer a powerful symbolisation of the female power.

In her treatment of incest, Gregory rewrites the second major 'not-said' in the eighteenth-century fictions she examined for her thesis, and uses it to destablise the explicit sexuality which is a feature of the erotic historical. Eighteenth-century fictions, she argued, display signs of a contemporaneous anxiety around the issue of incest which is repeatedly hinted at or explored in disguised forms in fictions such as the 1777 novel by Henry Mackenzie, *Julia de Roubigne* (Gregory, 1984, 228–31).[11] Gregory connects this anxiety to an intensification of family, especially sibling relationships, and to the new form of companionate marriage which necessitated a familiar well-loved partner as a spouse (1984, 228). In several of the texts she examines, a couple are brought up together as if they were siblings and then marry, while other texts focus on conflicts between siblings, often because of the power wielded by the eldest son. To counter this power, Beatrice engages in incestuous sex to manipulate her brother and thus make herself *de facto* Squire. Gregory explores the theme of incest again in *The Favoured Child* where their children Julia and Richard, who grow up thinking that they are cousins, marry secretly after Richard rapes Julia and leaves her pregnant.

In an article entitled 'Love Hurts', Gregory argues that the heroines of eighteenth-century fiction were 'pain specialists' whose suffering demonstrated their virtue (1996, 140). She goes on to argue that these conventions of female powerlessness and victimisation survive into the popular 'sex and shopping' novels of the 1980s, where the greater sexual freedom of the heroines leads to her sexual exploitation. Even in texts like Barbara Taylor Bradford's *A Woman of Substance* (1981) she argues, that the heroine's achievements are undercut and her worldly success is seen as being at the expense of love and happiness. Though Gregory does not mention the erotic historicals in this piece, they offer an extreme example of this valorisation of female sexual suffering. In both Rogers' *Sweet Savage Love* and Kathleen Woodiwiss' *The Flame and the Flower*, the heroine is raped and it is her ability to suffer which eventually wins her the hero's love.

In contrast, Gregory, although she includes the explicit sex scenes typical of the erotic historical, refuses to valorise female suffering in the same way. Beatrice is the dominatrix in sex with Harry, exploiting his liking for pain to manipulate him. Richard's rape of Julia is realistically painful (he breaks her wrist) rather than erotic, and an explicit attempt to dominate and control her. Gregory thus exposes the reality of the pain behind the rape fantasy of the erotic historical novels. Furthermore, through Julia in *The Favoured Child*, Gregory exposes the ideology which changes a 'wild free little girl into a young lady who could be shouted at, abused, and who would pride herself that she could return love for pain' (1989, 221). Julia internalises this ideology of female suffering and accepts Richard's mistreatment believing that this will retain his love for her, but it leads neither to his redemption nor their mutual love.

Through a prostitute called Julie (an explicit double for Julia), Gregory highlights the double sexual standard which ensured the chastity of gentry women by allowing gentlemen to use working-class women as sexual objects. Julie is one of the 'lost children' of Acre, children who are forcibly taken from the poverty-stricken village to provide child labour in the factories of the north, or to scrape a living as link-boys, chimney sweeps or exploited seamstresses in the cities. This is the child-slavery which, Marx notes, provided the labour for the manufactories (Marx, n.d., 709) and powered the Industrial Revolution. These children are the most vulnerable victims of the 'historical process' Harry Lacey so casually espouses. Unlike Marx, Gregory connects their exploitation to the sexual exploitation of working-class women. Julia rejects James Fortescue, a man of radical political beliefs whom she loves, because he admits that he has used working-class women for sex. Men of his class are taught, he concurs, 'to deal with lust as they would deal with hunger' and to separate it from love (1989, 364). This sexual double standard, Gregory has suggested, endures from the eighteenth century through to the 1980s where 'men are still less emotionally committed than their female partners' (1996, 143).

Gregory argues in her thesis that the most important development in eighteenth-century fiction was the arrival of the fiction of individual consciousness, which reflected new ideas about the importance of the individual (1984, 242). Her own texts rework this idea, ultimately turning back to an ideal of communality which is at odds with the economic individualism of the 1980s. Her use of first-person narration appears to foreground the development of a single individual. But, in fact, the three female protagonists – Beatrice, Julia and Meridon – can be seen as multiple expressions of the development of a kind of everywoman. Both Julia and Meridon have dreams in which they 'become' Beatrice. The cyclical form of the trilogy with Meridon finally returning to Wideacre reinforces this.

In the third volume, Meridon (*née* Sarah Lacey) experiences both poverty, in her early life as a gypsy and in a travelling circus, and then wealth, when she is recognised as heir to Wideacre and educated into 'ladyhood' by Lady Havering. Having 'seen both sides' (1991, 262), she finally rejects the life of the 'Quality' and chooses to live with Will Tyacke, descendant of the family which lived on Wideacre before the Norman invasion. In returning Meridon not to the Hall but to a cottage in the village where she will throw her lot in with the villagers, Gregory has her choose communality rather than economic individualism.

The 'message' of Gregory's trilogy, as summed up by Will Tyacke, has a particular resonance as a verdict on the idealisation of the market in the 1980s:

> I don't think people can be happy unless they are well-fed and well housed and have a chance at learning [. . .] And you'll never do that by opening the market place and saying it's free to all those with money to buy it. Some things are too important to be traded in a free market. Some things people should have as a right. (1991, 546)

Gregory's texts suggest that the major historical shifts – the eighteenth-century replacement of traditional agricultural practices by 'farming for profit', and then the closing down of the traditional industries in the 1980s – were validated by the development of economic theories which began with Adam Smith's *The Wealth of Nations* (1776), regarded as the progenitor of economic theory. 'Thatcherite' financial policy had its roots in a theory of economics which Margaret Thatcher saw as directly descended from Smith. 'The Scots invented Thatcherism, long before I was thought of', she declared, a comment which has been interpreted as a reference to the centrality of Smith's thought to the development of her own (Young, 1990, 528), although her immediate debts were to the Austrian economist Friedrich von Hayek and the American monetarist Milton Friedman.

In *Wideacre*, Celia attacks the theories of political economy which prioritise 'profit' and the 'market' at the expense of people. She draws a parallel between farming and mining, both of which entail 'ownership' by the rich who pay the poor for their labour to exploit the 'natural' riches of the earth. While Beatrice has come to espouse a kind of Thatcherite trickle-down economics – 'The way of the world is that the poor survive only if the rich prosper' (1987, 570) – Celia argues,

> All the people who write about the need for a man to have profit are rich people. All they wish to prove is that their profits are justified. [. . .] Why should the man who invests his money have his profit guaranteed, while

the man who invests his labour, even his life, has no guaranteed wage? [The miners] live like animals in dirt and squalor and they starve while the mine owners live like princes in houses far away from the ugly mines. (1987, 566).

The sudden introduction of mining into the debate, which initially seems out of place in a text so concerned with the rural, clearly has a particular resonance in relation to the miners' strike of 1984–1985, which was the direct result of the prioritising of profit over people's jobs. Celia concludes, 'it is an ugly world you and your political economists defend' (568). Gregory's texts suggest that economic theory in both the eighteenth and twentieth centuries developed as a discourse (closely related to historical narratives) which naturalised the ideals of 'profit' and the 'market' in order to serve the interests of the ruling class.

Will Tyacke, rephrasing Adam Smith, seems to state Gregory's position when he argues that 'the wealth of a country is its people' (1991, 333). Gregory also redefines the notions of 'wealth' and 'ownership': Meridon's most valuable lesson is that what she loves about Wideacre – the land, people, sky, birds, winds, sunshine – cannot be 'owned'. In emphasising 'people' rather than dehumanised 'labour', Gregory rejects the pursuit of individual advantage, substituting instead a validation of the human and the communal. Will's own endeavour has been to make sure that 'the wealth of the land could go to those who earned it' (1991, 488).

Gregory is also concerned with the erasure of the history of the working class and of women. The history of Wideacre has been a history of 'generation after generation of robbers' (1991, 490), taking the land from those there before them. 'But the worst theft of all', thinks Meridon, 'was to take some-one's history from them' (1991, 490). The children of the Havering estate believe that the rich have always been there and that they have no choice but to accede to the status quo and 'try to become rich [themselves]' (490). This echoes Marx's insight that capitalism is made 'natural' through an erasure of historical process: 'The advance of capitalist production develops a working class, which by education, tradition, habit, looks upon the conditions of that mode of production as self-evident law of nature' (n.d., 689).

Gregory's achievement in these texts is that she dissents from this natural-isation of the status quo as the inevitable product of history. She offers us instead an alternative picture of the late eighteenth century as a moment which leads to our own time but which holds other possibilities. In her thesis, Gregory notes the use of fiction as an 'educational device' to draw the readers' attention to the 'need for reform in public life' (1984, 4). Similarly, Gregory uses the popular historical novel to convey complex arguments about the morality of political economy, not as allegory but as an engage-ment with historical process. Her later novels explore Britain's culpability in the slave trade in *A Respectable Trade* (1995), and the relationship between colonisation of the 'New World' and environmental exploitation in *Earthly Joys* (1998) and *Virgin Earth* (1999).

The 'popular' status of Gregory's fiction both conceals and enables a Marxist understanding of history, which generates a strong and radical voice of dissent. However, Marxism was one of the meta-narratives being rejected by the postmodernist theories which increasingly informed the women's historical novels of the late 1980s. Postmodern historical novels, like those of Jeanette Winterson and Rose Tremain discussed below, display a greater self-consciousness in their representation of history. However, self-conscious formal experimentation does not, as I will argue in relation to A.S. Byatt in Chapter 9, necessarily indicate equally radical politics.

Postmodern histories: Rose Tremain and Jeanette Winterson

Both published in 1989, Rose Tremain's *Restoration* and Jeanette Winterson's *Sexing the Cherry* are postmodern historical novels which turn to the seventeenth century to offer a critique of the 1980s. Both writers are centrally concerned with the inter-related meanings of authority and narrative, and the function of leaders and heroes. To interrogate these questions they develop a historical fiction which is non-realist and at odds with the model of the nineteenth-century classical historical novel outlined by Lukács. They use narrative strategies typical of historiographic metafiction to expose the subjectivity of historical narratives and to question their 'authority' to represent 'reality'. They ask instead how ordinary people can 'authorise' their own stories without an appeal to a 'higher' authority, whether God, King, Emperor or even an explorer and horticulturalist like John Tradescant. In doing so, both authors display the potential of postmodernist fiction to move beyond apolitical gameplaying and challenge the consensual historical narrative established by the status quo.

Tremain has been explicit about her use of the Restoration period to write a coded critique of the greed and materialism of the 1980s:

> I grew up in the 60s and I was really dismayed when the Thatcher mindset came along but I also found it very difficult to write about, so I went searching for some other time in history that might be a mirror, or a parallel ... (Rustin, 2003, 23)

Her title signals her play with the varying meanings of 'restoration', one of which suggests the Conservative claim to 'restore' Britain to the continuum interrupted by the liberalism of the 1960s, a restoration which set off an explosion of materialism similar to that of the 1660s. 'We live in commercial times' is how Tremain's narrator describes his era (1990, 58). In *Sexing the Cherry*, Winterson makes her parallel with the 1980s explicit through a final section set in a post-Falklands Britain where the lakes and rivers are polluted with mercury from the activities of big business.

In turning to the seventeenth century, Tremain and Winterson offer important voices of dissent from the ideologies of consent identified by Simon Barker. Typically, Barker points out, the Civil War has been presented as an anomaly in the smooth continuum of history: 'The interregnum, it seems was a mere "hiccup" in the course of an English history which has served to secure our present freedom and democracy: the word is restoration not revolution' (1986, 181). Instead, Tremain and Winterson depict the seventeenth century as a period of crisis, instability and discontinuity within which we can identify the beginnings of much that is now recognisable in our modern world: the development of capitalism in the establishment of the Bank of England, of imperialism in the exploration of new worlds, of new understandings in science and medicine, and of new techniques such as grafting in horticulture. Any sense of progress, however, is fractured and problematic. In both texts the plague acts as a metaphor for the corruption of London and the country itself – in *Restoration*, the Quaker Pearce despairs of the 'greed and selfishness of our age which he believed was like a disease or plague, to which hardly any were immune' (1990, 290) – while the Great Fire offers the potential for cleansing and redemption.

Winterson's rejection of realism comes from her belief, expressed in *Art Objects* (1995), that it was developed by the Victorians and therefore coincides with 'a marked polarisation of the sexes' (28). She argues that our materialism and our ideas of both history and society are direct legacies from the Victorians: 'We live in a money culture because they did' (138). Winterson's first historical novel, *The Passion* (1987), was set against Napoleon's aborted attempt to invade England and the retreat from Moscow. It uses two narrators: Henri, who hero-worships Napoleon and becomes his chicken cook, and Villanelle, a Venetian girl with webbed feet. Napoleon's expansionist warfare leads Henri to the frigid wastes of Russia, where men freeze to death in a 'zero winter' (1988, 77). War imposes rigidly polarised gender roles: 'Soldiers and women. That's how the world is' (1988, 45). In addition, victory always leaves 'another defeated and humiliated people' (1988, 79), who will not appreciate the improvements Napoleon brings because they want 'the freedom to make their own mistakes' (103).

In rewriting the moment out of which Lukács argued the classical historical novel and the realist novel emerged, Winterson suggests that these forms are irrevocably linked to the rigid gender roles which solidified during that period. Against the frozen Russian plains, Winterson sets the fluidity of Villanelle's Venice, a fantasy space of masquerade. Villanelle's cross-dressing, her webbed feet, her love for another woman, and even her name, all signal her ambiguity, her ability to cross the boundaries between polarities: male/female, water/land, bird/human, poetry/prose, reality/fantasy. Henri's refrain is 'I'm telling you stories. Trust me' (1988, 5). Subjectivity, Winterson suggests, is constructed through narrative and that is why story-telling is important. 'Are real people fictions?' she asks in *Art Objects*, 'We mostly understand ourselves through an endless series of stories told to ourselves by ourselves and others' (1995, 59). At the end of *The Passion*, although he recognises the power of love to bring freedom and redemption, Henri, as Lynne Pearce notes, cannot write himself an alternative narrative (1995, 164). Like his hero Napoleon, he is obsessed with the past because he has no future and, like Napoleon, he remains trapped in an island prison.

The narrative strategies Winterson and Tremain use are typical of those of historiographical metafiction as it is described by Linda Hutcheon (1988, 113–15), which differs considerably from the model of the realist historical novel idealised by Lukács. Both novels play with the narrative voice – through the use of multiple narrators in *Sexing the Cherry*, and a naïve and split first-person narrator in *Restoration* – in ways which destablise the 'authority' of historical narratives and expose their subjectivity. Furthermore, both female authors use the historical novel to ventriloquise male narrators. This cross-writing, as I have suggested, is a kind of drag act which exposes gender as a performance which is historically contingent.

Lukács suggests that the protagonist of a historical novel should be an average man, a type representative of his historical moment. In contrast, Winterson and Tremain, like Angela Carter, use fantastic and marginal figures, whose grotesque bodies destablise polarised gender identities. Winterson's gigantic and Rabelaisian Dog Woman is larger and stronger than any man, and uses her body to terrorise men who threaten the things she cares for. Marked out as radically 'Other' by her body, Dog Woman is conservative in her Royalist politics and in her conception of herself as a mother. Elizabeth Langland suggests that Dog Woman's conservativism and her 'performance of gendered traits of tenderness, charity, and the maternal' are at odds with her unconventional physical presence in a way which 'destablises the conventional meaning of those terms and exposes their cultural construction' (Langland, 1997, 102). Like Butler's drag performer, Langland suggests, Dog Woman exposes the performative nature of normative gender but without implying that, as Butler's work has been misread to suggest, gender can be a 'voluntary performance' (102–3). The second narrator, Dog Woman's adopted son Jordan, feels less of a 'man' than his mother. He has 'lost' his identity in his mother because 'she is bigger and stronger than me and that's not how it is supposed to be with sons' (Winterson, 1990, 101). Hence his desire is to be a hero, like John Tradescant, who takes Jordan on his voyages, and his search for Fortunata, the dancer, is a search for a part of himself.

Tremain's Robert Merivel is a similarly marginal figure, de-masculinised by his position as a buffoon at court. Like Winterson's Henri, he is traumatised and fragmented by his powerless position within history. The first words of the text – 'I am, I discover, a very untidy man' (1990, 13) – establish and then immediately undermine the concept of a stable known identity and its relation to the body. His grotesque body is 'an affront to neatness' (13), and even suggests that he may not be his father's son, that is, may not be who he thinks he is. Through Merivel, Tremain undermines what, in Hutcheon's words, 'has been accepted as universal and transhistorical in our culture: the humanist notion of man as a coherent and continuous subject' (1988, 177). Merivel is neither coherent not continuous. His ignominiously good 'performance' (1990, 38) as 'paper groom' to Charles II's mistress expresses the extent to which he is constructed or 'written' by the King he worships. His identity fluctuates according to the recognition of the King. His subjectivity is not static but dependent on his status as subject to the King. Banished from the court and the King's affirming gaze, he falls from grace into a state of abandonment.

Shuttling between the two poles of his world – the luxurious materialism of the Restoration court dominated by the King and the abstemious and egalitarian society of the Quaker-run lunatic asylum where God is the only authority – he is split between his two identities as 'Merivel' and 'Robert'. The sharp discontinuity in tone and scene between these two worlds emphasises that there is no one essential version of 'the seventeenth century', no continuum which can be 'restored'. The duality of 'Robert' and 'Merivel' illustrates the social and cultural construction of identity. 'Who knows', the King tells him, 'whether, at some time in the future, History may not have another role for you?' (1990, 196). Merivel demonstrates, to borrow Hutcheon's words again, how 'the subject of history is the subject in history, subject to history and to his story' (1988, 177).

In her treatment of King Charles II, Tremain breaks another of Lukács' defining characteristics, his suggestion that world historical figures should play only a minor part in a historical novel. As Winterson does with Napoleon in *The Passion*, Tremain centralises the world historical figure but exposes him to us through the misperception of his adoring subject. This deployment of point of view provides a slanted and subjective view which deconstructs the heroic status of the world historical figure. Through the eyes of his chicken chef, we see Napoleon gorging on chicken as he gorges on the countries he conquers. And through the eyes of the fool he has cuckolded, we see Charles II, his head buried in the crotch of the woman he has bribed Merivel to marry, as an exploitative and amoral man rather than a being made divine by his kingship. The tragi-comic moral dilemma of *Restoration* comes from Merivel's recognition that, having been given all the material possessions he could want, he has broken the one rule on which this wealth depends: he has fallen in love with his own wife. Yet, given his iden-tification with the King, it is also inevitable that he can only desire what the King desires.

In *Sexing the Cherry*, Winterson appears to move further away from the conventional form of the realist novel than Tremain. 'History', Winterson wrote in her first novel, 'should be a hammock for swinging and a game for playing, the way cats play. Claw it, chew it, rearrange it and at bedtime, it's still a ball of string full of knots' (1985, 93). By splicing 'real history' with her rewritings of the fairytale of the twelve dancing princesses, she implies that history is only another form of the discourses by which we interpret the world, no more privileged than a child's story. Thus she plays fast and loose with her historical background, which seems at times to be a barely sketched-in cardboard setting for dreamlike fantasies.

Kate Hodgkin, for instance, has drawn attention to Winterson's misrepresentation of the Puritans as self-interested, male hypocrites driven by repressed lust: 'The idea that a Puritan might actually be a woman, or poor, finds no place in the novel's ferociously scurrilous depiction of radical religion' (Hodgkin, n.d., 8). As Hodgkin points out, this picture has much to do with Winterson's own experience of growing up lesbian in a fiercely repressive evangelical Christian family (fictionalised in *Oranges Are Not The Only Fruit*). Her fiction consistently seeks to recover and re-value the body denied by the church. 'Through the flesh we are set free [. . .] our desire for another will lift us out of ourselves more cleanly than anything divine' as she puts it in *The Passion* (1988, 154). However, her depiction of Puritanism in *Sexing the Cherry* is more indebted to easy stereotypes than to the historical reality of Puritanism as a politically radical religion. The same, of course, can be said of Ellen Galford's depiction of Puritans in *Moll Cutpurse*, where they are Moll's bête noire because of their hypocritical abuse of women. It is not until the 1990s and Stevie Davies' *Impassioned Clay* (1999) that radical religion is linked to radical lesbian sexuality.

In contrast to this, Tremain's depiction of the egalitarian Quaker community with its idealistic attempt to help poor and oppressed people looks both more authentic and more radical. Moreover, Tremain's novel offers far more of the historical detail – of clothes, food, customs, language – which Umberto Eco has argued is essential to the serious historical novel (Eco, 1984, 23). Her inspiration for the novel, she has recorded, came from reading Pepys' diaries (Tremain, 1999, 62–3), and *Restoration* has the kind of solidly physical materiality, as well as the bawdiness, which we associate with Pepys' writing. While she researches the historical background carefully, Tremain also admits to using deliberate anachronisms: 'Because the character is quite anarchic, so there is a small level of author anarchy there' (Ashby, 2002, 16). This is not the kind of 'necessary anachronism' which Lukács argues is allowable to clarify and underline the relationship between past and present (1983, 61). Instead, it is an inventive playfulness typical of postmodern writing, which draws attention to the fictionality of the historical novel.

However, Tremain's extensive use of historically verifiable detail conveys and acknowledges the otherness, the *difference*, of another historical period, which Winterson's work seems to deny or elide. Martha Tuck Rozett has argued that:

Some of this strangeness [of *Restoration*] is due to the very historicity of the novel, for Tremain manages to capture an aspect of the past that is utterly foreign to us: the quasi-sexual, lover-like devotion and absolute trust the subject feels for the king, regardless of his flaws, and the god-like intuitive knowledge that the king – again, despite his flaws – seems to possess. (1995, 160)

Oddly, it is Winterson who offers us a way of reading Tremain's use of the King as both a flawed man and a symbol of the divine in *Restoration*. In *Art Objects*, Winterson reminds us that the monarch's role is to inspire and lead their subjects: 'royalty is an *imaginative* function: it must embody in its own person, subtle and difficult concepts of Otherness' (1995, 141). At the end of *Restoration*, the King is, to borrow Winterson's formula, 'a bridge between the terrestrial and the supernatural' (1995, 140), who 'restores' Merivel by giving him the mysteriously empty room in his beloved Bidnold. This restoration can only happen, however, after Merivel has been refined through his experiences. He has come to terms with his parents by rescuing a woman from the Great Fire (re-enacting and correcting his failure to rescue his mother in an earlier fire), and he has himself become a parent. Thus it is as a symbol of divine otherness, not as a flawed human being, that the King authorises or affirms the restoration that Merivel has himself achieved.

Winterson is truer to history than her playful mixing of texts at first appears. The central image of her text – 'sexing the cherry' – comes from the practice of grafting, popularised in the seventeenth century by John Tradescant. Her novel, as Elizabeth Langland (1997) has shown, can be read as a parodic rewriting of Andrew Marvell's 'The Mower, Against Gardens'. Whereas Marvell's reactionary mower rails against the gardener's practice of grafting, maintaining that 'in the cherry he does Nature vex, / To procreate without a sex', Langland argues that Winterson uses grafting as 'one central means to escape the tired binaries of reproduction' (1997, 100). When she witnesses Jordan grafting a cherry, Dog Woman reproduces the Mower's conservatism, regarding the result as a monster, and saying that 'such things had no gender and were a confusion to themselves' (1990, 79). In contrast, the more open Jordan wants to 'have some of Tradescant grafted onto to me so that I could be a hero like him' (1990, 79). Grafting, in Winterson's novel, becomes an image for how what is regarded as the 'natural' order of things (the body, gender, history, time, matter, authority, heroism) can be re-imagined.

The two epigraphs to the novel ask questions which destablise two central concepts: time and matter. The first notes that the Hopi, an Indian tribe, have 'no tenses for past, present and future'. The second draws on Quantum Theory to posit the idea that 'Matter [...] is now known to be mostly empty space' (1990, 8). Winterson's novel explores how these understandings might change our concepts of time, space and matter. She uses them to challenge 'not only the authority of bodily materiality and the cultural meanings we ascribe to it but also the nature of time itself and a belief in linear progress' (Langland, 1997, 105). Thus she disrupts the linearity of the realist narrative by introducing the fantastic, the fairy tale and the myth. Linear history is further collapsed as Dog Woman and Jordan reappear in the final section as their twentieth-century incarnations: Nicolas Jordan and the unnamed woman who mounts a solitary protest against the pollution of the lakes and rivers by big business. Finally, the novel concludes:

> The future and the present and the past exist only in our minds [. . .] And even the most solid of things and the most real, the best loved and the well-known, are only hand-shadows on the wall. Empty space and points of light. (1990, 144)

For Winterson, however, this does not mean a morally empty universe but one which gives us the freedom to rethink the moral imperatives and priorities which we take for granted as 'natural'.

This is most obvious in the way in which she undermines the authority of the narratives of heroism which dominate our history of England as an imperial power. 'England is a land of heroes' (1990, 79), Jordan tells us, and his twentieth-century incarnation, Nicolas Jordan, is similarly obsessed by the men who appear in *The Boys' Book of Heroes*: William the Conqueror, Christopher Columbus, Francis Drake and Lord Nelson. These are, of course, the world historical figures who dominate our traditional historical narratives, which privilege the 'authority' of the fighter and the explorer. Nicolas comes to understand that the female environmental campaigner, who burns down the pollution-producing factory, is a hero. This involves a redefinition of the concept of heroism from the individual self-aggrandisement of the male fighter and explorer to the anonymous woman who sacrifices herself for the community: 'Heroes give up what's comfortable in order to protect what they believe in or to live dangerously for the common good' (1990, 138).

Both Tremain and Winterson celebrate the heroism of marginal figures unrecorded in conventional historical narratives. Both are associated with the cleansing power of fire. Dog Woman burns down the corrupt and plague-ridden city of London, while her twentieth-century reincarnation burns down the factory. Robert Merivel risks his life to save a woman he does not know from the Great Fire, an act which brings about his redemption. In validating such acts both the writers undermine the authority of the grand narratives of conventional history and show how the individual can authorise him or herself.

Like Angela Carter, Tremain and Winterson are interested in how identity, particularly gendered identity, is produced through performance, in Judith

Butler's terms, by a process of repetition, citation and imitation over time. Or, to put it slightly differently, identity is produced through the process of telling stories, which are produced through and in history. 'Our flesh comes to us through history' as Carter put it, but it is shaped by the narratives, both fictional and 'historical', we tell to explain it. If both history and identity ('real people') are fictions, Tremain and Winterson suggest, then we can invent, or 'authorise', our own narratives. If gendered identity is constructed, despite the materiality of the body, then we have a certain freedom to 'graft' a new identity.

In *Art Objects*, Winterson argues that art is not consolation but creation: 'energetic space which creates energetic space' (1995, 114). Because of this it has the power to 'create rooms for us, the dispossessed' (114). This is a particularly good description of the historical novel. At its best and most inventive, it brings together past and present in a dialogue which creates an 'energetic space' which allows us to imagine a better future.

9
Dialogues with the Dead: History and the 'Sense of an Ending', 1990–2000

The 1990s were, as Patricia Waugh put it, an 'era of belatedness, of a generalised "post"-condition' (1995, 33). Theorists talked about 'postmodernism', 'poststructuralism', 'postcolonialism', 'post-industrialism', 'post-feminism', 'post-nationalism', the 'post-human', 'late capitalism' and 'the end of history'. For Frederic Jameson, it was precisely this 'inverted millenarianism' with its 'senses of the end of this or that' which constituted postmodernism, defined as a radical break with 'the 100-year-old modern movement' (1991, 1). For women the 1990s were most obviously 'post-feminist', not in the sense that the battle for equality had been won, but because they found themselves facing an anti-feminist backlash.[1] The language of revolutionary feminism might be everywhere, co-opted by the global market in order to sell consumer goods, but the actual economic and political gains made by women often seemed illusory.

The ends of decades, of centuries and particularly millennia, as Frank Kermode noted much earlier in *The Sense of an Ending* (1967), tend to focus attention particularly acutely on endings in general and the possibility of the end of the world in particular. This was especially evident as the millennial-fever of the 1990s brought rumours of the 'Y2K' bug that would allegedly disrupt the computer systems which controlled everything from banks to the electricity grid in our machine age, bringing civilisation to an apocalyptic standstill at midnight on 31 December 1999. As Elaine Showalter pointed out in *Hystories: Hysterical Epidemics and Modern Culture* (1997), 'Epidemics of hysteria seem to peak at the ends of centuries when people are already alarmed about social change' (1998, 19). In retrospect, the furore over the 'Y2K' bug exemplifies just such hysteria, but Showalter drew attention to other 1990s 'hysterical epidemics', among which she included Gulf War Syndrome, recovered memory, chronic fatigue syndrome and multiple personality syndrome.

Humans need narratives that impose a sense of beginning, middle and ending, Frank Kermode suggests, because these give shape to the chaos of experience:

Men [*sic*], like poets, rush 'into the middest'... when they are born, they also die in mediis rebus, and to make sense of their span they need fictive concords with origins and ends, such as give meaning to lives and to poems. (Kermode, 1967, 7)

History, myth, religion, fiction and poetry are all ways of making meaning by imposing a structure on contingent experience. Thus world history is 'the imposition of a plot on time' (43). Such plotting requires an ending to 'bestow upon the whole duration and meaning' (46), but it also highlights the constructed and multiple nature of history. 'There is no history, says Karl Popper, only *histories*' (1967, 43, my emphasis). In the 1990s, then, it is hardly surprising that people's attention turned to history and to narratives of ending.

Francis Fukuyama controversially combined the two by maintaining that history had ended. In *The End of History and the Last Man* (1992), he argued that the collapse of communism signalled the triumph of democratic capitalism and the establishment of a global consensus. This meant the end of history as defined by Hegel, in the sense of a process of dialectical evolution through clashes between great civilisations. This was the notion of history, of course, which underpinned Lukács' theorisation of the historical novel. In retrospect, Fukuyama's book can be seen, in David Usborne's words, as 'a hymn to liberalism, capitalism and unrestricted trade' (2003, 5) – a narrative of wishful thinking.

In the millennial 1990s, 'serious' women writers increasingly turned to the historical novel, or rather to new versions of the genre which they shaped to reflect their sense of history as subjective, multiple, contingent and fragmented. Commenting on the general turn to history for subject-matter (in male and female writers), Maggie Gee was typical of several reviewers in seeing it as a failure of nerve, a retreat from the urgencies of the contemporary. It was, she thought, 'easier to cling on to the coat-tails of fact, to write historical reconstructions, or novelised biographies, or fictional autobiographies' (1997, 10), than to attempt the more difficult task of assimilating the accelerated change in their own time. This perhaps reflects the still low standing of the historical novel at this point as, in Melvyn Bragg's phrase, 'the genre which dare not speak its name' (Cuthbertson, 2001, 34).[2]

But Gee also misses the centrality of history and its *representation* to the postmodern thinking which informed these novels. As Jameson puts it:

[Postmodernism is] an attempt to think historically in an age that has forgotten how to think historically in the first place. [...] the postmodern looks for breaks, for events rather than new worlds, for the terrible instant after which it is no longer the same [...] for shifts and irrevocable changes in the *representation* of things and of the way they change. (1991, ix)

This has particular relevance for the historical novel as a genre. The post-modern historical novel, Jameson argued, 'can no longer set out to represent the historical past; it can only "represent" our ideas and stereotypes about the past (which then becomes "pop" history)' (1991, 25). The past thus becomes not 'the organic genealogy of the bourgeois collective project', as Lukács defined it, but 'a vast collection of images, a multitudinous photographic simulacrum' (Jameson, 1991, 18).

Within this context, the woman's historical novel of the 1990s looks less like a nostalgic retreat into the past than a complex engagement with the ways in which representations of history change over time and their relation to structures of power, not least those of gender. In particular, writers turned to historical periods where Jameson's 'breaks [...] shifts and irrevocable changes' were especially obvious: the first millennium in Moy McCrory's *The Fading Shrine* (1990); the French Revolution in Hilary Mantel's *A Place of Greater Safety* (1992); the seventeenth century, but focusing on the fractures of the English Civil War rather than the 'Restoration', in Philippa Gregory's *Earthly Joys* (1998) and *Virgin Earth* (1999), and Stevie Davies' *Impassioned Clay* (1999b); the nineteenth century in a host of novels, such as Elaine Feinstein's *Dreamers* (1994) about the 1848 revolutions or Sarah Waters' lesbian fantasy *Tipping the Velvet* (1998), which emphasised repressed and contested discontinuities rather than the consensual continuity invoked by Margaret Thatcher; and the First World War as the beginning of modernity in Pat Barker's *Regeneration* trilogy (1991–1995) and several other novels.

Given the poststructural recognition that the past itself as a 'referent' is always unobtainable and accessible only through textual representation, the woman's historical novel during this decade does not seek straightforwardly to represent history in the sense of mirroring or reproducing it. To borrow Linda Hutcheon's words, 'fiction is offered as another of the discourses by which we construct our versions of reality, and both the construction and the need for it are what are foregrounded in the post-modernist novel' (1988, 40). The novels of the 1990s, like those of the 1980s, contest the idea of a single unitary and linear history. They emphasise the subjective, fragmentary nature of historical knowledge through rewritings of canonical texts, through multiple or divided narrators, fragmentary or contradictory narratives, and disruptions of linear chronology.

Even texts which are ostensibly 'realist', such as Pat Barker's *Regeneration* trilogy (1991–1995), Hilary Mantel's *A Place of Greater Safety* or Penelope Fitzgerald's *The Blue Flower* (1995), are less straightforward than they appear. Instead of producing a single narrative of the French Revolution, for instance, Mantel writes it as the stories of three central figures: Georges-Jacques Danton, Maximilien

Robespierre and Camille Desmoulins. The effect is to situate the reader within multiple and subjective points of view on the confusing and violent flood of events, rather than producing an 'overview' or 'complete account' (Mantel, 1998, ix). Mantel often renders dialogue in script form which disrupts the usual practice of the realist novel and thus draws attention to its fictionality. 'The past is not something that you can retrieve', Mantel points out, 'You have to *reinvent* it, it has to be strenuously reimagined' (Galván, 2001, 31). 'History is fiction', as Robespierre maintained (Mantel, 1998, 24).

Mantel, like Fitzgerald, is particularly interested in the disjunctions between the private early lives of these men, when little is known of them, and their public personae as world historical figures. When people become public persons, she suggests, they 'step as it were not just into history, but into myth' and 'their story is in some sense confiscated from them' (Galván, 2001, 36). Mantel's title reflects her belief that novelists can get beyond these stereotypes and provide 'a place of safety for the dead, where they can show their faces and be recognised' (Galván, 2001, 37).

In *The Blue Flower*, Fitzgerald is similarly concerned to tell the story of Fritz von Hardenberg, the young man who became the great Romantic poet and philosopher Novalis. She does this through a fragmented narrative made up of scenes or snapshots from his early life, which foreground ordinary domestic detail (laundry, food, Christmas celebrations). She also tells the stories of the real women – his mother, his sister, Karoline Just who loved him unrequitedly, his fiancée Sophie who died at the age of 15 – whose needs and desires he disregarded in his pursuit of the ideal. Fitzgerald takes as her epigraph Novalis' statement that 'Novels arise out of the shortcomings of history.' Like Mantel, then, she privileges imaginative fiction for its ability to go beyond the surface facts of history.

However, these texts are concerned not to represent a transcendent or authentic 'truth' of the past, but rather, in Hutcheon's words, to urge a revaluation of and 'dialogue with the past in the light of the present' (1988, 19). The notion of a 'dialogue' between past and present comes up repeatedly in the work of both the writers and critics during the 1990s. Steven Connor, for instance, argues that in the face of the collapse of confidence in authoritative histories, postmodern novels are concerned with 'constructing the terms of a conversation or structure of address between the past and the present' (1996, 164). This dialogue is perhaps most explicit in the many novels – *Impassioned Clay*, *The Fading Shrine* and Michèle Roberts' *In the Red Kitchen* (1990) to give just three examples – which use parallel narratives to juxtapose past and present.

The re-imagining and re-evaluation of women's lost histories or 'herstory' is still an important part of this contestatory dialogue with traditional history but by the 1990s it has been accepted into mainstream fiction. Sara George's *The Journal of Mrs Pepys* (1998), for instance, re-imagines the story of Pepys' much-tried wife, Elizabeth – 'one of the many women half-hidden from history by their dominant menfolk', as Margaret Forster puts it in the cover blurb of the paperback edition. Alison Fell's *The Mistress of Lilliput* (1999) rewrites Swift's *Gulliver's Travels* as the adventures of Gulliver's wife. Hilary Bailey's *Cassandra: Princess of Troy* (1993) retells the fall of Troy from the point of view of the legendary prophetess. Geraldine McCaughrean's *The Ideal Wife* (1997) tells the story of two girls brought up by Robin Wootton (probably based on Thomas Day) according to Rousseauian principles in order that he may choose one for his wife. The Irish writer Emma Donoghue weaves an imaginative fiction out of the fragmentary evidence about Mary Saunders, a servant girl hung for murdering her mistress in 1763 in *Slammerkin* (2000). Rosalind Miles retells the Arthurian legends in her *Guenevere* trilogy (1998–2000), making not only women but Goddess-worship central to the story. These texts all privilege the female point of view and thus expose the subjective and phallocentric nature of mainstream history.

Perhaps the most radical examples of this project are Sarah Waters' *Tipping the Velvet* and *Affinity* (1999), which explicitly set out, as she put it, to 'reclaim the Victorian period [...] for a modern lesbian agenda' (Boyce, 2002, 3). Waters completed a PhD on the idea of history in gay and lesbian writing, and this research (as with Philippa Gregory) informs her fiction. In the 1980s and 1990s, as in the 1920s and 1930s, the relationship between feminist historical research and historical fiction is close and productive. Alex Owen on spiritualism, Elaine Showalter on hysteria and Marjorie Garber on cross-dressing, for example, have all been influential.[3] Waters' novels draw on her historical research to foreground what is repressed in Victorian fiction, the sexual desire and behaviours which are 'not-said' in the novels of Charles Dickens, Wilkie Collins or the Brontës. The extent to which what had been radical or academic feminism has now been assimilated by the mainstream and appropriated by the commercial is indicted by the fact that *Tipping the Velvet* was made into a television drama, scripted by Andrew Davies and shown on BBC2 in October 2002.

In the 1990s and in the face of the coming millennium, writers interrogated the ways in which subjective 'fictions' (including history) are used to impose meaning and structure upon the past with a particular concern for the reasons why such meanings were *needed* by human beings. This 'need' for narratives of meaning is particularly clear in two themes that appear frequently in these novels. The first is a concern with religion as a narrative which imposes meaning on history, particularly through the notion of an apocalypse or a Second Coming, what Walter Benjamin called 'Messianic time' (1973, 265). The second theme is a concern with spectrality and spiritualism and with the medium as a figure who connects past and present.

The coming millennium is clearly the inspiration behind much of the interest in religion as a shaping narrative. Moy McCrory's *The Fading Shrine*, for instance, is the story of the destruction of a convent during the tempests, floods and calamities around the time of the first millennium, seen as apocalyptic by the scribes. The body of women's knowledge, particularly about childbirth and abortion, the convent holds is thereby lost to history. The mystery of the painting which the present-day nun cannot decipher symbolises the unreadable traces of the past, as 'Facts become submerged after the passage of time' (1991, 286). Jane Rogers' *Mr Wroe's Virgins* (1991) retells the story of John Wroe, leader of the Christian Israelites in Ashton in the early nineteenth century. A nihilist himself, Rogers' Wroe prophesies the end of the world and the beginning of a New World as a kind of consolatory 'fantasy' (1992, 225) in which he himself cannot believe. The story is told through the sometimes contradictory voices of five different women, the 'virgins' of the title. Through the experience of Martha, an abused child who has to learn language as an adult, Rogers shows how language is used to name and therefore 'invent' reality (1992, 252–3), and to shape time into past, present and future. Memory, like religion, is a narrative which is used to order contingent experience. However, the linear Messianic time prophesied by Wroe is contrasted with the cyclical time (what Kristeva would call 'women's time') experienced by the women through their monthly bleeding (1992, 193).

The silencing of women's experience, particularly lesbian experience, and the possibility of a female prophet are explored in Stevie Davies' *Impassioned Clay* (1999b). This came out of Davies' own research into female radical religion for *Unbridled Spirits: Women of the English Revolution, 1640–1660* (1998). In the introduction, she draws attention to an explicit parallel between the 'hysterical' 'anti-female backlash' of the seventeenth century and the 'present "crisis of family values"' (1999a, 3), and these are replicated in the parallel narratives of the novel. Davies' need to write two texts – one historical, the other fictional – illustrates the ways in which imaginative writing can fill in the gaps in historical fact; or, perhaps, can create the kind of 'history' the writer wishes had existed.

Davies' fictional seventeenth-century Quaker protagonist Hannah Emanuel is executed for the transgression of developing a theology of a female god, claiming that, 'The Spirit, she is in me [...] *she's me*' (1999b, 205). Egalitarian, outspoken and lesbian, Hannah is, Kate Hodgkin has remarked, 'the prophet all feminist scholars would have liked to have found' in their research (n.d., 16). As such, like Galford's *Moll Cutpurse*, she says more about *our* desires than those of the seventeenth century. Hannah's final 'crucifixion' – she is hung wearing the 'brank' or scold's bridle to silence her – positions her as a second (and female) Christ. The novel recovers a lost matrilineal genealogy as the present-day narrator, Olivia, discovers that Hannah is her biological ancestor through her mother's line. The concepts of voice and dialogue are central to Davies' engagement with the past. *Unbridled Spirits* is framed in terms of listening to lost and silenced voices, 'voices from which our own tongue derives' (1999a, 6). This is repeated in *Impassioned Clay* where Olivia hears the voices of the dead: 'the dead spoke to me' (1999b, 32). The brank becomes a particularly potent symbol of the erasure of women's history: 'History, gagged and branked, struggles in the silences that are left when dissident voices have been silenced' (1999b, 141).

The women in these texts – Davies' Hannah, the nuns in McCrory's convent, Rogers' Joanna, who wants to set up a woman's church following in the footsteps of the earlier prophetic writer Joanna Southcott – recall the 'defeated' women who represent lost possibilities in the woman's historical novel of the 1930s. Davies and McCrory, however, use the parallel narrative of the present day to suggest that some advances have been made.

The second central theme, then, is the concern with spectrality and spiritualism, and with the medium. The interest in spiritualism that emerged at the end of the nineteenth century can be seen as a response to the Darwinian theory of evolution and the subsequent crisis of faith. In a secular age, postmodernism, as Peter Middleton and Tim Woods suggest, 'is haunted by memory: memories of disaster, genocide, war, the Holocaust and the persistent destruction of human possibility by economic and political means' (2000, 81). Postmodern historical novels often use spectrality to figure the ways in which the present is haunted by the past. Dialogue is again a central motif. The seventeenth-century prophet was engaged in a dialogue with God (as Davies puts it, revolutionary tracts can be seen as a version of 'I-said-to-God-and-He said-to-me' [1999a, 8]), and often presented herself as a passive mediator relaying His voice. Similarly, the spiritualist medium was engaged in a dialogue with the dead who haunt the present, mediating between dead and living, past and present.

In the work of several novelists, including Pat Barker, Sarah Waters, Michèle Roberts and A.S. Byatt, the female medium becomes a suggestive figure for the historical novelist herself, ventriloquising the voices of the past. As Waters notes, in the nineteenth century, women 'were seen as being particularly prone to making good mediums because femininity was considered to be rather passive, so they would make good vehicles for the spirits' (Boyce, 2002, 3). Thus, mediumship, as Alex Owen (1989) shows, became one of the few 'professions' open to women.

In her novella, 'The Conjugial Angel' in *Angels and Insects* (1992), A.S. Byatt creates two women, Mrs Papagay and Sophie Sheeky, who make their living through séances. Michèle Roberts based her professional medium, Flora Milk, in *In the Red Kitchen*, on the furore around the life of the real nineteenth-century figure of Florence Cook. The novel links together the often conflicting voices of five different women: Flora, her sister Rosina, their patron Minny Preston, Hat an Egyptian princess, and Hattie King, a former prostitute and writer of cookery books in the present. The inter-weaving of these voices breaks down linear historical chronology and thus makes connections between women across history. In the Gothic *Affinity*, Sarah Waters brings together the theme of spiritualism and women's imprisonment. Her medium, Selina Dawes, is imprisoned in Millbank Prison for fraud and assault during a séance that went wrong. The women's prison, 'which has so many separate lives in it, and is so curious a shape, and must be approached, so darkly, through so many gates and twisting passages' (1999, 7), becomes a figure for History itself and the difficulty of shaping it into a coherent story.

The question of authenticity – of history and of fiction – is central to these texts, focused through suspicions that the medium herself is fraudulent. Byatt's medium, Sophie, is genuine (despite the suspicions of those who attend her séances) and her conjuring up of the bodily form of Arthur Hallam allows Byatt to explore the fear, both Victorian and present-day, that the body, mouldering after death, is all there is. The protagonist of *Affinity*, Margaret Prior, who falls in love with Selina and arranges her escape from prison, comes to believe in Selina's powers and is brutally disillusioned. But the novel ultimately leaves the reader in doubt as to whether her ability as a medium is a fraud.

Similarly, Roberts' Flora Milk may or may not be a 'hysteric who suffers from delusions' (1990, 130). She is exhibited as such by Dr Charcot at the Salpetrière Hospital in Paris, and Roberts thus explores the links between the bodily 'performances' or possession of the hysteric and the medium. Through her use of multiple and competing narrators, Roberts leaves open the question of whether Flora is genuine, and the victim of male manipulation, or a fraudulent exploiter as her sister Rosina maintains. The lack of resolution suggests, in Rosie White's words, 'the absence of a final, signified, historical truth' (n.d., 148). But the novel also strongly suggests the erasure of female history, most explicitly through the erasure of the hieroglyphs which spelt out Hat's name on her sepulchre: 'I have been unwritten', she mourns, 'Written out. Written off. Therefore I am not even dead. I never was' (Roberts, 1990, 133).

The medium who connects past and present, and who gives a voice to the dead who have been erased from history, is a particularly suggestive figure for the female historical novelist. Writing historical fiction is itself, in Waters' words, 'a sort of confidence trick, it is just whether you can make it sound authentic' (Boyce, 2002, 3). A.S. Byatt and Pat Barker, as I will argue below, use the medium to think about the function of the historical novelist, and the ways in which she creates a dialogue with the dead.

Given that the historical novel has offered women writers a space within which they can cross-write as men, the other suggestive figure for the historical novelist, as I suggested in the Introduction, is the girl masquerading as a boy. In the 1990s, both Sarah Waters and Patricia Duncker have used the historical novel to explore the theme of cross-dressing as an enabling fantasy for women. Their work reflects the importance of the theorisation of gender as performative in Judith Butler's *Gender Trouble* (1990). Indeed, the blurb on the cover of the 1999 paperback edition of Waters' *Tipping the Velvet* quotes a review from the *Independent on Sunday* which makes this connection explicit: 'Imagine Jeanette Winterson on a good day, collaborating with Judith Butler to pen a sapphic Moll Flanders.' What is perhaps most interesting here is the assumption that the general reader will recognise the significance of Butler's name.

Waters' Nancy King is an oyster girl in the 1890s who becomes a male impersonator in the music-halls, a 'rent-boy' on the streets of London, the kept 'boy' of a wealthy lesbian lady, and finally an East End 'tom' and Socialist speaker living with the girl she loves. Although it is informed by Waters' research into Edwardian male impersonators such as Vesta Tilley and Hetty King, and the beginnings of gay communities in the 1890s, *Tipping the Velvet* is, as Waters herself admits, 'historical fantasy' not social history (Boyce, 2002, 3). As such, like *Impassioned Clay* and *Moll Cutpurse*, it is most informative about the fantasies of the present, and the fact that, partly thanks to Waters, the figure of the historical lesbian has moved out of the shadows into mainstream fiction and television.

The most sustained and serious exploration of male impersonation is Patricia Duncker's *James Miranda Barry* (1999), which re-imagines the historically documented story of an army doctor and medical reformer who was discovered after his death to have the body of a woman. Duncker takes liberties with Barry's life, altering dates and imagining a woman for him to love. Alice Jones is a scullery maid who becomes an actress playing boy's parts on stage, and then a professional medium. When Barry wants to reveal his impersonation, it is Alice, the professional performer, who dissuades him, telling him, 'Nothing's absolutely genuine [...] It's all a performance, [...] You are what the world says you are' (Duncker, 2000, 358–9). As Alice reflects, 'You can't suddenly become a woman. It takes years of practice' (368). This accords with Butler's argument that gender, as the practice of drag reveals, is imitative, performative and contingent.

However, it is not the secret of Barry's 'real' gender or, indeed, the reasons for his impersonation which are the most interesting things about the book. Duncker resists what Marjorie Garber has identified as the critical tendency to look *through* rather than *at* the cross-dresser (1993, 4). In the film *Tootsie*, Garber has argued, 'Dorothy's power inheres in her blurred gender, in the fact of her cross-dressing, and not [...] in *either* of her gendered identities' (1993, 1). The same is true of James Miranda Barry. Barry's cross-dressing offers what Garber calls a 'third term' (10), which challenges the binary categories of 'male' and 'female'. Cross-dressing thus becomes an enabling fantasy for women because it demonstrates that: 'Gender exists only in representation [...] This is the subversive secret of transvestism, that the body is not the ground but the figure' (Garber, 1993, 374). It is in the historical novel, even the popular (and heterosexual) romances of Georgette Heyer, that women writers have had the freedom to explore this understanding.

Ventriloquising the past: A.S. Byatt's romance with history

The Booker Prize-winning *Possession: A Romance* (1990) was the novel that transformed A.S. Byatt into a major bestseller. Representative of its period in interesting ways, *Possession* has attracted a considerable amount of critical attention which repeatedly positions it as a typically 'postmodern' text and as an example of historiographic metafiction.[4] Byatt herself prefers to call her fiction 'self-conscious realism' (Byatt, 1993a, 4), but in *Possession* she explores the pleasures of what might be called self-conscious historical romance.

Byatt is interesting in relation to the development of the woman's historical novel for two reasons. First, she is one of the few serious writers to have paid tribute to the skill of Georgette Heyer as a 'superlatively good writer of honourable escape' (Byatt, 1993a, 258). *Possession* is, among other things, a historical romance influenced by Heyer,[5] and it is a celebration of the *pleasures* of reading, especially of reading well-crafted women's historical fiction. Byatt recognised that Heyer's books satisfied the reader's 'perennial need for a happy ending' (increasingly unavailable in 'serious' writing) and her curiosity about 'historical facts of daily life and thought' (1993a, 259). But further to this, Heyer, Byatt suggests, achieved a 'clever balance between genuine romance and a saving comic mockery of romance within romance' (1993a, 261). In this ironically self-reflexive gameplaying with the conventions of romance, Heyer's novels are far closer to historiographic metafiction than their status as popular romance suggests. Their pleasure for the reader lies in this 'precise balance [...] between romance and reality, fantastic plot and real detail' (Byatt, 1993a, 265). In this they provide an important model for Byatt's own self-consciously metafictional historical romance with its wealth of literary historical detail and its happy ending.[6] Thus, in Byatt's writing we can trace the subterranean importance of Heyer through the century.

Secondly, in her critical study, *On Histories and Stories* (2000), Byatt has written an important defence of the historical novel as a form which she argues is, despite the disapproval of critics and reviewers, undergoing a renaissance which makes it of central importance to our understanding of contemporary literature. She asserts, I think wrongly, that discussion of the form has been limited by being 'confined within discussions of Empire or Women, or to the debate between "escapism" and "relevance"' (2000, 3). The 'new map [...] of recent British writing' (2000, 3) which Byatt attempts to establish in *On Histories and Stories* is an idiosyncratic one which (perhaps inevitably) tells us more about Byatt's own practice than the wider picture. But it does draw attention to writers such as Hilary Mantel and Penelope Fitzgerald who have been relatively neglected, partly because their use of the historical novel form does not fit either mainstream or feminist accounts of contemporary fiction in immediately obvious ways.[7]

Byatt's own earlier novel *The Virgin in the Garden* (1978) was explicitly conceived as a historical novel along the lines of *Middlemarch* (Kenyon, 1988, 75) in the sense that it was an attempt to write what Lukács called 'self-experienced history' (1983, 84). Set in 1952–1953, it used the coronation of Elizabeth II and a production of a verse drama about her earlier namesake, the 'Virgin Queen', in order to explore the difference between the original and the 'New' Elizabethan Ages. The Eliotesque realism of the novel is countered by an intertextual exploration of Renaissance myth and symbolism. The effect of this is that the rich colour of the past, as it is experienced through the literature of the so-called 'Golden Age', continually over-shadows the present. As Byatt put it later, the 'ruddy and shining' figure of Elizabeth I 'presides over the pale world of her successor' (Byatt, 1991a, xiv).

Even in the modern setting of *The Virgin in the Garden* there is a trace of Heyer's influence. The unusual name of the protagonist, Frederica (who plays the virgin queen), recalls Heyer's own novel of that name, published in 1965. *Frederica* features one of Heyer's most independent heroines, acting as *de facto* head of a family of engaging siblings after the death of her parents. In her 1969 essay on Heyer, Byatt particularly admires the accurate historical detail in *Frederica*. Byatt's own highly intelligent Frederica, anxious for both intellectual and sexual experience, seems to be both a version of Byatt herself and a kind of everywoman whose life is at the centre of the two succeeding novels, *Still Life* (1985) and *Babel Tower* (1996). Byatt's trilogy is an ambitious attempt to write the present, or at least the very recent past, as 'history'.

Possession continues this inter-weaving of realism and mythic allusion, past and present, in ways which engage directly with contemporaneous debates around postmodernism and the representation of history. Like *Impassioned Clay* and *In the Red Kitchen*, it uses the popular technique of parallel past and present narratives, as well as the motif of the recovering of the hidden past. Here the parallel narratives are used primarily to foreground a disjunction between past and present, where the past is, as in *The Virgin in the Garden*, presented as richer and more whole than the present. But the text also re-establishes a lost matrilineal genealogy, as the female protagonist discovers the story of a foremother.[8] Again typically of the 1980s–90s, *Possession* turns to the Victorian period for its setting. Dana Schiller includes it in a discussion of 'neo-Victorian novels': novels 'at once characteristic of postmodernism and imbued with a historicity reminiscent of the nineteenth-century novel' (1997, 538). Byatt herself locates it in what Sally Shuttleworth calls the genre of 'retro-Victorian novels', inspired by the postmodern era's nostalgic desire for the drama of a loss of faith which drove Victorian writing (Byatt, 2000, 78).

In the present day narrative of *Possession*, two literary critics – Roland Michell, a part-time researcher based in the British Museum, and Maud Bailey, a lecturer at Lincoln University – track down the textual evidence which provides proof of a brief but artistically formative love affair between two imagined Victorian poets, Randolph Ash (based on Browning, Tennyson and a dash of Meredith[9]) and Christobel LaMotte (based on Emily Dickinson with a hint of Christina Rossetti). What they discover, through using their skills as literary critics to turn detective, is not only proof of the affair but that the couple had a daughter, May, making Maud, who had previously believed herself to be only indirectly related to LaMotte, her direct descendent and literary heiress. While LaMotte and Ash are parted when he returns to his unconsummated marriage, the novel concludes with the union of Roland and Maud, who hope to find a 'modern way' of love (1991b, 507) within which they will both be able to retain their 'self-possession' (506). The happy ending provides the traditional pleasures of 'coherence and closure', answering those 'deep human desires', Roland thinks, 'which are presently unfashionable' (1991b, 422).

In tandem with these, however, Byatt also provides the pleasures of postmodern metafiction. *Possession* 'plays serious games with the variety of possible forms of narrating the past', including several forms of romance (both 'high' and 'low'), the detective novel, the campus novel, the epistolary and forged manuscript novels, biography and fairy tale (Byatt, 2000, 48).[10] Byatt also plays with the various meanings of the word 'possession' – daemonic, sexual, economic – but particularly the notion of possession of/ by the past. For her writers, historians, biographers and literary critics, this possession of/by the past is enacted in and through texts.

Byatt herself turns to fictional and mythic forms to write her historical novel. The subtitle *A Romance* and the epigraph from Hawthorne draw attention to the text's status as romance rather than realist novel. In Hawthorne's words, 'Romance' is a genre which attempts 'to connect a bygone time with the very present that is flitting away from us.' Byatt's parallel narratives enact precisely that connection between past and present. By writing the past as 'romance', Byatt (like Heyer and many other women writers) is able to include the women who have been left out of traditional historical narratives. But she also, like Naomi Mitchison and Philippa Gregory, turns to myth as a way of imagining female powers and autonomy which have rarely been central to 'factual' history. Thus Byatt's LaMotte argues that, 'Romance is a proper form for women' (1991b, 373), and her 'Fairy Epic' about Melusina is 'not grounded in historical truth, but in poetic and imaginative truth [. . .] where the soul is free from the restraints of history and fact' (373). For women especially, Byatt suggests, fiction and poetry have been a way of breaking out of the limits of 'history and fact'.

In keeping with the postmodern belief that we can only know the past through texts, the recovered story of Ash and LaMotte is almost all told through texts: the letters, poems, fairy tales, diaries and so on left by the people concerned, as well as contemporary literary critical and biographical interpretations of their work, all read and interpreted (sometimes wrongly) by the modern-day critics. All of these texts, including a considerable amount of *faux*-Victorian poetry, have been skillfully pastiched by Byatt. The exceptions are three passages told through an omniscient narrator, which reveal things never discovered by the contemporary couple. Crucially, what they do not discover, but Byatt reveals in a 'Postscript', is that Ash did meet the daughter they believe he never knew existed.

The poetry and its interpretation introduce a rich mythic level which reinforces the central themes of matrilineal genealogy and female creativity through foregrounding the myth of Demeter/Ceres and her lost and recovered daughter Persephone, and the story of Melusina, the subject of LaMotte's epic fairy poem. The castle-building Melusina, who is revealed as a lamia when her husband spies upon her in the bath, functions as an important image of female self-possession and autonomous creativity. She is linked to both LaMotte and Maud through a web of imagery, including water, the colour green, towers and serpents/dragons.

Persephone or Proserpina, the subject of Ash's *The Garden of Proserpina*, is an equally important mythic female figure. The book opens with Roland reading Ash's own annotated copy of Giambattista Vico's *Principj di Scienza Nuovo* (first published in 1725 and then in new editions in 1730 and 1744) in the London Library. Vico, Roland remembers, 'had looked for historical fact in the poetic metaphors of myth and legend; this piercing together was his "new science"' (Byatt, 1991b, 2). Vico interprets Proserpina as 'the corn, the origin of commerce and community' (3). And Roland's supervisor, Blackadder, believes that for Ash she became 'a personification of History itself in its early mythical days' (3). Vico's emphasis on the importance of narrative and figurative language has obvious attractions for a historical novelist but it has also been influential for postmodern historians, such as Hayden White, interested in the past as a textual product constructed through language – history as 'fiction'.[11]

In engaging with 'the variety of possible forms of narrating the past', including romance, myth and poetic metaphor, *Possession* is also explicitly engaging with such poststructuralist theories about history. As I have noted above, *Possession* is usually characterised as a typically 'postmodern' text. On the surface this looks like an accurate description. Byatt's extensive, possibly even excessive, use of allusion transforms her novel into a model of inter-textuality. It seems to epitomise Roland Barthes' description of the text in 'The Death of the Author' as: 'a multi-dimensional space in which a variety of writings, none of them original, blend and clash [...] a tissue of quotations drawn from the innumerable centres of culture...' (Barthes in Walder, 1990, 230).

Indeed, it is this very 'tissue of quotations' from a wide range of Romantic and Victorian writers which makes Byatt's text so seductive to literary critics. *Possession*, as Louise Yelin has acknowledged, 'flatters us by offering us the pleasures of recognising the inter-textual allusions and revisionary rewritings out of which it is made' (1992, 38). Yet at the same time the text is scathing about scholars who seek to 'possess' writers and their texts in what Byatt clearly regards as the *wrong* way: Mortimer Cropper and his avid collection of Ashiana, Fergus Wolff with his aggressively deconstructionist criticism, Leonora Stern and her claiming of La Motte for a lesbian tradition. Roland

and Maud are presented as primarily textual scholars, driven by narrative hunger and the pleasure of reading.

However, Byatt might be better categorised not as a postmodern writer but as a *recovering* postmodernist. *Possession*, which looks like the most postmodernist of her texts, is in fact perhaps the most resistant to postmodern ideas. Despite its putative feminist themes, *Possession* is perhaps the most conservative, indeed even Thatcherite, of Byatt's texts. In an important essay, Jackie Buxton has argued that far from being a postmodern text, *Possession* 'exhibits a strong suspicion of that epistemic condition, even a condemnation of it' (1996, 212). The final Postscript recording Ash's meeting with his daughter suggests that it is only the omniscient narrator who can reveal the final 'truth' of the past. Thus *Possession* is determined to recover the 'authority' of the writer Barthes pronounced dead and to reclaim him/her as a privileged medium between past and present.

'When I was young', Byatt writes in *Passions of the Mind*, 'I was excited by the idea that history, biography, autobiography, were fictions' (1993a, 23). Her fiction has been consistently preoccupied with 'the problems of the "real" in fiction and the adequacy of words to describe it' (1993a, 4). Her earlier novels – *The Game* (1967), *The Virgin in the Garden* (1978), *Still Life* (1985) – engage with these ideas in complex and interesting ways. *The Game* is particularly concerned with the powers and dangers of fiction. 'Fictions are lies, yes, but we don't ever know the truth', says her character Cassandra, 'We see the truth through fictions – our own, other people's' (1983, 225). By the 1980s and 1990s, however, Byatt seems to have come to see the post-modern argument that we cannot know the past *except* through texts as having hamstrung writers. In *On Histories and Stories* she comments, 'There has been a general feeling during my writing life that we cannot know the past – often extended into the opinion that we therefore should not write about it' (2000, 37).

Moreover, she argues that there has been 'an increasing gulf' between current literary criticism, informed by such theories, and the text it discusses:

> Modern criticism [...] imposes its own narratives and priorities on the writings it uses as raw material, source or jumping off point. [...] Such secondary cleverness distresses both the reader and the writer in me. (2000, 45, 46)

Possession is Byatt's critique of such critics. In *Possession*, postmodern concepts of language, the self and the ultimate unknowability of history have not only ham-strung Roland and Maud as critics, but have also debilitated their emotional capacities. They are a generation who are saturated in the theory of sexuality and desire, but who therefore 'mistrust [...] love, "in love", romantic love, romance *in toto*' (1991b, 423). Maud notes, 'We never say the word Love, do we – we know it's a suspect ideological construct – especially Romantic Love' (1991b, 267). For Byatt, 'part of the whole joke of the novel' is that 'the dead are actually much more alive and vital than the living' because the 'poor moderns' are so given to questioning everything they say and do in the light of the fact that 'language always tells lies' (1993, quoted in Buxton, 1996, 212). The past is not only better than the present but, she suggests, more 'authentic' because it is past.

At the end of the novel, Roland is transformed through his love of language and of Maud from a postmodern sceptic into a poet:

> He had been taught that language was essentially inadequate, that it could never speak what was there, that it only spoke itself. [. . .] What had happened to him was that the ways in which it could be said had become more interesting than the idea that it could not. (1991b, 473)

This clearly echoes Byatt's own feelings, and what seems to be her determination to resurrect the author, rescuing 'him' from the clutches of theorists like Barthes. It is interesting, I think, that it is Byatt's *male* protagonist who moves from the secondary position of literary critic to the primary position of poet.

Possession is a text which is driven by nostalgia, which looks back from a present moment it perceives as fractured and alienated to a past which appears to represent stability and wholeness. In this sense it could be argued that it does illustrate (though not interrogate) a nostalgia for the perceived authenticity of the past which lies at the heart of postmodernism. The relationship between past and present is one of discontinuity and crisis, a disjuncture which, for Byatt, can only be healed by the right 'reading' of the literature of the past. In this, *Possession* is very much a text of the 1980s and replicates the Conservative project to 'restore' Britain to its former greatness. Indeed, the *deus ex machina* of *Possession*, rather bizarrely, is Euan McIntyre, a poetry-loving Yuppie solicitor who figures as a benign emblem of Thatcherite economic individualism. The novel, as Louise Yelin has noted, 'elides politics and sexual politics' and leaves out of its account of critical theory Marxism, new historicism and any other form of 'oppositional criticism or cultural materialism' (1992, 40). Byatt's otherwise extensive play with the notion of 'possession' evades the political implications of the desire for material 'possessions'.

The ostensibly radical experimentalism of Byatt's 'historiographic metafiction', unlike that of Winterson or Tremain, masks a conservative content even when it comes to *Possession*'s sexual politics. The novel's recuperation of the heterosexual happy ending is presented as radical because it is 'unfashionable' but it is done at the expense of the lesbians in the text. Christabel LaMotte's defining relationship as a writer is not the long-term relationship she has with Blanche Glover but the brief affair with Ash.

Blanche's suicide erases her from the text. Moreover, Leonora Stern, the twentieth-century lesbian, reverts to heterosexuality with Blackadder. As Yelin notes, both heterosexual romance and cultural change are 'made possible [...] by a suppression of homoeroticism or a redirection of women's desire from women to men' (1992, 39). In relation to this it is interesting that Byatt's historical models for the woman writer are Rossetti and Dickinson, women who enabled their writing through a retreat into the private sphere, rather than the far more openly political Elizabeth Barrett Browning. Furthermore, Mary Wollstonecraft figures only as a model for Blanche Glover's suicide. The lesbian and the woman poet seem to exist only in the past and are thus perhaps made safe.

Byatt has made several comments which suggest ambivalence about feminism and relations between women and their effects on fiction. In 1996 she commented:

Then you got the women's movement and a kind of group prescription of what you ought to be writing about – for women, by women, about women. What happened was we got a generation of absolutely wonderful male novelists [...] and lots of women who seemed quite content to write about what lesbians felt in their women's groups. (Brace, 1996, 7)

This surely rather reductive account of the effects of feminism seems to indicate a fear of being trapped as a writer in 'women's subjects'. *The Game* was, Byatt has written, 'about the fear of the "woman's novel" as an immoral devouring force' (1991a, xii).[12] In a scathing review of Monique Wittig's *The Lesbian Body* in 1974, she compared Wittig's violent rupturing of gendered language unfavourably with Margaret Thatcher's method of dealing with the generic 'he' by maintaining that, in lawyer's terminology, 'He embraces she' (1993a, 272). Byatt would 'rather take Mrs Thatcher's way': 'I like change not revolution', she asserted, 'I like subtle distinctions with a continuing language, not doctrinaire violations' (1993a, 276). This preference for 'change not revolution' dovetails with the 'smooth historical continuum' used by Thatcherism itself to promote consensus and neutralise resistance, as I argued in Chapter 8.

Byatt's answer to the problems of postmodernism and of being a woman writer seems to lie in the notion she develops of writing as ventriloquism. She glosses this as 'love for the dead, the presence of literary texts as the voices of persistent ghosts or spirits' (2000, 45). Her depiction of Ash as 'The Great Ventriloquist' draws heavily on Robert Browning with his 'resurrection' of dead voices from the past in dramatic monologues, particularly in *The Ring and the Book* which Byatt discusses at length in an essay in *Passions of the Mind* (1993a, 29–71). Browning is himself ventriloquised by Byatt in a short story 'Precipice-Encurled' in *Sugar* (1987) which is a precursor of *Possession*. In Browning's 'Mr Sludge, the Medium', which provides the second epigraph to *Possession*, the medium's fraudulent ventriloquism of dead voices is compared to the 'fictions' of historians, biographers, and poets whose 'lies' make a 'portly truth'. For Byatt, Browning and Ash, as ventriloquists, provide a model of the author as a 'medium' between the living and the dead, the past and the present. As such they have the 'authority' to ventriloquise both male and female voices. The female medium of 'A Conjugial Angel' is not a fraud like Mr Sludge, and thus she offers a more potentially positive model for the female writer.

Byatt's ventriloquising of the past, however, is extremely problematic. She uses the term 'ventriloquism' specifically, she has said, to evade the implications of the words pastiche and parody (2000, 43). Further, she has said that she wrote *Possession* because she wanted to 'rescue [...] the complicated Victorian thinkers from the modern diminishing *parodies* like those of [John] Fowles' (2000, 79, my emphasis). There are problems with this. Chris Baldick points out that 'Pastiche differs from parody in using imitation as a form of flattery rather than mockery' but he cites *The French Lieutenant's Woman* as an example of *pastiche* (1991, 162).

The terms are clearly slippery. Jameson argues that parody implies a critique of the original forms whereas:

> Pastiche is, like parody, the imitation of a peculiar or unique, idiosyncratic style, the wearing of a linguistic mask, speech in a dead language. But it is a neutral practice of such mimicry, amputated of the satiric impulse [...] Pastiche is thus blank parody, a statue with blank eyeballs [...] (1991, 17)

In our postmodern world, he argues, parody has been replaced by pastiche because, following the collapse of modernist style, writers 'have nowhere to turn but to the past: the imitation of dead styles' (17–18).

Fowles' replication of Victorian realism in *The French Lieutenant's Woman* carries a strong critique of nineteenth-century hypocrisy and repressed sexuality, which suggests his text is parody not pastiche. His two central characters are sympathetic to modern readers because they are, as it were, born out of their age and are themselves recognisably 'modern' in their desires. Byatt regards Fowles' understanding of Victorian life and literature as 'crude' (2000, 174). I would certainly agree that to impose our sexual values back into the past is to falsify it. However, although Byatt re-imagines the history of female autonomy and creativity which has been left out of both traditional accounts and Fowles' novel, her recreation of the Victorian past, an 'imitation of dead styles', is also distorted because it is ultimately a flattering pastiche.

Byatt's use of the term 'ventriloquism' depoliticises her repetition of past forms. Like Modernists such as T.S. Eliot (himself a patchworker of voices from the past), her experimental form conceals conservative politics. Discussing the recent developments in fiction in 1988, Maureen Duffy argued that they represented a 'retreat into history' which was carried out not to 'illuminate the present but to dazzle, like entering a kind of Aladdin's cave of glittering objects' (quoted in Onega, 1995, 93). This is an excellent description of *Possession* which dazzles to deceive, plundering the past for an array of glittering quotations which conceal the fundamental conservativism of its attitude to the present. Byatt is an important writer and a perceptive critic, not least in her recognition of Heyer's skill. However, while Byatt astutely analyses the pleasures of Heyer's fictions, she does not interrogate the politics of those pleasures in either Heyer's work or her own.

Hystorical men: Pat Barker's *Regeneration* trilogy

Women writers over the last years of the twentieth century have been fascinated by the First World War. Pat Barker's trilogy – *Regeneration* (1991), *The Eye in the Door* (1993), and *The Ghost Road* (1995) which won her the Booker Prize – is based on the historical facts of the treatment of Siegfried Sassoon and Wilfred Owen for 'shellshock' by W.H.R. Rivers, an army psychologist and anthropologist, at Craiglockhart hospital in 1917. Sassoon was sent to Rivers for treatment after writing his 'A Soldier's Declaration', a protest against the prolongation of the war for political ends, and the trilogy opens with this historical document. Using extensive research, Barker then skilfully interweaves the documented facts about the two soldier poets with the story of a fictional soldier, Billy Prior, a working-class and bisexual officer who is finally killed, with Owen, attempting to cross the Sambre Canal a week before the Armistice.

Barker's trilogy is probably the best-known woman's historical novel about the war and its effects but it is not an isolated example. Others include: Susan Hill's *Strange Meeting* (1971) and *How Many Miles to Babylon?* (1974) by the Irish writer Jennifer Johnston, Nicky Edwards' *Mud* (1986), Helen Dunmore's *Zennor in Darkness* (1993) and *A Spell of Winter* (1995), Esther Freud's *Gaglow* (1997), and Jane Thynne's *Patrimony* (1997).

The fascination of war for women is perhaps that it is one of the most powerful signifiers of gender difference: men fight, women do not. The critic Terry Castle (2002), in exploring her own obsession with the war, has suggested that women are haunted by the sense of their own 'cowardice' compared to the courage displayed by the men who walked towards death across No Man's Land. So powerful are the taboos surrounding the ideology that war is a male preserve, however, that the historical novel is one of the few places where women have been able to explore the relationship between gender and war. In times of war, women have frequently turned to the historical novel, depicting past wars as a coded way of writing about con-temporaneous issues.

One of the interesting things about the coverage of the Gulf War in 1990–1991 was how little commentary by women on the gendered nature of the war made its way into the media. The turn to the First World War in women's historical fiction in the 1990s can be seen as a way of engaging with issues which could not be aired in a more overt way. However, it also reflects a shift in feminism itself which, having been preoccupied with femininity in the 1980s, began to explore masculinity in the 1990s and to theorise it as equally constructed.

The First World War was one of the catalysts, as I argued in Chapter 2, which made women aware of their own existence as subjects within history. As a former suffragette, thrilled by her sudden freedoms, puts it in *The Eye in the Door*: 'for women, this is the first day in the history of the world' (1994, 101). Yet that liberation came at a huge cost. The war was also, as Barker's Billy Prior reminds us, 'the last [day] for a lot of men' (101), who were slaughtered in their millions in the confines of the trenches. As Barker's trilogy admirably demonstrates, the war was both the most 'masculine' of activities and simultaneously the activity which put 'masculinity' under the most intense pressure.

By the 1990s the war was itself part of history. In retrospect, it could be seen as what Mary Lascelles calls a 'watershed' moment, on one side of which lies 'the familiar and intelligible landscape of the present' (1980, 34) and on the other the difference of the past. Dale H. Porter has argued that 'historicity' hinges on our sense of 'the *otherness* of the past, of discontinuity and qualitative change' after which (here he cites Barbara Tuchman on the First World War) 'the old world was never seen again' (1993, 330). He suggests that this sense of historical change is most intriguing to readers when it is set two or three generations back to the time of their grandparents or great-grandparents, rather than their parents. This combination of relatedness and discontinuity, he argues, produces what Eric Hobsbawm called the 'twilight zone between history and memory' (1993, 332). It is this 'twilight zone' of the First World War (often the time of their grandparents) which seems to draw so many women writers in the 1990s, within which they can explore the ways in which war makes gender difference so starkly extreme and yet so tenuously contingent.

The First World War represents an especially stark disjunction between past and present. In retrospect, it can be seen as marking the real beginning of the twentieth century and the birth of a modernity which was already in process but was agonisingly hastened by the experience of the war. The certainties of the Victorian period, particularly the notions of civilisation and history as progress, were violently shattered. Previously rigid class and gender boundaries were broken down. The authority of the older generation was increasingly rejected by the younger generation who saw them as respon- sible for the slaughter. The concept of a unified and essential consciousness or subjectivity, already questioned by Freudian theory, was irrevocably destablised. The war, W.H.R. Rivers argued in *Instinct and the Unconscious*, was 'a vast crucible in which all our preconceived views concerning human nature have been tested' (quoted in Showalter, 1987, 189).

'More than the Holocaust', Barker has suggested, '[the First World War was] when the modern world started and people woke up to what human beings were capable of' (Jaggi, 2003, 19). The Somme 'revealed things we cannot come to terms with and cannot forget. It never becomes the past' (Jaggi, 2003, 16). The motif of spectrality is central to her trilogy, suggesting the ways in which the trauma of the war still haunts our national psyche. The soldiers, like Siegfried Sassoon, both hallucinate 'ghosts' and are themselves 'ghosts in the making' (Barker, 1996, 47), treading the 'ghost road' of the title. They are 'mate' in the words of the tribe Rivers studies, 'a state of which death was the appropriate outcome' (1996, 134). What Barker's trilogy explores is a watershed between a lost past and a present which is not 'familiar and intelligible' but fractured and haunted by the trauma of that past.

The title *Regeneration* refers in part to a nerve experiment conducted by Rivers with Henry Head where they severed and sutured Head's radial nerve and then charted the progress of regeneration over a period of 5 years. It is this process of violent severance at the level of individual and society, mind and body, which Barker is exploring. Her concern is the 'bedrock in the human capacity for destruction', she has said, and 'the real question is whether transformation – regeneration – is possible' (Taylor, 2000, 40). She depicts Rivers' Freudian-influenced work with shell-shocked soldiers as a similar attempt at regeneration, using the 'talking cure' to help them to repair the psychic fractures caused by the trauma of war experience. The moral irony of his work is that, as a doctor and 'external conscience [and] father confessor' (1994, 238) to these men, he must do this in order to send them back to probable death in the trenches. Sassoon suffers, in Rivers' phrase, from an '*anti*-war neurosis' (1992, 15). His protest, Rivers suggests, was 'an entirely valid, sane response to the situation we're in [...] *wrong*, of course' (1994, 270). The trilogy ends with Rivers' interpretation of the seemingly meaningless cry of Hallett, a dying soldier whose jaw has been shot away: '*Shotvarfet*' [...] 'It's not worth it' (1996, 274). The human pain of this cry undercuts the moral judgement of Rivers' earlier '*wrong*, of course'.

As a genre the historical novel lends itself to series of novels, usually to cover change over long periods of time. Barker's entire trilogy, in contrast, covers just 17 months – from Sassoon's 'Soldier's Declaration' in July 1917 to Owen's death in November 1918 – an indication of the hugely transformative nature of the relatively brief moment she is charting. At one point Sassoon tells Rivers how impossible it is to write about the war because it's so 'big': 'you'd have to be Tolstoy' (1994, 220). Yet the First World War has become known, as Anne Whitehead reminds us, as the 'literary war' because of the extraordinary amount of writing it produced as people attempted to make sense of their experiences by transforming them into narrative. 'The act of remembering one's own experience', she suggests, 'is inherently the act of telling a story of the past' (1998, 691). Sassoon himself wrote obsessively about his war experience. As Barker shows in the novels, writing is a form of memory, a way of attempting to re-member or re-order and control or exorcise traumatic experience by transforming it into narrative.[13] Here this is often an experience which is so terrible that the mind can only survive by forgetting (as in Prior's amnesia and mutism) or alternatively that is compulsively re-enacted through somatic symptoms such as the nightmares, stammers and tics so common in other patients at Craiglockhart.

But why write a novel about something already so extensively written about, especially since Barker makes considerable intertextual use of these prior texts, particularly those of Rivers, Sassoon and Owen? One reason is that, typically of women's historical fiction, Barker gives a voice to experience unrecorded or misrepresented in those texts, particularly that of the working-class men represented by Prior. She is concerned with representations of the war, both written and remembered, and the ways in which these are inflected by class and gender assumptions. Much of the trilogy consists of re-imagined dialogues between Rivers and his patients during which memories are transformed into narrative rather than being repressed and acted out through somatic symptoms. At one point, Rivers describes the differences between neuroses suffered by officers, who tend to stammer and have elaborate nightmares, and those of private soldiers whose symptoms are usually physical: mutism, paralysis, blindness, deafness and so on. Rivers attributes the elaborate dreams of the officers to their 'more complex mental life', the result of their public-school-education (1992, 96). This was the interpretation offered in one of Rivers' books, as Elaine Showalter notes in *The Female Malady* (1987, 174–5), an important source for Barker's *Regeneration*, acknowledged in her 'Author's Note'.

Prior's ridicule of this interpretation lays bare the class assumptions of Rivers' thinking, and that of much of the writing about the war. Prior's insistence on asking questions transforms his therapy sessions with Rivers into two-way dialogues which undermine Rivers' position as privileged interpreter of the war experience and disrupt the received assumptions in contemporaneous accounts. Writers like Sassoon and Owen, Barker notes, 'thought they were writing on behalf of the inarticulate soldier' but he was and is only perceived as inarticulate 'because nobody is prepared to listen' (Jaggi, 2003, 19). This point is made most brutally in *Regeneration* when Dr Yealland uses electric shocks to force a mute soldier to speak but tells him: 'You must speak but I shall not listen to anything you say' (1992, 231). As Rivers recognises, what Yealland does is only a more obviously brutal version of what he himself does, symbolised by Rivers dragging a spoon across the mute Prior's tongue. Both doctors silence the unconscious protests of the soldiers, acted out through their bodily symptoms, in order to return them to active duty. Prior's own self-awareness counters Rivers' interpretations, and gives a voice to the silenced.

In Prior, Barker re-imagines how the war might have been experienced by a very self-aware working-class and bisexual officer, a 'temporary gentleman' (1994, 19), whose self-evidently 'complex' mental life straddles the divides of class and sexuality. It is Prior who recognises that this 'period of terribly rapid change' is remarkable for people's 'awareness' of its transitional nature, and it is not just the educated middle classes, Barker thus implies, who are aware of this (1994, 100). 'Equally *not* at home' (1994, 110) in the officer's mess or the back streets of Salford, Prior is torn by divided loyalties to his fellow soldiers and to the working-class community from which he comes, members of which are involved in pacifist activities which reject 'the bosses' war' (1996, 6). Equally divided sexually, he shifts from passive object (his earliest sexual experience was being raped by a priest) to an active subject self-aware enough to understand that his impulses towards sadism are intertwined with the fact that combat makes him feel 'sexy' (1992, 78). Barker's explicit treatment of the effects of the war on Prior's sexuality counters Rivers minimising of the sexual drive in Freudian theory which, Showalter suggests, 'helped domesticate it for an English audience' (1987, 189).

Like all the central male characters in the trilogy – Rivers, Sassoon and Charles Manning – Prior is a deeply divided man. As Rivers recognises, 'most of us survive by cultivating internal divisions' (1994, 233) but this is especially the case with homosexual or potentially homosexual men in a homophobic society. Rivers himself seems to have completely repressed his own sexuality, while Manning lives a double life as heterosexual family man and secret homosexual. Such divisions are exacerbated by the fractures of the war. Sassoon copes by being 'two people' – the anti-war poet and the bloodthirsty officer (1994, 233).

The epigraph to *The Eye in the Door* from Stevenson's *Dr Jekyll and Mr Hyde* stresses the 'thorough and primitive duality of men', but suggests that the human being encompasses *both* sides of that duality. 'Even if I could rightly be said to be either [of his two contending natures]' Stevenson's protagonist says, 'it was only because I was radically both...'. Prior takes this Jekyll and Hyde performance to an extreme, and develops a split personality with a 'warrior double' born in the trenches (1994, 245) in order to dissociate the parts of himself he finds unacceptable. His dissociation involves a damaging denial of capacities within himself, which can only be healed, Rivers suggests, not just through memory but through 'recognition. Acceptance' (1994, 249) of the otherness within himself.

Barker's ventriloquism of male voices offers a second reason for her, as a woman, to write about the First World War. Previously known for feminist novels about working-class women's lives, Barker's shift to 'male' subject-matter in the trilogy was much commented on by critics. A.S. Byatt, for instance, suggests that Barker 'found her great subject partly because she was a woman avoiding the constraints of prescribed feminist subject matter' (2000, 31). While the misogynist perception that Barker was finally writing about something 'serious' and 'important', which clearly appealed to male readers, has much to do with the high profile of the trilogy (and, of course, the Booker prize it garnered), this misrepresents what Barker is doing. Asked about the lack of female protagonists in the trilogy, she pointed out, 'There *is* a woman on every page – me' (Jaggi, 2003, 19). As a woman writer ventriloquising male voices, like Mary Renault, she exposes the contingent and mimetic nature of masculinity which we can now see so vividly laid bare in the accounts of men made 'hysterical' by their experience of the war.

While women suddenly found their lives opening up during the war, men found their lives narrowed down to the confines of a few months in a mud-filled trench before an early and brutal death. As Barker's W.H.R. Rivers puts it:

> Mobilization. The Great Adventure. They'd been *mobilized* into holes in the ground so constricted they could hardly move. [...] The war that had promised so much in the way of 'manly' activity had actually delivered 'feminine' passivity, and on a scale that their mothers and sisters had scarcely known. No wonder they broke down. (1992, 107–8)

As Elaine Showalter shows in *The Female Malady* (1987, Chapter 7), faced with men exhibiting the symptoms previously associated with women to the extent that they were given the name 'hysteria' (from the Greek for womb), doctors quickly came up with the more acceptably 'masculine' (though inaccurate) term 'shellshock'.

Barker's act of ventriloquism puts 'masculinity' into question. It enables a sustained and complex exploration of the ways in which 'masculinity', epitomised by the legendary British 'stiff upper lip', is built on the repression and silencing of 'feminine' emotions. In attempting to get men to acknowledge that their 'hysterical' symptoms are a valid reaction to the horror and fear of war, Barker's Rivers understands that he is 'setting himself against the whole tenor of their upbringing' which has trained them to 'identify emotional repression as the essence of manliness' (1992, 48). It can only be done 'at the cost of redefining what it meant to be a man' (48).

Two central recovered memories make this explicit. The first is Prior's memory, recovered through hypnosis, of the experience that made him mute: after one of his men had been blown to pieces, Prior, picking up the pieces, had come across a disembodied eyeball. His comment – 'What am I supposed to do with this gob-stopper?' (1992, 103) – figures the way in which the war has 'stopped' his mouth. The image of the eye, which runs through the trilogy, is an excellent example of how Barker's putative 'realism' contains complex layers of symbolic meaning. The 'eye in the door', again disembodied, of the second volume is literally the eye painted around the spyhole in prison doors, used for the surveillance of conscientious objectors and other prisoners who thus never know when they are being watched. It symbolises the internalisation of ideology, the 'eye' of the super-ego which polices individual behaviour. In this volume this is particularly clear in the case of the homosexual men living double lives who are 'whipped back into line' (1994, 160) by fear of exposure and prosecution during and after the Pemberton-Billing libel case.[14]

The second recovered memory is Rivers' own recollection of a childhood incident following a trip to the barber's, during which the 4-year-old Rivers had cried and been slapped by his father. Afterwards Rivers' father had showed him the picture of his ancestor and namesake, William Rivers, the man who shot the man who shot Nelson at Trafalgar, having his leg amputated without anaesthetic. '*He* didn't cry. [...] *He didn't make a sound*', Rivers' father tells him (1996, 95). That imposed silence – the 'resolutely clenched mouth' (95) at the centre of the picture – causes Rivers' lifelong stammer and the repression of his visual memory. As Prior tells him, he 'blinded' himself so that he would not recall that memory: 'You put your mind's eye *out*' (1994, 139). In Lacanian terms, Catherine Lanone suggests, the incident of the painting 'triggers a perverse mirror stage where identification occurs with a split, sacrificed body, not a whole one' (1999, 265). Later, as a psychologist, Rivers' job is to 'read the body as a text' (Lanone, 1999, 265). The bodies he 'reads' repeatedly re-enact that clenched mouth. Masculinity is produced at the cost of the silencing of the male voice and the violent fragmentation of the male body, ultimately represented in the shattering of Prior's reflection in the canal as he dies.

It is also reproduced through the sacrifice of sons by their fathers. Lanone has drawn attention to the centrality of the story of Abraham and Isaac in the trilogy. This echoes Owen's poem, 'Parable of the Old Man and the Young', where Abraham refuses the angel's offer of the ram as substitute, and slays 'his son, / And half the seed of Europe, one by one' (Lanone, 1999, 260). Barker parallels the Christian story with a custom Rivers finds among the Melanesians, where a surrogate father brings up an illegitimate boy and then, as the boy is about to kill a sacrificial pig, crushes the boy's skull with a club (1996, 103–4). Rivers compares this to the representation of Abraham and Isaac in a window in Rivers' father's church where God is about to intervene to prevent the sacrifice. 'The two events', Rivers thinks, 'represent the difference between savagery and civilisation' (1996, 103). The Melanesians are a 'people perishing from the absence of war' (1996, 207), since the 'civilised' white men banned their head-hunting. Yet Western 'civilisation', as Barker makes clear, produces the wholesale slaughter of millions of young men, Rivers' own surrogate sons Billy Prior[15] and Wilfred Owen among them, on a scale unimaginable to the Melanesians.

'History', Barker has said, 'is never a judge but a dialogue between past and present. The answers change because the questions change, depending on our preoccupations' (Jaggi, 2003, 19). Like Byatt, Waters and Roberts, Barker is interested in the medium as a model for the author as a ventriloquiser of dead voices. Both medium and writer, she has said, 'balance between conviction and sincerity and trickery' (McCrum, 2001, 17). The trilogy contains two séances, one in Manchester where a medium relays the voices of dead sons killed in the war to their grieving relatives. The second is a native ceremony attended by Rivers and his colleague on Eddystone as part of his anthropological fieldwork. As Rivers reflects, the questions asked of the two white men by the spirits, like those of the ghost seen by Sassoon at Craiglockhart, become 'more insistent, more powerful for being projected into the mouths of the dead' (1996, 212). By ventriloquising the voices of dead men, Barker is able powerfully to insist that we address the questions her texts ask about the relationship between war and gender, between violence and the construction of masculinity.

The trilogy ends with Rivers' vision of Njiru, the Eddystone witchdoctor, walking the ward of the Empire hospital repeating the words of the exorcism of the spirit Ave, 'the destroyer of peoples' (1996, 268), who presages epidemic disease and war. The exorcism prophesies 'the end of men' (276). This suggests, John Brannigan has argued, that 'History is over', and Rivers and all of us belong to 'the land of the living dead, and to the haunted time of post-history' (2003, 53). Another way of reading this is to take the generic 'men' at its face value. This is the end of 'men' in terms of the end of a certain kind of imperialist and capitalist masculinity, which leads, Barker shows, only to the dead end of the trenches. The ambivalent openness of the ending suggests that it is up to us to address the questions – about the possibility of transformation and regeneration – which Barker so powerfully asks, in the hope that we can write our own history differently.

Postscript

Women's historical novels have been critically dismissed or, perhaps worse, ignored because they have been perceived as nostalgic, escapist, irrelevant or simply as 'trash'. In fact, as I have shown, the genre encompasses an extraordinarily wide variety of forms – from Georgette Heyer's romances to Pat Barker's re-imagining of the trenches of the First World War. Moreover, the shapes taken by the woman's historical novel across the century have shifted back and forward across the 'low-brow'/'high-brow' binary, from Baroness Orczy's swashbucklers through to the postmodern histories of Rose Tremain, Jeanette Winterson and A.S. Byatt. In the 1960s and 1970s, the form was strongly associated with women's popular fiction in ways which probably account for the fact that it is still to a certain extent, in Melvyn Bragg's phrase, 'the genre that dare not speak its name'. Yet in the 1990s it became a high-brow genre again, invigorated by a new self-reflexiveness about the constructed nature of history.

One thing these texts do have in common is the pleasure provided by a good story-teller. 'Escapism' has become a dirty word in critical terms but I do not think that we should under-estimate its importance. One of the very few fan letters Georgette Heyer kept was from a women who had been a political prisoner in Rumania for 12 years. She wrote to tell Heyer that she had kept herself and her fellow prisoners sane by retelling the story of *Friday's Child* (1944) again and again (Hodge, 1985, 160–1).

The historical novel, perhaps more than any other genre, has allowed women writers to transcend the constraints of gender and the limitations of the romance plot and the domestic novel. It has allowed women writers and readers the considerable pleasures of cross-writing and cross-reading – of trespassing in time to masquerade as a highwayman, a pirate, a Jacobite rebel or Merlin himself.

It has also allowed women writers to re-imagine women's history in order to recover a matrilineal genealogy which has been erased from what Austen called 'real solemn history'. In the stories of 'captive women' in the 1960s and the 'herstories' of the 1980s, women writers offered a historical consciousness-raising that contributed in important ways to second-wave feminism.

From the 1920s onwards (and probably well before), women writers like Naomi Mitchison and Sylvia Townsend Warner used the historical novel as a political weapon, taking advantage of the 'mask' it provided to write about subjects which were otherwise taboo for reasons of either politics or gender. It is interesting that it still seems to be the alignment of the genre with the popular which enables writers like Philippa Gregory in the late twentieth century to produce politically radical texts under the guise of entertainment.

If the twentieth century really began (as Barker suggests) with the First World War, then in retrospect it can be seen to have ended, not at midnight on 31 December 1999, but with the fall of the twin towers in New York on 11 September 2001. While not the 'end of history', it was a moment of fracture which made us sharply aware of ourselves as subjects within history again. The questions which some of the best of these novelists – Naomi Mitchison, Sylvia Townsend Warner, Mary Renault, H.F.M. Prescott, Pat Barker – ask about the relationships between gender, power, nationality, sexuality, religion and violence are still, sadly, all too relevant.

Notes

1 Introduction

1. These include Avrom Fleishman, *The English Historical Novel: Walter Scott to Virginia Woolf* (1971), Nicholas Rance, *The Historical Novel and Popular Politics in Nineteenth-Century England* (1975), Andrew Sanders, *The Victorian Historical Novel 1840–1880* (1978), Mary Lascelles, *The Story-Teller Retrieves the Past: Historical Fiction and Fictitious History in the Art of Scott, Stevenson, Kipling, and Some Others* (1980), Harry E. Shaw, *The Forms of Historical Fiction: Sir Walter Scott and his Successors* (1983), and Harold Orel, *The Historical Novel from Scott to Sabatini: Changing Attitudes to a Literary Genre, 1814–1920* (1995). Harry B. Henderson's *Versions of the Past: The Historical Imagination in American Fiction* (1974) offers a different story in relation to America but it is again concerned with a male tradition. Neil McEwan's *Perspective in British Historical Fiction Today* (1987) discusses twentieth-century writers but Mary Renault is the only female writer he includes.
2. As forerunners, Radcliffe is mentioned in Sanders, and Maria Edgeworth in Fleishman (who also mentions Clara Reeve and footnotes Jane and Anna Maria Porter), Rance and Lascelles. Fleishman offers detailed discussions of George Eliot's *Romola* (1863), and Virginia Woolf's *Orlando* (1928) and *Between the Acts* (1941), and briefly mentions Naomi Mitchison, Mary Renault and H.F.M. Prescott, while dismissing Georgette Heyer. For the nineteenth century, Rance and Sanders include *Romola* and Elizabeth Gaskell's *Sylvia's Lovers* (1863), while Rance adds Charlotte Brontë's *Shirley* (1849) and Eliot's *Felix Holt* (1866). Shaw includes *Romola* in what is really a detailed study of Scott's form, and Orel likewise mentions *Romola* but his real interest is in the male-authored historical romance as an adventure story. Many other obviously 'historical' novels by women, such as Mary Shelley's *Valperga* (1823) or *Perkin Warbeck* (1830), are ignored.
3. See, for instance, his comment that, 'Avoiding escapism of the popular kind, the serious artist tends to withdraw from the horror of the present to contemplate the horror of the past' (Fleishman, 1971, xvii).
4. There were, in fact, stories that Mary had miscarried twins, fathered by Bothwell, at Lochleven in 1567 (Bowen, 1971, 302).
5. Examples include Scott's *The Abbott* (1820), Schiller's tragedy, *Maria Stuart* (1800), a trilogy by Swinburne beginning with *Chastelard* (1865), and Maurice Hewlett's *The Queen's Quair* (1904).
6. I have borrowed this term from the work of Berthold Schoene-Harwood (2000).

2 Entering into history: the woman citizen and the historical novel, 1900–1929

1. Criticism of Heyer includes Jane Aiken Hodge's *The Private World of Georgette Heyer* (1984), and essays by A.S. Byatt (1991), Kathleen Bell (1995) and Carmen Callil (1996), and a collection of materials edited by Mary Fahnestock-Thomas (2001), while jay Dixon is working on a forthcoming critical study.

2. Eve Kosofsky Sedgwick (1985) has suggested that homosocial bonds between men, which exclude women or use them as objects of exchange, provide the central plot structure underpinning much of Western literature.
3. The Irish agitation for Home Rule had caused particular concern in August 1914. Armed rebellion was averted only by the outbreak of the First World War. The Easter Rising of 1916 had, after Britain's summary executions of the leaders, garnered increasing support. From 1920 when the Black and Tans arrived, there was guerrilla warfare between them and the Irish Republican Army (IRA). In 1920, 24 Irish 'rebels' were executed by the British. The Anglo-Irish Treaty signed by Michael Collins in 1921 precipitated the country into a Civil War which did not end until 1923.
4. In this satirical play, two disillusioned Athenians, Pisthetaraerus and Euelpides, persuade the birds to establish a state of their own, called Cloud Cuckoo Land, in the air between the gods in heaven and the men on earth. Their search for an ideal state proves an impossible utopia, as Cloud Cuckoo Land itself becomes not an escape but a reiteration of the old ways but this time with Pisthetaraerus wielding power. Bird rebels, at the end, were roasted for his wedding feast.
5. I am indebted to Gill Spraggs for locating and translating this epigraph, as well as for giving me the benefit of her wide knowledge of Greek history and literature in relation to this text.
6. I am indebted to Gill Spraggs for this information.
7. The accounts of the Peloponnesian War by Thucydides (who appears briefly in the novel) and Xenophon, which were Mitchison's sources, offered influential models for subsequent historians.
8. Two other early accounts, Jean Rhys' *Voyage In the Dark* (1934) and Rosamond Lehmann's *The Weather in the Streets* (1936), both post-date Mitchison's novel by over a decade.
9. In the 1920s, Mitchison was involved in work with the North Kensington birth control clinic in London, and during her 1932 visit to the Soviet Union she witnessed an abortion (1979, 172).

3   Histories of the defeated: writers taking sides in the 1930s

1. Ray Strachey's *The Cause* (1928) was followed by her *Millicent Garrett Fawcett* (1931) and *Our Freedom and its Results* (1936), Sylvia Pankhurst's *The Suffragette Movement* (1931), Emmeline Pethick-Lawrence's *My Part in a Changing World* (1938), Holtby's *Women* (1934), and Lady Rhondda's *This Was My World* (1933). There were also numerous articles in *Time and Tide* and other periodicals, such as Vera Brittain's report on the Suffrage Exhibition held by The Six Point Group in London in 1930 (Berry and Bishop, 1985, 102–5).
2. It received 530 reviews and went into 29 editions in England, while hardback sales in the US were over 40,000 (Bentley, 1962, 73). Vera Brittain's diaries of the 1930s give an idea of Bentley's new-found status as a literary 'celebrity' (Brittain, 1986, 39).
3. Other examples include Storm Jameson's *The Triumph of Time* (1933) focusing on Yorkshire ship-builders, Clemence Dane's *Broome Stages* (1931) centred on a theatrical family and, slightly later, Marguerite Steen's huge *The Sun is My Undoing* (1941), depicting a family of Bristol slavers.
4. *Summer Will Show*, in particular, has attracted important commentaries by, among others, Barbara Brothers (1989), Terry Castle (1993), Sandy Petrey (1991), Thomas Foster (1995), Chris Hopkins (1995) and Janet Montefiore (1996).

5. The novel invokes not only *Sentimental Education* but *Sense and Sensibility, Mansfield Park, Jane Eyre, Wuthering Heights, Daniel Deronda, Great Expectations* and *The Mill on the Floss*.
6. Diana left her first husband in 1932 to become the mistress of Oswald Mosley, a notorious womaniser and founder of the British Union of Fascists. She married him in 1936 in Berlin in the presence of Goebbels and Hitler. Her younger sister Unity fell in love with both Nazi Germany and Hitler and attempted to commit suicide when war broke out.

4 Writing the war and after: wicked ladies and wayward women in the 1940s

1. Because of the war, *English Social History* was first published in the US in 1942, and then published in Britain in 1944.
2. Unlike the films discussed by Harper, these latter three films were made in the US. *Frenchman's Creek* (1944) was directed by Mitchell Leisen and starred Joan Fontaine; *Forever Amber* (1947) was directed by Otto Preminger and starred Linda Darrell; *Gone With the Wind* (1939) was directed by Victor Fleming and starred Vivien Leigh, Clark Gable and Leslie Howard. For an important discussion of the cultural impact of *Gone with the Wind* see Helen Taylor's *Scarlett's Women* (1989).
3. For a discussion of the English domestic novel of these years see Phyllis Lassner (1990).
4. Recent work on Daphne du Maurier has begun to reassess her status as a writer. Alison Light's ground-breaking chapter in *Forever England* (1991) importantly discusses her work in relation to romance and historical fiction, while Avril Horner and Sue Zlosnik (1998) have explored its Gothic affinities.
5. See, for instance, the coverage included in the Reader's Digest video, *Years to Remember: Remembering the Forties* (1993).

5 Hollow men and homosexual heroes: exploring masculinity in the 1950s

1. Alison Light (1987) has looked at historical fictions in the 1950s by writers such as Margaret Irwin, Jean Plaidy and Anya Seton in relation to their construction of femininity. She suggests that these novels offer evidence of the desire to re-examine and make sense of the social and sexual divisions disrupted by the war which needed to be re-ordered if 'a new middle class consensus [was] to be enabled' (1987, 67). The narratives of these novels, she asserts, offer resistance to the conventions and construct alternative subjectivities, most importantly through a 'femininity where sexual desire is taken as crucial and mobilising' (1987, 68). My own chapter focuses on women writers' exploration of masculinity because this offers a resistance to the national consensus which is, if anything, more radical.
2. See, for instance, Reston (2001).
3. Recent biographies by David Sweetman (1993) and Caroline Zilboorg (2001) have provided valuable new contextual material.
4. Renault herself disliked, for instance, Peter Wolfe's rather reductive Freudian readings of her work (Wolfe, 1969). Wolfe, moreover, presented her as predominantly a writer who looked back to the concerns of the 1930s rather than recognising her contemporaneous relevance. More usefully, Bernard F. Dick (1972) drew attention

to the centrality of Greek myths and philosophy to all her work, while Neil McEwan (1987) illuminated her scholarly and imaginative use of historical and archaeological sources and her technical craftsmanship. McEwan's commentary is an example, like that of Landon C. Burns (1964), of how an otherwise perceptive discussion of Renault's work can be flawed by a failure to engage with the central issue of homosexuality. Burns considers this element 'negligible' (1964, 104), while McEwan's comment that Renault makes the 'perverse' love affair between Alexander the Great and the eunuch Bagoas in *The Persian Boy* seem 'natural' (1987, 72) suggests a discomfort with the same-sex love which was central to both Renault's work and her life. On the other hand, Terry Castle has criticised Renault for a 'retreat into homophobic convention' in *The Friendly Young Ladies* and suggests that in contrast to her positive depictions of male homosexuality, Renault 'never attained corresponding imaginative freedom, paradoxically, regarding female same-sex love' (1993, 42). Julie Abraham (1996, Chapter 2) offers an important reading of Renault's treatment of same-sex love in relation to history. She argues that love is the crucial term in Renault's histories, but she also concludes that Renault suggests that to be female is to be inescapably disqualified from participation in history. Ruth Hoberman's chapter on Renault in *Gendering Classicism* (1997), and articles by Erin G. Carlston (1996) and Kathleen Bell (2003) have also offered theoretically informed analyses which suggest that Renault's conceptualisation of both gender and sexuality is far more fluid than earlier readings suggest.

5. Renault uses the spelling 'Sokrates' rather than the more usual 'Socrates'. For the sake of consistency I have used her spelling throughout.

6. I would like to thank Kathleen Bell for letting me see a copy of this paper before publication.

7. See, for instance, Fletcher and MacCulloch (1997, Chapter 4) and Hoyle (2001).

8. The influential work of the medieval historian Eileen Power, particularly *Medieval English Nunneries* (1922), made available a body of historical information which may have helped encourage women like Prescott and Warner to use nunneries as settings in their historical novels.

6   The return of the repressed: maternal histories in the 1960s

1. Bloom notes that Ian Fleming had been sold in this way since the 1950s (2002, 75).

2. Several of the novels Scanlan discusses, such as those by Doris Lessing, deal with events within the author's adult lifetime. They are novels of the present as history rather than historical novels as such.

3. Kamensky was based on the real figure of Ezno Azeff (Glendinning, 1988, 230).

4. As 'Philippa Carr' in the 1970s and 1980s, Hibbert went on to combine the two, writing 'historical gothics', which trace a family through several generations.

5. For readings of the modern gothic, see Joanna Russ (1973), Kay Mussell (1974, 1981), Janice Radway (1981), Juliann Fleenor (1983) and Tania Modleski (1984).

6. The pseudonym 'Victoria Holt', of course, appropriately recalls the 'Victorian period'.

7. This is true of all the books I have looked at from this period, *Mellyn*, *Menfreya*, *Pendorric*, *The Shivering Sands* (1969), *The Secret Woman* (1970), as well as later texts like *The Demon Lover* (1982).

8. Interestingly, when Hibbert did use first-person narration for a book centred on a real historical personage, as in *My Enemy the Queen* (1978), narrated by Lettice Knollys, it was published under the name 'Victoria Holt'. The exception to this is

the 'Queens of England' series, started in 1984 under the Plaidy name, which all use first-person narration.
9. See Brontly (1997) for an interesting discussion of metaphors for history, including chess.
10. Dunnett was also a portrait painter.
11. jay Dixon notes the emergence of the 'alpha-man' as hero in the Mills and Boon novel in the 1960s. She suggests that in a period of unrest, romances were portraying 'a strong authority figure to provide an element of certainty in an uncertain world' (1999, 63). Dunnett is doing something rather different with Lymond but this interest in leaders in this period is clearly evident in a range of texts.
12. Dunnett returned to many of these themes and motifs in her Niccolo series (1986–2000) which traces the story of Lymond's ancestor. This repetition suggests the archetypal nature of the psychological patterns she is mapping.

7 Selling women's history: popular historical fiction in the 1970s

1. Several of Cookson's novels have been made into television dramas, most memorably *The Mallens* by Granada in 1979 but also *The Dwelling Place*. Howatch's *Penmarric* was serialised by the BBC in 1979, while Stewart's *The Crystal Cave* was also made into a BBC television series (Wynne-Davies, 1996, 222).
2. Thurston's analysis of the 'erotic historical' focuses on the independent heroine and its sexual content, which reflects contemporary not historical social values and mores (Thurston, 1987, 76). She does not address its relation to other forms of the historical novel.
3. In 1972, Mills and Boon sold 27 million books in Britain (Dixon, 1999, 21). Today, according to their website, they sell 200 million books per annum worldwide (www.millsandboon.co.uk).
4. jay Dixon argues that sales of Mills and Boon's historical romances were 'miniscule' compared to those with contemporary settings (1999, 34). However, given overall sales, this proportion is still significant and, especially added to the high profile of Barbara Cartland's work, makes the historical romance an interesting phenomenon.
5. This 'oral' quality is not surprising given that Cartland famously dictated her novels to a secretary.
6. *Penmarric* covers the period from 1890 to 1945; *Cashelmara* from 1859 to 1891; while Cookson ends *The Mallen Trilogy* just after the First World War.
7. In April 2003, *The Guardian* reported that Catherine Cookson's 22-year reign as the 'most borrowed author' in public libraries was 'expected to end soon' (*The Guardian*, 11 April 2003). The figures produced by the Public Lending Rights scheme, since it started in 1983, offer an extraordinary testament to the popularity of Cookson's fiction. Between January and July 1983, for instance, 33 of the top 100 most-borrowed books in the PLR list were by Cookson (Goodwin, 1994, 311), and this level of popularity has been sustained. In 1998, her books accounted for one-third of all popular fictions borrowed from public libraries (Bloom, 2002, 196). Public libraries have been especially important in keeping available historical fiction by women which is out of print, but Cookson still has a strong presence in bookshops. Ninety million copies of her books were sold between the publication of her first novel in 1950 and her death in 1998 (Bloom, 2002, 196).
8. The exception is Charlotte Guest's translation of *The Mabinogi*, discussed by Marion Wynne-Davies.

9. There were a few earlier texts (see Taylor and Brewer, 1983) but none as influential. In the 1950s and early 1960s there were also a handful of texts with Arthurian or Dark Age settings, such as Meriol Trevor's *The Last of Britain* (see Ashe, 1971, 198), Bryher's *Ruan* (1961) and Anya Seton's *Avalon* (1965).

10. This included work like *Arthurian Literature in the Middle Ages* (1959) edited by Roger Sherman Loomis, Richard Barber's *King Arthur: Hero and Legend* (1961), and Geoffrey Ashe's *From Caesar to Arthur* (1960) and *The Quest for Arthur's Britain* (1968).

11. See, for instance, Barber (1990, 198) and Knight (1983, 212) who also praise Stewart, and Nastali (1999, 19).

12. Edith Pargeter's *The Brothers of Gwynedd Quartet* (1974) is another example of a 1970s' text by a woman concerned with issues of leadership and nationhood, which uses an illegitimate first-person male narrator.

13. Stewart does not mention Sutcliff's novel in the interview with Raymond H. Thompson (1989), where she discusses T.H. White's *The Once and Future King* as the forerunner from which she wanted to differentiate her own novels. However, there are echoes and conceptual similarities which may simply be the result of two women authors using the same source material, or may indicate that Stewart knew Sutcliff's novel and was reworking it.

14. The Welsh name Emrys is derived from Ambrosius.

15. The most influential of these has been *The Mists of Avalon* (1983) by the American Marion Zimmer Bradley, which is fantasy (rather than historical fiction), and is obviously 'feminist' in its centralising of the female characters. However, as Marion Wynne-Davies shows, Bradley constructs a simplistically essentialist binary opposition between a universally timeless female power and 'hostile male otherness' (Wynne-Davies, 1996, 182).

8   'Herstory' to postmodern histories: history as dissent in the 1980s

1. The film of John Fowles' *The French Lieutenant's Woman* (1969), directed by Karel Reisz and released in 1981, stimulated renewed interest in Fowles' novel and contributed to the 1980s interest in the Victorian period. Umberto Eco's *The Name of the Rose* (1980, published in English translation in 1983) was important in helping to make the genre of historical fiction respectable again (see Rozett, 1995, 145). Eco's novel has almost no women characters. Fowles makes Sarah Woodruff the enigmatic 'Other' of his novel, the object not the subject of history and of the male gaze. While Ackroyd's novels portray male homosexuality, as in *The Last Testament of Oscar Wilde* (1983), they show a similar lack of interest in women's history.

2. This trajectory from feminist confessional realism to historical novel can be traced in the writing of individual authors. Michèle Roberts is a particular case in point as Rosemary White (n.d.) has shown.

3. See, for instance, Paulina Palmer (1989) and Patricia Duncker (1992). This is particularly noticeable in Anne Cranny Francis' *Feminist Fiction: Feminist Uses of Generic Fiction* (1990) which examines several genres, including romance, science fiction and the detective novel, but not the historical novel. Lyn Pykett (1987) is one of the few critics to discuss women's historical novels in the 1980s.

4. First published as *The Century's Daughter*.

5. Feminist and lesbian detective novels have, in contrast to the historical novel, attracted a considerable amount of critical attention. See, for instance, Gill Plain (2001).

6. See Hayden White, *Tropics of Discourse* (1978), where he argues that historical narrative can be emplotted according to the literary tropes of romance, comedy, tragedy or satire, and that each of these accords with an ideological implication, here respectively, anarchist, conservative, radical and liberal (1985, 70).

7. Patricia Waugh defines metafiction as 'fictional writing which self-consciously and systematically draws attention to its status as artefact in order to pose questions about the relationship between fiction and reality' (1988, 2).

8. The Nag Hammedi gospels were a major source for Roberts' novel. Their potential interest for feminist theorists had been explored by Elaine Pagels' *The Gnostic Gospels* (1979).

9. In relation to her stress on historical accuracy, Gregory has even said that she does not read historical novels in case she inadvertently recycles an incorrect historical 'fact' in her own fiction (Zigmond, 2003, 4–5).

10. See Pierre Macherey, *A Theory of Literary Production* (1978). Gregory's secondary material includes Arnold Kettle and Raymond Williams but not, for instance, E.P. Thompson or Marx himself.

11. *Pace* Ackroyd, Gregory's use of names suggests the 'calculated' or artful, rather than naïve, nature of her fiction. For instance, 'Julia', for her unwittingly incestuous protagonist, recalls *Julia de Roubigne*, while 'Celia', meaning 'blind' (*Collins*, 1975, 67), is appropriate for the character who is 'wilfully blind' (Gregory, 1989, 589).

9   Dialogues with the dead: history and the 'sense of an ending', 1990–2000

1. In the early 1990s, several influential texts by American feminists – Susan Faludi, *Backlash: The Undeclared War Against Women* (1992), Marilyn French, *The War Against Women* (1992), Naomi Wolf, *The Beauty Myth* (1990) – as well as Linda Grant's *Sexing the Millennium: A Political History of the Sexual Revolution* (1993) made it clear that the battle was still ongoing. In 1997, Natasha Walter's *The New Feminism* attempted to celebrate the new freedoms enjoyed by young women. But, as she admitted, women still lacked real economic and political equality.

2. When the Historical Novel Society was set up in 1997, its founder Richard Lee recalled, the genre 'was sneered at, even by authors. "A bit like hanging baskets," said one review' (Cuthbertson, 2001, 34).

3. Alex Owen, *The Darkened Room: Women, Power and Spiritualism in Late Victorian England* (1989), Elaine Showalter, *The Female Malady: Women, Madness and English Culture, 1830–1980* (1985) and Marjorie Garber, *Vested Interests: Cross-Dressing and Cultural Anxiety* (1992) appear in the Author's Notes to several novels. Owen is cited as a source by A.S. Byatt for *Angels and Insects* (1992), for instance, and by Michèle Roberts for *In the Red Kitchen* (1990). Roberts also cites Showalter who is important for Pat Barker's *Regeneration* trilogy. Patricia Duncker cites Garber in the notes to *James Miranda Barry* (1999).

4. Kathleen Kelly, for instance, calls it a 'virtuoso postmodern exercise' (1996, 78), while Susanna Onega includes it in her list of British historiographic metafictions (1995, 94).

5. In a piece on the writing of *Possession*, Byatt writes, '[*Possession*] should learn from my childhood obsession with Georgette Heyer, to be a Romance' (www.asbyatt. com/Posses.htm [accessed: 26/10/2001]).

6. Byatt has also cited Umberto Eco's *The Name of the Rose* and Iris Murdoch (Kenyon, 1992, 19) as influences in the writing of *Possession* but far less attention has been paid to the equally important Heyer connection.
7. The writers Byatt explicitly sites at the centre of her 'map' are Anthony Burgess, William Golding, Muriel Spark and Penelope Fitzgerald (2000, 3–4). I have, for obvious reasons, concentrated on the female writers she discusses.
8. Two other important examples of texts which recover matrilineal genealogies are Ruth Prawer Jhabvala's *Heat and Dust* (1975), where the narrator pieces together and partially re-lives the story of her step-grandmother, and *L.C.* (1986) by the American author Susan Daitch, which Hutcheon (1988) discusses as an example of women's historiographic metafiction.
9. Louise Yelin (1992) has pointed out the significance of Meredith as an inspiration.
10. Byatt's phrasing here tellingly echoes her earlier comment that Heyer is 'playing romantic games with the novel of manners' (1993a, 261).
11. White includes a chapter on Vico's 'New Science' in *Tropics of Discourse* (1978).
12. Some of this ambivalence may be to do with Byatt's notoriously problematic relationship with her sister, the novelist Margaret Drabble, whose novels would clearly be categorised as 'woman's novels' in the sense Byatt is using the term here.
13. Barker's exploration of the relationship between memory and history as trauma has important affinities with Toni Morrison's *Beloved* (1987), one of the most important historical novels of the twentieth century, and where Morrison develops the concept of 're-memory' in order to re-imagine the unimaginable in her recreation of the horror of slavery. Two incidents in *Regeneration* suggest that Barker may have been influenced by *Beloved*: Prior and Sarah nearly make love on a tombstone on which she can just make out the word 'Beloved' (1992, 93), and later Rivers remembers the use of bits in silencing American slaves (238).
14. This was a libel case brought by Maud Allen against the MP Noel Pemberton Billing as a result of an article he had allegedly written which clearly implied that she was a lesbian. The article, 'The Cult of the Clitoris', suggested that the list of sub-scribers to a private performance of *Salome*, given by Allen, would include the names of 'The First 47,000'. These were the names of 47,000 people listed in a 'Black Book', allegedly owned by a German Prince, who were a risk to British national security because of their double sexual lives. Gay Wachman suggests that the case effectively silenced lesbian women who therefore wrote about their sexuality in oblique ways throughout the 1920s (2001, Chapter 1). In contrast, Barker's Rivers thinks that 'Maud Allen was in the firing line almost by accident. The real target was men who couldn't or wouldn't conform' (1994, 161).
15. Prior's first name recalls Melville's *Billy Budd*, another image of youthful innocence sacrificed to patriarchal values. Catherine Lanone has drawn attention to the way in which the 'wordless murmur' of support of Hallett's '*Shotvarfet*' / 'It's not worth it' echoes the 'strange human murmur' elicited by Billy's execution in Meville's text (Lanone, 1999, 266).

Bibliography

Primary sources

Ackroyd, Peter, 1983, *The Last Testament of Oscar Wilde: A Novel*, London: Hamish Hamilton.
Aiken, Joan, 1978, *The Smile of the Stranger*, London: Victor Gollancz.
——, 1988 [1987], *Deception*, London: Grafton.
Amis, Kingsley, 1954, *Lucky Jim*, London: Victor Gollancz.
Aristophanes, 1959, *The Birds and The Frogs*, trans. Dudley Fitts, New York: Heritage.
Austen, Jane, 1985 [1818], *Northanger Abbey*, Harmondsworth: Penguin.
Bailey, Hilary, 1995 [1993], *Cassandra: Princess of Troy*, London: Pan.
Bainbridge, Beryl, 2001 [1985], *Watson's Apology*, New York: Carroll & Graf.
Barker, Pat, 1986 [1986], *Liza's England* (first published as *The Century's Daughter*), London: Virago.
——, 1992 [1991], *Regeneration*, Harmondsworth: Penguin.
——, 1994 [1993], *The Eye in the Door*, Harmondsworth: Penguin.
——, 1996 [1995], *The Ghost Road*, Harmondsworth: Penguin.
Bedford, Sybille, 1960 [1956], *A Legacy*, New York: Meridian.
——, 2000a [1963], *A Favourite of the Gods*, Washington: Counterpoint.
——, 2000b [1968], *A Compass Error*, Washington: Counterpoint.
Bell, Marguerite, 1977, *A Rose for Danger*, London: Mills & Boon.
Bentley, Phyllis, 1932, *Inheritance*, London: Gollancz.
——, 1937 [1936], *Freedom, Farewell!*, London: Gollancz.
——, 1948, *Life Story*, London: Gollancz.
Bowen, Marjorie, 1906, *The Viper of Milan: A Romance of Lombardy*, London: Alston Rivers.
Bradford, Barbara Taylor, 1981 [1980], *A Woman of Substance*, London: Panther.
Bradley, Marion Zimmer, 1993 [1983], *The Mists of Avalon*, Harmondsworth: Penguin.
Brittain, Vera, 1936, *Honourable Estate*, London: Victor Gollancz.
Brontë, Charlotte, 1967 [1847], *Jane Eyre*, London: Pan.
——, 1985 [1849], *Shirley*, London: Penguin.
Brontë, Emily, 1981 [1847], *Wuthering Heights*, Oxford and New York: Oxford University Press.
Broster, D.K., 1927 [1925], *The Flight of the Heron*, London: Heinemann.
——, 1929, *The Dark Mile*, London: Heinemann.
——, 1968 [1927], *The Gleam in the North*, Harmondsworth: Penguin.
Bryher, 1961, *Ruan*, London: Collins.
——, 1966, *This January Tale*, New York: Harcourt Brace & World.
——, 1968 [1957], *The Player's Boy*, London: Hodder & Stoughton.
Butts, Mary, 1974 [1935], *Scenes from the Life of Cleopatra*, New York: Ecco.
Byatt, A.S., 1983 [1967], *The Game*, Harmondsworth: Penguin.
——, 1985, *Still Life*, London: Chatto & Windus.
——, 1988 [1987], *Sugar and Other Stories*, Harmondsworth: Penguin.
——, 1991a [1964], *The Shadow of the Sun: A Novel*, London: Vintage.
——, 1991b [1990], *Possession: A Romance*, London: Vintage.

——, 1993b [1992], *Angels and Insects*, London: Vintage.
——, 1994 [1978], *The Virgin in the Garden*, London: Vintage.
——, 1997 [1996], *Babel Tower*, London: Vintage.
Carter, Angela, 1984, *Nights at the Circus*, London: Chatto & Windus.
Cartland, Barbara, 1976, *No Time for Love*, London: Pan.
——, 1979, *Love has His Way*, London: Robert Hale.
Comyns, Barbara, 1981 [1959], *The Vet's Daughter*, New York: Dial.
Cookson, Catherine, 1973 [1971], *The Dwelling Place*, London: Corgi.
——, 1975 [1974], *The Mallen Litter*, London: Corgi.
——, 1977, *The Girl*, London: Heinemann.
——, 1979a [1973], *The Mallen Streak*, London: Corgi.
——, 1979b [1974], *The Mallen Girl*, London: Corgi.
——, 1984 [1953], *Colour Blind*, London: MacDonald.
——, 1993a [1950], *Kate Hannigan*, London: Corgi.
——, 1993b [1967], *Katie Mulholland*, London: Corgi.
Daitch, Susan, 2002 [1986], *L.C.*, Chicago and Normal: Dalkey.
Dane, Clemence, 1931, *Broome Stages*, London: Heinemann.
——, 1944, *He Brings Great News: A Story*, London and Toronto: Heinemann.
Davies, Stevie, 1999b, *Impassioned Clay*, London: Women's Press.
de Guise, Elizabeth, 1977, *Puritan Wife*, London: Mills & Boon.
de La Fayette, Madame, 1961 [1678], *The Princess of Cleves*, trans. Walter J. Cobb, New York: Signet.
Dell, Ethel, M., 1922, *Charles Rex*, London: Hutchinson.
Donoghue, Emma, 2001 [2000], *Slammerkin*, London: Virago.
Drabble, Margaret, 1967 [1962], *A Summer Birdcage*, Harmondsworth: Penguin.
du Maurier, Daphne, 1945 [1941], *Frenchman's Creek*, London: Gollancz.
——, 1974 [1946], *The King's General*, London: Pan.
——, 1975 [1938], *Rebecca*, London: Pan.
——, 1992a [1951], *My Cousin Rachel*, London: Arrow.
——, 1992b [1969], *The House on the Strand*, London: Arrow.
——, 1994 [1931], *The Loving Spirit*, London: Arrow.
Duncker, Patricia, 2000 [1999], *James Miranda Barry*, London: Picador.
Dunmore, Helen, 1994 [1993], *Zennor in Darkness*, Harmondsworth: Penguin.
——, 1996 [1995], *A Spell of Winter*, Harmondsworth: Penguin.
Dunnett, Dorothy, 1973a [1966], *The Disorderly Knights*, London: Sphere.
——, 1973b [1969], *Pawn in Frankincense*, London: Sphere.
——, 1986 [1962], *The Game of Kings*, London: Arrow.
——, 1999a [1964], *Queens' Play*, London: Penguin.
——, 1999b [1971], *The Ringed Castle*, London: Penguin.
——, 1999c [1975], *Checkmate*, London: Penguin.
Eco, Umberto, 1992 [1980], *The Name of the Rose*, trans. William Weaver, London: Minerva.
Edgeworth, Maria, 1980 [1800], *Castle Rackrent*, intro. George Watson, Oxford: World's Classics.
Edwards, Nicky, 1986, *Mud*, London: Women's Press.
Eliot, George, 1980 [1863], *Romola*, Harmondsworth: Penguin.
——, 1988 [1866], *Felix Holt*, Harmondsworth: Penguin.
Evans, Margiad, 1978 [1932], *Country Dance*, London: John Calder.
Farnol, Jeffery, n.d. [1913], *The Amateur Gentleman*, London: Sampson Low.
Feinstein, Elaine, 1994, *Dreamers*, London: Macmillan.
Fell, Alison, 1999, *The Mistress of Lilliput*, London: Doubleday.

Fitzgerald, Penelope, 1996 [1995], *The Blue Flower*, London: Flamingo.
Flaubert, Gustave, 1964 [1869] *Sentimental Education*, Harmondsworth: Penguin.
——, 1977 [1862], *Salammbô*, Harmondsworth: Penguin.
Fowles, John, 1977 [1969], *The French Lieutenant's Woman*, London: Triad/Granada.
Freud, Esther, 1998 [1997], *Gaglow*, Harmondsworth: Penguin.
Galford, Ellen, 1985 [1984], *Moll Cutpurse: Her True History*, Ithaca: Firebrand.
——, 1994 [1986], *The Fires of Bride*, London: Women's Press.
Galsworthy, John, 2002 [1922], *The Forsyte Saga*, London: Granada.
Gaskell, Elizabeth, 1982 [1863], *Sylvia's Lovers*, Oxford: World's Classics.
——, 1970 [1854–5], *North and South*, Harmondsworth: Penguin.
George, Sara, 1998, *The Journal of Mrs Pepys: Portrait of a Marriage*, London: Review.
Gregory, Philippa, 1987, *Wideacre*, Harmondsworth: Penguin.
——, 1989, *The Favoured Child*, Harmondsworth: Penguin.
——, 1991 [1990], *Meridon*, Harmondsworth: Penguin.
——, 1996 [1995], *A Respectable Trade*, London: HarperCollins.
——, 1999 [1998], *Earthly Joys*, London: HarperCollins.
——, 2000 [1999], *Virgin Earth*, London: HarperCollins.
Hall, Radcliffe, 1982 [1928], *The Well of Loneliness*, London: Virago.
Henty, G.A., n.d. [1892], *Beric the Briton*, London: Blackil.
Heyer, Georgette, 1959 [1923], *Powder and Patch*, London: Pan.
——, 1964 [1940], *The Spanish Bride*, London: Pan.
——, 1965 [1921], *The Black Moth*, London: Pan.
——, 1966 [1951], *The Quiet Gentleman*, London: Pan.
——, 1971 [1968], *Cousin Kate*, London: Pan.
——, 1977 [1929], *Pastel*, New York: Buccaneer.
——, 1991 [1965], *Frederica*, London: Arrow.
——, 1992 [1940], *The Corinthian*, London: Arrow.
——, 1997 [1926], *These Old Shades*, London: Arrow.
——, 1998 [1959], *The Unknown Ajax*, London: Arrow.
——, 1999 [1949], *Arabella*, London: Arrow.
——, 1999 [1953], *Cotillion*, London: Arrow.
——, 2000 [1928], *The Masqueraders*, London: Arrow.
——, 2001 [1937], *An Infamous Army*, London: Arrow.
Hill, Susan, 1974 [1971], *Strange Meeting*, Harmondsworth: Penguin.
Hodge, Jane Aiken, 1976, *Judas Flowering*, Greenwich, CT: Fawcett Crest.
——, 1980 [1978], *Red Sky at Night*, London: Hodder & Stoughton.
Holt, Victoria, 1963 [1960], *Mistress of Mellyn*, London: Fontana.
——, 1965 [1963], *Bride of Pendorric*, London: Fontana.
——, 1968 [1966], *Menfreya*, London: Fontana.
——, 1972 [1970], *The Secret Woman*, London: Fontana.
——, 1980 [1978], *My Enemy the Queen*, London: Fontana.
——, 1984 [1982], *The Demon Lover*, London: Fontana.
——, 1993 [1969], *The Shivering Sands*, London: HarperCollins.
Howatch, Susan, 1972 [1971], *Penmarric*, Greenwich, CT: Fawcett Crest.
——, 1975 [1974], *Cashelmara*, London and Sydney: Pan.
Irwin, Margaret, 1941, *The Gay Galliard: The Love Story of Mary Queen of Scots*, London: Chatto & Windus.
——, 1966a [1931], *Royal Flush*, London: Pan.
——, 1966b [1934], *The Proud Servant*, London: Pan.
——, 1966c [1937], *The Stranger Prince*, London: Pan.

——, 1968 [1924], *Still She Wished for Company*, London: Chatto & Windus.

——, 1998 [1944], *Young Bess*, London: Allison & Busby.

——, 1999a [1948], *Elizabeth, Captive Princess*, London: Allison & Busby.

——, 1999b [1953], *Elizabeth and the Prince of Spain*, London: Allison & Busby.

Jameson, Storm, 1933, *The Triumph of Time*, Leipzig: Bernhard Tauchnitz.

——, 1942, *Then We Shall Hear Singing*, London: Cassell.

Jesse, F. Tennyson, 1981 [1927], *Moonraker*, London: Virago.

Jhabvala, Ruth Prawer, 1976 [1975], *Heat and Dust*, London: Futura.

Johnston, Jennifer, 1988 [1974], *How Many Miles to Babylon?*, Harmondsworth: Penguin.

Joyce, James, 1971 [1922], *Ulysses*, Harmondsworth: Penguin.

Kaye-Smith, Sheila, 1934, *Superstition Corner*, Chicago: Henry Regnery.

Kennedy, Margaret, 1985 [1953], *Troy Chimneys*, London: Virago.

King-Hall, Magdalen, 1946 [1942], *Life and Death of the Wicked Lady Skelton*, New York: Rinehart.

Kipling, Rudyard, n.d. [1906], *Puck of Pook's Hill*, in John Beecroft, ed., *A Selection of His Stories and Poems*, Vol. I, New York: Doubleday.

Le Carré, John, 1980 [1963], *The Spy Who Came in from the Cold*, London: Pan.

Lee, Sophia, 2000 [1783], *The Recess*, ed. April Alliston, Lexington: University Press of Kentucky.

Leslie, Doris, 1944, *Polonaise*, London: Book Club.

——, 1946, *The Peverills*, London: Hutchinson.

Lofts, Norah, 1951, *The Lute Player*, London: Michael Joseph.

——, 1968 [1946], *To See a Fine Lady*, London: Corgi.

——, 1969, *The Lost Queen: A Tragedy of a Royal Marriage*, New York: Doubleday.

——, 1972 [1944], *Jassy*, Greenwich, CT: Fawcett Crest.

Macaulay, Rose, 1965 [1923], *Told by an Idiot: A Novel*, London: Collins.

——, 1982 [1932], *They Were Defeated*, Oxford: Oxford University Press.

——, 1986 [1916], *Non-combatants and Others*, London: Methuen.

Mantel, Hilary, 1998 [1992], *A Place of Greater Safety*, New York: Henry Holt.

McCann, Maria, 2001, *As Meat Loves Salt*, London: Flamingo.

McCaughrean, Geraldine, 1997, *The Ideal Wife*, London: Richard Cohen.

McCrory, Moy, 1991 [1990], *The Fading Shrine*, London: Flamingo.

Melville, Herman, 1967, *Billy Budd, Sailor and Other Stories*, Harmondsworth: Penguin.

Miles, Rosalind, 1998, *Guenevere, Queen of the Summer Country*, New York: Crown.

——, 2000, *The Knight of the Sacred Lake*, New York: Three Rivers Press.

——, 2001, *Guenevere: The Child of the Holy Grail*, London: Pocket Books.

Mitchell, Margaret, 1958 [1936], *Gone With the Wind*, New York: Pocket Books.

Mitchison, Naomi, 1932 [1923], *The Conquered*, London: Jonathan Cape.

——, 1927 [1924], *When the Bough Breaks and Other Stories*, London: Jonathan Cape.

——, 1928 [1925], *Cloud Cuckoo Land*, London: Jonathan Cape.

——, 1933 [1929], *Barbarian Stories*, London: Jonathan Cape.

——, 1983 [1931], *The Corn King and the Spring Queen*, London: Virago.

——, 1997 [1947], *The Bull Calves*, London: Virago.

Molière, 1997, *Don Juan*, trans. Kenneth McLeish, London: Hern.

Morrison, Toni, 1997 [1987], *Beloved*, London: Vintage.

Muntz, Hope, 1949 [1948], *The Golden Warrior: The Story of Harold and William*, Foreword by G.M. Trevelyan, London: Chatto & Windus.

Murdoch, Iris, 2002 [1965], *The Red and the Green*, London: Vintage.

Myers, Elizabeth, 1945, *The Basilisk of St James's: A Romance*, London: Chapman & Hall.

O'Brien, Kate, 1946, *That Lady: A Novel*, London: Heinemann.

Orczy, Baroness, 1980 [1905], *The Scarlet Pimpernel*, London: Knight.
Page, Kathy, 1987, *The Unborn Dreams of Clara Riley*, London: Virago.
Pargeter, Edith, 1989 [1974], *The Brothers of Gwynedd Quartet*, London: Headline.
Plaidy, Jean, 1966 [1949], *Murder Most Royal*, London: Pan.
——, 1967a [1955], *Royal Road to Fotheringay*, London: Pan.
——, 1967b [1963], *The Captive Queen of Scots*, London: Pan.
——, 1974 [1961], *Daughters of Spain*, London: Pan.
——, 1975a [1967], *The Princess of Celle*, London: Pan.
——, 1975b [1968], *Caroline, The Queen*, London: Pan.
——, 1975c [1968], *Queen in Waiting*, London: Pan.
——, 1976 [1969], *The Third George*, London: Pan.
Power, Maggie [Margaret], 1994, *Lily*, London: Simon & Schuster.
Power, Margaret, 1987, *Goblin Fruit: A Novel*, London: Journeyman.
Prescott, H.F.M., 1958 [1932], *Son of Dust*, London: Eyre & Spottiswoode.
——, 2002 [1952], *The Man on a Donkey*, London: Phoenix.
Radcliffe, Ann, 1980 [1794], *The Mysteries of Udolpho*, Oxford: Oxford World's Classics.
Reid, Hilda, 1928, *Phillida: Or the Reluctant Adventurer*, Boston and New York: Houghton Mifflin.
Renault, Mary, 1961 [1958], *The King Must Die*, London: Four Square.
——, 1973 [1962], *The Bull From the Sea*, Harmondsworth: Penguin.
——, 1984a [1944], *The Friendly Young Ladies*, New York: Pantheon.
——, 1984b, *The Alexander Trilogy: Fire from Heaven* (1970); *The Persian Boy* (1972); *Funeral Games* (1981), Harmondsworth: Penguin.
——, 1986a [1956], *The Last of the Wine*, London: Sceptre.
——, 1986b [1966], *The Mask of Apollo*, London: Sceptre.
——, 1993 [1953], *The Charioteer*, San Diego, New York, London: Harcourt Brace.
Rhys, Jean, 1968 [1966], *Wide Sargasso Sea*, Harmondsworth: Penguin.
Roberts, Michèle, 1985 [1984], *The Wild Girl*, London: Methuen.
——, 1990, *In the Red Kitchen*, London: Methuen.
Rogers, Jane, 1992 [1991], *Mr Wroe's Virgins*, London: Faber & Faber.
Rogers, Rosemary, 1974, *Sweet Savage Love*, Ontario: Mira.
Sabatini, Rafael, 2001 [1921], *Scaramouche: A Romance of the French Revolution*, New York: Signet.
Scott, Walter, 1906a [1814], *Waverley*, London: Dent.
——, 1906b [1818], *The Heart of Midlothian*, London: Dent.
——, 1906c [1821], *Kenilworth*, London: Dent.
Seton, Anya, 1961 [1954], *Katherine*, London: Hodder.
——, 1966 [1965], *Avalon*, Greenwich, CT: Fawcett Crest.
Simpson, Helen, 1948 [1935], *Saraband for Dead Lovers*, London: Pan.
Smith, Eleanor, 1941, *The Man in Grey: A Regency Romance*, London and Melbourne: Hutchinson.
——, 1943, *Caravan*, London: Book Club.
Steen, Marguerite, 1942 [1941], *The Sun is My Undoing*, Philadelphia: Blakiston.
Stewart, Mary, 1971 [1970], *The Crystal Cave*, London: Coronet.
——, 1974 [1973], *The Hollow Hills*, London: Coronet.
——, 1980 [1979], *The Last Enchantment*, London: Coronet.
——, 1984 [1983], *The Wicked Day*, London: Coronet.
Styron, William, 2002 [1967], *The Confessions of Nat Turner*, New York: Random House.
Sutcliff, Rosemary, 1959, *The Lantern Bearers*, Oxford: Oxford University Press.
——, 1963, *Sword at Sunset*, London: Book Club.

——, 1981 [1959], *The Rider of the White Horse*, London: Book Club Association.

——, 1993 [1954], *The Eagle of the Ninth*, Farrer, Straus, Giroux: Sunburst.

Thackeray, William, 1993 [1847], *Vanity Fair*, Ware: Wordsworth.

Thynne, Jane, 1997, *Patrimony*, London: Fourth Estate.

Tremain, Rose, 1990 [1989], *Restoration*, London: Sceptre.

Vaughan, Hilda, 2002 [1948], *Iron and Gold*, Dinas Powys: Honno.

Waddell, Helen, 1950 [1933], *Peter Abelard*, London: The Reprint Society.

Warner, Sylvia Townsend, 1978 [1929], *The True Heart*, London: Virago.

——, 1987 [1936], *Summer Will Show*, London: Virago.

——, 1988 [1948], *The Corner that Held Them*, London: Virago.

——, 1989 [1938], *After the Death of Don Juan*, London: Virago.

——, 1993 [1926], *Lolly Willowes: Or the Loving Huntsman*, London: Virago.

——, 1997 [1954], *The Flint Anchor*, London: Virago.

Waters, Sarah, 1998, *Tipping the Velvet*, London: Virago.

——, 1999, *Affinity*, London: Virago.

Webb, Mary, 1928a [1917], *Gone to Earth*, intro. John Buchan, London: Jonathan Cape.

——, 1928b [1924], *Precious Bane*, intro. Stanley Baldwin, London: Jonathan Cape.

West, Rebecca, 1966, *The Birds Fall Down*, London: Macmillan.

——, 1980 [1929], *Harriet Hume: A London Fantasy*, London: Virago.

White, T.H., 1969 [1958], *The Once and Future King*, London: Fontana.

Whyte-Melville, J.G., 1911 [1863], *The Gladiators*, London: Dent.

Wilby, Jane, 1977, *Eleanor and the Marquis*, London: Mills & Boon.

Winsor, Kathleen, 2000 [1944], *Forever Amber*, Chicago: Chicago Review Press.

Winterson, Jeanette, 1985, *Oranges Are Not The Only Fruit*, London: Pandora.

——, 1988 [1987], *The Passion*, Harmondsworth: Penguin.

——, 1990 [1989], *Sexing the Cherry*, London: Vintage.

Woodiwiss, Kathleen, 1972, *The Flame and the Flower*, New York: Avon.

Woolf, Virginia, 1968 [1937], *The Years*, Harmondsworth: Penguin.

——, 1977 [1928], *Orlando: A Biography*, London: Granada.

——, 1978a [1941], *Between the Acts*, London: Grafton.

——, 1978b, *The Pargiters*, London: Hogarth.

Secondary sources

Abraham, Julie, 1996, *Are Girls Necessary? Lesbian Writing and Modern Histories*, New York and London: Routledge.

Adam, Ruth, 1975, *A Woman's Place: 1910–1975*, New York: Norton & Co.

Allen, Trevor, 1967, 'Jean Plaidy's Novelised History', *Contemporary Review*, 210 (March), 157–60.

Anderson, Linda, 1990, 'The Re-imagining of History in Contemporary Women's Fiction', in Linda Anderson, ed., *Plotting Change: Contemporary Women's Fiction*, London: Edward Arnold, 129–41.

Anon., 2000 [1845], 'The Historical Romance', in E.J. Clery and Robert Miles, eds, *Gothic Documents: A Sourcebook, 1700–1820*, Manchester: Manchester University Press.

Ashby, Melanie, 2002, 'Interview: Rose Tremain', *Mslexia*, 15 (October, November, December), 14–16.

Ashe, Geoffrey, 1960, *From Caesar to Arthur*, London: Collins.

Ashe, Geoffrey, ed., 1971 [1968], *The Quest for Arthur's Britain*, London: Paladin.

Auden, W.H., 1966, *Selected Shorter Poems*, London: Faber & Faber.

——, 1977, *The English Auden*, ed. Edward Mendelson, London: Faber & Faber.

Bainbridge, Beryl, 1999 [1987], *Forever England: North and South*, New York: Carroll & Graf.

Baker, Niamh, 1989, *Happily Ever After: Women's Fiction in Postwar Britain, 1945–60*, Basingstoke and London: Macmillan.

Bakhtin, Mikhail, 1994, *The Bakhtin Reader: Selected Writings of Bakhtin, Medvedev, Voloshinov*, ed. Pam Morris, London: Edward Arnold.

Baldick, Chris, 1991 [1990], *The Concise Oxford Dictionary of Literary Terms*, Oxford: Oxford University Press.

Barber, Richard, 1990 [1961], *King Arthur: Hero and Legend*, Woodbridge, Suffolk: Boydell.

Barker, Simon, 1986, 'Images of the Sixteenth and Seventeenth Centuries as a History of the Present', in Francis Barker *et al.*, ed., *Literature, Politics and Theory: Papers from the Essex Conference 1976–84*, London: New York.

Barthes, Roland, 1970, 'Historical Discourse', in Michael Lane, ed., *Structuralism: A Reader*, London: Jonathan Cape.

——, 1975 [1970], *S/Z*, trans. R. Miller, London: Jonathan Cape.

——, 1990, 'The Death of the Author', in Dennis Walder, ed., *Literature in the Modern World*, Oxford: Oxford University Press.

——, 1993 [1980], *Camera Lucida: Reflections on Photography*, trans. Richard Howard, London: Vintage.

Bassnett, Susan, 1997 [1988], *Elizabeth I: A Feminist Perspective*, Oxford and New York: Berg.

Batsleer, Janet, 1981, 'Pulp in the Pink', *Spare Rib*, August 1981, 109, 52–5.

Beauman, Nicola, 1983, *A Very Great Profession: The Woman's Novel 1914–39*, London: Virago.

Beddoe, Deirdre, 1989, *Back to Home and Duty: Women Between the Wars, 1918–1939*, London: Pandora.

——, 2000, *Out of the Shadows: A History of Women in Twentieth-Century Wales*, Cardiff: University of Wales Press.

Beer, Gillian, 1970, *The Romance*, London: Methuen.

——, 1999, 'Sylvia Townsend Warner: The Centrifugal Kick', in Maroula Joannou, ed., *Women Writers of the 1930s: Gender, Politics and History*, Edinburgh: Edinburgh University Press.

Beer, Patricia, 1968, *Mrs Beer's House*, London: Macmillan.

Bell, Kathleen, 1995, 'Cross-dressing in War-time: Georgette Heyer's *The Corinthian* in its 1940 Context', in Pat Kirkham and David Thomas, eds, *War Culture: Social Change and Changing Experiences in World War Two*, London: Lawrence and Wishart.

——, 2003, 'Writing a Man's World: An Exploration of Three Works by Rosemary Sutcliff, Mary Renault and Cecil Woodham Smith', in Jane Dowson, ed., *Women's Writing 1945–1960: After the Deluge*, Basingstoke and London: Palgrave, 148–61.

Benjamin, Walter, 1973 [1940], 'Theses on the Philosophy of History', *Illuminations*, London: Fontana.

Bentley, Phyllis, 1941, *The English Regional Novel*, London: George Allen & Unwin.

——, 1962, *O Dreams O Destinations: An Autobiography*, London: Victor Gollancz.

Benton, Jill, 1992 [1990], *Naomi Mitchison: A Biography*, London: Pandora.

Berry, Paul and Alan Bishop, eds, 1985, *Testament of a Generation: The Journalism of Vera Brittain and Winifred Holtby*, London: Virago.

Blackett, Monica, 1973, *The Mark of the Maker: A Portrait of Helen Waddell*, London: Constable.

Bloom, Clive, 2002, *Bestsellers: Popular Fiction since 1900*, Basingstoke and New York: Palgrave.

Boucier, Richard S., 1986–7, 'Scott and Historical Fiction: The Case of *Ivanhoe*', *Selected Papers and Medievalism*, 1–2: 11, 150–9.

Bowen, Marjorie, 1971 [1934], *Mary Queen of Scots*, London: Sphere.

Boyce, Lucienne, 2002, 'Those Rude Victorians: An Interview with Sarah Waters', *Solander*, 11, 6: 1 (May), 2–5.

Brace, Marianne, 1996, 'That Thinking Feeling' (interview with A.S. Byatt), *The Guardian*, 9 May, 6–7.

Bradbury, Malcolm, 1987, *No, Not Bloomsbury*, London: Andre Deutsch.

Brannigan, John, 2003, *Orwell to the Present: Literature in England 1945–2000*, Basingstoke and New York: Palgrave.

Bridgwood, Christine, 1986, 'Family Romances: The Contemporary Popular Family Saga', in Jean Radford, ed., *The Progress of Romance: The Politics of Popular Fiction*, London: Routledge, 167–93.

Brittain, Vera, 1935 [1933], *Testament of Youth*, London: Victor Gollancz.

——, 1986, *Chronicle of Friendship: Vera Brittain's Diary of the Thirties, 1932–1939*, ed. Alan Bishop, London: Victor Gollancz.

Brontly, Susan, C., 1997, 'Painting Clio's Portrait: Metaphors on the Postmodern Pallette', *Clio*, 26: 3, 297–322.

Brothers, Barbara, 1989, 'Writing Against the Grain: Sylvia Townsend Warner and the Spanish Civil War', in Mary Lynn Broe and Angela Ingram, eds, *Women's Writing in Exile*, Chapel Hill and London: University of North Carolina Press, 351–68.

Brownmiller, Susan, 1975, *Against Our Will: Men, Women and Rape*, London: Secker & Warburg.

Brumm, Ursula, 1969, 'Thoughts on History and the Novel', *Comparative Literature Studies*, 6, 317–30.

Brunt, Rosalind, 1984, 'A Career in Love: The Romantic World of Barbara Cartland', in Christopher Pawling, ed., *Popular Fiction & Social Charge*, London: Macmillan.

Bryher, 1920, 'The Girl-Page in Elizabethan Literature', *Fortnightly Review*, CVII (January–June), 442–52.

——, 1963, *The Heart of Artemis: A Writer's Memoirs*, London: Collins.

——, 1972, *The Days of Mars: A Memoir, 1940–1946*, New York: Harcourt Brace Jovanovich.

Burns Jr, Landon C., 1964, 'Men are only Men: The Novels of Mary Renault', *Critique* VI: 3, 102–21.

Butler, Judith, 1990, *Gender Trouble: Feminism and the Subversion of Identity*, New York and London: Routledge.

Butterfield, Herbert, 1924, *The Historical Novel: An Essay*, Cambridge: Cambridge University Press.

——, 1951 [1931], *The Whig Interpretation of History*, New York: Charles Scribner.

Buxton, Jackie, 1996, '"What's Love Got to do With it?" Postmodernism and *Possession*', *English Studies in Canada*, 22: 2 (June), 199–219.

Byatt, A.S., ed., 1993a [1991], 'An Honourable Escape: Georgette Heyer' *Passions of the Mind*, London: Vintage, 258–65.

——, 1993a [1991], *Passions of the Mind: Selected Writings*, London: Vintage.

——, 2000, *On Histories and Stories: Selected Essays*, London: Chatto & Windus.

Caesar, Julius, 1957, *The Gallic War and Other Writings*, trans. Moses Hadas, New York: Random House.

Caine, Barbara, 1997, *English Feminism: 1780–1980*, Oxford: Oxford University Press.

Callil, Carmen, 1996, *Subversive Sybils: Women's Popular Fiction this Century*, London: The British Library.

Cam, Helen, 1961, *Historical Novels*, London: Published for the Historical Association by Routledge & Kegan Paul.

——, 1963, 'Historical Novels: Fact or Fiction?', *The Listener*, 30 May, 914–15.

Carlston, Erin G., 1996, 'Versatile Interests: Reading Bisexuality in *The Friendly Young Ladies*', in Donald E. Hall and Maria Pramaggiore, eds, *Re-presenting Bisexualities: Subject and Culture of Fluid Desire*, New York and London: New York University Press.

Carter, Angela, 1979, *The Sadeian Women: An Exercise in Cultural History*, London: Virago.

Castle, Terry, 1993, *The Apparitional Lesbian: Female Homosexuality and Modern Culture*, New York: Columbia University Press.

——, 2002, 'Courage, mon amie', *London Review of Books*, 24: 7, 3–11.

Caveliero, Glen, 1977, *The Rural Tradition in the English Novel 1900–1939*, London and Basingstoke: Macmillan.

Clery, E.J. and Robert Miles, eds, 2000, *Gothic Documents: A Source Book, 1700–1820*, Manchester: Manchester University Press.

Cockburn, Claud, 1972, *Bestseller: The Books that Everyone Read 1900–1939*, London: Sedgewick & Jackson.

Collins Gem Dictionary of First Names, 1975, London and Glasgow: Collins.

Connor, Steven, 1996, *The English Novel in History 1950–1995*, London and New York: Routledge.

Cookson, Catherine, 1999, *My Land of the North: Memories of a Northern Childhood*, London: Methuen (first published as *Catherine Cookson Country*, 1986).

Cranny Francis, Anne, 1990, *Feminist Fiction: Feminist Uses of Generic Fiction*, Cambridge: Polity.

Cuthbertson, Sarah, 2001, 'HNS Conference Report 2001', *Solander*, 10, 5: 2 (December), 34.

Davies, Stevie, 1999a [1998], *Unbridled Spirits: Women of the English Revolution 1641–1660*, London: The Women's Press.

Dick, Bernard F., 1972, *The Hellenism of Mary Renault*, Carbondale and Edwardsville: Southern Illinois University Press.

Dixon, jay, 1999, *The Romance Fiction of Mills and Boon, 1909–1990s*, London: UCL Press.

Dowson, Jane, ed., 1996, *Women's Poetry of the 1930s*, London: Routledge.

——, 2003, *Women's Writing, 1945–1960: After the Deluge*, Basingstoke and London: Palgrave.

du Maurier, Daphne, 1972 [1967], *Vanishing Cornwall*, London: Penguin.

——, 1981, *The Rebecca Notebook and Other Memories*, London: Gollancz.

——, 1989, *Enchanted Cornwall*, London: Michael Joseph/ Pilot Productions Ltd.

Dudgeon, Piers, 1998 [1997], *The Girl from Leam Lane: The Life and Writing of Catherine Cookson*, London: Headline.

Duffy, Martha, 1971, 'On the Road to Manderley', *Time*, April, 97: 12, 65–6.

Duncker, Patricia, 1992, *Sisters & Strangers: An Introduction to Contemporary Feminist Fiction*, Oxford and Cambridge, MA: Blackwell.

DuPlessis, Rachel Blau, 1985, *Writing Beyond the Ending: Narrative Strategies of Twentieth Century Women Writers*, Bloomington: Indiana University Press.

Eco, Umberto, 1984 [1983], *Postscript to The Name of the Rose*, trans. William Weaver, San Diego, New York, London: Harcourt Brace Jovanovich.

Faderman, Lillian, 1985 [1981], *Surpassing the Love of Men: Romantic Friendship and Love Between Women from the Renaissance to the Present*, London: The Women's Press.

Fahnestock-Thomas, Mary, ed., 2001, *Georgette Heyer: A Critical Retrospective*, Saraland, AL: Prinny.

Faludi, Susan, 1992, *Backlash: The Undeclared War Against Women*, London: Chatto & Windus.

Ferris, Ina, 1989, 'Re-positioning the Novel: *Waverley* and the Gender of Fiction', *Studies in Romanticism*, 28 (Summer), 291–301.

Fetterley, Judith, 1978, *The Resisting Reader: A Feminist Approach to American Fiction*, Bloomington: Indiana University Press

Fiedler, Leslie, 1984 [1960], *Love and Death in the American Novel*, Harmondsworth: Penguin.

Firestone, Shulamith, 1972 [1971], *The Dialectic of Sex: The Case for Feminist Revolution*, London: Paladin.

Fleenor, Juliann, ed., 1983, *The Female Gothic*, Montreal and London: Eden.

Fleishman Avrom, 1971, *The English Historical Novel: From Walter Scott to Virginia Woolf*, Baltimore and London: Johns Hopkins Press.

Fletcher, Anthony and Diarmaid MacCulloch, 1997, *Tudor Rebellions*, 4th edn, London and New York: Longman.

Forster, Margaret, 1994 [1993], *Daphne du Maurier*, London: Arrow.

Foster, Thomas, 1995, '"Dream Made Flesh": Sexual Differences and Narratives of Revolution in Sylvia Townsend Warner's *Summer Will Show*', *Modern Fiction Studies*, 41: 3–4 (Fall–Winter), 531–62.

Fowler, Bridget, 1991, *The Alienated Reader: Women and Popular Romantic Literature, in the Twentieth Century*, Hemel Hempstead: Harvester Wheatsheaf.

Frazer, J.G., 1957 [1890–1915], *The Golden Bough*, London: Macmillan.

French, Marilyn, 1992, *The War Against Women*, London: Hamish Hamilton.

Freud, Sigmund, 1959 [1909], 'Family Romances', *The Standard Edition of the Complete Psychological Works*, Vol. IX, London: Hogarth, 237–41.

——, 1977, 'Female Sexuality', *On Sexuality: Three Essays on the Theory of Sexuality and Other Works*, Vol. 7, Harmondsworth: Penguin.

——, 1977, *On Sexuality: Three Essays on the Theory of Sexuality and Other Works*, Vol. 7, Harmondsworth: Penguin.

Friedan, Betty, 1982 [1963], *The Feminine Mystique*, Harmondsworth: Penguin.

Fries, Maureen, 1977, 'The Rationalization of the Arthurian "Matter" in T.H. White and Mary Stewart', *Philological Quarterly*, 56 (Spring), 258–65.

Fukuyama, Francis, 1992, *The End of History and the Last Man*, London: Hamish Hamilton.

Galván, Fernando, 2001, 'On Ireland, Religion and History: A Conversation with Hilary Mantel', *The European English Messenger*, X: 2 (Autumn), 31–8.

Garber, Marjorie, 1993 [1992], *Vested Interests: Cross-Dressing and Cultural Anxiety*, London: Penguin.

Garside, Peter, 1991, 'Popular Fiction and National Tale: Hidden Origins of Scott's *Waverley*', *Nineteenth Century Literature*, 46, 30–53.

Gavron & Hannah, 1983 [1966], *The Captive Wife: Conflicts of Housebound Mothers*, London: Routledge & Kegan Paul.

Gee, Maggie, 1997, 'Clinging to the Coat-tails of Fact', *Times Literary Supplement*, 12 September, 10.

Geoffrey of Monmouth, 1966, *The History of the Kings of Britain*, trans. Lewis Thorpe, Harmondsworth: Penguin.

Gerrard, Nicci, 1989, *Into the Mainstream: How Feminism has Changed Women's Writing*, London: Pandora.

Gilbert, Sandra M. and Susan Gubar, 1984 [1979], *The Madwoman in the Attic: The Woman Writer and the Nineteenth-Century Literary Imagination*, New Haven and London: Yale University Press.

Glendinning, Victoria, 1988 [1987], *Rebecca West*, London and Basingstoke: Macmillan.

Goodwin, Cliff, 1994, *To be a Lady: The Story of Catherine Cookson*, London: Century.

Grant, Linda, 1994 [1993], *Sexing the Millennium: A Political History of the Sexual Revolution*, London: HarperCollins.

Green, Peter, 1962 [1958], 'Aspects of the Historical Novel', *Essays by Diverse Hands*, 31, 53–60.

Greenfield, Barbara, 1985, 'The Archetypal Masculine: Its Manifestations in Myth, and Its Significance for Women', in Andrew Samuels, ed., *The Father: Contemporary Jungian Perspectives*, London: Free Association Books.

Greer, Germaine, 1993 [1971], *The Female Eunuch*, London: Flamingo.

Gregory, Philippa, 1984, 'The Popular Fiction of the Eighteenth-Century Commercial Circulating Libraries', PhD Thesis, University of Edinburgh.

——, 1996, 'Love Hurts', in Sarah Sceats and Gail Cunningham, eds, *Image and Power: Women in Fiction*, London and New York: Longman.

——, 2004, 'My Favourite Lesson', *The Guardian*, 3 February, 7.

Gubar, Susan, 1987, 'This is my Rifle, This is my Gun: World War II and the Blitz on Women', in Margaret Higonnot *et al.*, eds, *Behind the Lines: Gender and the Two World Wars*, New Haven and London: Yale University Press, 227–59.

Harman, Claire, 1991 [1989], *Sylvia Townsend Warner: A Biography*, London: Minerva.

——, 1995 [1994], *The Diaries of Sylvia Townsend Warner*, London: Virago.

Harman, Claire, ed., 1981, 'Sylvia Townsend Warner: 1893–1978: A Celebration', *PN Review*, 23, 8: 3.

Harper, Sue, 1983, 'History With Frills: "Costume" Fiction in World War II', *Red Letters*, 14, 14–23.

——, 1987, 'Historical Pleasures: Gainsborough Costume Melodramas', in Christine Gledhall, ed., *Home is Where the Heart is: Studies in Melodrama and the Women's Film*, London: BFI Publishing.

Harrison, Jane, 1927 [1912], *Themis: A Study of the Social Origins of the Greek Religion*, 2nd edn, Cambridge: Cambridge University Press.

Hartley, Jenny, 1997, *Millions Like Us: British Women's Fiction of the Second World War*, London: Virago.

Hartley, Jenny, ed., 1994, *Hearts Undefeated: Women's Writing of the Second World War*, London: Virago.

Harvey, Elizabeth, 1992, *Ventriloquised Voices: Feminist Theory and English Renaissance Texts*, London: Routledge.

Heath, Stephen, 1986, 'Joan Riviere and the Masquerade', in Victor Burgin, James Donald and Cora Kaplan, eds, *Formations of Fantasy*, London and New York: Routledge, 45–61.

Heilbrun, Carolyn, 1979, *Reinventing Womanhood*, London: Victor Gollancz.

Henderson, Harry B., 1974, *Versions of the Past: The Historical Imagination in American Fiction*, New York: Oxford University Press.

Henderson, Leslie, ed., 1990, *Twentieth Century Romance and Historical Writers*, 2nd edn, Chicago and London: St James Press.

Hennessy, Peter, 1993 [1992], *Never Again: Britain 1945–51*, London: Vintage.

Hiller, Bevis, 1998 [1983], *The Style of the Century*, 2nd edn, New York: Watson Guptill.

Hoberman, Ruth, 1997, *Gendering Classicism: The Ancient World in Twentieth-Century Women's Historical Fiction*, New York: State University of New York Press.

Hodge, Jane Aiken, 1985 [1984], *The Private World of Georgette Heyer*, London and Sydney: Pan.

Hodgkin, Kate, n.d., 'The Witch, the Puritan and the Prophet: Historical Novels and Seventeenth Century History', unpublished paper.

Hole, Christina, 1947, *English Home-Life: 1500–1800*, London: Batsford.

Holmes, T. Rice, 1931 [1909], *Caesar's Conquest of Gaul*, 2nd edn, London: Oxford University Press.

Holtby, Winifred, 1934, *Women*, London: John Lane, The Bodley Head.

Hopkins, Chris, 1995, 'Sylvia Townsend Warner and the Historical Novel', *Literature and History*, 4: 1 (Spring), 50–64.

Horner, Avril and Sue Zlosnik, 1998, *Daphne du Maurier: Writing, Identity and the Gothic Imagination*, London and Basingstoke: Macmillan.

Hoyle, R.W., 2001, *The Pilgrimage of Grace and the Politics of the 1530s*, Oxford: Oxford University Press.

Hubback, Judith, 1957, *Wives Who Went to College*, London: Heinemann.

Hughes, Helen, 1993, *The Historical Romance*, London and New York: Routledge.

Humm, Maggie, 1998, 'The Business of a 'New Art': Woolf, Potter and Postmodernism', in Judy Simons and Kate Fulbrook, eds, *Writing: A Woman's Business; Women, Writing and the Market Place*, Manchester: Manchester University Press.

Hutcheon, Linda, 1988, *A Poetics of Postmodernism: History, Theory, Fiction*, New York and London: Routledge.

Irigaray, Luce, 1985 [1977], *This Sex Which is Not One*, trans. Catherine Porter with Carolyn Burke, Ithaca, NY: Cornell University Press.

——, 1991, *The Irigaray Reader*, ed., Margaret Whitford, Oxford: Blackwell.

Jaggi, Maya, 2003, 'Dispatches from the Front' (interview with Pat Barker), *The Guardian*, 16 August, 16–19.

Jameson, Frederic, 1991, *Postmodernism or the Cultural Logic of Late Capitalism*, London and New York: Verso.

Jameson, Storm, 1984 [1969], *Journey From the North*, Vol. I, London: Virago.

Jenkins, Elizabeth, 1958, *Elizabeth the Great*, London: Companion Book Club.

——, 1961, *Elizabeth and Leicester*, London: Gollancz.

Jones, Ann Rosalind, 1986, 'Mills and Boon Meets Feminism', in Jean Radford, ed., *The Progress of Romance: The Politics of Popular Fiction*, London and New York: Routledge & Kegan Paul, 195–218.

Jones, Gwyn and Thomas Jones, 1974 [1949], *The Mabinogion*, London: Dent.

Julian of Norwich, 1961, *The Revelations of Divine Love*, trans. James Walsh, London: Burns & Oates.

Kaplan, Cora, 1990 [1986], *Sea Changes: Culture and Feminism*, London: Verso.

Kearns, Cleo McNally, 1990, 'Dubious Pleasures: Dorothy Dunnett and the Historical Novel', *Critical Quarterly*, Spring, 32, 36–48.

Kee, Robert, 1995 [1980], *Ireland: A History*, London: Abacus.

Kelly, Kathleen Coyne, 1996, *A.S. Byatt*, New York: Twayne.

Kenyon, Olga, 1988, *Women Novelists Today*, Brighton: Harvester.

——, 1992, *The Writer's Imagination*, Bradford: University of Bradford Print Unit.

Kermode, Frank, 1967, *The Sense of an Ending*, New York: Oxford University Press.

Knight, Stephen, 1983, *Arthurian Literature and Society*, Basingstoke and New York: Palgrave.

Knights, Ben, 1999, *Writing Masculinities: Male Narratives in Twentieth-Century Fiction*, London: Macmillan.

Kristeva, Julia, 1997 [1981], 'Women's Time', in Robyn R. Warhol and Diane Price, Herndl, eds, *Feminisms: An Anthology of Literary Theory and Criticism*, Basingstoke: Macmillan, 860–79.

Laing, R.D. and Esterson, A., 1964, *Sanity, Madness and the Family*, London: Tavistock.

Langland, Elizabeth, 1997, 'Sexing the Text: Narrative Drag as Feminist Poetics and Politics in Jeanette Winterson's *Sexing the Cherry*', *Narrative*, 5: 1 (January), 99–107.

Lanone, Catherine, 1999, 'Scattering the Seed of Abraham: The Motif of Sacrifice' in Pat Barker's *Regeneration*, and *The Ghost Road*, *Literature and Theology*, 13: 3 (September), 259–68.

Lascelles, Mary, 1980, *The Story-Teller Retrieves the Past: Historical Fiction and Fictitious History in the Art of Scott, Stevenson, Kipling and Some Others*, Oxford: Clarendon.

Lassner, Phyllis, 1990, 'The Quiet Revolution: World War II and the English Domestic Novel', *Mosaic*, 23: 3, 87–100.

Leavis, F.R., 1962 [1948], *The Great Tradition*, London: Penguin.

Lerner, Gerda, 1979, *The Majority Finds its Past: Placing Women in History*, Oxford: Oxford University Press.

——, 1994 [1993], *The Creation of Feminist Consciousness: From the Middle Ages to 1870*, Oxford: Oxford University Press.

Lewis, Jayne Elizabeth, 1995, '"Ev'ry Lost Relation": Historical Fictions and Sentimental Incidents in Sophia Lee's *The Recess*', *Eighteenth Century Fiction*, 7: 2 (January), 165–84.

Lewis, R.W.B., 1993 [1975], *Edith Wharton: A Biography*, London: Vintage.

Light, Alison, 1987, 'Towards a Feminist Cultural Studies: Middleclass Femininity and Fiction in Post-Second World War Britain', *English Amerikanische Studies*, 1, 58–72.

——, 1989, '*Young Bess*: Historical Novels and Growing Up', *Feminist Review*, 33 (Autumn), 57–71.

——, 1991, *Forever England: Femininity, Literature and Conservatism Between the Wars*, London: Routledge.

Lister, Anne, 1988, *I Know My Own Heart: The Diaries of Anne Lister 1791–1840*, ed., Helena Whitbread, London: Virago.

Loomis, Roger Sherman, ed., 1959, *Arthurian Literature in the Middle Ages: A Collaborative History*, London: Clarendon.

Lucas, John, 1999 [1997], *The Radical Twenties: Writing, Politics and Culture*, New Brunswick, NJ: Rutgers University Press.

Lukács, Georg, 1983 [1962], *The Historical Novel*, trans. Hannah and Stanley Mitchell, London: Methuen.

Macaulay, Thomas Babington, 1968, *Lays of Ancient Rome and Miscellaneous Essays and Poems*, London: Dent.

Macherey, Pierre, 1978, *A Theory of Literary Production*, London: Routledge & Kegan Paul.

Mantel, Hilary, 2002, 'No Passport Required', *The Guardian*, 12 October, 4–6.

Marcus, Jane, 1984, 'A Wilderness of One's Own: Feminist Fantasy Novels of the Twenties: Rebecca West and Sylvia Townsend Warner', in Susan Merrill Squier, ed., *Women Writers and the City: Essays in Feminist Literary Criticism*, Knoxville: University of Tennessee Press.

Marwick, Arthur, 1970, *The Nature of History*, London and Basingstoke: Macmillan.

Marx, Karl, n.d., *Capital*, Vol. I, Moscow: Progress.

Marx, Karl, 1979, *The Essential Marx: The Non-Economic Writings*, New York: New American Library.

Marx, Karl and Friedrich Engels, 1985, *The Communist Manifesto*, Harmondsworth: Penguin.

Maslen, Elizabeth, 1999, 'Naomi Mitchison's Historical Fiction', in Maroula Joannou, ed., *Women Writers of the 1930s: Gender Politics and History*, Edinburgh: Edinburgh University Press.

——, 2001, *Political and Social Issues in British Women's Fiction, 1928–1968*, Basingstoke and New York: Palgrave.

Masterman, C.F.G., 1909, *The Condition of England*, London: Methuen.

McAleer, Joseph, 1992, *Popular Reading and Publishing in Britain 1914–1950*, Oxford: Clarendon Press.

McCrum, Robert, 2001, 'Pat Barker: The Books Interview', *The Observer*, 1 April, 17.

McEwan, Neil, 1987, *Perspective in British Historical Fiction Today*, Basingstoke and London: Macmillan.

Middleton, Peter and Tim Woods, 2000, *Literatures of Memory: History, Time and Space in Post-war Writing*, Manchester and New York: Manchester University Press.

Miller, Jane, 1986, *Women Writing About Men*, London: Virago.

Mitchell, Juliet, 1975 [1974], *Psychoanalysis and Feminism*, Harmondsworth: Penguin.

——, 1984 [1966], *Women: The Longest Revolution: Essays on Feminism, Literature and Psychoanalysis*, London: Virago.

Mitchison, Naomi, 1928, *Anna Comnena: Representative Woman*, London: Gerald Howe.

——, 1934, 'New Cloud-Cuckoo Borough', *Modern Scot* (June), 30–8.

——, 1935, 'Writing Historical Novels', *The Saturday Review of Literature*, 27 April, XI, 41, 645–6.

——, 1975, *All Change Here: Girlhood and Marriage*, London: Bodley Head.

——, 1979, *You May Well Ask: A Memoir 1920–1940*, London: Victor Gollancz.

——, 1985, *Among You Taking Notes: The Wartime Diary of Naomi Mitchison*, ed. Dorothy Sheridan, London: Victor Gollancz.

Modleski, Tania, 1984, *Loving with a Vengeance*, London: Methuen.

Montefiore, Janet, 1996, *Men and Women Writers of the 1930s: The Dangerous Flood of History*, London, New York: Routledge.

Morrison, Elspeth, 2001 [1994], *The Dorothy Dunnett Companion*, Foreword by Dorothy Dunnett, New York: Vintage.

——, 2002, *The Dorothy Dunnett Companion II*, New York: Vintage.

Morton, H.V., 1944 [1927], *In Search of England*, 31st edn, London: Methuen.

Mulford, Wendy, 1988, *This Narrow Place: Sylvia Townsend Warner and Valentine Ackland: Life, Letters and Politics, 1930–1951*, London: Pandora.

Murray, Margaret, 1921, *The Witch Cult in Western Europe*, Oxford: Clarendon.

Mussell, Kay, 1974, 'Beautiful and Damned: The Sexual Woman and Gothic Fiction', *Journal of Popular Culture*, 9 (Summer), 84–9.

——, 1981, *Women's Gothic and Romantic Fiction: A Reference Guide*, Westport, CT and London: Greenwood.

Nastali, Dan, 1999, 'Arthur Without Fantasy: Dark Age Britain in Recent Historical Fiction', *Arthuriana*, 9: 1, 5–22.

Onega, Susana, 1995, 'British Historiographic Metafiction', in Mark Currie, ed., *Metafiction*, London: Longman.

Orel, Harold, 1995, *The Historical Novel from Scott to Sabatini, Changing Attitudes to a Literary Genre, 1814–1920*, London: Macmillan; New York: St Martin's Press.

Orwell, George, 1966 [1938], *Homage to Catalonia*, Harmondsworth: Penguin.

Owen, Alex, 1989, *The Darkened Room: Women, Power and Spiritualism in Late Victorian England*, London: Virago.

Pagels, Elaine, 1979, *The Gnostic Gospels*, London: Weidenfeld & Nicolson.

Palmer, Paulina, 1989, *Contemporary Women's Fiction: Narrative Practice and Feminist Theory*, Hemel Hempstead: Harvester Wheatsheaf.

Pankhurst, Sylvia, E., 1977 [1931], *The Suffragette Movement: An Intimate Account of Persons and Ideals*, London: Virago.

Pearce, Lynne, 1995, '"Written on Tablets of Stone": Jeanette Winterson, Roland Barthes and the Discourse of Romantic Love', in Suzanne Raitt, ed., *Volcanoes and Pearl Divers: Essays in Lesbian Feminist Studies*, London: Onlywomen Press.

Pethick-Lawrence, Emmeline, 1938, *My Part in a Changing World*, London: Victor Gollancz.

Petrey, Sandy, 1991, 'Ideology, *Écriture*, 1848: Sylvia Townsend Warner Unwrites Flaubert', *Recherches Semiotiques/Semiotic Enquiry*, 4: 2–3, 159–79.

Philips, Deborah, 1986, '"True Romance": an interview with Barbara Cartland', *Women's Review*, 13, 28–9.

Plain, Gill, 1996, *Women's Fiction of the Second World War: Gender, Power and Resistance*, Edinburgh: Edinburgh University Press.

——, 2001, *Twentieth Century Crime Fiction: Gender, Sexuality and the Body*, Edinburgh: Edinburgh University Press.

Plath, Sylvia, 1968 [1965], *Ariel*, London: Faber & Faber.

Plato, 1951, *The Symposium*, trans. W. Hamilton, Harmondsworth: Penguin.

——, 1973, *Phaedrus and Letters VII and VIII*, trans. Walter Hamilton, Harmondsworth: Penguin.

Plumb, J.H., 1966 [1956], *The First Four Georges*, London: Fontana.

Porter, Dale, H., 1993, 'The Gold in Fort Knox: Historical Fiction in the Context of Historiography', *Soundings*, 76: 2–3 (Summer/Fall), 315–50.

Power, Eileen, 1922, *Medieval English Nunneries*, Cambridge: Cambridge University Press.

Prescott, H.F.M., 1940, *Spanish Tudor: The Life of Bloody Mary*, London: Constable.

Pugh, Martin, 2000, *Women and the Women's Movement in Britain 1914–1959*, Basingstoke and London: Macmillan.

Punter, David, 1996, *The Literature of Terror*, Vol. I, 2nd edn, London and New York: Longman.

Pykett, Lyn, 1987, 'The Century's Daughters: Recent Women's Fiction and History', *Critical Quarterly*, 29: 3, 71–7.

Radford, Jean, ed., 1986, *The Progress of Romance: The Politics of Popular Fiction*, London: Routledge.

Radford, Jean, 1999, 'Late Modernism and the Politics of History', in Maroula Joannou, ed., *Women Writers of the 1930s*, Edinburgh: Edinburgh University Press, 33–45.

Radway, Janice, 1981, 'The Utopian Impulse in Popular Literature: Gothic Romances and "Feminist" Protest', *American Quarterly*, 140–62.

Radway, Janice A., 1987 [1984], *Reading the Romance: Women, Patriarchy & Popular Literature*, London and New York: Verso.

Rance, Nicholas, 1975, *The Historical Novel and Popular Politics in Nineteenth-Century England*, London: Vision.

Rattenbury, Arnold, 1981, 'Plain Heart, Light Tether', in Claire Harman, ed., 'Sylvia Townsend Warner: 1893–1978: A Celebration', *PN Review*, 23, 8: 3, 46–8.

——, 1996, 'Literature, Lying and Sober Truth: attitudes to the work of Patrick Hamilton and Sylvia Townsend Warner', in John Lucas, ed., *Writing and Radicalism*, London, New York: Longman, 201–44.

252 Bibliography

Reader's Digest, 1993, *Years to Remember: Remembering the Forties*, Video.

Rehberger, Dean, 1995, '"Vulgar Fiction, Impure History": The Neglect of Historical Fiction', *Journal of American Culture*, 18: 4, 59–65.

Renault, Mary, 1968, 'Notes on *The King Must Die*', in Thomas McCormack, ed., *Afterwords: Novelists and their Work*, New York, Granston and London: Harper & Row, 81–7.

Reston Jr, James, 2001, *Warriors of God: Richard the Lionheart and Saladin in the Third Crusade*, New York: Doubleday.

Rhondda, Lady, 1933, *This Was My World*, London: Macmillan.

Richter, David H., 1992, 'From Medievalism to Historicism: Representations of History in the Gothic Novel and the Historical Romance', *Studies in Medievalism*, IV, 79–104.

Riviere, Joan, 1986 [1929], 'Womanliness and Masquerade', in Victor Burgin, James Donald and Cora Kaplan, eds, *Formations of Fantasy*, London and New York: Routledge.

Robinson, Lillian S., 1978, 'On Reading Trash', in *Sex, Class and Culture*, Bloomington and London: Indiana University Press.

Rowbotham, Sheila, 1976 [1973], *Hidden From History: Rediscovering Women in History from the Seventeenth Century to the Present*, New York: Random.

——, 1997, *A Century of Women*, London: Penguin.

Rowse, A.L., 1941, *Tudor Cornwall*, London: Cape.

——, 1963 [1946], *The Use of History*, London: English University Press.

Rozett, Martha Tuck, 1995, 'Constructing a World: How Postmodern Historical Fiction Reimagines the Past', *Clio*, 25: 2, 145–64.

Russ, Joanna, 1973, 'Somebody's Trying to Kill Me and I Think It's My Husband: The Modern Gothic', *Journal of Popular Culture*, 6 (Spring), 666–91.

Rustin, Susanna, 2003, 'Costume Dramatist' (interview with Rose Tremain), *The Guardian*, 10 May, 20–3.

Sage, Lorna, 1992, *Women in the House of Fiction: Postwar Women Novelists*, Basingstoke and London: Macmillan.

——, 2001 [2000], *Bad Blood*, London: Fourth Estate.

Sanders, Andrew, 1978, *The Victorian Historical Novel: 1840–1880*, London and Basingstoke: Macmillan.

Scanlan, Margaret, 1990, *Traces of Another Time: History and Politics in Postwar British Fiction*, Princeton, NJ: Princeton University Press.

Schiller, Dana, 1997, 'The Redemptive Past in the Neo-Victorian Novel', *Studies in the Novel*, 29: 4 (Winter), 538–60.

Schoene-Harwood, Berthold, 2000, *Writing Men: Literary Masculinities from Frankenstein to the New Man*, Edinburgh: Edinburgh University Press.

Scott, Bonnie Kime, 1990, *The Gender of Modernism: A Critical Anthology*, Bloomington and Indianapolis: Indiana University Press.

Sedgwick, Eve Kosofsky, 1985, *Between Men: English Literature and Male Homosocial Desire*, New York: Columbia University Press.

Sellar, W.C. and R.J. Yeatman, 1989 [1930], *1066 and All That*, London: Methuen.

Shattock, Joanne, 1994, *The Oxford Guide to British Women Writers*, Oxford: Oxford University Press.

Shaw, Harry E., 1983, *The Forms of Historical Fiction: Sir Walter Scott and his Successors*, Ithaca and London: Cornell University Press.

Shils, Edward and Michael Young, 1953, 'The Meaning of the Coronation', *Sociological Review*, 1: 2, 63–81.

Showalter, Elaine, 1987 [1985], *The Female Malady: Women, Madness and English Culture, 1830–1980*, London: Virago.
——, 1998 [1997], *Hystories: Hysterical Epidemics and Modern Culture*, London: Picador.
Simons, Judy and Kate Fulbrook, eds, 1998, *Writing: A Woman's Business: Women, Writing and the Market Place*, Manchester: Manchester University Press.
Sinfield, Alan, 1997, *Literature, Politics and Culture in Postwar Britain*, London: Athlone.
Sitwell, Edith, 1946, *Fanfare for Elizabeth*, London: Macmillan.
——, 1962, *The Queens and the Hive*, London: Macmillan.
Sked, Alan and Chris Cook, 1993, *Post-War Britain: A Political History 1945–1992*, 4th edn, Harmondsworth: Penguin.
Smith, Adam, 1979 [1776], *The Wealth of Nations*, Harmondsworth: Penguin.
Smith, Bonnie G., 1984, 'The Contribution of Women to Historiography in Great Britain, France and the U.S.', *American Historical Review*, 89, 709–32.
Spencer, Jane, 1986, *The Rise of the Woman Novelist: From Aphra Behn to Jane Austen*, Oxford: Basil Blackwell.
Spraggs, Gillian, 2001, *Outlaws and Highwaymen: The Cult of the Robber in England from the Middle Ages to the Nineteenth Century*, London: Pimlico.
Squier, Susan Merrill, ed., 1984, *Women Writers and the City: Essays in Feminist Literary Criticism*, Knoxville: University of Tennessee Press.
Steedman, Carolyn, 1989, 'True Romances', in Raphael Samuel, ed., *Patriotism: The Making and Unmaking of British National Identity*, Vol. 1: *History and Politics*, London and New York: Routledge.
Strachey, Lytton, 1928 [1918], *Eminent Victorians*, London: Phoenix.
——, 1928, *Elizabeth and Essex: A Tragic History*, London: Chatto & Windus.
Strachey, Ray, 1931, *Millicent Garrett Fawcett*, London: Murray.
——, 1936, *Our Freedom and its Results*, London: Hogarth Press.
——, 1978 [1928], *The Cause: A Short History of the Women's Movement in Great Britain*, London: Virago.
Sutherland, John, 1981, *Bestsellers: Popular Fiction of the 1970s*, London, Boston and Henley: Routledge & Kegan Paul.
Sweetman, David, 1993, *Mary Renault: A Biography*, London: Chatto & Windus.
Taylor, A.J.P., 1970 [1965], *English History 1914–1945*, Harmondsworth: Penguin.
Taylor, Beverley and Elisabeth Brewer, 1983, *The Return of King Arthur: British and American Arthurian Literature since 1900*, Cambridge: D.S. Brewer; Totowa, NJ: Barnes & Noble.
Taylor, D.J., 1994 [1993], *After the War: The Novel and England since 1945*, London: Flamingo.
Taylor, Debbie, 2000, 'Pat Barker: Interview', *Mslexia*, 5 (Spring–Summer), 39–40.
Taylor, Helen, 1989, *Scarlett's Women: Gone With the Wind and its Female Fans*, London: Virago.
Thatcher, Margaret, 1993, *The Downing Street Years*, London: HarperCollins.
Thompson, Raymond, H., 1989, 'Interview with Mary Stewart', www.lib.rochester.edu/camelot/intrvws/stewart.htm [accessed: 28/08/03].
Thurston, Carol, 1987, *The Romance Revolution: Erotic Novels for Women and the Quest for a New Sexual Identity*, Urbana and Chicago: University of Illinois Press.
Tindall, Gillian, 1985, *Rosamond Lehmann: An Appreciation*, London: Chatto & Windus.
Tremain, Rose, 1999, 'Tremain's Terrain', *History Today* (October), 62–3.
Trevelyan, G.M., 1946 [1942], *English Social History: A Survey of Six Centuries, Chaucer to Queen Victoria*, London, New York and Toronto: Longmans, Green & Co.

Trodd, Anthea, 1998, *Women's Writing in English: Britain 1900–1945*, London and New York: Longman.

Trumpener, Katie, 1993, 'National Character, Nationalist Plots: National Tale and Historical Novel in the Age of *Waverley*, 1806–1830', *ELH*, 60, 685–731.

Turner, Joseph, W., 1979, 'The Kinds of Historical Fiction: An Essay in Definition and Methodology', *Genre*, XII (Fall), 333–55.

Usborne, David, 2003, 'The Future Ain't What it Used to Be', *The Independent Review*, 7 April, 4–5.

Wachman, Gay, 2001, *Lesbian Empire: Radical Crosswriting in the Twenties*, New Brunswick, New Jersey and London: Rutgers University Press.

Waddell, Helen, 1934 [1927], *The Wandering Scholars*, London: Constable.

——, 1948 [1929], *Medieval Latin Lyrics*, London: Constable.

Wallace, Diana, 2000, *Sisters and Rivals in British Women's Fiction, 1914–39*, London: Macmillan.

Walter, Natasha, 1998, *The New Feminism*, London: Little, Brown.

Warner, Sylvia Townsend, 1982, *Letters*, ed., William Maxwell, London: Chatto & Windus.

——, 1990 [1959], 'Women as Writers', in Bonnie Kime Scott, ed., *The Gender of Modernism: A Critical Anthology*, Bloomington and Indianapolis: Indiana University Press.

Warner, Val and Michael Schmidt, 1981, 'Srylvia Townsend Warner in conversation', in Claire Harman, ed., 'Sylvia Townsend Warner: 1893–1978: A Celebration', *PN Review*, 23, 8: 3, 35–7.

Waugh, Patricia, 1988 [1984], *Metafiction*, London: Routledge.

——, 1995, *Harvest of the Sixties: English Literature and Its Background 1960–1990*, Oxford and New York: Oxford University Press.

Wells, H.G., 1980 [1909], *Ann Veronica*, London: Virago.

Welsford, Enid, 1962, *The Court Masque*, New York: Russell & Russell.

West, Rebecca, 1952 [1949], *The Meaning of Treason*, London: Macmillan.

——, 1978 [1974], 'And They All Lived Unhappily Ever After', in *Rebecca West: A Celebration*, Harmondsworth: Penguin, 460–5.

Westland, Ella, 1995, 'The Passionate Periphery: Cornwall and Romantic Fiction', in Ian Bell, ed., *Peripheral Visions: Images of Nationhood in Contemporary British Fiction*, Cardiff: University of Wales Press.

White, Hayden, 1985 [1978], *Tropics of Discourse: Essays on Cultural Criticism*, Baltimore and London: Johns Hopkins University Press.

White, Rosemary, n.d., 'Michèle Roberts: An Interview', *Bête Noire*, 14/15, 125–40.

——, n.d., 'Five Novels as History: The Lives and Times of Michèle Roberts', *Bête Noire*, 14/15, 144–57.

Whitehead, Anne, 1998, 'Open to Suggestion: Hypnosis and History in Pat Barker's *Regeneration*', *Modern Fiction Studies*, 44: 3 (Fall), 674–94.

Williams, Gwyn, A., 1994, *Excalibur: The Search for Arthur*, London: BBC Books.

Wilson, Elizabeth, 1980, *Only Halfway to Paradise: Women in Postwar Britain: 1945–1968*, London and New York: Tavistock.

Winterson, Jeanette, 1995, *Art Objects: Essays on Ecstasy and Effrontery*, London: Jonathan Cape.

Wolf, Naomi, 1991 [1990], *The Beauty Myth*, London: Vintage.

Wolfe, Peter, 1969, *Mary Renault*, New York: Twayne.

Woodward, C. Vann, with Ralph Ellison, William Styron and Robert Penn Warren, 1969, 'The Uses of History in Fiction', *The Southern Literary Journal*, 1, 57–90.

Woolf, Virginia, 1977 [1929], *A Room of One's Own*, London: Granada.
——, 1979, *On Women and Writing*, ed. Michèle Barrett, London: Women's Press.
——, 1986 [1938], *Three Guineas*, London: Hogarth.
——, 1990 [1906], 'The Journal of Mistress Joan Martyn', in Bonnie Kime Scott, ed., *The Gender of Modernism: A Critical Anthology*, Bloomington and Indianapolis: Indiana University Press.
Wright, Patrick, 1985, *On Living in an Old Country: The National Past in Contemporary Britain*, London: Verso.
Wynne-Davies, Marion, 1996, *Women and Arthurian Legend: Seizing the Sword*, London: Macmillan.
Yelin, Louise, 1992, 'Cultural Cartography: A.S. Byatt's *Possession* and the Politics of Victorian Studies', *The Victorian Newletter*, 81, 38–41.
Young, Hugo, 1990 [1989], *One of Us: A Biography of Margaret Thatcher*, London: Macmillan.
Zigmond, Sally, 2003, 'Historically Accurate Page-Turners: How does She Do it?' (interview with Philippa Gregory), *The Historical Novels Review*, 26 (November), 4–6.
Zilboorg, Caroline, 2001, *The Masks of Mary Renault: A Literary Biography*, Columbia and London: University of Missouri Press.

Index